UNIQUE

A UNIQUE WORLD

&

A UNIQUE LIFE

BY

APRIL FLOYD

FLOYD BOOKS PUBLISHING CO.

Some Editing by Sheila Banks
Cover Design by Anna Spies

To purchase this book in bulk, inquire about a presentation, inquiry about the film, or interviews based on this story, please contact the author at **http://www. aprilfloydbooks.com** or email author at **Floydbookspublishing@gmail.com**, **FEG. floydentertainmentgroup@gmail.com**

Copyright © 2010 by April Floyd

ISBN-13:978-0991564705
ISBN-10: 0991564707
LCCN-2014903298

Family & Relationships / Conflict Resolution / Erotica Fiction / General
Published by Floyd Books Co.
Manufactured in the United States of America.

TABLE OF CONTENTS

Part I: Unique World

Part 2: Unique Life

HOW READERS ARE RESPONDING TO 'UNIQUE'

"I read April Floyd's book, Unique, and I loved it. I literally couldn't put it down! I laughed, cried, and was wowed throughout the entire book."

~Lisa Anderson

"I thought I was watching a movie as I read. This book is *Awesome*; a must read! The characters were very powerful; and they seemed real. I could not put the book down! I loved it!"

~Deon Layton

"Unique by April Floyd was too damn good! I loved it. I recommend that everyone read it—no matter what they usually read—because the story relates to so many. It is inspiring; as well as entertaining."

~Barbra Jackson

"I would have never picked up this book because it was completely out of my genre. But, I was spellbound from cover-to-cover. I can see Unique this book as a Lifetime movie. Great Book!"

~Ricky Jones

ADVANCE PRAISE FOR UNIQUE

UNIQUE, APRIL FLOYD'S DEBUT novel, introduces readers to six-year-old Unique, a little girl who has witnessed much more than any young eyes ever should.

In telling Unique's story, April Floyd draws upon her life experiences and observations as a mother, daughter, godmother, nurse's assistant and a public school bus driver, as her muses. These varied experiences amongst a diverse population have provided April with a rich source of inspiration. Her characters are full of life and down-to-earth causing each reader to correlate.

Unique is the uplifting story of a young girl who is seemingly engulfed in insurmountable hardships. Instead of being drowned under the burden of her dysfunctional family and surroundings; she rises above the chaos, and in the process, also raises the lives and expectations of those who are around her.

The story of how Unique rises above other people's low expectations of her is inspiring as well as relevant. So many people struggle with disabilities, and yet, with determination and strength of character, anything is truly possible, even with those for whom the bar has been set low; those who are seen by the world as "different."

The character Unique defies those assumptions; the cards dealt her by life and, with the help of those who believe in her, finds a way to achieve her success through her undying determination and the strength of her character.

Unique is a modern novel that will draw you into Unique's world. One out of five Americans may feel especially touched by this book, but everyone can relate to it.

It is a whirlwind of emotion, drama, intrigue, and, most of all, passion. It is, indeed, a book that you will not be able to put down or forget.

DEDICATIONS

To my husband, Eddie Floyd Jr.

Thank you for seeing my talent and encouraging me to write again.
The support and love went beyond anything ordinary. I love you with
my all; and, I dedicate my first published novel to you.

To my mother, Carolyn Ford

You always believed in me, supported me and loved me.
I could never give up because you wouldn't allow me too. Promises made
will be kept. You were my everything, Mama. Rest-In-Heaven
and Thank you, Mommy.

To my father, Benautry Ridgnal

Thank you for your love and support. Rest-In-Peace, Dad.

To my children: Malissa, Terry & Walter, Jr.

Your strength is inspiring. Use the examples of others
as your cheat-sheet to life. Mommy loves you.

To my mother-in-law, Rachel Pinkney

When I told you I wanted to write, you encouraged me.
You showed me some of your poems you've written and published.
You loved me as soon as I said hello; and, I love you for that.
I learned that it doesn't take long to know when you have met one
of God's angels. You were my mother, my friend and my counselor.
I miss you.

To my father-in-law, Eddie Floyd

Your character and strength are a gift to all that know you.
It makes us stronger and wiser a wonderful gift.
Thank you for your love.

SECRET TO LIFE ~ QUOTES

"Next to God, family is the best thing."

~April Floyd

"Life teaches that it can be complex, but we each can make choices that determine our destiny!"

~April Floyd

PROLOGUE

DOROTHY WOKE UP WITH no appetite. She looked down at her full belly and thought, 'Is this the day?' Rubbing her stomach, she walked out from her bedroom to the front room into total chaos. All her children were auguring, and no food was in the apartment to feed them. The smell of burning candles filled the place. They had to rush to complete the needed tasks before sundown because there was no electricity. A knock on the door broke the augments and Dorothy went to the door. It was Al, father to the child still in Dorothy's belly. They had a rocky past relationship, and they hardly exchanged many words due to a fear of arguing. Al brought groceries for them all. As the children helped carry the bags in the house, the lights popped on, and the television started to play. Al smiled, looked at the lights, then Dorothy.

Dorothy said, "Thanks." She knew it wasn't the first time Al had helped her out and still hated the detachment. But with her life, she knew she couldn't blame him. He then handed her an envelope with some money to help her out. He rubbed her stomach and walked back to his car. Dorothy shut the door thankful but resentful at the same time. She walked to the kitchen to check the bags. "Let's see what we got?" She reached into a bag a paused; she noticed water streaming down her legs. Next, sharp pain crossed from her back to her belly. It was clear—Dorothy was in labor! But, Al had already gone, so she called her friend, Diane.

Diane, she came right away and took Dorothy to St. Louis Regional Hospital.

ↂ

Moans from pain bubbled forth from Dorothy at the hospital. Dorothy was happy this was no false labor, and her baby was coming. Several hours later, a little girl was born.

Dorothy noticed the whispers between the doctor and the surgical tech. "What's wrong!" Dorothy grunted trying to lift herself up, leaning to peer at the staff who were working on the child. "Tell me!"

Hearing her baby cry and doctors motioned a small sign of relief gave Dorothy a brief comfort. They wrapped the baby up and allowed Dorothy to hold her new baby girl. As all mother do, Dorothy began checking and counting fingers and toes. "What's wrong with her! Why is her arm like this! I didn't do drugs, drink or smoke with her so why in the fuck is she messed up!" Dorothy was wailing. Diane couldn't comfort her friend this time.

Doctors waited until she calmed a bit and explained the condition of her child and why. Depression set in fast, and Dorothy asked everyone to leave.

Later, that evening a nurse asked if she wanted to hold her baby. Dorothy agreed. It was then that she looked into those unique eyes and smiled. "You are unique." She quietly whispered. Holding the baby up to smell her. She said, "Unique, that's your name—Unique."

PART I

UNIQUE WORLD

TAKE A LOOK

CHAPTER 1

THE VILLAIN'

IT WAS A GLORIOUS spring day in New York City. The sun showed off, beaming through the floor-to-ceiling windows of Victoria's luxurious penthouse suite like lasers. A gentle breeze puffed through her partially opened bedroom bay windows, ushering in the sweetness of the morning dew. A bright sun ray stroked Victoria's face, and she quickly awakened in bed with a sense of urgency. She gave no notice to the morning beauty freely given her. Instead, she grabbed her Blackberry before even washing her face or brushing her teeth. This was atypical behavior for Victoria. Vanity usually came before phone calls. While punching in the numbers to reach her assistant, Victoria's mind raced. How much is this secret going to cost me? How far will I go to keep the life I've worked so hard to build? I'm a celebrity, dammit! Victoria was frantic. She needed her assistant, Brenda. And, she needed her now to discuss with her assistant how the latest news could affect her lifestyle, and ultimately her celebrity status. Just thinking about what the media would do with the information was

driving Victoria crazy. She was becoming frustrated at the number of rings it had taken before her assistant answered her phone.

"Answer the damn phone!" She barked aloud, impatiently.

Brenda was indispensable to Victoria; ever available for the diva's most trivial demands. She always had the right answer for, and perfect solution to, every one of Victoria's crises—big or small.

"Oh, hell no," Brenda mumbled, groggily. "That overbearing, egotistical bitch is calling me this early in the morning? I just went to sleep."

Jason rolled over to his back. "Brenda," he moaned, "I keep telling you, hanging with me and working for that ice princess is going to leave you tired all the time. Don't act surprised."

"If I have to give up something, it won't be you. You are safe. If Victoria had a man, she wouldn't be wound so damn tight."

"Victoria is always working, never got a man, never happy and is always calling you. It sounds to me like she's a lesbian, and she wants you. Tell that ice princess—I'm your man. Stop hiding us, baby; and maybe she'll finally give you some time to yourself."

"She's a workaholic. I'm sure she's not gay; Jason, so you're safe on that end. I left the phone in the other room. I'd better find out what Victoria's ass wants this early."

"Hello," Brenda finally responded, letting out a yawning sigh.

"Why does it take you so long to answer your phone?" Victoria griped. Brenda could hear Victoria's anxiety over the phone. She occasionally spoke to her boss as though soothing a third grader; this was one of those times.

"Victoria, it's early; and I don't expect to answer my phone until after I have washed. Listen, you need to calm down. Whatever, you're frantic about can wait until I have taken my shower. By the way, I can smell your breath through the phone. Brush your teeth and do your morning thing. I'll be right over; so we can talk at breakfast."

Crimson crept up Victoria's face, embarrassed because her breath was funky; and, Brenda called her out. She checked herself, huffing puffs of bad breathe in her hand for smelling, chuckled and agreed. Trashing her natural routine was entirely against the model diva commandments; so she quickly switched gears to get back on track post haste.

Brenda didn't want to admit it, but her curiosity had heightened. She wanted to know what had Victoria so frantic? Somehow, this episode of histrionics seemed more real than any of her past 'Help me, Brenda' moments.

While waiting for Brenda, Victoria pressed the call button to summon Ms. Ruth to prepare breakfast for the two of them. Ms. Ruth had been Victoria's housekeeper—and, occasional den mother—since the beginnings of her high-profile career. After swiftly correcting her disgraceful violation of the most basic model diva rules, Victoria realized she was too depleted to go through her full morning pampering routine. She flung one arm into her favorite comfortable white robe; intensely exhaling while looking into the mirror. Finally, she placed the other arm in its sleeve. After sliding into her sparkly house shoes; she strolled to the breakfast area.

Victoria sat at the breakfast table, leisurely sipping her special brew green tea and perusing the morning news when she heard the doorbell ring.

Brenda had rushed to catch the elevator up to Victoria's suite, arriving in record time to hear and put out her boss' latest fire. Ms. Ruth chuckled at Brenda's nervousness when she opened the white double doors. As much as she genuinely cared for Victoria, Ms. Ruth lived in the real world, with real problems. It tickled her to witness yet another of Victoria's and Brenda's so-called "emergencies." She welcomed the young woman, shaking her head while formally directing Brenda, "Right this way."

Even though Brenda certainly knew the way, Ms. Ruth nonetheless escorted her into the breakfast room. The older woman served Brenda's usual breakfast; and thoughtfully repositioned the freshly picked lilies on the table so that the two younger women could better see each other, then excused herself.

Brenda exhaled as she picked up her fork to plow into the delicious cheese-filled omelet. Starting the conversation, Brenda asked, "Do you think I should change my favorite breakfast? I am sure the calories are sticking somewhere. Maybe on these thighs?"

Brenda's eyes widened ogling Victoria because she gave no response to the vicious 'C' word. After a few bites and a silent Victoria, Brenda

began to realize that Victoria was severely stressed out over whatever the situation was. 'This must be severe,' Brenda speculated.

"What's the big news, Victoria?" Brenda asked, getting to the point. "I rushed up here and canceled our morning appointments; so this had better be good."

Victoria quietly wondered if she had exaggerated her situation a bit. She felt defensive. Brenda's question irritated her.

"Brenda, it's important to me."

Brenda's facial expression changed, deciding to keep the sarcasm to a minimum. Brenda knew Victoria was extremely sensitive. She gestured to her to continue with a nod, to go on.

"Brenda, I have a sister. I made certain I never told anyone about her."

"I have members of my family I don't claim either," Brenda interrupted. "So what? That's normal…"

Victoria screwed up her face with obvious annoyance. Victoria was baffled at Brenda's ability to continue to interrupt. She just wanted Brenda to listen to her. Brenda examined Victoria's expressions, got the message, apologized for interrupting and encouraged Victoria to go on.

Victoria's upturned lip and frowned brow seemed to say, 'Finally, you'll listen and stop yapping.'

"This sister is not like any other sister." Victoria continued, "I have always been ashamed of being her relative. I hoped no one would ever know she was my sister; and, I did everything to keep things private. I acted like she never existed. And, for a while—she didn't—at least, not to me.

One day she showed up at a mall where I was making an appearance. I think she was about sixteen. All the major radio and television stations were there to see me. As soon as I spotted her approaching with some of her friends and random extended family, I had to call security and have all their asses removed; especially hers. I remember telling security that I had no idea who she was. I lied that she and her group were a threat to me. That was enough for the security guard to take immediate action. They never got close. "

Victoria continued to rant, "You may think I was wrong to do that; but, I'm a famous supermodel! My sister, my blood relative, is a disabled,

handicapped retard. I didn't want that type of attention then; and, I don't want it now." In a desperate attempt to justify her shameful actions, Victoria added, "She's only my half-sister, my father's daughter. I don't understand how she got into the modeling and fashion business anyway—the way she looks abhors... And, I mean... It's crazy! Why? How?"

Brenda shook her head, "The modeling business? How did you find out that she was in the modeling business?"

"Informants," Victoria stated, flatly.

Brenda snickered, placing her hands on her hips while leaning back in her chair. "Informants! What informants? I thought I knew all your contacts."

Victoria gave no eye contact continuing to cover up where she had gotten her information.

"Why are you laughing? I have informants. Moreover, no, you do not know everyone I know. A girl has to have some secrets." Victoria changed the subject back to the situation at hand and, went on to tell Brenda about the major charities and foundations that were involved with her sister's new fashion show for the disabled.

"Victoria, I heard about that event; and, it's a big damn deal! I had no idea that your sister was the catalyst behind that show's creation. WOW! So many prestigious people and organizations are going to be there, supporting the cause."

Victoria did not appreciate Brenda's overwhelming enthusiasm regarding the sister she did not want to acknowledge. She grabbed her butter knife, stabbed it into the fat-free cream cheese, smearing it sparsely on her gluten-free, low-carb, mini bagel half; slowly sliding the blade across the toasted bagel, apparently deep in thought.

"What's going to happen when the media finds out I'm her sister?" Victoria demanded, waving the knife at her semi-friend and assistant. "I didn't have anything to do with her success. The embarrassment! Brenda, Help! What to do? I don't know—."

Brenda tossed her long, black hair away from her face. "Well, I'm not sure not claiming your sister is as big of a problem as you're making it, Victoria. Think about it for a minute. You might just be able to benefit from your situation; although you don't have a lot of time. If

you do nothing, and the media gets hold of the story, you know it won't be anything positive. My advice would be to get involved now. Spin a negative into a positive, you see?"

Victoria held her head down, sighing in exasperation. She would have to face the shame she had been running away from her entire career. Victoria knew Brenda was dead-on, but she wasn't happy about it. Rolling her eyes up in her head, Victoria acquiesced and said, "Okay! Okay! Okay! You're—probably—right. Now, Miss Know-It-All, where do we start?"

Brenda moaned begrudgingly before laying out her strategy. "Pretend you know nothing about the upcoming events. Call your sister. Ask her how she's doing. She lives in St. Louis, right? Do you remember that station in St. Louis that was relentlessly hounding you for an interview? Well, I think it's time you accept. I'll set things up. Tell your sister you'll be in town and would like to see her. Once you do, she will likely bring up the "Unique People; Special Lives" runway charity event. You offer her a hand in the project; or, a substantial donation. Be the supportive, generous sister."

Victoria's expression changed instantly. She looked as if she had seen a ghost; and, her skin turned bright red. "Brenda, NO! NO! That's going too far! Can't I lend my support without actually getting involved?"

"No, you can't. You've got to approach this the right way; so it appears that you've been a part of your sister's life all along. Unique's show isn't just another runway show or charity event, Victoria. It's going to be one of the largest events for people with disabilities there's ever been. All the major broadcast and cable outlets will be there. Either do it the way I strongly recommend, or it will blow up in your face."

Victoria rolled her eyes.

"May I speak frankly, Honey?" Brenda continued. "You do not want to come off as the insensitive sister that has something against people with disabilities. And one more suggestion, Victoria— you probably should stop calling your sister a retard. First, it is entirely not politically correct. Second, if Unique has accomplished all she has without your help, she is clearly not a 'retard.' I'm just giving you something to think about."

"Wait a second. Okay, I'll do this, but you'd better help me out when I stumble. I know my sister isn't a retard literally, but I do not have a

sympathetic bone in my body for my sister or the other cripples in the world. I am exhausted from hearing about the mental and physical retards, including my sister."

Victoria could see Brenda's flesh crawl as she spoke. Even though her boss' cruel words made her sick, Brenda managed to keep her composure; and, gave Victoria assurance of her loyalty.

"Victoria, I'm here now, right? I'll be here through it all, good or bad, rise or fall. You know that. I have to go. I will call you when I nail down the date and time of that interview. Don't worry; it will be all right."

Victoria believed Brenda and was finally able to calm down. She would do whatever it took to keep her image spotless in front of the paparazzi.

"I believe you, thanks. Call me when you obtain the details of that interview."

Brenda nodded okay as she exited Victoria's suite.

❧

Though Victoria followed Brenda's suggestions to the 't,' neither of them could have anticipated what they were about to face. Other than the mall incident, Victoria had failed to mention to Brenda how horrible she had consistently been to her sister. Unique, however, vividly remembered it all. Even with Cindy's teachings, forgiveness was a difficult pill to swallow.

When Unique received the call from her estranged sister, she was not surprised. In fact, she expected it. She only thought it would have come sooner. Not mentioning the upcoming event, she played the role of 'grateful-to-hear-from-my-famous-big-sister' for just a little while.

Unique lived in a modest home with her adoptive family. It had four bedrooms, two baths and was full of love. When the phone rang, she was sitting at the kitchen table with her two younger brothers, Jerry and Maury, cracking up at their jokes. She ran down the hallway to the foyer and answered the phone with laughter still in her voice.

"Unique?" Victoria asked.

"Yes, this is Unique. May I ask who you are?"

"Hi Unique, it's your sister Victoria. How are you?"

"Victoria—my sister, Victoria?"

"Yes, sweetie, it's me. I know I haven't called in a while. How are you?"

"I'm all right, Victoria. What made you call? Is our father okay?"

"Oh yes, Dad's okay… All is well on this end. I'm coming to St. Louis soon. I'm scheduled for an interview there, and I just thought it would be fun if we could spend some time catching up. Are you available on Saturday? My interview is over at noon. So we could grab lunch; my treat."

"Well, that sounds good. I'll let my mom know; and, I'll leave that day open. It's nice hearing from you."

"See you soon, Unique. Bye, for now…"

Unique told her mom about the surprise call from her sister as soon as Cindy walked through the door, her arms full of grocery bags. Jerry and Maury seemed to eat their weight in everything every day. Unique grabbed two bags out of her mom's arms before Cindy could close the door, spilling the details of her surprise call from Victoria. Cindy wiped her brow, smiling at her daughter's excitement. On the inside, though, she was concerned. Cindy's thoughts quickly drifted back to the past and, how poorly Unique's biological family had treated her. Even though their callousness toward the girl upset her, Unique's excitement brought Cindy back to the reality of forgiveness. It was one of the critical life lessons she had repeatedly drilled into her daughter's head; to forgive. She knew the days would come when Unique would have to face the demons of her past. Cindy had done all she could do, said all that needed to be told to her daughter, regarding how she would deal with her birth family. She trusted that she had done an excellent job teaching and guiding Unique to be independent, and to make her own well-thought-out decisions. Cindy was sure Unique knew without a doubt that, no matter what she chose, she had her mom's approval.

☙

Saturday arrived so quickly. Unique was excited about meeting her sister for lunch. She tried on a dozen different outfits for Cindy, undecided on the perfect one. After trying on yet another blouse, Unique asked her mom again how this one looked.

Cindy smiled, giggling, and said, "The last time I saw you this nervous about your appearance was when you were getting ready for your high school prom." She smiled broadly at Unique's latest choice, assuring and calming her, "It doesn't matter—honey. You always look beautiful."

Unique stared at herself in her bedroom's full-length mirror.

"I still look like a teenager. Why have I always been so small? I want to look more like a respectable businesswoman, not a kid." Unique couldn't help but want to impress Victoria.

Cindy lovingly and reassuringly placed her hands on Unique's shoulders to slow her down. "Look Unique, great things come in small packages, and you're a great business lady. You have already accomplished more at your age than most people have in a lifetime. You're not just dreaming about your goals; you are acting on them. No one—including your famous sister—can deny that. Just finish getting ready, sweetheart. She'll be here soon."

Suddenly, a horn blew. Unique rushed to her bedroom window and peeped through the curtains.

Victoria had pulled up in an ivory Cadillac limo. Not realizing she was speaking aloud, Cindy commented, "A limo for lunch… What's up with this? Victoria must think this is "Pretty Woman" or something."

Unique grimaced slightly in response. Cindy looked at the apparent mien on Unique's face and checked herself. She didn't want to become overprotective. She kissed Unique and sent her on her way.

❦

When Victoria saw her sister, she immediately noticed the resemblance in their features, traits she had not seen when they were younger. She and Unique shared the same eyes; nearly identical to those of their father, Al. They both had full cherry lips and long silky hair. Unique took a deep breath and climbed into the back of the limo with a woman who was nearly a stranger. Victoria signaled the driver to go.

"Wow! There you are!" Victoria exclaimed enthusiastically. "It's been so long since I've laid eyes on you, little sister. I almost forgot how beautiful my sister is!"

Victoria had already decided to woo Unique; but, realized she was nearly as nervous as her sister and was laying it on a bit over-the-top. Unique sat up straight. She wanted to appear taller.

"Victoria, if you hadn't noticed, I'm not a kid anymore, so stop with the little sister routine. Where are we going for lunch?"

Victoria was almost impressed with her sister's directness. "Well, alrighty then… I want to surprise you. After we eat, I'm taking you to meet some of my closest friends. Then, we're going shopping. I want a whole day with you before I get back on the road."

"Wait, what's up, Victoria? Seeing you again sounds fascinating and exciting; but, I hoped for you to do this throughout most of my teenage years. You know—when it really would have meant something? Now I am grown. I have my own clothes, and friends and family who have already done the teenage thing with me. The time for sisterly bonding has come and gone. So, from little sister to big sister, what's really up? You must know I'm not the same gullible sister that you had your security to remove from the mall, when all I wanted was to say hello to my big sister, right?"

Unique stared down Victoria, fighting back the tears and a blizzard of mixed emotions. Part of Unique was ashamed for holding on to her anger and hurt, ignoring the ingrained lessons of forgiveness. Victoria had caused pain for Unique most of her entire life. That echoing pain continued to drive Unique, giving her the confidence to unleash it on her sister now.

Victoria could not look her sister in the eyes. "You're still holding that against me? I remember that day. And yes, I see, you are all grown up now. Look Unique; I just wanted to make up for some of the wrong I know I have done to you."

"Okay, Victoria, I'm okay with that, but I must ask, why now? Tell me the truth—you're never truthful with me. I want a relationship with you, Victoria, more than anyone does. I always have, because family means everything next to God. Believe it or not, our dad taught me that; but, somehow I felt you never wanted to acknowledge that I was your sister. I had no part of your life. So, yes, I want the truth! Why now? Suddenly you recognize me as a sibling? Truth, Victoria! Tell me the truth!"

After Unique relentless pounding about the truth; Victoria sank deeper into her seat and released a heavy sigh. "Fine, you want the truth? You got the truth. First, we will eat lunch at my hotel; then the day will be spent telling you the truth, Unique."

Victoria directed the limo driver to return to her hotel. She called the hotel and ordered room service for both of them; never asking Unique what she wanted. It would be waiting by the time they arrived. Next, she called Brenda and openly discussed going to "Plan B," right in front of Unique. Brenda didn't even have the chance to say a word before Victoria ended the call.

Meanwhile, Unique sat in the limo fumbling with her hands. Nervousness swapped places with her dissolving confidence while watching her sister's frantic actions. Not knowing what Victoria was up to, Unique grabbed her stomach in response to what felt like fear. She remembered she was still the little sister. The unwanted, ignored little sister that Victoria was always ashamed to be around. It looked like the real Victoria was bursting through that nicey-nice façade. They arrived at the hotel precisely in fifteen minutes. Room service arrived ten minutes after that. Victoria hung the 'do not disturb' sign on the door; and, the truth was about to be told.

Victoria began after Unique burrowed in the farthest end of the couch. "Unique, the fact is this. I think you got into the fashion industry to embarrass me. You knew this business was my domain, and you just had to hitch your wagon to my star to be seen. Hoping some of what I have; will spill over onto you. You're waaay out of your league, Little Girl."

Unique stood up and laughed; suddenly empowered. Somehow—her older, super-model sister didn't intimidate her anymore.

Unique stared Victoria up and down, "Victoria, you are so vain, it's pathetic. My accomplishments have absolutely nothing to do with you. Embarrassment! Embarrassment? You are an embarrassment to me. Sure, some of your exterior features are different from mine. I said, different; not better! Because there are some parts, I have that your frail behind doesn't. And, heads up, big Sis. Your personality—sucks —big time! No one really likes you, Victoria.

You think everything is always about you. If you would just stop and look at the people in your life, you would see that they are only there because you pay them to be there. They tell you what you want to hear because they're on your payroll. Or, they want something you have. NO—ONE—LIKES—YOU—FOR WHO YOU ARE, VICTORIA! Let the truth be told—God forgive me—but you are a self-righteous ass-wipe that never knew how to treat anyone, not even Dad. NO! ONE! LIKES! YOU! That's what's sad. The truth is you are alone, and people like you die alone. People love me. I know this because I can't buy them. They choose to be in my life. I know what love is. And, I have joy in my life. Yes, I have a mental challenge and physical limitations at times; but, I'm on my way to stardom. You're not embarrassed—Victoria; you're jealous.

I will let myself out so you can go back to your fake, paid-for-friends and your pathetic life. "

Unique grabbed her designer handbag, stopped, pierced Victoria and said, "I design—you wear." Unique strutted over to the table to snatch a piece of chicken with a napkin. She then plucked her cell phone from her purse and called a cab, staring at Victoria the entire time. Unique stormed out of the suite's door, slamming it behind her.

A stunned Victoria froze in place on the sofa, eyes wide and mouth agape in disbelief, as she watched Hurricane Unique make her dramatic exit. She raised up momentarily, then plopped back down, reddening and unable to breathe. 'Who was that and what the hell just happened?' Victoria was completely outdone and amazed by Unique's chutzpah—and, poise—while essentially cussing her out! She slowly stood again, walked to the table, speared and scooped some of the leftover food; then pitched the entire plate into the trash, thinking aloud, "This is not how I expected things to go."

Victoria proceeded to her usual behavior. She dug around in her purse for her cell, tucked her hair behind her right ear and called Brenda; bending her assistant's ear with her version of the brief time assemble with Unique. Secretly, Brenda's stomach tickled about Unique having the audacity to tell her sister off; but, she also knew Victoria's ego wasn't going to stay humbled for long with anyone. Victoria asked Brenda to come to her suite, needing to talk in person about the conversation between her

and her sister. She wasn't sure how to handle the situation now and needed to know what to do next.

Staying in the same hotel as Victoria, Brenda arrived minutes later. Brenda entered placing her belongings on the sofa next to Victoria.

"Victoria, first of all, you must control your temper. Clearly, Unique is a lot smarter than you gave her credit for and had not forgotten how you treated her. It's also evident that she's influenced by some things from your past—holding it against you. For my own understanding, I need you to go further into your relationship with your sister—why you never claimed her as your sibling?"

Victoria paused briefly. "Brenda, how long do you have?"

"I have as long as it takes Victoria. You know that."

Brenda's eyes were pierced and adjoined Victoria so as not to miss a word. Victoria cooed as she spoke truths to Brenda.

"When I was just a child, my dad wanted me to know all about my sister and her connecting half sisters and brothers. He made a point to take me to her house to spend time with her. I hated those visits; the way her mom's house looked and smelled was disgusting to me. Even worse, my sister was a crippled retard; she had a disease called Erb's Palsy, and a mental illness called bipolar disorder."

"I know what being bipolar is," Brenda interrupted. "I had a cousin who struggled with that; but, my cousin didn't make it. He committed suicide when he was nineteen. What is Erb's Palsy? I don't think I've ever learned of that."

"I only know because my dad talked about it while Unique was growing up. It's caused by the stress of a vaginal delivery when a baby's shoulders get hung up in the birth canal; injuring the nerves that stimulate the muscle of the arm. Simply put, one of Unique's arms is smaller than the other, and doesn't work properly. But, the point is—I had to spend time with her."

"Excuse me, but how is that about you?" Brenda wondered out loud, forgetting it was Victoria, her boss that she was speaking.

Victoria ignored her, too caught up in her story and continued, "One day we went outside to play, and the neighborhood kids started teasing her and throwing rocks at her. I saw it, but I didn't want them to know she

was my sister. I was ashamed of her and afraid; so I joined in and threw rocks at Unique, too. One of my rocks hit her in her face. She still has the scar. This stuff happened all the time. Even her other sisters and brothers fought her and teased her. It got to the point that bullying her became my entertainment-of-choice every time I visited."

Brenda studied Victoria as she spoke. 'Was it possible that was actual remorse in her voice?'

"Then my dad decides to be a fucking hero or some rescue ranger, by bringing her home to live with us. He told me it was over some custody shit; but, I didn't care what was going on. Unique was officially in my personal space, and I hated it. Dad put us in the same school because her mom could not take care of her. I thought I was going to die when my dad told me."

'Nope, no remorse...' Brenda sighed while Victoria continued.

"All my friends learned she was my sister. I tried threatening her, telling her not to talk to me, walk with me, or tell anyone we were related. Then the worst thing happened one day at school. I had a big crush on this boy, Martez. I've never been able to forget him I still wonder about him today with his fine self—smooth, dark skin and soft curly hair. His eyes were so brown they cast a spell on me whenever I looked into them. Whenever he talked, his lips seemed to say, 'taste me.' And, whenever he walked me to my locker, he always carried my books. One day another student found out Unique was my sister. That word got to Martez. He asked me about Unique. He said he'd heard she was my sister, and he needed to know if it was true. I denied it. I told him I didn't know where that came from and that I didn't have a sister. I didn't realize Unique was right behind me, listening to me trying to plead my case with Martez. She started crying and yelling that, 'She wishes she wasn't my sister.' Martez stopped talking to me after that—and, the other kids started teasing us both. They called us the retard sisters. I hated her."

Victoria sat up straight and continued. "After that, I went back to stay with my mom so that I could start a new life in a new school without my sister. My father still made me keep in touch with Unique; but, the visits became fewer and fewer. I was happy about that. The truth is, I've had her removed from events more than once. Anytime she tried to speak

with me in public; I asked security to put her ass out, ASAP. I treated her like she was nothing but an unwanted fan."

Silence filled the room momentarily. Brenda continued to listen intently. Victoria took a deep breath, a bit choked up and began to speak again. Slowly.

"Talking about the past and saying a thing truthfully out loud compelled me to know what I've done. The potency of seeing and hearing Unique today forces me to see what I missed out on in her life—both our lives. I see now how much I hurt her. How could I have been so evil? How could I have been so cruel to my own sister? The sad thing is— nothing has changed with me."

Unexpected tears trickled down Victoria's flawlessly painted face.

"I'm thinking of the strength it took to go through life like that— and, with all her challenges," Victoria corrected herself. "And, to achieve what she has. I have a sister, Brenda, whom I made fun of all her life. Worse than that—I denied her the right to having a relationship with her big sister for all these years. Unique is correct; I have been jealous of her all her life. I was jealous when I had to share my dad. I was jealous when I saw her with two mothers both loving and fighting for her. My mother wasn't a role model at all, and she never protected me. My mom blamed and punished me for looking and acting like my dad. That's the truth. Now, it's too late."

Victoria sobbed now, holding her face in shame. Brenda couldn't stop her mind's short, catty question: Did hell just freeze over? For the first time, Brenda saw a vulnerable side of Victoria. A much softer side—a part of Victoria Brenda never knew existed. Brenda remained quiet, handing Victoria a box of tissues, giving her time to let all of her emotions out.

"It's too late," Victoria wailed. "She has grown into a smart, talented, gifted, young woman; and, I had nothing to do with that." She blew her nose. "Funny how I never knew my sister until today when she confronted me about myself. I can never take back all the terrible things I've done to her. But, I know now I have to, need to try. For myself, I need to seek her forgiveness. I just don't know where to start. Oh God! I don't know where to start!" Fresh tears flowed, completely ruining her make-up. But, for the first time in her life, Victoria didn't even care.

Brenda took Victoria's hand, snatched new tissues out of the box and wiped her tears, and compassionately said, "I've got a feeling you will figure it all out. One thing is for sure. I believe you will do what's best for you and your sister. I'm going to go now, Victoria. You need some time to think about things. Lie down and rest up a bit. If you need me, just call me. Okay?"

Victoria nodded, 'yes' as they both got up and headed for the door. "Thanks, Brenda. You know I appreciate you coming to hear my problems. Oh, and tell Jason I said hello."

Brenda stopped in her tracks with a startled and embarrassed expression, closing the door before she fully opened it. She turned to face Victoria.

"What? How did you know he was here?"

"Girl, I know you can't go five days without your Boo."

"That's not all I can't do without." Brenda sniggered.

The two shared a good laugh as Brenda exited the beautiful suite, leaving Victoria alone with her thoughts.

CHAPTER 2

THE BETRAYAL

COMPLETELY OUT OF VICTORIA'S piercing eyesight, Brenda gently closed the door behind her. Still holding on to the doorknob, she lingered for a moment with a sinful expression on her face; not knowing how to process all the personal information Victoria just revealed to her. What she did know was Victoria did not quickly open herself up to anyone. On the one hand, Victoria had touched Brenda with her trust in confiding in her with such a personal matter. On the contrary, everything in her was bursting at the seams to take advantage of the opportunity to make big bucks from Victoria's secret family.

Brenda let go of the doorknob and hurried to her lavish suite. She swiped her card and opened the double doors. Brenda loved flowers. Their fragrance greeted her as soon as she opened her door. Her suite was filled with a thick scent of white Gardenias, and the white, pink, and yellow Oriental Lily; mixing them with colorful Calla Lilies because these

were her favorites. After Inhaling and exhaling the pleasant fragrance, she headed toward the white Chippendale sofa in search of her briefcase.

Brenda was so preoccupied with finding her briefcase that she didn't even notice the rose petals scattered on the French parquet floors leading into the master bedroom. That's where Jason had set the perfect romantic scene. Champagne and strawberries awaited her. His gorgeously sculpted body sprawled erotically across the king size bed, clad only in a tuxedo thong. Wouldn't Brenda be deliciously surprised? The anticipation of taking her in his arms and, so much more—was thrilling. Tired of waiting he stood and admired his reflection in an adjacent mirror. Broad shoulders, magnificently muscular chest, green eyes, and amazingly abundant hair.

"Jason? Jason!" Brenda called from the living room.

Jason posted back on the bed and pretended he didn't hear her, mumbling under his breath, "Damn, baby, haven't you noticed the rose petals? Come on, find me. Don't ruin the mood. Please."

Minutes passed — still no Brenda. So now—Jason was merely out of the romantic mood. Deflated in more ways than one, he jumped up out of bed and grabbed his bathrobe; snatching the belts to tie, now yelling in the direction of her voice.

"What?"

Jason found Brenda bent over as she searched wildly through her Louis Vuitton attaché. Because Brenda's black skirt was hiked up almost to her crotch, she inadvertently gave Jason an eyeful. Jason licked his lips, focusing on her thick thighs, shapely legs, a tiny waist, and her round apple-shaped bottom. Her ivory silk blouse hugged her thin waist so tight. Suddenly, Jason was back in the mood. Just as an Irish Setter hunting dog's tail points instinctively when it strikes scent, the lower half of Jason's levitated pointing him in the direction of Brenda. Jason glanced down at his pointer, grinned, stroked it and headed toward his prey.

"There you are," she snapped, whipping around from her briefcase with a satisfied expression. Brenda only then noticed the lovely rose petals thoughtfully strewn on the floor just for her. Jason's standing very close to her; pressed his pointer against her body. There was no denying what Jason wanted. As he leaned in for a kiss, she pecked Jason on the lips and ran her fingers along one of his perfectly chiseled cheeks and uttered words he didn't care to hear.

"Not now, honey… I'm sorry, but something has come up."

"What? Besides me?" He looked down at his pointer and said, "Sorry boy, false alarm." To Brenda, he complained, "Something always comes up when dealing with that damn ice princess. Victoria needs this. Victoria needs that. Then, you're off and running. I'm getting tired of this shit, Brenda."

Brenda then held up a business card, flipping it between two beautifully manicured fingers—back and forth.

"Jason, Do you know what this is?"

Continuing to rub himself down, he replied, "Yeah, it's a business card. So what?"

Brenda playfully batted her long lashes at Jason and slithered over to him until the tips of her breasts brushed his chest. Eyes big, bold and seductive, Brenda cooed, "It's not just a business card. This person has been waiting for a story on Ms. Victoria. I never called because there wasn't anything juicy enough to share, until now. As I just told you this morning, if I had a way out, I would leave that bitch in a heartbeat."

Brenda could tell by Jason's seductive smile that her words were music to his ears. Suddenly, Jason glanced around the over-priced suite, sucked in his teeth, the smile faded, and Jason held her by the shoulders at arm's length.

"I hope you have a complete plan, 'cause I've kinda gotten used to rolling like a baller; thanks to you catering to that bitch's every whim. You're a top paid assistant, babe. That's not exactly an easy job to find."

Jason paused, processing the information before continuing.

"Whoa, Sugar-puff—slow down, there. Are you saying what I think you're saying? Victoria, the ice princess, does have a secret. Damn! I never thought this day would come." Jason enthusiastically pumped his arm. "Yes, I didn't believe that you'd ever be able to dig up dirt on her ass—not even on hands and knees with a magnifying glass. So, don't keep me in suspense. What is it and how'd you get it?"

Brenda spilled everything Victoria had confided in her. Any fleeting compassion she might have felt for her employer's sob story had dissolved. Jason could barely contain his excitement. He and Brenda fantasized about all the benefits they would reap from Brenda's betrayal—If the plan worked.

One thing, though, was still nagging at Jason.

"Brenda, babe, you sure you have all this thought-out? Once you do something like this, there is no turning back."

"No, not yet; but, I'm not making or taking any calls until I do. "

Jason's shoulders relaxed. He had to trust that Brenda had it handled. The lifestyle to which they had become accustomed, thanks to Ms. Victoria—was at stake. Hanging with Brenda allowed him to meet upscale clients and provide significant revenue for his marketing firm.

"All right, baby, I know you'll do what you gotta do. I am sure everything will work out," Jason assured himself, reaching for her hands. "Just one more question, then I will let it go." He took a deep breath. "Any chance you might cave with a change of heart?"

Brenda didn't hesitate for a moment, almost snarling as she broke away from Jason. "No way in hell! I remember everything that egotistical, overbearing bitch has put me through. She had me running dumb-ass, unnecessary errands all the damn time. Do you remember when she told me I couldn't go to the Bahamas with you because she needed me?"

Jason nodded, 'yes,' swiping his fingers across his right brow, recalling the headache of Victoria's dissembling the vacation he and Brenda had planned for a year.

Brenda looked into Jason's eyes, her anger and resentment coming to a boil as she continued, "Well, I never told you why I had to cancel our third-anniversary celebration trip. Queen Victoria made me stay with her that weekend to do her feet—her feet! While she talked about upcoming schedules, I was rubbing toes—HER TOES! She had always tried to get in our way when I needed time off to spend with you. That's why I started requiring a separate suite so you can travel with me sometimes. Doing so is the only way I get a chance to see you. It's like because she doesn't have anyone in her life, she wants me to have no one in mine; certainly not you. By the way, she knows you're here."

Lustfully licking his lips while eyeballing Brenda, Jason responded in a low, throaty growl, and said, "Good. I'm happy she knows I'm here. Let's rub our love all up in her face until she fuckin' chokes with jealousy."

Jason flicked off Brenda's cell to ensure no interruptions. He wanted Brenda. He was determined not to allow Victoria to interrupt their

lovemaking ever again. He grabbed Brenda by her waist with one hand and with the other; he pushed her long hair behind her ears. Looking into those bold eyes of Brenda's made Jason crave her lips. Primitively, he kissed them; then devouring her lips and tongue with passionate kisses and gentle bites—continuing to kiss all over her body. Jason, removing one item of Brenda's clothing at a time along the way as he skillfully guided her to the bedroom.

℣

The following week, Jason and Brenda spent rare time at their modest home in Atlanta. One morning, he awakened to an empty bed. Without donning a stitch of clothing, Jason padded into the kitchen, where Brenda was already dressed and sipping espresso at the breakfast table. Jason leaned over and tenderly planted a wet kiss on her neck.

"Morning, babe… Why are you up and ready to go so early?"

"Busy day. I'm meeting with that magazine rep this morning to find out how much my intel on Victoria is worth. Later on, I have an interview with another top model who happens to be in need of an assistant. Keep your fingers crossed, baby; because if these two things go well, we are on our way to being done with the ice princess."

Jason's lips curled up with pleasure.

"Do what you gotta do, babe. Let me know how it goes." Jason peeped the time on the microwave. "Oops, I have to get ready for a meeting, myself. I'll tell you about it later."

Jason quickly pecked Brenda on the cheek and sprinted toward the shower. Brenda sipped the last of her espresso and headed for the door.

Brenda was feeling antsy about both meetings. She desperately hoped her prospective new employer would be nothing like Victoria.

She and the magazine rep met at a secluded restaurant. The food was horrible; but, so was the nature of the meeting. The other woman was cold and pleased with Brenda's information. She reached into her bag and handed Brenda an envelope stuffed with a substantial amount of cash. Discretion and no paper trail were part of the deal. Pleased with

herself and armed with a new shot of confidence, Brenda lingered at the restaurant after her magazine contact left; and leisurely prepped for the interview.

Brenda and Marisa, the new third stream top model, hit it off immediately. Brenda thanked God this girl was nothing like Victoria. She was smart, in any case. She'd already done a thorough background check on Brenda and asked all the right questions. Marisa was impressed with what she heard and saw, not hesitating to offer Brenda the job. Brenda would start in three weeks from the day. She was as thrilled as a kid in a candy store. The only thing left for the new employer to do is to call Brenda's references; however, Brenda requested that she hold off for a few weeks. Stating that she needed time to break away properly from her current employer. Marisa thought that gesture was Brenda way of saying she had a special bond with her boss and so agreed to wait.

Brenda felt things were definitely looking up, and, that she and Jason were well on their way.

Later that evening—Brenda made it back to her place and chilled on the sofa with her purse beside her, mentally processing all the events that had unfolded that day. She couldn't wait to share her news with Jason.

Suddenly, it dawned on Brenda that her phone had been on vibrate the entire day. She knew Victoria was going to take pissed-off to a whole other level. Brenda grabbed her purse, rummaging for her phone. After finding it, her eyes widened. "Shit!" There they were—eighteen missed calls and eighteen messages from Victoria. Never mind that Brenda had requested, and received the day off to take care of personal business. Victoria was so needy and demanding; she expected Brenda to answer her calls no matter what or when.

Brenda was just relieved she would no longer have to deal with Victoria's obnoxious, demanding spirit much longer. She resigned herself to getting it over with; so, Brenda decided to call the ice princess to find out what was so damn urgent now. Although, she knew it was probably nothing important; Brenda took a deep breath.

"Hello, Victoria, what's going on?"

"You haven't answered my calls all day."

"Victoria, I asked for time off because I had some important business of my own to take care of."

"Whatever! I needed the last date of that show we did in Chicago. I've got people asking me all kinds of questions about dates and times of events. I pay enough money for my assistant to handle these issues. Even if you're going to be off, I still expect you to at least answer your phone and be available to respond to questions. I shouldn't have to be bothered by this. I thought I made it clear four years ago that being my assistant would be your life. Nothing stands still in this business. That's why we get the big bucks. You like the big bucks, right?"

"Yes, Victoria, I like the big bucks. I am sorry for not answering my phone. Thanks for letting me take care of my affairs."

"You're welcome. I allowed you to go and take care of whatever your personal business was, because of friendship. However, as for—me, my brand, my bread, and butter—you had better remember that this is a business; and my business takes precedence. I need to make sure you understand that."

"I understand. I will take the next flight out to you tomorrow."

"Good, I'll see you then."

Brenda disconnected and laughed, talking to herself out loud, "Whoo, chile, I deserve an award for that act. That Ice Princess Victoria has no clue her world is about to turn upside down—I can't wait! Three more weeks of this bullshit, then I'm done."

❧

The next day, Brenda arrived early in the morning at the one-and-a-half-story penthouse suite in Chicago to meet with Victoria.

Victoria gawked at Brenda, and said, "Well, hello."

Following Victoria's gaze, Brenda turned to look over her shoulder.

"I was expecting your shadow," Victoria continued sarcastically, turning and sashaying into the den.

"Jason is not my shadow," Brenda argued. "He isn't with me."

"Why? Did you two fight? He's usually everywhere you are to run up my bill. Hell, his room service tab alone is half your salary."

Brenda felt her temper flaring.

"About that—Jason will not be accompanying me on any more trips. Also, to answer your question, no, we aren't fighting. We are very much in love."

Brenda had to pause and dig her nails into her palms to prevent herself from exploding.

"It's just—I took this job—not Jason. So it's not right to hold him to our abusive schedule. It's also not fair for you to pay his way for everything. So, Jason will not be tagging along as a 'shadow' anymore."

"I'm sorry, Brenda," Victoria checked herself, feeling Brenda's rising temperature; no matter how subdued. "I didn't mean it like that. It's just that I am under lots of pressure right now, dealing with this thing about my family, and I hate it when I need to talk to you but can't."

"That's okay; I understand the pressure you are under, Victoria. What's the latest development on that front?"

Victoria indicated she had better take a seat. Brenda sat in a chair near the sofa where Victoria had lounged. She rubbed her temples with the realization that she was Victoria's everything—including her therapist. Pretending to be a best friend and faithful confidant felt wrong to Brenda; but, she wanted and needed every tidbit of information, so she played her role.

Supermodel Victoria was oblivious to any and everyone, other than herself. She just needed someone to vent to and seemed thrilled to have a listening ear.

"Brenda, I have pondered this in my brain over and over again. I have no clue what I should do about my sister. I admit, my image has pretty much been the most important thing to me. Until now—for the first time in my life, my conscience is haunting me. Also, I feel terrible about how I've treated Unique. You were right. It would be a PR and an image-killing nightmare if I continued to pretend as though my sister doesn't exist. But, here's the thing—for the most part, I don't care about that. I do genuinely care about my sister succeeding in what she is trying to achieve. What she has decided to do with her life is a good thing. I pulled every article about her, and I am amazed at her accomplishments. Swear to God; I wish I had done everything differently. Wish I could take it all back. Now she'll think that I have a hidden agenda."

'What the hell? Why a fucking conscious now!' Brenda internally said because she needed more dirt, not Victoria turning into some bleeding-heart, goody-two-shoes.

"I understand where you are coming from, Victoria." Brenda pleadingly said, "I do. However, your sister wants nothing more to do with you. Can you blame her? You called her jealous and said yourself that you treated her like shit her entire life. Even though she is clearly intelligent, you call her a retard. Why would she want you to have anything to do with her—or her show—now? Was there ever a time in your lives when you did right by your sister?"

Victoria was heartbroken—and, looked it. Brenda was right. There wasn't a single instance she could think of when she had treated her sister as a person or shown her any kindness. She melted once more into tears.

"Oh my god! Brenda, you're right. I can't think of one time when I did the right thing by Unique. I've never been a sister to her."

'No, no, no!' Internally Brenda screamed because her plan was falling apart. Brenda continued clutching Victoria's hand until a clear plan of deceit came to mind, and she said, "Okay… Honey— Calm down—this is how I see it. You need to do everything in your power to stop Unique's show. All you have to do is make some calls using your popularity and influence, and that shit will be dead in the water. Can you imagine what a disaster you and your brand would be if this gets out? You know it's true. You've said it all along. It's either you or Unique. It's your choice, Victoria. Forget her dreams! What about yours? So really, I thought you said you didn't have a sensitive bone in your body for the 'retards' and 'cripples' in the world. Where is all this crazy talk about conscious coming from all of a sudden?"

Hearing her own words repeated back to her, stung. Victoria felt sick to her stomach about how cruel and selfish a person she had become and had always been. Victoria shook her head sadly, and admitted, "Yeah… that's what I said. I felt that I didn't have a sympathetic or sensitive bone in my body for human beings with any physical or mental challenge. I always referred to them as the retarded, lame, handicapped, mentally challenged, or anyone in that category. I'm ashamed! These are human beings, Brenda. How could I have been such a monster? I'm not that monster anymore.

I've been thinking about all that my sister said to me. And, I don't want to die alone. I thought about everything she's accomplished—despite all her challenges.

All I did was trash, bully or ignore her every step of the way. Also, It's not just me, either. I acted just like millions of other ignorant, hateful people out there. We don't want to see; so we make excuses. We build a wall, so we become blind to others in the world. Unique doesn't have that luxury, and serious challenges are part of her reality. Instead of focusing on her pain, my selfless sister reached out to other people who are different and in similar situations. More importantly, she is waking up individuals like me. Suddenly, because of Unique's strength and determination, I can finally see the real world—the pain, the joy, the power, the love, and the blessings that come with helping. "

By now, Victoria was pacing the floor with tears, and blowing mucus in a handkerchief.

"Unique said I was selfish. She was right to get in my face. It's as though she held up a mirror so that I could see myself for the first time. I've been selfish all my life. Brenda, I can and will change. Changing starts with me; and, I want to begin now by putting myself aside and helping my sister with this project. No matter what the media says and, I'll make sure that they don't mention my name. I'll hang in the background, anonymous."

'Dear God, what have I done?' Brenda's mind screamed internally, ashamed of herself after listening to Victoria; witnessing her powerful, change-of-heart transformation right before her eyes. Brenda had such a shameful expression on her face. She realized she had made a major mistake by selling Victoria's story and going to the magazine rep, but it was too late. Brenda wanted to take it all back and make a change like Victoria was doing; but, was afraid and it was too late. Realizing her damage was invalidated: she panicked, not sure what to do next. Then, she listened to the little voice that told her she had to go through with her plan, or her career would be the one to crash and burn. Brenda reached into her purse to turn off the hidden recorder, grabbing a mint to offer Victoria as her cover. Brenda popped a mint into her mouth before continuing.

"Victoria, wow… That took a lot of guts. I must say, I'm proud of you. Wow—you put it all out there—willing to change. Now, that takes

guts. I hope it all pans out for you. You okay? You got yourself pretty worked up. You hungry? Let's get some lunch," Brenda suggested gently. "Then we can work on that Chicago deal."

"Yeah, I guess I could use a bite, thanks. I also have a special assignment for you. I want you to help me find out exactly what my sister needs to make sure her show is the hottest of the season!"

Brenda enthusiastically agreed to get right on it; even though she knew she wouldn't see it to completion. She had less than three weeks left, working with Ms. Victoria. Brenda suggested a favorite spot she knew of near a post office for lunch. That way, she could both eat and mail a package, killing two birds with one stone.

CHAPTER 3

THE TRUTH REVEALED

It was Victoria who had been pulling most of the behind-the-scenes-strings for Unique's runway show because Brenda had called in sick for the past six days. Victoria felt something was 'off' with Brenda; but, she couldn't be certain of it. Victoria had been on the phone constantly, pulling all her contacts and resources together, when her doorbell rang. Victoria's' live-in house worker, Ms. Ruth hurried to check the peephole.

Victoria watched as the still-attractive, middle-aged woman stopped in amazement, staring at—rather than opening—the door. "Ms. Ruth, don't just stand there. Is something wrong? Who is it?"

"Uh, it's your father, Ms. V. I haven't seen him since the Jamaica trip."

Victoria laughed knowingly, "Oh, I remember that trip. You and my dad got kinda close. So, don't just stand there, Ms. Ruth! Let the man in!"

Ms. Ruth smoothed her uniform and hair; as if, he was coming to visit her. She then slowly opened the door.

"Hello Al, it's been a while since I've seen you."

"Hello, Ruth. And, you are still looking as good as…"

Victoria cleared her throat—loudly—interrupting before her dad could say things to Ms. Ruth which she didn't care to hear.

"Hi Dad, what a surprise! I mean, it is great to see you; but, what brings you to Florida? St. Louis, too cold for you?" Victoria chuckled. Every time her father was in her presence, she felt like a little girl.

"No, honey, I flew out just to see you. Don't you remember giving me your schedule, so I'd know when you were home?"

Victoria looked a bit concerned. Her dad was always welcome; but, she remembered the last time he made a surprise visit, he had bad news. She suspected it was bad news now, too.

"Honey, it wouldn't have mattered where you were. I needed to see you."

She hugged her father, noticing he had no bags. "Come on into the study with me, Dad, so we can relax and talk. Can I get you something to drink? You hungry?"

Father and daughter sat down across from each other in the cozy, sunny room. Al sat on the butter-soft, brown leather sofa, and Victoria curled up on the matching love seat across from him. Now, face-to-face and comfortable Victoria was just like her dad in getting straight to the point.

Long, colt-like legs folded under her, Victoria asked, "So, Dad, what's up? Everything—Okay?"

"I've got something I want you to see; but, first I need to talk to you about your sister, Unique."

Victoria sucked in her breath. Thoughts of harm that may have come Uniques way panicked her imagination. Whatever Dad was about to say wasn't good. "Okay, Dad."

"Your sister gave me a call. She was very upset, Victoria. Again! You! Again! This time she's had to deal with constant calls, texts, emails and even surprise visits from reporters and producers about allegations of her being a secret family member to you. All the questions have been about you being her sister and hiding her under the rug."

Victoria was speechless, looking like a deer caught in the headlights. Al realized that his oldest child had no clue what was happening.

After wiping his brow, Al continued to explain. "The media have you on audio calling your sister a 'retard,'" Al continued sadly. "It was your voice saying you don't have a sensitive bone in your body for disadvantaged people; referring to them all as 'cripples' or 'retards' like your sister."

Tears of hurt and disappointment pooled in Al's eyes as his blood seem to boil inside. He took a deep breath and wiped his beard with his right hand and said, "And, yes… I am well aware of all the times you've had her removed from your public appearances. Unique just wanted to see you—see her sister, Victoria. How in God's name could you be so cruel to your own flesh and blood?"

Al, crossed his legs, "It's partly my fault because I always made excuses for you and your 'ways.' I ask myself, where did I fail you? You have hurt the thing I instilled in you most, family. The truth is, there's never any reason for denying your family. And, there's never a reason to be so damn mean to anyone! I know I taught you all about the importance of family, how family keeps you balanced in life. I tried so hard to foster a relationship between you and your sister. I know you hated going over Dorothy's house to visit Unique, but I made you—to avoid days like this—right here! "

Al pointed his finger to the floor and continued to discipline Victoria. "Your mother has always been a selfish, and mean-spirited one. I prayed that you would be different from her. But, you're not. You've acted just as hateful as your mama. I'm very disappointed in you, Victoria. And, I'm sorry—I must have failed you somewhere along the way—for you to be like this, is beyond me."

Victoria burst into sorrowful tears. Al was taken aback. Victoria crying caught Al's attention because that was unlike Victoria. He'd only known his daughter to be tough as nails. Victoria had hardly ever cried.

Victoria could barely speak between her near-hysterical dam burst of emotion and sobbing. "Oh, Daddy, I am so very sorry, I promise you. Yes, I did do all those horrible things to my little sister, and I am so ashamed of myself. But, I swear to you, my heart and mind started changing the moment Unique went off on me. I never saw her so strong and feisty. God knows I deserved it and have had it coming for a long time. It was at that moment when I saw my sister for the first time. I realized how much I

loved and respected her. I do. Unique was so strong and beautiful. Dad, I can never adequately express to you or Unique how deeply sorry I am— for everything. But, I am most sorry for the years I've thrown away with my sister. I know this hurts you too; and, I am so sorry, and Daddy you have never failed me. It wasn't you! My mom failed me and I don't want to be like her at all. Do you think Unique will ever be able to forgive me? Even though—I understand if she can't. I don't deserve her forgiveness. Dad, will you forgive me, too?"

Victoria hung her head in shame and blew her nose. That was the only sound to pierce the momentary, deafening silence in the room. Al felt compassion for his lost child.

"Baby, I'm your dad, and there is nothing that would cause me not to forgive you. However, your sister, Unique is the one you need to talk to about her forgiveness."

Victoria's demeanor expressed concern. Al's eyes soften, and he said, "Don't worry— she'll let this go because she loves you just as I. We are family, child."

Victoria's mind slipped back to the audio. "Dad, I can't figure out how the media would have gotten me saying those bad things about Unique when I changed the moment I…" She looked up in an "ah-ha" moment.

"OH! MY! GOD! Dad! My assistant, Brenda, must have recorded me on her phone and leaked it to the media. She's the only one I've talked to."

Al nodded in acknowledgment with the tilt of his head. As an attorney, Al did not feel it's lawful to accuse someone without legitimate proof. He was a real egalitarian and believed everyone had equal rights to defend themselves. He taught his children to take responsibility for what they do in life. Al looked at Victoria, shook his head because Victoria wasn't displaying his teachings.

"That may be true; but, don't blame your assistant. Even if it was Brenda who ratted you out; this is on you, baby-girl."

"But Dad— She betrayed me! I didn't know."

"So what, she betrays you! She couldn't have recorded your voice unless you said it." Al adjusts himself in his seat to relax a bit, then continued, "Okay, it's clear to me she's likely responsible for the leak. But, you, Victoria, have to take responsibility for your words and actions. You

are the one who has to straighten this mess out, starting with Unique. Here's the video that's going viral... I'm surprised you haven't seen it already. Watch it. Then, fix this! Don't make me fly down here again over you disrespecting a family member, young lady."

Just as when Victoria was small, she had the reverential respect for and natural fear of her father. She replied to his command while wiping her tears away. "Yes, Sir, I will get things straightened out. I'll make it right with my sister. I promise."

Al stood up first, then Victoria followed. Al opened his arms to Victoria. She gratefully flew into them, fresh tears of sorrow—and relief—flowing. Al held her and kissed his daughter on the forehead, reassuring her of his love for her—no matter what.

After a few precious moments, Al tilted Victoria's chin up with a gentle fingertip, "Go get a facial. All those salty tears make a face puffy. And, you've shed more than your share today. I love you, baby-girl, just as I love your sister, Unique. Call me when you make things right with her. As for the media, trust your ole' Dad to handle them. I will consult other partners in my firm about all our legal options with those vultures. The media edit and turn stories around all the time; It's what they do. Trust me; I got this part. You fix the relationship with your sister."

Victoria knew she had a lot of work to do for Unique to ever forgive her. She just hoped and prayed that it wasn't too late. Walking her dad to the door, she promised herself not to give up on repairing their broken relationship; no matter what. Al kissed her goodbye and left as swiftly as he came; but, not before him giving Ms. Ruth a playful tap on the bottom as he exited. Ms. Ruth blushed as she shut the door behind him.

❧

Victoria sat on the sofa rehearsing over and again all the right, possible words she would say when she finally has the opportunity to speak to her sister. She went over and over them again until Ms. Ruth walked in. Tired of the repetition, she decided to help.

"Ms. V, if you don't mind, just speak from the heart when you talk to your sister. She may not forgive you right away. But, she will forgive

you—because she loves you. I've been around long enough to know your father pretty well. He is an exceptional person. He raised both you girls to love and instilled in you the ability to forgive. Trust me, Unique will be happy to hear from you. Just call her and stop with the rehearsing. I'm about to burn your dinner with listening to you go on and on."

Victoria laughed aloud. And, it felt good. "I guess you're right, Ms. Ruth. I'm sorry—get back to your food. We don't want any burned meals."

❧

Victoria picked up her phone to dial Unique, but it rang before she got the chance. It was Brenda. "Hello, B. Just the person I wanted to talk to."

Brenda wasn't sure if Victoria had heard the news or yet seen the video, but She knew it was time to quit. She didn't want to be fired first. That would be on her record—and, under public scrutiny—forever.

Her questions were answered when Victoria got right to the point. "I need to talk to you, so I'll be at your place within the hour."

Victoria was even more curt than usual and disconnected directly. "She knows," Brenda said out loud—nervous. Not knowing how Victoria was going to react; she'd wished she could take it all back.

Victoria instantaneously called out to Ms. Ruth, who detected the apprehension in Victoria's voice, responded swiftly, "What is it, Ms. V?"

"I'm going out to see Brenda at her hotel. Can you stick my dinner in the fridge for later? I've got a quick piece of business to take care of."

Ms. Ruth didn't like the sound of Victoria's stern voice; but, said nothing and did what she was requested.

Victoria grabbed her handbag and rushed out the door.

❧

As promised, Victoria arrived at Brenda's hotel within the hour. Victoria's knock on the door was aggressive and bold. Brenda braced herself. Victoria's expression went beyond anger. It reflected rage, hurt and betrayal. With a lump in her throat, Brenda wasn't so sure she even wanted to risk having

this really—pissed-off—Victoria in her room. Momentarily, unable to move or speak; she just stood there until Victoria asked.

"Well, can I come in, Brenda," which was an unnecessary ask, because Victoria had already slipped past Brenda and into the room.

"Sure you can. Uh, yeah… I'm just surprised that you came to see me for—uh—a visit."

Victoria laughed mockingly, "A visit? Is that what you think this is? Well, let me correct you. This is no damn visit. You had to be the one who leaked my private conversation with you—and you only—to the media. It is in the magazines, on the TV and splashed all over the Internet. It was you! Wasn't it? Tell the truth!"

Brenda cleared her throat and lied, "No, Victoria, I would never do that to you. I have no idea how they got that information. And, yes, I saw the article. And, the video… I knew you were going to be upset by…"

The fury blazing in Victoria's eyes shut Brenda right up. Those eyes glared at Brenda with complete disbelief.

"I repeat… You— Brenda, were the only one with whom I discussed my family." Victoria moved closer to Brenda's face. "If… I find out you were the one behind this shit— may God help you and will forgive me for what I'll do. At any rate, I know I can no longer trust you; so, I am relieving you of your position."

"You're firing me?"

"Ding, ding, ding… Yes, you got it. See, you're a bright girl!" Victoria's sarcasm turned into deadly seriousness. I want the laptop I gave you, any hard drives or thumb drives with all work and contacts related to me. Immediately… I want any hard copies as well. I will mail your last paycheck. And, I'm sure you don't expect any severance pay.

On a personal note, Brenda, I hope you weren't the one to betray me for money. It's not worth it. Once I get my hands on concrete proof—and, I will—you will never work in this industry again. As anyone's assistant or trash collector. I'll make sure of it. "

Victoria strode to the door, turning to face Brenda again before she walked out.

"If you did do this, I might be able to eventually forgive you; but, I will never forget. There's no way in hell I will allow you to rip someone

else's life apart like you tried to do to mine. See, here's the thing. If this was you—and, I'd bet my life that it was—you've failed! Failed—Brenda, because my family is stronger than you gave us credit for. We just get stronger, that's all. By the way, all my personal contact numbers have already been changed. Oh, and, one last thing. I expect you checked out of this hotel by morning. Goodbye, Brenda…"

Brenda slid to the floor as Victoria slammed the door behind her, coming to grips with the reality that she had destroyed her entire life. There was no future for her. She killed it.

CHAPTER 4

THE ART OF
FORGIVENESS

VICTORIA DID JUST AS her father had not-so-subtly-suggested. After her confrontation with Brenda, Victoria treated herself to a late-night facial and a much-needed massage to de-stress. Once home—she called her sister Unique.

"Unique, hi… This is Victoria."

Unique was still hurt and furiously replied, "Why are you calling me? I know it's not to talk to the 'retard.' Before you say another word, I asked Dad just to leave it alone. I knew he would try to make excuses for you, like always."

Victoria pleaded. "Please Unique, just hear me out. I am so sorry. God, you have no idea how sorry I am. For everything, I've ever done and said to hurt you. I know this sounds crazy—but, I never wanted to hurt you. Hell, I was so thoughtless and self-absorbed, it never even occurred

to me that, of course, you would be hurt. The problems were all me. You were right to call me selfish, not to mention all the other things you said. I deserved it. The bottom line is this: I never really knew you until the day you told me about myself. It was as if I saw my little sister for the very first time. You have indeed grown up into a fabulous, intelligent, tough—and beautiful—woman that I admire. I couldn't be prouder of the woman you've become. I am sorry to admit; I had no part in that. I know it's too late to go back to the past. But, if we could put it behind us and if you allow me to be your big sister now, I promise; I will never disappoint you again. We're still young and although we can't change our past; we can build an unbreakable bond as we ride into our future—together. Please Unique, can you forgive me?"

Victoria's heart sank when Unique said nothing after her contrition. Bombarded with emotions running the scope from anger to love and everything in-between, Unique suddenly remembered her mom, Cindy's constant teaching and preaching, 'If you want Jesus to forgive you, you must forgive others.' Forgiveness was an endless lesson from both her parents and the pastor at their church. She had gotten good at it, too. Unique could hear her father's words in her head. 'Next, to God, the family is the most critical love.'

Unique had forgiven her birth mother; Dorothy, so many times for so many things. She had learned to ask Jesus to forgive her for her wrongs. She especially remembered asking God to forgive her for almost giving up on her sister, Jamie's dreams.

After what felt like forever to Victoria, Unique spoke.

"My mom—Cindy, always said, 'If you don't forgive, you give power to the devil and your enemy.' Vickie, having you in my life is all I ever wanted. Of course, I forgive you. I never stopped hoping my big sister would want to be a part of my life."

Victoria practically exploded with relief, shrieking with joy and thanking her sister profusely for her absolution. When she heard Unique call her Vickie, she knew it was all going to be okay. But, one thing still ate away at Victoria so she said, "Unique, can I ask you a question?"

"Yeah, sure—What is it?"

"Brenda said I had never done anything nice for you. To be perfectly honest, I can't remember one time I did right by you. God knows I have to live with my actions forever. But, is there a time I ever treated you like a person?"

"Vickie, the past is the past. I forgive you for all the past, just as Jesus forgives. But, you know what, big Sis? You must be getting old 'cause your memory is kinda cloudy," Unique teased.

After Victoria had laughed in protest, Unique explained, "Don't you remember? You treated me great most of the times when we were little. Do you remember when I had got sick one day, Dad was at work and the nanny wasn't around. I think she was in the yard somewhere. Anyway, you ran to get some towels, soaked them in fresh water and put them on my head so gently. You must have been afraid because you held me close to you with my head in your lap. You rocked me until the nanny came back in. You never hated me, Vickie. I always knew you loved me—even when you got too full of yourself—so, don't let anyone put that in your head."

"Omigod, I did forget." Victoria was relieved, she started crying all over again. Her heart pulsated with joy as some of their childhood memories jolted back into her soul. Their childhood memories were like precious jewels to her now, and excitement filled her.

"I remember that! And, I also remember us running and playing in the house, even though we were repeatedly warned not to; breaking Dad's table in the process."

For the first time in years, Al's girls laughed together.

"You were afraid he was going to be angry," Unique chimed in. "So I told him I did it. We both laughed when he said…"

Victoria finished the sentence and the story, "Thanks. That table was ugly."

"He said, 'he was waiting for an excuse to get rid of it,'" Unique added, chuckling. There were quiet smiles and a short pause on both ends of the phone call, as the girls relived the memory. Unique's next lower and softer spoken words substantiated her love for her sister. "You see, Vickie? You were there for me when we were younger."

Victoria lowered her voice, "Wow, I was, wasn't I? Thank you, Unique. I actually had forgotten the good times we shared. You held on to them for both of us. Thank you for giving them back to me."

Unique teased, "You're welcome. Wait. You're not going to start crying again, Are you?"

"No… But, I do have another favor to ask you."

"What is it?"

"Can I come there, so we spend one whole day together shopping?"

"Really?" Unique asked in excitement, "Cool, I would love that! The only thing is, I am kind of busy with my show coming up; but, for my big sister? Sure, I'll find the time! I hope it's fabric, furniture or food shopping! Memo-to-sister… I design clothes."

Victoria laughed at the thought and asked another question dear to her heart. "I want to help you with your show, too. But, before you say anything, I'll only do it if you promise you do not mention my name. Your show is all about you and your visions for this world. I just want to be part of what you are doing."

Unique grinned from ear-to-ear when she heard Victoria say the magic words: that she wanted to help. Unique was grateful—especially since her little fashion show had evolved into a giant, runway event! Unique knew she could use all the help she could get.

"Sure, I would like that."

They said their 'good nights,' 'I love you(s)' and hung up; happy to be a family again.

&

Victoria wasn't done for the night, though. She needed to check with Dad on the media front, confident that he and his law firm would make the problem go away. But, in the meantime, Victoria needed to do some fixing of her own, like making sure she didn't falsely accuse Brenda without substantial evidence. She decided to call a press conference. After calling her PR advisors, it was unanimous. They all agreed a press conference was a good idea to set the record straight. The released audio was somehow altered. The new Victoria claimed responsibility for saying some vile things—but, some of what the public heard was edited. The media needed to hear everything from her own mouth. A press conference would also bring more attention to her sister's upcoming show.

The news conference was a good choice. Victoria owned up to her mistakes and feelings about dealing with a sister with special needs, right up front. She mentioned Brenda only as her former assistant; making no judgment, no accusations. People could draw their own conclusions on how the media got the story in the first place. She also hit everyone with her thoughts on the stigmatization of mental and physical disabilities. Before taking questions, Victoria bragged about her sister's show, stressing how critical it was to spread awareness of and foster compassionate action in support of the millions of people whose only difference was in the kinds of challenges they have to face every day.

The news generated from the press conference inspired legions of people to donate or purchase tickets to Unique's event on the website Victoria had created. It was also the driving force for Brenda being fired on the spot from her new assistant gig. No one with half a brain wanted her as a personal assistant now. Brenda made the wrong choice, a greedy choice; and dug her own professional grave. She foolishly convinced herself that there would be no consequences, only because she denied it. She forgot that people don't need proof to believe something and are good at reading between the lines. Brenda, also, mistakenly counted on people loathing Victoria, once her secret hit the light of day. She thought wrong. Most importantly, especially for anyone considered to be any celebrity, an assistant had to be utterly loyal and must be faithful and trustworthy. In most instances, confidentiality agreements are signed before employment even begins, but Victoria trusted Brenda—a mistake.

Brenda also had mistakenly thought that Jason would be there for her through it all, good or bad, right or wrong, ride-or-die; but, he was MIA (Missing In Action). He didn't like the mountain of negative fall-out from Brenda's scheme. He saw the part of the press conference where Victoria implied—but, didn't have to say—that her assistant Brenda, stabbed her in the back.

Sure, at the time, Jason cheered Brenda on with her plan; happy to cash in on it with her. But, now, she was more of a liability than an asset. Jason had only heard Brenda's side of the story. She had conveniently left out the part about Victoria being remorseful, eventually sickened by having been such a bitch to her sister, and changing into a caring human

being. But, Brenda knew; and, she tried to take down Victoria anyway. Jason thought, 'Fuck that kind of drama and cray-cray in a possible marriage partner!' So—he dumped her, unceremoniously breaking off the engagement.

Because his own guilt was eating away at him, sometimes Jason reflected on the many nice things Victoria, the 'ice princess,' had done for Brenda and him. It did not add up to Jason when he compared the wrong of Victoria to the good. There was the time when Brenda had pneumonia and was hospitalized for several weeks. Victoria had placed her life on hold, staying right there with Brenda, almost around-the-clock as her nurse and friend. Brenda was spoiled; her room filled with flowers and balloons. Victoria mothered Brenda, assisting her with bathing, hair coming and whatever else she needed or wanted. The supermodel put her life on hold and mothered Brenda the entire way and until she got well.

Jason remembered the vacation Victoria paid for to make up for the one he and Brenda were forced to cancel. Hell, those kinds of personal sacrifices came with the damn territory. He and Brenda blew it. A nagging little voice also reminded Jason of all the times he sponged off Victoria when she and Brenda traveled, and never giving it a second thought. Next thing Jason knew, he was privately making a substantial donation to Unique's foundation.

Jason got the promotion he had been waiting for at his company, and he was a single man again.

Even though no one besides Jason had proof—Brenda was responsible for the leak to the media and Brenda's life only continued its downward spiral. She had nowhere to turn, and nowhere to be, no man shoulders to cry on and comprehensively disconsolate.

CHAPTER 5

UNIQUE'S BIG DAY

IT WAS ANOTHER EXTRAORDINARY day for Unique and her family. The morning sky had just begun to light up. Soon the sun rays were beaming through Unique's curtains onto her half-asleep face.

Her mother awakened her with the usual morning greeting, "Rise and shine Sleepy Butt!"

She was half-asleep; but, the other half was wide-awake. Unique was bursting with excitement. She had run herself ragged in preparation for this day. It had finally arrived and, come in style. The weather was perfection. Sitting up in bed and padding to the bathroom, Unique felt an overwhelming sense of achievement, gratification, and gratitude in her life. She knew this day was going to be an adventure—an adventure that would change her life forever. She prayed that remarkable change would spill over onto and blessedly impact the lives of everyone involved.

Her mother knew she would be rushing Unique along throughout her day, so she jumped right on in. "Unique! You are taking too long in the bathroom. Move it, babe! We've got a long day ahead of us."

As Unique brushed her teeth, she thought of all the hard work her mom—Cindy, had put in to help make her dreams become a reality. She happily yelled back, right after she rinsed the chalky, minty toothpaste from her mouth. "Okay, Mom, just a minute."

"Unique, please hurry! Breakfast is ready. Come down to eat before it gets cold."

Unique's two younger brothers were already sitting at the table, uncharacteristically eating in silence. They were acutely aware that this day was big, and had no time for the usual morning chatter. Unique practically skipped her way to the kitchen to grab a bite. Her mom was running a very tight ship.

After breakfast, Cindy snapped them into action, "Boys, load the cars and tell your dad we are ready to go."

The youngest Maury took off running to give their father the message. The other, Jerry—started loading the cars. Packing, lifting, and loading all that stuff might have been tough, physical labor for most folks—but, not Jerry. He was a wrestler, track and football star at his high school, jumping at any physical challenge he could find. For just the tiniest, most satisfactory moment, Cindy stopped and actually looked at her children with awe and wonder. Could anything be more fulfilling than appreciating that you've been an excellent mother?

They arrived at the concert hall for the runway show later that morning. When Unique walked in, she was amazed by the hundreds of workers already buzzing around the place. Close to three hundred people were there preparing the room for the show. Yep—it takes a village, for real! Pulling it all together takes a whole lot of work, she smiled to herself. Standing in the middle of the giant space, Unique slowly realized that the dreams she and her sister, Jamie, had held dearest were about to become a reality. It was a reality, taking shape right now! She sorely missed her sister more than ever today, quickly brushing a renegade tear from her eye before anyone spotted it. No tears today! Jumping back into the reality of all the activity swirling around her, Unique noticed the lighting grip dropping some equipment and cursing at no one in particular. The sound engineer inadvertently wrapped himself up in a maze of cables and cords. The assistant show director was running back and forth, telling the

small army of hairdressers and makeup artists—who seemingly came all together, all at once—where to set up.

Security had already been there for hours with the sniffing canine 'officers,' scouring every crevice of the building inside-out and top-to-bottom, for any possible threat.

Tyrone, the show's coordinator, tripped on some of the cords before they were bound into place with electrical tape and thick plastic mats, which would be camouflaged by strategically placed carpet pieces. Embarrassed, he quickly bounced back before anyone—other than Unique—noticed. He scurried along, wrangling the models, "Move it, ladies! Chop, chop!" Snapping his fingers and clapping his hands, Tyrone locked them all in place, just like the Shetland Shepherds who herd their sheep into the proper formation.

At Tyrone's shrill insistence, the models were settling into their places backstage, each hunting for her assigned dressing table where the magic happened. The musical director, Ralph, was a redbone who turned red from the irritation of Tyrone and his models. To Ralph, they were all in the way and were working his last nerve. Peeping Unique, and every bit as high-strung as the rest of the creative crew, he demanded to know where he and his artists were to gather for the final dress rehearsal. Unique pointed him toward the rear of the building.

Upon arrival, to Ralph's pleasant surprise, things were all set up. There was a private soundproof booth teched-out with audio equipment, a fully loaded board, microphone, earplugs, the works. Ralph was delighted and to be so far away from Tyrone's motley crew—even better. Unique looked back and could see the gleam of Ralph's smile from where she stood. She felt as powerful as Scandal's Olivia Pope. Handled.

Unique checked and double checked the clothing in their order of appearance, to make sure there was not one item left behind. Her fashion show was groundbreaking. She not only designed clothes for the challenged-in-one way-or-another runway models; she also created colorful and fun, yet highly functional accessories for children with physical and mental disabilities. Wheelchairs, walkers and other types of equipment featured detachable clips or strapping to match whatever the child was wearing.

The medical staff had arrived and were searching for their station to set things up. Unique was taking no chances with the distinct possibility of someone getting sick, falling, stumbling or suffering a seizure. She wanted to make sure her special guests had the care they needed if they were to become overwhelmed by the show in any way. She also had a backup plan in place to keep the show running seamlessly, in the unlikely event of the unexpected snafu. If any participants new to runway modeling were to get sick or become frightened before going on stage, she had understudies all lined-up, willing and ready to fill in—if necessary. Each adult runway model was paired with a child model to escort onto the stage, displaying each child's outer and inner beauty through the universal language of fashion. After they returned to the rear of the stage together, an assistant would take each little girl and boy to enjoy the rest of the show; The caregiver model would then do her pivot on the catwalk, fully showing off her gorgeous piece from Unique's elegantly designed clothing line.

Unique stepped onto the stage, still putting out event-related fires and supervising last minute stage prep for the final dress rehearsals. The pressure was on big time, now. You can do this—Unique, she coached herself mentally. Just stay calm—breathe. One of the video production crew had a question about the exact placement of the large screens he was getting ready to anchor on each side of the stage securely. Unique recognized this guy. Those screens were supposed to have been installed long before today; along with the other stage designs. With anxiety building, she was about to go off on this mope—when her mother stepped in at just the right time. Cindy had been proudly watching her daughter in action from the sidelines when she saw Unique's frustration level climbing, just by the expression on her daughter's face. That man needed to be rescued from what was building up to be Hurricane Unique. Victoria's help had been invaluable; but, she and the crew had tweaked the screen's placement a bit and forgot to tell Unique. Happily, Mama Bear—Cindy was on top of it and jumped in between Unique and the production assistant, "I got this one." Unique had complete gratitude for her mother because she did not like getting fussy with anyone, but would if she felt pushed. Cindy patiently directed the P.A., knowledgeably answering all his questions.

Unique leaned over and whispered, "Mom, where is Victoria? She said she would beat us here. That was hours ago."

Cindy still had her hair tied up with her favorite head wrap. With all the running around she'd been doing, it had slid half off her head. Unique didn't think she'd ever seen her mother look so worn out. Cindy's appearance was always crisp and put together, even when working in her garden. With the head wrap looking crazy; Unique couldn't help but giggle at her mom's expense.

"And, what, may I ask is so funny?" Cindy asked, feigning insult, putting her hands on her hips, playfully cutting her eyes at Unique. She tapped her toe waiting for an answer.

"Nothing Mom, I just love you. By the way, your scarf is about to slide right off."

Cindy snatched off the colorful fabric and re-tied it. "Oh, sorry—sweetie… I forgot to tell you Victoria called. She said she was picking up some last minute surprises for you."

Unique shook her head. "More surprises! Mom, she's already done so much. Do you know she wanted her name to stay out of this? Vickie, of all people, not wanting any of the limelight! Can you believe it?"

Cindy was thrilled with the changes she'd seen in Victoria. Especially, for her daughter's sake… It was evident Victoria was sincere and had no ulterior motives for getting involved. She came through for Unique with this show. Cindy smiled, inwardly acknowledging how God always works it out. And, is always right on time. "I am so proud of Victoria. She's done a complete 180."

"Mom, I had never thought the day would come when Victoria and I would talk the way we do now. After she fired that ratchet assistant, I believe she confides more in me now. She is starting to feel more like my best friend, besides an older sister. Vickie even made sure the media didn't stalk me after that messed-up audio recording was leaked. I never thought poorly of the press until they started hunting us for a response to the accusations."

Something had puzzled Cindy for a while, so she had to ask. "Victoria mentioned it was something you said that woke her up and made her take a hard look at how she treated you in the past. She said your kindness and

determination opened the window of change for her. What exactly did you say, baby?"

Unique shrugged her shoulders, "I said so much, Mom. I can't remember exactly—I just know it wasn't very nice. And, I'm so happy to have my big sister back. Being Besties is a bonus. Better late than never, right, Mom?" Unique winked at Cindy.

"That's right, sweetheart…" Cindy smiled and pecked Unique on the cheek, "I'm just happy you've got your sister back, too."

"I do wonder what she's got up her fancy sleeves, though," Unique thought out loud.

Cindy, of course, knew. But, she'd promised Victoria she wouldn't tell.

Unique looked away from Cindy just in time to catch her adopted dad, Chuck, getting ready to arrange the centerpieces in the wrong place on the tables. Running over to him, she cried out just in time, "Dad! Hey, thanks. Let me help." Hands full—Unique whipped her head back toward Cindy, "Mom, let me know if Victoria calls again, okay?" and continued helping her dad.

CHAPTER 6

UNIQUE TAKES
A LOOK BACK

UNIQUE STOOD ON STAGE before the show, watching the happy, well-orchestrated chaos in final prep for the runway. She felt herself drifting into a daze, fading from the reality. The cavernous space was unrecognizable, magically transformed into the manifestation of all her—and Jamie's—dreams. She looked back to how it all began. Astonished that she had made it as far as she had—despite everything. Reminiscences went far back as her memory would take her.

❧

Unique's memories traveled back to when she was six years old in that wretched residence. It was a small house with three, first-floor entry doors,

converted from a two-family flat. A door leading to stairs connected to the upper level and lower levels from the inside. The place stood out from the other houses on the street. In addition to being the smallest, it was the only house with blue painted bricks.

Unique remembered wandering into the kitchen for something to eat. She looked in the refrigerator. There was nothing but old rotting potatoes and a jar of mayo. She turned to explore the contents of the cabinets and reached for the last of the dry cereal, jumping back from the scattering roaches running swiftly out the cupboard. Little Unique sat at the kitchen table that tilted at her every move, because of one of its broken legs. Her tummy growling from hunger, Unique reached into the box and devoured the last of the dry cereal.

At two a.m., thumping on the door woke up Unique. It wasn't unusual to hear knocks and other noise at that time of the morning in their neighborhood. She covered her head with the sticky feathered pillow, praying her mama would allow her to stay in her bed this time; but, that prayer went unanswered. Again—instead, Unique's mother, Dorothy, stormed into the room. She talked fast but quietly, telling Unique to wake up and put her shoes on. Unique pleaded with her mother, "Mommy please, can I stay in bed this time? Alternatively, can I sleep on the floor in the front room? Please?"

Dorothy stood there, fragile, with her hair all over her head. She had on the usual male tee shirt and jeans. Dorothy continued rubbing her nose until it was red. Her only thought was of the treats on the other side of that knock at her door; so she looked down at little Unique clenching that sticky pillow and tried to cajole the child, "Go for only a little bit, honey. You know I don't want you anywhere around when my guests come over."

Dorothy put Unique out the door as the strange man entered, glancing down at the child as if she were nothing.

Unique backed away from the front door, looking around, wondering, 'Where to go tonight.' Unique was minuscule for a six-year-old. The cold, pre-dawn, morning dew seemed to be seeping right through her tiny bones. She was in agony; undersized and underdeveloped for her age because she didn't have the food and rest that a growing child needed. Her stomach continued to ache with loud hunger noises. Unique tried

to use her imagination when she heard the growl from her belly. She pretended the noise was a lost animal in the woods that needed her help. Usually, while on the street, she would make up little adventures to go on. However, this morning, her little body wasn't up to an adventure—even just in her head. She needed food, sleep, and to be warm, dry and safe.

Wearing nothing but a thin cotton gown dotted with cigarette holes and worn-down slippers, this time, Unique decided to walk across the street to a neighbors' house, who had recently moved in. She had only seen the family from a distance, watching them through her foggy window as they entered and exited their home. Curious Unique wanted to know more about them. However, she knew that wouldn't happen because she was too shy to approach them.

Unique reached the rear of her neighbors' house. As she looked around the wooden gate, she noticed a comfortably padded swing on the back porch. It looked so inviting to her; even better than the stained bed she slept in with her Mommy. Unique needed to sleep so badly. Also, thinking that she might even be able to warm up a bit by balling up on the quilted swing.

She slowly scanned her surroundings and decided to make her move. The swing squeaked as she curled up in the corner of it. Unique knew she was outside, but she felt more comfortable in that swing than she ever felt at home.

Mrs. Woods, the neighbor who lived in that home with the cozy swing, couldn't sleep again. As usual, she made her way to the kitchen for a warm cup of milk. Reaching into her cabinet for a mug, she heard a noise on her porch. It sounded like the swing squeaking. She assumed it was a stray cat or raccoon, maybe the wind picked up a bit. She padded over to look out the window. "I got to oil that swing. It's working on my nerves," Mrs. Woods complained to herself.

That's when she saw the little girl in a ragged gown and house shoes, curled up in the corner of her swing. In a hurry to open up her door, she fumbled with the lock. "Oh my goodness," she exclaimed to herself. "Why would this child be out here alone in the middle of the night hours?"

She realized this was the same child she had noticed walking the streets. The door opening startled Unique. She jumped in fear and immediately began apologizing.

Mrs. Woods saw that she was terrified, and immediately jumped in to reassure her, "It's okay. It's okay, honey." She gently invited Unique inside the house, asking if the little girl would like to join her for a warm glass of milk.

"Yes," Unique responded enthusiastically. Then she hung her head, remembering that it was wrong to talk to strangers, let alone go into their houses. Understanding what the child was probably thinking, Mrs. Woods, held out her hand. Unique took it with her tiny hand and walked with her friendly neighbor into the house.

While drinking the milk, Mrs. Woods noticed the child was small for her age, not much larger than a toddler losing its baby fat. It looked as though she had not eaten in a while. Her hair was matted, and the cotton gown she wore was threadbare and covered with cigarette burns. How did that happen? She wondered. Mrs. Woods looked down at the child's little feet dangling from the chair, slipping out of dirty house shoes that were falling apart. Her heart broke for this little girl, tears gathering in the corners of her eyes. Before one tear could drop, she jumped up from her chair to fix this child something to eat. The quickest thing she could make was a thick peanut butter and jelly sandwich.

"You know what goes well with milk?"

Unique continued drinking without pause or looking up.

"Peanut butter and jelly. How about I make you a sandwich?"

Unique remained silent, still sipping on the milk. Mrs. Woods placed the sandwich on a plate and sat the dish on the table in front of Unique, who finally murmured, "Thank you, Miss."

Unique took a big ole, bite. Mrs. Woods smiled, watching her enjoy it. Cindy could tell from the child's expression that it was the best thing she'd ever tasted.

Now Mrs. Woods needed some answers. She started to ask questions. "What's your name, sweetheart? And, how old are you?"

Unique lifted her little head and giant, golden, puppy-dog eyes from her feast, waiting until she swallowed to speak, "My name is Unique, and I am six years old." She stared intently at Mrs. Woods, "Miss, what do I call you?"

Mrs. Woods' heart melted. Not only was this baby cute as a button—all she needed was a little soap and water—she was respectful, as well. "Well, how do you do, Unique? So happy to meet you. My name is Cindy Woods. You can call me, Mrs. Woods or Mrs. Cindy—whichever one you want. How's that?"

In addition to being small for her age, Cindy noticed that Unique was not showing her left side to her. So, Cindy pretended not to notice. Instead, she asked several questions.

"May I ask you something else?"

Unique bobbed her head up and down and thought, 'This is a nice lady.'

"Why are you out this time of the morning all by yourself? It's too dark and maybe even not safe for a little girl to be out alone. Not even most grown-ups like to be out this late—or, early. Depending on how you look at it, I suppose."

Unique giggled. Miss Cindy was funny.

"Where's your mommy, honey? Does she know you're out of the house?"

Unique knew she would get into trouble with her mommy if she were caught walking around. Dorothy had told her to stay close to the house, mainly the backyard, until she was done. Unique respectfully but carefully answered. "I like walking. My mama knows I walk around, but she doesn't mind."

Cindy knew there had to be much more than that to the story; but, she certainly wasn't going to upset the child by giving her the third degree. She was just a baby, after all. A child who apparently wasn't being cared for properly. "You know what, Unique? People tell me all the time that I talk too much, sometimes calling me a chatterbox. So, how about I practice listening—and, you do the talking. About anything you want."

Unique explained that she didn't have anything special to talk about at that moment. She wanted to know more about Miss Cindy. The two new friends sat at the kitchen table, nibbling, sipping and chatting until daybreak. In that time, Unique learned more about the three children she watched, playing in the yard; observing them from her foggy window. Mrs. Woods discovered why Unique always tried to keep her left side hidden.

After they'd been sitting and getting to know each other better, Unique fell silent for a moment, stood up to face Miss Cindy, turning so that her left side was in full view. Cindy said nothing. She just watched,

fighting back the tears. Unique slid her flimsy gown off her left shoulder, exposing her bare left arm.

Unique's left arm was half the size of her right arm. The stub of her arm was small, and it almost looked shriveled. Unique's left hand curled under as if it withered away. Cindy lovingly reached out, guiding Unique into her arms. Unique rested her head on Cindy's shoulder and sighed. Eyes closed, the tears snuck out this time; rolling down Cindy's face as she held this beautiful, brave little girl as tightly as she could.

When it was time for Unique to go home—daylight - Mrs. Woods invited Unique to come over anytime she felt the urge to walk or enjoy a PB & J sandwich. Cindy was also suggesting she take Unique for a drive instead of her late hour walks, thinking it's safer that way. Unique left Mrs. Woods' home with something unfamiliar pasted on her face—a smile. Mrs. Woods was a lovely lady. Also, she smelled good. With the smile came another different feeling, happiness. Unique was so happy she decided to take a nap on that swing. She was even glad her mama made her leave.

❧

Unique awakened the next day with a bit more enthusiastic about her day than she'd ever experienced in her entire, short life. Being excited or looking forward to anything were other "different" feelings that took her by surprise. It was Sunday and unusually quiet in her house. With nothing else to do, Unique perched herself again at her foggy window, where she could watch the whole world. Lots of neighbors left their houses dressed up for Church—or, maybe they were going to a party, Unique mused.

She figured Mrs. Woods and her kids would be going to church too. "Ah Ha! There they were all dressed up with bibles in their hands." Unique smiled. She couldn't wait to see and talk to Mrs. Woods again. Maybe she would get to meet the rest of the family. Unique wondered if Mrs. Woods' kids knew what a nice mommy they had. She sighed, pulling herself from the foggy window view.

Unique brushed her hand across the old paint peeling off her bedroom wall. As chipped paint pieces fell to the floor, she noticed a small, fresh

cut on her right hand. She stuck out her tongue and licked the blood, grimacing. "Ouch! That stings!"

The comforting lick of her tongue was Unique's Band-Aid. She opened her bedroom door while staring at her wound and walked directly into her mommy's belly. Dorothy glared down at her.

"Hey, Lil girl, where did you run off to last night? You know you not s'posed to go too far. But, guess what? When I looked out for you last night; I saw you nowhere. I don't even know what time you came back to the house. I fell asleep waiting for you."

Unique was afraid her mommy was going to slap her like she often did. Alternatively, worse—if she found out about Mrs. Woods, she might get mad and never let her see her new friend, again. So, she said nothing.

"Where'd you go?" Dorothy asked again.

Unique fumbled with her hand a bit longer before responding, "I just walked around." Unique's tone voiced that her mother's questions were irritating. She hoped her mother would get bored and drop it.

Dorothy was not letting her off that easy. "You know what I said about that. You s'posed to stay close to the house."

Dorothy smacked Unique on the bottom, calling her a 'hardheaded little girl.' Usually, Unique whined every time she was spanked or slapped; but not this time. Dorothy's face screwed up in bewilderment, fleetingly wondering why Unique didn't put up a fight for the first time, ever.

Not really caring one way or the other, Dorothy pulled deeply on the cigarette dangling from her lips, coughing and hacking. "Go sit yo' ass down somewhere."

Unique smiled on the inside this time. Fine by her. She was happy to obey her mom and plopped in front of the TV in what passed as the 'front room' before the rest of her siblings got up. They always beat her to the TV, but not this time. Unique wished they would sleep all day. When they were awake, her three older sisters and baby brother were nothing but mean to her. Not a nice one in the bunch: May was the oldest at 17, Jasmine was 8, Sarah was 9, and Ben was 5. She also had a half-sister who lived with her Father, Al. Victoria was 10. Emotionless May, took care of things but had no time for conversation. Messy Fashions, Jasmine and Sarah, always fought about clothing because they were close

in size and teased Unique often. Busy Ben was just in the way and taking over everything. Sadly, at times Vickie was the worst of them all with her egocentric self, teasing, and bullying Unique had become a norm.

Unique knew she was sitting too close to the television—she'd been hollered at enough about it—but, she wanted to be able to change the channels. Besides, Jasmine and Sarah were up and already in a deafening disagreement about their clothes. To drown out the yelling, Unique scooted even closer to the screen and turned up the volume. Sarah ran to Unique—insisting that Unique take her side in the battle with Jasmine for the fluffy pink blouse. Sarah asked Unique to 'tell Jasmine about the pink shirt.' She wanted Unique to say it was a gift from one of Mama's friends. She'd seen her mom's friend give it to her. Jasmine countered insisted that it was always hers.

Unique just wanted to watch TV in peace; but, she knew there was no such thing. She rolled her eyes, refusing to take sides. Unique looked at them and then the television and grunted. She knew they both would attack her if she did not pick a side. She decided to stay a bit in the neutral zone by saying, "If you ask me—that silly blouse is ugly! I can make one way better."

Sarah and Jasmine looked at each other and fell out laughing.

Jasmine hooted, "Any blouse she makes for us would only have one arm!"

Sarah high-fived Jasmine, howling even louder, "Well, at least she could wear it!"

Unique said nothing; but, hated the jokes. She was serious about making stuff. Ben zoomed into the room and changed the channel. She knew her television time was over. Ben always just took over everything including food. Unique got up, ignored her siblings and trudged to her room. Once again, loneliness shrouded the little girl in sadness, making her feel what she almost felt all the time: there was no place in that house for her. Still tired from being put out of the house in the middle of the night, again, she fell on top of the stained, smelly, sheet-less bed, and— mercifully—fell asleep.

CHAPTER 7

PAINFUL DRAMA

CINDY RUSHED UP THE stairs to the stage where Unique stood in a daze. She called aloud to get her attention.

"Unique! Unique! Are you okay, honey? Unique!"

Suddenly, Unique snapped back to the present, surveying the crew moving about preparing the show and approaching her—a concerned mother.

Cindy walked over to Unique calmly, enfolding the girl in her arms, knowing precisely what her daughter was thinking, and feeling.

"Heady stuff, huh?"

Unique leaned back into Cindy, ever grateful—for everything.

"Sure is—but, I'm okay, Mom—just the teeniest bit overwhelmed. Thanks, again—I couldn't have done any of this without you; and, I love you so much. How are we doing?"

Cindy sighed and released her.

"Well, we have the nurses here ahead of schedule and waiting to check in with you."

Unique was back and ready to roll.

"On my way! Thanks, Mom."

Cindy closed her eyes for a fraction of an instant. Sometimes, she was so in awe of, and caught up in, what a strong, smart, impressive, accomplished young woman Unique had become. Cindy had to remind herself that Unique had to jump hurdles to battle her mental and physical disabilities successfully—that she sometimes had limitations. Most of the time, Unique made it look easy. However, Cindy knew first-hand that it was anything—but. It was Cindy's job as Unique's mom always to be aware and in tune with her special daughter—this was one of those times.

"Know what? I got this, sweetheart. Why don't you go backstage and relax for a few minutes?"

Unique thanked Cindy and retreated to one of the private rooms backstages. One of the doors has her name emblazoned on it. She knew she didn't order that. Once inside, Unique laughed and clapped in delight, recognizing that this was Vickie's special surprise. The intimate space was beautifully and thoughtfully appointed specially for Unique, with everything she loved. The creamy, full sofa was deliciously comfy, draped with a faux-fur throw and colorful pillows. Roses and daisies, Unique's favorite combo, filled vases on the vanity and small tables. A dazzling array of chocolate-covered, fresh fruit arranged in a crystal bowl in the middle of the coffee table. A mini-fridge was full of drinks and finger-food. A masseuse stood by to soothe away any tension, as she was pampered and painted for the show by her very own beauty squad. Her prodigal sister loved her and spoiled her with luxuries she would never have allowed herself. Her essentials for the evening; makeup, jewelry, shoes, clothing, and all her personal possessions—were positioned neatly in the well arranged backstage dressing room.

✥

Sinking into the cushions of the sofa, snuggled in the throw, Unique closed her eyes and drifted away.

She was eight-years-old this time. It was 1:00 a.m. on a Friday morning. The room was so hot that Unique's little body drenched with

sweat. The heat and humidity were stifling. Unique could barely breathe, let alone rest. The familiar knocking began. However, this time, it was different—more aggressive. The stranger knocked with urgency; much like a policeman. Unique knew the routine all-too-well. Get up, stay out of Mama's way and get out. She got up, looked at her mother, and began to leave her only place to sleep. Her siblings were practically piled on top of each other on the crowded second floor, so that wasn't an option. Unique had no desire to be with them because at least one fight was guaranteed to break out. With nowhere in that house to rest her head, Unique prepared to walk.

Even though the child was exhausted from the lack of sleep, the silver lining was her oasis across the street. She was always happy to visit her neighbors who had become her new best friends and refuge. It had been almost two years since her official meeting with Mrs. Woods.

Dorothy knew what was up. Sure, she was high most of the time; but, wasn't blind. She said nothing, secretly grateful knowing Unique would be safe when Dorothy handled her business with her 'visitors.' Dorothy peeped Unique's new clothes, happier disposition and the ice-cream from the daily ice-cream truck. The kid wasn't even skin and bones anymore. Dorothy saw Mrs. Woods' affection for the child, so when her guests came, Dorothy knew Unique would be safe.

Right now, Dorothy's hard nose rubbing and sniffles were a definite sign she's in desperate need of a fix and so pointed her little girl to the door.

The knocking grew louder, and a man yelled out, "Open up bitch! Or don't get these treats! Your choice!"

Pushing sleepy little Unique along, Dorothy rushed her out the bedroom and hurried to the front door. As Dorothy unlocked and opened the door, Unique cringed at the sight of the hairy stranger. To her, he looked just like the werewolf, with furry hair covering his bare arms and back. His long, greasy, straight hair hung to the back of his knees. He was a thin but tall man wearing a musky wife beater and gross jeans with holes near the crotch. Unique eyed the scary, red eyes and rotted teeth stranger with contempt. Also, he smelled terrible; like Unique imagined a skunk would. The stinky, werewolf stranger blocked the doorway when Unique tried to squeeze through.

He winked at Unique and said, "Hey! Where you think you goin?"

For a moment, Dorothy remembered to be a mother and intermediately said, "This is my child, Jesse, and she's leaving."

Jesse pushed Unique away from the door, shut and locked it. Running his dirt-caked fingers through his nasty hair and said, "Oh, no! I think we're gonna have a little fun first—if you want these treats." Dangling the drugs in Dorothy's face, taunting her.

Dorothy was shaking. She looked at Unique and pleaded with her nasty guest. "Aww, come on baby. You know I got all you need for the treats. Stop playing."

Jesse turned his lip up and said, "Playing? Playing! Do I look like I'm playing?"

The werewolf picked up a table and hurled it against the wall, particle board flying everywhere and continued to make his demands, "I want you and your little-crippled retard knurling all over me—or, no deal. That's the only way you gonna get my shit, bitch!"

Dorothy panicked as Jesse began rubbing himself right in front of Unique. He eyed Unique with lust, and she ran closer to Dorothy looking for protection. Dorothy rubbed her nose even harder clearly showing the need for the drugs or treats Jesse held in his hand. He teased again, dangling the bag of potions.

Dorothy raised her voice at the sick twisted thoughts of the pervert and said, "NO, Jesse. I said, NO! She's just a baby, and not here for that! You freak! Get the hell out my damn house and take yo damn treats with you! With yo sick ass! Get the hell out! Now! I mean it!"

Dorothy saw Jesse gravitated toward Unique and despite her addiction, she had the presence of mind to pull Unique behind her back. Putting on her parental protection coat despite her needs wasn't easy. Knowing Jesse's rep for being violent, Dorothy was taking a significant risk. Telling Jesse, 'No,' was not an answer he accepted. Dorothy recognized the dangerous twitch in his eyes. She knew then; Jesse had been using meth again. That poison always compounded his crazy. There was no reasoning with him under meth's grip. Holding Unique behind her, Dorothy tried to nudge her back to the door leading upstairs. Dorothy thought, If she moved fast, Unique could unlock the door then relocked it behind her, safe from Jesse.

Jesse was no fool. He had been to Dorothy's house so many times he knew where all the doors led. Jesse saw Dorothy headed for the door; he leaped to push them away from the exit. However, Jesse was meaner and faster than Dorothy. He picked up a lamp, yanked its cord and pitched it to her. Dorothy dodged it, and it clashed with the wall, but she fell to the floor. Unique was petrified, taking the brief distraction to run to the front door.

Jesse caught sight and said, "Come back here, you raggedy little bitch!"

"Leave her alone, Jesse! Please!" Dorothy pleaded, pulling herself up off the floor.

Jesse grabbed the back of Unique's hair and slapped her across the back, knocking her frail little body against the golden metal TV stand. Unique's nose hit the stand's sharp edge, breaking the bridge and tearing the skin open. Blood gushed, and she could barely breathe.

Dizzy from the blow, Unique held her nose, crying, "Mommy, Mommy, help me." She attempted to stand, slowly pulling up off and away from the TV stand, grunting. Trying to catch her breath was getting harder by the second. She felt her strength leaving her body. Blood clotted all over her new PJs that Mrs. Woods had bought her. Her eyes widened, horrified. She held her nose and started crying even louder, "Mommy, Mommy, PLEASE!"

The rage at observing her baby hurt trumped Dorothy's addiction. Witnessing her child's bleeding and hearing her cries caused Dorothy to fight back even harder. She picked herself up off the floor and grabbed Ben's wooden bat, swinging it at Jesse's head while yelling telling Unique to run out the door as fast as she could! The racket had roused the children upstairs—but, they couldn't get to Dorothy. Dorothy had locked the door from her side. They ran out the second front door but couldn't get in through the first front door, for it too was bolted.

Unique's watched her mother swing that bat, and although she was hurt, Unique managed to open the front door and ran out. Concurrently the other siblings moved in, grabbing everything and anything to join in the fight against Jesse.

Jesse didn't stand a chance against all of Dorothy's other kids who had come armed with anything heavy they could carry; and, were beating the hell out of him. Reaching Mrs. Woods' house, breathless, Unique

hammered at the door. The porch light came on immediately. Cindy was horrified when she saw Unique holding her nose, blood dripping from her tiny fingers onto the front porch. She fumbled in a panic to unlock her door, but within moments, Cindy flung open her door and caught a bloody Unique, who fainted into her arms. Cindy carried the child inside, yelling at her husband to call 911!

"Unique—baby! What happened?"

Groggy and blood-soaked, Unique barely opened her eyes. Unique was weak from the blood loss as it continued running from her nose. Mrs. Woods sat her down on the sofa. She called out for her husband to hurry with the towels and ice. Mrs. Woods tried to get the nosebleed to stop by pitching her nose. It wasn't working. Unique managed to speak.

"My mom's hairy guest attacked my mom and me. I ran out; but, they're still fighting."

Cindy's husband flew into the living room with ice and towels for Unique's bleeding nose and said, "The paramedics are on their way—and, the police."

Having a pretty good idea of the horrors going on in the house across the street, Cindy started crying. Even with ice, she couldn't get Unique's nosebleed under control. Cindy called out for her husband's assistance again.

"Honey, look after Unique because I need to get dressed."

Putting on her clothes, she started to cry while thinking of the horror it must be living with a family like that. Every fiber of her being ached to help this precious baby in any way possible, but her hands were tied because she was not the parent and could not overstep her boundaries. She fully understood how tough it was for Dorothy trying to raise all her children alone. However, she was most concerned for Unique. Cindy was dressed and back on the sofa with Unique.

The police and paramedics arrived. Cindy helped the EMTs carefully secure Unique in the ambulance; sharing with them the little data she knew. Cindy needed more information and permission from Dorothy to take care of Unique. Assuring Unique that she'd be right back, Cindy ran across the street just in time to witness the police escorting him out the house in cuffs. She was amazed at his face and body. It looked as if two wolves, one bear, and a Rottweiler dog on the side had attacked him. She shook her head, disgusted.

Cindy self-acclaimed, 'Wow! Looks like that animal messed with the wrong family. They beat him down.'

The door was open. Calling out for Dorothy, Cindy found May comforting Sarah and Jasmine. Sarah and Jasmine's hair was all over the place, and they both were still breathing hard from the struggle. May, being the oldest, was calm, but you could sense she did the most damage. Ben was responsible for the bug spray in Jesse's eyes. Little Ben was still holding on to the can of Raid.

May walked over to little Ben to retrieve the can. She shook it in the air applauding Ben's efforts and said, "Roaches checked in, but they didn't check out. You've been exterminated fool!"

If all of this weren't so tragic, Cindy's sense of humor would have had a hearty laugh at that girl. Instead, she proceeded to look for Dorothy.

Dorothy, fragile, haggard and worn out, was being questioned by the police in the kitchen. Dorothy appeared so frail and worn out from the fighting.

"I'm so sorry to interrupt, Dorothy, officers. But, we need your permission and some information so the EMTs can take Unique to the hospital."

Dorothy gave Cindy a written statement and the signed guardianship papers and all Unique's information. Dorothy nodded, grateful to Cindy for doing what she couldn't. She stayed with the police for further questioning and said she would meet Cindy at the hospital when done. Cindy climbed in the back of the ambulance to comfort Unique, held her small hand, and said, "Unique, I need you to be a big girl. I'll be right behind you. Don't worry, okay."

The medic interjected, "I'll take care of her."

Cindy kissed Unique, got in her car, and followed the ambulance.

&

Cindy was at Unique's side during the examination, X-rays and CT scan. By the time Dorothy arrived, the pediatrician and otolaryngologist were ready to give their prognosis.

"As we suspected, Unique suffered a severe fracture of her nasal septum."

Catching Dorothy's confusion, the pediatrician kindly explained, "Commonly known as a broken nose."

"To avoid future complications like a septal hematoma, which would make it difficult for Unique to breathe," The otolaryngologist added, "We firmly recommend surgery,"

Dorothy gave her consent to proceed. Social workers showed up in the waiting room to question Dorothy about the safety of the child. Dorothy knew the process too well. Excusing herself momentarily, she grabbed Cindy's arm, walking her to a smaller anteroom. With so many strikes already against her with Social Services, Dorothy knew she could lose Unique this time, maybe all her children. Things would go seriously wrong if their stories didn't add up when talking to the social workers. Frightened, frustrated, hopeless and ashamed of her life choices, Dorothy struggled to find the right words; words that Mrs. Woods might understand. Looking at the beautiful painting of paradise on the wall, she wished she could hide in it from all the problems she faced now. Dorothy sat there holding her head down between her seriously skinny legs.

Cindy deserved more credit than Dorothy gave her. She saw the tortured pain and sorrow in Dorothy's eyes and told her to take her time. Silent tears flowed, non-stop. Cindy reached into her bag, pulled out a pack of tissues and offered them to the damaged woman.

Dorothy had blown her nose before she found her voice. She looked Cindy in the eyes. "I want to thank you for all you've done for my little girl—not just tonight; but, for all the time. I know you love her. Unique is a special one. I knew it as soon as she entered the world. That's why I gave her the name, Unique. When I first found out she was physically challenged, I wanted to give her up—at first. I knew to raise that child, wasn't going to be easy; but Unique's eyes pierced and snatched my heart and soul. I know I ain't been the best mama. But, I love her. Have always loved her, no matter what. Something special about those eyes of hers—isn't it?"

Dorothy wiped her eyes and continued, "You looked into her eyes. I know you love her, too. I see it in your eyes. You demonstrated your love

with the clothes, the food you provided her and the time you spend with her. She told me you help her with homework, besides feeding her and all the cute clothes. I never have the time for that. Unique lights up when she talks about you and your family. At first, I admit, I was a bit jealous. I sure wished she could feel like that about me."

New tears streamed down Dorothy's face. "I wanted her to view me and mine as she sees your family, but we're a hot mess of a family—that's the truth. But, who am I to be jealous? I know I ain't done the best for my kids. And, the other children—they've teased and bullied Unique her whole life. And, I really ain't tried to stop 'em. What kinda Mama does that make me? My house is full of chaos all the time. For what it's worth, I am so thankful that she goes to you when, well—you know."

Dorothy rubbed her thin thighs and said, "I did try though, Mrs. Cindy, you gotta know that. Tried over and over again. It's just—I got a habit I can't kick. I'm so very sorry. I never wanted my baby to get hurt. Unique has special needs that the others don't have. She needs more than what I can give. I'm not fit to be Unique's mother. "

Dorothy started crying harder. She was sweating because her body was still in need of the drugs she craved, and tears from the emotional pain that she was experiencing had begun falling like raindrops she couldn't hold back. Dorothy's thoughts were racing through her mind, as she thought about Unique from the time she was born until the present.

Cindy felt Dorothy's pain, led her to a couch and slid her arm around her shoulders. Trying to comfort her any way she could. Dorothy understood the beast that rode a person's soul within. She has seen its ugly face many times. Cindy sighed, knowing the only person who could fight Dorothy's demons was Dorothy herself—with the unfailing mercy of God. Cindy was conscious of the fact that Unique was innocent and suffering from her mother's demons and monsters as well.

Dorothy pulled away and swallowed the lump in her throat, mustering the nerve to ask Cindy for help.

"Mrs. Cindy, I told the police we were Jesse's victims. I didn't know him, and he broke in to rob the place. The social workers are digging all up in my records. They'll find plenty to justify throwing Unique in foster care—and my other children."

Cindy cut her off, "I understand. I'd never see Unique again… Just tell me what to say. But, Dorothy, what are you going to do to stop this madness? Unique shouldn't have to suffer because of your demons, and are you going to keep letting men like Jesse try to have their way with your baby?"

"Of course not!" Dorothy's body was shaking and sweating from temporary deprivation of the drugs. Broken and distraught—she wiped her tears as she continued, "Don't you think I wanna get clean? This damn demon won't leave me the fuck alone! I'm beyond help."

"Oh honey, no! That's not true—there's always hope. I didn't mean to sound so judgmental. You have got to remember that hope and grace are there for you if you grab hold of it. I am just asking you to focus on the immediate decisions you need to make regarding Unique. I am really concerned about Unique."

Dorothy wiped tears, sweat, and snot, "Can I ask you something?"
"Of course."
"Why do you love Unique so much?"

Cindy smiled, "Because she's easy to love. Loving Unique is as natural as breathing. Loving her feels like my heart has finally been completed. And, I didn't even know anything was missing. Such a sweet child doesn't have to ask to be loved. It is given her because she freely loves. And yes, those eyes—you named her well, Dorothy. She's also bright, strong and unyielding. She deals with life challenges that would bring a grown man to his knees. Oh, but not Unique; she keeps going."

"Thank you for that." Dorothy looked directly into Cindy's eyes for the first time—her own jaundiced eyes filling up again with tears. "I—uh, have another question. And, if you can't do it, I completely understand… Would you and your family please take care of Unique, take care of her? I just can't let anything like this—or, worse—happen to her again. I can't give her what she needs… God—forgive me. I have to protect my baby from her own mother. And, foster care would be even worse than living with me because she's special and all. I'm happy to give you all the money I can to help support her. "

Dorothy cried harder, shaking her skinny knees up and down in extreme rhythm. Her hands were sweaty, trembling and fidgeting.

"I love her enough to ask for a chance for her. I see that opportunity with you and your family, not in some home or foster care."

Cindy dabbed at her tears. "Neither my husband or I usually make any big decisions without first consulting the other. But, knowing him and knowing how he feels about Unique, I'm sure I speak for him when I say, 'Absolutely, resoundingly, YES! We would love to take care of Unique; but, there are a couple of conditions you'll need to agree to before we can do so. First, you use your money to take care of you and those four other precious babies. We got this. Second, and this is critical, Dorothy. Moreover, there's no coming back into her life—playing 'Mommy,' under pretenses that you're better. Please get yourself clean and sober! Visits are fine—I encourage them. But, if you are high or drunk, you can't come in. Okay? Can you do that for Unique? And, for yourself? You have my promise that we will love and raise Unique the same way we do our own. That means we make all the decisions. You must trust us, and you can never involve yourself with our choices as long as they don't hurt Unique."

Dorothy sniffed, "Thank you. Yes, whatever you say. I trust you completely. Mrs. Cindy, this means the world to me. Thank you so very much—again."

Cindy pulled Dorothy into a hug, soothingly rubbing her back, "No, thank you! It's all gonna work out, honey. I know it will. How about we wait to talk details, hmm? Right now, let's go have a nice chat with those social workers; and, wait together for our little girl to get out of surgery?"

Dorothy and Cindy quelled any concerns from Social Services. The designated social workers seemed satisfied—at least for now. And, that was all that mattered until they could legalize Cindy and Chuck's guardianship of Unique.

Unique's procedure was relatively standard, so it didn't take too long. The surgeon walked in smiling, assuring Dorothy "Your daughter will be just fine. Meanwhile, she's in recovery for a few hours and when the anesthesia has worn off, and she's drinking okay; you can take her home. Her nose will be sore, swollen, bruised and packed with cotton to control the bleeding. You are to remove the cotton a day or two after surgery. I'll give you a prescription for the pain. You can get it filled right here in the hospital. Now, after you get home and you see anything obstructing her

breathing—come back immediately. Would you like me to take you to her?"

Relieved, both women thanked the doctor and followed him into the recovery area where nurses were waking up Unique. The senior recovery nurse explained to them both that this was a simple procedure usually done as an outpatient unless significant complications emerged. Unique was all right. She woke up enough for her favorite drink—apple juice. She took a sip from the straw eased between her lips.

"Good, good," the nurse smiled at Unique. She cocked her head toward Dorothy and Cindy, still tending to the child.

"You see, she's fine," said the nurse. "You have a little champ here. She's a tough one. I'll grab her things, and get her paperwork ready so you can dress her to go home. Now, she will remain sleepy from the anesthesia; that's normal."

Cindy and Dorothy thanked the nurse and fussed over Unique. Dorothy then became withdrawn. She didn't want to get in the way of the best decision she ever made for Unique. Excusing herself to go to the restroom Dorothy said, "Cindy could you finish with Unique? I'll be back."

Dorothy was very remorseful, and she begged God for forgiveness as she held up on the restroom sink. She wanted forgiveness for many reasons. She memorized her baby's birth clearly. Her heart ached, and at the same time she wasn't released from the mental agony, and her drugs were what she craved. She screamed, "THIS DAMN DEMON! LEAVE ME ALONE!"

The nurse came in with Unique's bloody clothes and said, "Why don't we just pitch these, and you take her home in what she's wearing."

Cindy looked at the bloody mess and said, "Yes, get rid of those."

"Okay, here's the instructions and her prescription." The nurse rubbed Unique's head, "Fill the script right away because the pain can get out of control for this baby."

"I understand."

Dorothy came back and said, "Okay, that's that, huh."

The nurse looked at Dorothy and knew she had other places she'd rather be and said, "Okay, I'll let you fine people be on your way."

Once the nurse had gone, Cindy asked Dorothy again, "Are you sure? There's no turning back from this decision. Can you ride home with us?"

"No, I already asked my brother to come and get me."

"I didn't know you had a brother." Cindy realized that brother was just a cover for the dope man coming to get her and didn't press Dorothy's buttons.

Dorothy's bloodshot, already swollen eyes filled again as she looked from Unique and kissed her very gently. I'm sure what's best for her is neither me nor my life. I'm sure I have a fight that I can't win right now. Yes, Cindy, I'm sure. You are not only what she needs; it's what she wants. I love her too much to be selfish. Plus, I know when to accept the gift God gives when he gives it. You are my gift. "

Cindy picked Unique up from the bed wrapped in blankets, held her in her arms and looked up at Dorothy. "I am here for you too. If you need help to get better and you succeed at killing the beast that rides you. Unique can come back to you. Again, Dorothy—Are you sure? There's no turning back from this decision. I will take her now."

"I love her more than myself, Cindy. I'm sure."

With Unique in arms, the two hugged. She could only imagine the devastation and heartache this broken, young woman was suffering. Cindy rewrapped Unique in the blanket and walked out of the room with the child in her arms.

Dorothy walked out of the room a few moments behind Cindy, giving Cindy a chance to get down the hall with Unique. Dorothy leaned against the wall holding her stomach. She howled like a wounded animal and slid down the hall wall. Her scream pierced the walls of the hospital. This cry Dorothy uttered was one all mothers dread, for it means the loss of a child.

Cindy heard Dorothy scream and wanted to turn back. But she looked at the child and asked herself, 'I wouldn't leave a child who needed me. Unique and Dorothy both need me. Stay strong—do what's right.' Her heart sensed Dorothy's pain, and she was nearly blinded by tears that just wouldn't stop. Then she continued to walk out of the hospital saying a quick prayer for Dorothy.

CHAPTER 8

A NEW START

MRS. WOODS HANDED HER valet parking ticket in for her vehicle to be fetched. Finally, a blockhead young man arrived driving her new Blazer out of control—bullwhipping his ass around corners. Cindy snatched her keys and thought, 'Boy, if I wasn't a Christian!' Fretful—the attendant dropped the keys into her hand. Mrs. Woods put Unique in the car and strapped her in comfortably. Unique was still very sleepy from the anesthetic. Before Cindy drove off, she decided to break the news to her husband by telephone. Exhaling, she picked up her Blackberry and started calling home. Cindy told her husband the whole story about Unique's visit to the hospital, the social workers and ultimately, why she felt the need to bring Unique home permanently. Cindy and Chuck usually saw eye to eye on most issues, and she was almost sure her husband's reaction would be the same as hers. It turned out; she was right on target. He only said he would have her spot set up in Jamie's room.

Jamie's room was a little girl's wonderland. She loved Barbie dolls, and Teddy bears, so her room was full of them. They lived on the top

and bottom bunk of Jamie's bed. In preparation for Unique, Chuck temporarily relocated the Barbies and Care-Bears the night before to put clean, matching sheets on both beds. Jamie had to see Barbie everywhere. She had Barbie everything, from sheets and towels to lamps and electrical outlet covers. Even her ceiling fan was Barbie. Jamie caught her dad taking the sheets off.

"Daddy, why are you taking Barbie away?"

Chuck kissed her and put her on the top bunk and said, "Sweetheart, Barbie needs a bath, but she'll be back in the morning. Dad needs you to sleep on the top bunk for now on okay."

"But why?"

Chuck laughed. "Because Unique is coming over and you must let her rest because she's sick."

"Okay, Daddy. I'm gonna be really quiet."

"That's my girl…" Chuck took more sweet kisses from his baby and put her to bed.

The anesthesia had long worn off; but, still, Unique remained asleep as Cindy gently placed her in Chuck's arms. He carried her into the house, up the stairs and into Jamie's room; which was now hers as well. The child was merely tired. Tired from years of sleep deprivation; restorative sleep that every child needed to grow, develop and thrive.

Upstairs, Jamie had completely passed out. Chuck unwrapped Unique and gingerly tucked her into the bottom bunk. When Chuck stepped back, Cindy artfully propped Teddy bears all around her new daughter. She had chosen a few new ones for Unique.

❧

Cindy and Chuck hadn't had lots of time to talk after she'd returned home late yesterday afternoon. Everything had happened so fast. They would talk specifics later; but, agreed that the priority was to prepare the children. Because change can sometimes be scary for little ones, they decided to call a family meeting over pizza. Jamie, Jerry, and Maury jumped up and down with excitement. Whatever, this family meeting was about, it must be fun, 'cause this wasn't even pizza night!

Unique's moving in with them was an easy sell because the children all adored her, too. So Jamie was thrilled to have a sister finally—one who doesn't cause her pain. After calming down their crew, Chuck explained that Unique was sick. He and Cindy made all three pinky swear that they would be as quiet as mice until Unique was feeling better.

Unique's new family anxiously waited for her to join the family. Even though Daddy said Unique was sick, Jamie, Jerry, and Maury had hoped she'd at least be awake.

After making sure Unique was okay, Chuck asked Cindy to join him in the bedroom so they could finally talk. Cindy gathered Jamie, Jerry, and Maury into the family room, downstairs. To their delight, she popped a "Winnie The Pooh" video in the VCR. Before leaving, she brought her index finger to her lips, reminding the children to "Shhhh" that Unique could rest.

She headed back upstairs to talk to Chuck, praying that the video would buy them at least an hour to talk, uninterrupted. She entered the bedroom slowly, hoping she hadn't upset her husband by making such a significant life decision with talking it over with him first like they usually did.

"Hey, sweetie—is everything okay? "Cindy asked panicked.

She realized this was the first time she decided without consulting him first, and it was a big decision too. After all these years together, Chuck knew his wife was nervous; so he squeezed her tight and playfully nipped her on the neck so she would relax.

Chuck softened his eyes and said, "Well, I think everything is probably going to work themselves out—they always do, babe. But... Really—we haven't had a chance yet to talk about all of this. Honey, I am so proud that you want to help Unique. Your limitless heart is one of the reasons I love you so much. And, I realize the sad circumstances demanded an immediate solution. You and I have tried to be proactive in every area of our lives; so, I think we should identify any potential problems that might arise. This decision is not a small matter and will affect all of us. We need to factor in the cost of taking care of another child with challenges; not to mention Unique's physical health, her mental health, and her family. Oh—the drama will be a mess. Are you ready for all that? Are we? I don't

want to shortchange this little girl. I love her, too. But, we already have our plates full with Jamie being mildly developmentally delayed. Then there's dealing with Maury's ADHD and dyslexia."

Cindy finished the thought. "And, even though Jerry has only been diagnosed with slow learning abilities, he still has a lot to handle. Little Unique has both a physical disability and a mental illness." Cindy took a breath, cocking an eyebrow at Chuck, half-playing. "So, what's your point?"

"My point is—a physical disability brings a whole different set of difficulties. It's nothing like our three children with mental challenges. There are going to be new provocations we're not used to handling. Are you ready for that? That's the question we both need, to be honest about."

Cindy sighed, "Honey, this is us… It's what we do." Cindy smiled for him to relax. "Of course, I know this isn't going to be easy. But, when have we ever done 'easy'?" We're the Woods', and we laugh in the face of difficulty and challenge. I prayed on this. I always allow the Lord to guide me in my everyday decisions. He was very clear about this one. And, no— He (God) didn't say it was going to be painless. I know the Lord wants us to help this baby! Otherwise, He wouldn't have guided her to our porch that night. And I just happened to be sleepless on the same evening, at the same time? That was not a coincidence. That was all God. Unique came to our porch, out of all the houses and all the porches in the neighborhood. That's how I know the Lord has His hand in all of this!

No, it's going to be complicated most days! I know because most things in Christ aren't a picnic. But, with God, it all works out. I believe this, Baby, do you? I also know I never want to look back and see that baby suffering, knowing we could have done something about it. Just as we are making it work with our three, we can make it with the four, now. But if you think it's too much for us, baby, I will do whatever you think is best. You know that. "

"I love your confidence in me, baby. Love your faith in God even more. And, yes—you know we share the same belief in God and all that is possible through Christ. I'm just thinking out loud; making sure we're both on the same page. I want what's best for Unique as much as you do. So I have worried about that child too. Plus, truth be told—I had

already gotten used to her being around. Three runts—now four—what's the difference? We got this."

Cindy and Chuck sealed their conversation and their commitment to Unique with a kiss. Cindy broke away first. "Hey, we need to go shopping for Unique. Other than her new stuffed buddies and the hospital-issued toothbrush, she doesn't have anything here.

Chuck laughed, "Oh, so now we have a new reason to shop, huh? Do I have to go? Not my favorite sport—"

Cindy shot him 'the look.'

"Yes, Ma'am... I'm going. Let's call Kate to sit with the kids."

There was a light tap at the bedroom door. It was Jamie.

"Daddy, can't Unique play now?"

Reaching down, Chuck picked her up and placed her on his hip, kissing Jamie on the forehead. "Not now, Sugar... know what? The longer you let Unique rest, the faster she'll feel better so she can play with you and all of your Barbie buddies. Won't that be fun?"

Jamie enthusiastically bobbed her little head up and down, "Yes!"

"So, can you keep super-duper quiet 'till she wakes up? "

"Okay, then we can play?"

"You bet! Now, scoot back to that video you were watching with your brothers."

There was a knock on the front door. Cindy threw it open, expecting Kate. It was Dorothy. She was twitching and holding on to some plastic trash bags.

"I wanted to bring you Unique's things. Also, I signed the written agreement like I said I would. I'm leaving today..."

"Leaving? Where are you going? Why so fast?"

"Yeah, I know it's sudden—but it's best for me. I think it's also best for you and Unique if I am not across the street, anymore. I want her to be able to move on. I just wanted to tell you I was leaving; and, if you don't mind, is it okay if I call from time to time just to see how she's doing?"

Chuck joined Cindy at the door with some questions of his own. Chuck had a distinctive voice, deep vocal power. When he spoke, you heard a symphony of the bass; combining his authority, humbleness, and love all at once.

Clearing his throat, he asked, "Are you going to be okay with this arrangement, Dorothy? I don't want my family to be put through the wringer. We all love Unique. When you leave, she will be part of our family. I don't want my family getting any more attached more than they already are if you're going to ride back into town and snatch her back into your life. We would have invested so much and for that to happen wouldn't be cool at all. This decision to raise Unique affects my children. And, to be clear, I do not play games when it comes to my family's life and well-being. I know you understand what I mean—right? Also, what about Unique's father? Are you sure he wants no part of his child's life? I'm not playing games with my family, Dorothy! I mean it! Did you get me? "

Dorothy appreciatively eyeballed Chuck from head to toe. "Wow, Cindy gurl! I ain't never seen a man like this one you got! Ever!"

Chuck and Cindy didn't want to embarrass Dorothy any more than she was embarrassing herself. So, they let it go, exchanging a single look that said the same thing.

Dorothy scored her daily fix. "And—Yes Sir, Chuck—I got you—all right." Dorothy's drug-inspired attempt at being flirty was sad; especially when she wiped her index finger across her nose afterward. "So, yeah—right... I'm gone for good. Oh, and don't worry. Unique's sorry ass daddy won't be a problem. Trust me. That stuck-up, sorry excuse of a man doesn't want nothing to do with his 'handicapped' child. Cause she ain't perfect like his little princess, he got at home. I have full custody anyway because he never asked for her. I hate I put his name on her birth certificate. He hasn't tried to even help me out with food in years. That bitch makes me sick! Remember, I'm gonna call from time to time to check in on Unique. Y'all take good care of my baby, okay? That's all I ask."

Chuck cleared his throat. After seeing and listening to this poor, lost woman, his heart was now confident he and Cindy were doing the right thing for Unique.

"Sure, Dorothy... We have no problem with you calling anytime. I do have another question before you go."

"What?" Dorothy asked, irritated.

Chuck stood up straight. "About Unique's father—what's his name so we can be sure?"

"It's like I already told Cindy. He didn't want Unique then; and, he won't want her ever! Unique got a little shrunk up arm and what they call Bipolar. Her daddy claims he ain't got no disabled or retarded kids. Told you... He'd be the last person trying to claim Unique. That bastard's name is on her certificate, but it won't matter because He! Don't! Want! Her! And, that's that! But, if you want to help Unique—keep her away from his sick ass!"

Chuck shook his head, disgusted, thinking that men like Unique's deadbeat dad were the lowest scum of the earth.

"Sure, I get it. It's men like that who makes it hard for women to trust the good ones. If you ever talk to him again, tell him that his child is neither handicapped nor is she retarded. I also ask that you never use—or, repeat—those degrading terms ever again when referring to Unique."

Dorothy was mesmerized by Chuck's voice. She winked at Cindy, grinning. "Wow, gurl, you better put a leash on this one. It's hard as hell to find this kind."

Cindy smiled, knowing how blessed she was. "Did you want to see Unique before you go?"

Dorothy pinched her nose and sniffed to make sure Cindy knew she was high; and, was honoring their agreement. "Nah, Thanks, though... It's better if I just go. You tell her I love her, please? When she wonders why I left, you tell her I had to because I loved her. Will you do that for me?"

Cindy thought about the other children. It wasn't like she could take them in too, but her heart had to know they were okay also. "Wait, Dorothy. Are the others children leaving too?"

"Hell yeah, they're going with me." Dorothy was unsettled with Cindy's question. "What—you want them too? They don't have issues like Unique, and I don't need your help with them. My oldest, May, can give me a hand with them. So rest your damn eyes, Cindy. My other kids are fine. Now, Bye! Damn!"

Dorothy turned and walked away. Her last request—before she went left, hit Chuck and Cindy like a ton of bricks. That was something they hadn't thought about or even discussed. Whenever Unique did ask about her mother, what were they supposed to say to her?

Kate arrived to sit with the children. Shopping gave them more opportunity to talk with no little ears around.

When they got back home, Kate reported that Unique ate a little chicken noodle soup, drank a full glass of apple juice and was full of questions. Kate had told her to hold tight until they returned. Kate asked no questions. It was none of her business. She left as soon as Cindy paid her.

Chuck and Cindy walked upstairs to the girls' room. Unique was in bed holding on to one of Jamie's stuffed bears. Her eyes were wide open. Chuck and Cindy both saw the confusion on her little face, even though bandages covered most of it. Chuck remained standing.

Cindy sat on the side of the bed, taking Unique's hands in hers and said, "Hey, how are you feeling after all that good sleep? You look better—ready to take on the world!" She joked.

Unique blinked from the bandage near her eyes. "My nose is hurting."

Cindy made a frowny face. "I know, baby. It's time for your medicine to make it stop hurting, that's why." She asked Chuck to get it from the pharmacy bag that was sitting on their dresser.

Unique remembered that something bad had happened to her mother and the hairy man—and panicked, "Why am I here? Where's Mommy?"

Just then, Chuck walked back in with Unique's pain pill and more apple juice. He handed them to his wife.

"Here, honey," Cindy cooed. "Can you swallow this for me like a big girl? It will make you feel better."

Unique hated taking pills; but, she had gotten used to it. After she had swallowed, Cindy knew it was time to explain. "Unique, baby, you're going to be staying with us."

"Why, where is my mommy?"

Cindy glanced up at Chuck before answering, "Honey, she had to leave."

"When is she coming back? Did that hairy, werewolf man hurt her?"

"No, your mother wasn't hurt by the dangerous man. She just thought it would be best for you to stay here with us. Is that okay with you?"

"How long do I get to stay, Mrs. Woods?"

"Well, how does forever sound, baby."

Cindy could tell by the puzzled expression in Unique's eyes that she didn't understand what Cindy was saying; so, she tried to explain it further. She knew it would hurt Unique; and, she hated that. But, the child needed and deserved the truth. Cindy chose her words carefully to lessen the sting as much as possible.

"Well, you know how your mommy was sick sometimes? She wanted to get better and make all the bad things that happened to go away. She loves you so much that she didn't want any more bad things to hurt you. And, the only way to do that was by letting you stay with us and be part of our family. I'm sorry—she doesn't live across the street from us anymore. But, it's okay because we are your family now. Is that okay with you? Unique, honey, you know you can tell me anything. Do you want to tell me how you feel about all this?"

Cindy and Chuck couldn't see much of Unique's face; but, they could read those expressive eyes. Usually bright and soulful, now they looked flat. Dazed. Chuck was frozen in place, praying that Unique wouldn't scream for her mother. He didn't know if he was prepared to handle that.

"My mother is gone? She left me?" Unique asked in disbelief.

"Yes, because she loved you so much," Cindy replied as simply as possible.

"And you're my new family?"

"Yeah."

Tears spilled from Unique's now-empty eyes. "Will you leave me too if I'm bad?"

Cindy kissed Unique on the forehead gently. "No, sweetie... and, you didn't do anything wrong to make your mother go away. She was sick and wanted to get better and fix all the bad stuff. She just couldn't do it here, across the street. We love you, too, Unique and we won't ever leave you."

Unique started sobbing in great heaves. Cindy pulled her from the covers and onto her lap, holding Unique's head close to her chest. With her world turned upside down, Unique needed reassurance and asked Mrs. Woods to pinky swear promise not to leave her, too. Chuck knelt next to them, looking the child in the eyes, lovingly. Mr. and Mrs. Woods both promised Unique they were in for the long haul.

"We will never go, we promise."

Unique was satisfied with that and stopped crying. Chuck and Cindy carefully dabbed at her tears, trying not to touch her nose.

❧

Eventually, Unique very naturally slipped into calling Mrs. and Mr. Woods "Mom and Dad," just like the other kids did. Although Unique loved hanging out with her brothers, Jerry and Maury, she and Jamie were inseparable. Together, they spent hours playing with their Barbie dolls. They loved dressing them and making clothes for them out of any material their mom was throwing away. Both girls were blessed with extraordinary creativity and imagination, each fueling the other with determination and passion. They could transform bits and pieces of old clothes, sheets or towels into mini-masterpieces with scissors, a needle, and thread.

An observant mother who nurtured the interests and strengths of all her children, Cindy was impressed with her daughters' inventiveness with their designs. Both were obsessed with clothes and everything about them. Not just to wear—but, how they were made; and, how to reproduce their own from the gallery of pictures in their heads. When Unique was eight and Jamie was seven, they had already decided what they wanted to do when they grew up. The 'dynamic duo' had run to their parents breathless with the exciting news.

"Mom! Dad! Me and Jamie have something important to say,"

Cindy interceded, "It's… Jamie and I - sweetheart."

Unique started again but began solemnly—with a 'grown-up' face—as she and Jamie practiced. "Jamie and I have an important announcement."

Cindy and Chuck stopped what they were doing, exchanged proud glances with their eyes. Shocked how quickly Unique sought the need to speak plainly and gave the girls their full attention.

Unique said, "We want to make clothes,"

Jamie continued, proudly, standing as straight as she could and trying not to giggle. "Awesome! Clothes."

Cindy interjected, after a beat, to make sure her daughters knew she was taking them quite seriously. "But, you already make clothes, beautiful clothes for your Barbies."

Unique expounded, ready to explode with excitement for their 'ah-ha' decision. "Yes, Ma'am... But, we mean we want to do it when we grow up. We want to be designers."

Chuck smiled, looking from one amazing little girl to the other, bobbing his head in acknowledgment of the genesis of their collective dream, which he could already envision as their future. His Unique and Jasmine embodied all the God-given gifts of talent and determination to make anything happen. "Wow, you young ladies are something else, you know? That is an exceptional career choice. Mom, I think you need to find more material for our aspiring designers so they can practice with their Barbies."

Unique's and Jamie's unwavering penchant for the design was growing faster than their little bodies. Cindy gave them all she thought her baby girls would need to create their doll clothes collection. She spent hours teaching them how to use a sewing machine, the differences in fabric, threads, tools, notions, seam finishing, stitching, and so much more. By the time they were nine and ten, Unique and Jamie were making their own clothes. They rarely wanted to wear store-bought anything, which was a bonus for the family budget.

When she realized that the talent of her girls went far beyond her knowledge and abilities, Cindy began to explore advanced training options for them. Strolling through a local outdoor craft fair one rare Saturday morning—alone—she stumbled upon the booth of a self-taught fashion designer named Naomi.

Naomi looked like a fashion model. Thirty-seven, she was a tall, lithe, caramel-colored, black woman with enormous hazel eyes. It was no surprise to Cindy that Naomi was a free spirit with no husband or children. The love of her life was creating exotic, one-of-a-kind designs. Her passion exemplified in her smooth style and her gorgeous, colorful, ever-present head-wraps. It was Naomi's great joy—and part of who she was to share her beacon and extensive knowledge of the art of design with anyone who wanted to master their gifts. But, she knew that before anyone could learn, the love of the art had to be emblazoned in one's soul. Naomi's practical side had just earned her MFA in design so that she could teach design at the university level.

Cindy approached with a smile and told her all about the girls. Time seemed to fly by as they chatted. Everything in Naomi's spirit knew Cindy Woods was directed to her booth at this random fair by divine intervention. Cindy's daughters sounded remarkable.

Naomi shook Cindy's hand and said, "Yes, I would be honored to meet, guide and nurture your little girls so their passion could fly.

❧

Jamie and Unique created as a team; never as competitors. They praised and encouraged each other with every lovely piece produced. After effectively making a blouse they were especially proud of, Unique and Jamie vowed to never turn from what they loved.

In the excitement, Unique said, "This top is awesome, Jamie."

Jamie placed the creation against her frame. "I know; I like the color fabric we chose. Unique, I want to try that on."

Admiring each other's work during a typical weekend afternoon of creating in their room, Jamie randomly announced that she wanted to wear the clothes, as well as make them.

Unique beamed in approval. "You mean like a supermodel?"

"Exactly like a supermodel," Jamie giggled, teetering to balance herself in a pair of mom's high heels she had 'borrowed.' "But, how do they walk in these heels? Would you help me practice?"

"Course I'll help." Unique helped to secure Jamie's stands.

"Good, because I want to be like the models we see on TV," Jamie stumbled in the heels. "I think walking like the models in these heels can be hard."

Unique got excited. "We'll design 'em."

"What! Heels?"

"Yes, everything and you'll model 'em. We'll even have our own company! Deal?"

"Deal!" The sisters pinky swore with their right hands.

Cindy couldn't wait to tell the girls about Naomi. After kissing the boys and Chuck when she got in, she tore up all fifteen stairs, out of breath

by the time she reached Unique's and Jamie's room. Her jaw dropped as soon as she opened the door. "Wow, girls! This blouse is a masterpiece. Are those the pants that go with it? Did you do all this today?"

"Mom, you like them?" Jamie asked.

Cindy bursting with joy said, "Like them? I love them! You young ladies blow my mind with your talent and your sheer determination. And, you know I'm not just saying that because I'm your Mom, right?"

The sisters beamed at each other.

Cindy invited them to perch on the lower bunk with her. "I've got a surprise for you. I met a grown-up designer, right here in St. Louis today. She sells her own line at her own store. Isn't that cool?"

"Way cool," Unique and Jamie agreed in unison.

"Guess what? She is going to be a design professor at one of the colleges. And, you two are going to be her first students!"

The girls looked at each other, confused. "We have to wait until we go to college first?"

Cindy laughed, "No, I'm sorry. She wants to teach you right now! When I told her all about my amazingly talented design prodigies, she couldn't wait to share all of her knowledge and techniques with you. So— how does going to her shop after school every Tuesday and Thursday, sound?"

"Seriously?" Unique asked with eyes as big as saucers. She and Jamie screamed with excitement, hugged mom, and then hopped off the bed to jump up and down. Jamie clapped her hands. Unique pumped her right arm victoriously in the air. They were deafening, Jerry and Maury ran into the room to investigate all the racket.

The girls continued singing together in a harmonizing tone while jumping around. "We're going to be designers! We're going to be designers!" They sang.

Cindy was grateful that her daughters could experience the critical feeling of accomplishment with designing. In school, both were behind their grade levels in reading and math. Ideally, immersing themselves in the technicalities of design would ultimately help with both subjects. As for their ability to design, there was no way to measure their talent. It was unlike anything anyone has ever seen in young ones. Cindy knew the

designs the girls came up with was a gift in both of them. As their mom, she was ready to prepare them for the world. It broke her heart to prick a hole in their balloon; but, she had no choice. She finally had to remind them of what the real world was going to throw at them.

"Listen, girls, we need to talk a little bit about something else."

Uh-oh, Mom sounded serious. The girls stopped jumping and sat cross-legged on the floor at her feet.

"You know how sometimes the kids can tease and be mean a school?" Cindy began. Unique dropped her head, cringing inside from her rush of terrible memories living in the house across the street with her sisters and brother.

"I thank God every day that the two of you are so kind and so strong. I want you both to always hold tight to that strength when you get out into the real world. Even in the world of design and fashion; some people will do their best to discourage you from going for what you want because of your differences. Your talent is a gift, and that makes you unique. It's nothing wrong with being different. Differences are why we can see so many things in the world."

Unique interrupted and said, "Yeah, like colors are different, and I love them all."

Jamie then said, "Yeah, and I like different fabric because it feels different when you wear it. "

Cindy jumped back in and said, "I want you both to remember how beautiful, smart, gifted and extraordinary you are. Always be willing to fight for what you want and what you believe in this life. And, never take 'No' for an answer. Never, ever let someone tell you 'you can't,' because you know you can. When things get tough—and, they will—I want you to dig into the problem like you're figuring out a puzzle. Never quit trying and never give up, okay? Promise?"

They both responded solemnly, "Okay, Mom." After a beat of letting Cindy's talk sink in, the jumping and sing-song affirmation started right back up.

My amazing little girls, Cindy smiled. She was so proud of them both. Cindy left their latest creations in hand.

The following Tuesday after school, Cindy kept her word as she always did, bringing Unique and Jasmine to Naomi's boutique for their first class in Design 101. It was love at first sight between Naomi and her young protégées. She had genuinely been blown away when she carefully examined their latest work. The pieces were exquisite. She could not believe Cindy's girls had any learning or physical disabilities at all. Once getting to know Unique, Naomi never gave a second thought to her left arm. Kindred spirits. Both of these young queens were genius visionaries.

It was the beginning of a whole new wonderful world for all of them. Naomi learned more from Unique and Jamie than she ever taught them.

CHAPTER 9

FAMILY TIES

IT WAS SUMMER, AND the Woods family was gearing up for one of their favorite warm-weather, family traditions, barbecuing. Chuck grilled regularly; but, this was the granddaddy of them all, the annual 'Woods Family Barbecue' that included the entire extended family—grandparents, aunties, uncles, and cousins who were sometimes several times removed. Cindy, Chuck, and the kids loved going all out for their party. The large backyard was everyone's favorite feature of the property. The Woods home might have been considered modest in size by some; but, the yard space more than made up for it. Over the years, Chuck had wisely purchased parcel after parcel, eventually making their backyard large enough to build four more homes if they wanted to. It was worth it to Chuck as much for his family's enjoyment as it was a substantial real-estate investment. Besides consuming copious amounts of barbecue, every possible side dish and beverage imaginable—there was a slew of fun, all-day activities. If you didn't want to boogie to the continuous music, there were board games

like Monopoly and Sorry, cards games, including Uno, Spades and Bid Whist; plus basketball, softball, football, and volleyball.

Chuck had his special barbecue ritual for the annual event. Just for his immediate family, Chuck used a standard grill. However, for the big blowout, he fired up his large, industrial-size grill the evening before to smoke the meat overnight, making the entire neighborhood smell like a delicious smokehouse. The hot dogs, smoked sausages, bratwurst, pork chops, pork steaks, beef steaks, hamburgers, and turkey burgers were accompanied by containers of his secret-recipe, homemade sauce. Only Cindy was privy to the secret ingredients.

Since all the meats were slow-cooked, Chuck was always right there to help Jerry and Maury put up the volleyball nets and football cones. Over-the-top excited, because they were about to have the time of their lives. The boys would always circle back and ask, "What's next, Dad?" Chuck hoped they were doing things correctly.

The girls liked playing outdoors as well; but, for the barbecue, their favorite thing was to help Cindy with preparing the sides—baked beans, potato salad, pasta, coleslaw, green salad, and the green bean casserole. Cindy's mom, and the world's best grandma, Carolyn did all the baking, which was just fine with everyone; because no one on the planet could put their foot in caramel, pound, lemon and chocolate cakes like Grandma—or—reproduce her famous sweet potato pies! Nothing like them in the world.

It seems the annual Woods Family Barbecue got better and better every year. While the large family chatted and played, Unique walked around slowly, savoring every precious moment of the festivities, taking mental pictures and videos to treasure forever in her memories. She had never seen anything like it before, except on TV.

She laughed at the menfolk competing playfully on their different sports teams. They were knocking each other so hard in the football scrimmage, though, she grimaced and had to turn away. That looked painful. Some of the teenagers played volleyball, each side slapping high fives when points were scored, teasing the opposing team in good fun. The card tables seemed to be the most raucous. Folks had a ball hooting, hollering and throwing shade at each other with choice names. Unique

skillfully dodged the water-play area. A small army of the other children, including her brothers, were hurling water balloons and spraying giant, colorful water guns at each other.

The big gathering of people was a family. And now—she was a part of it. Unique had never felt such love, joy, and gratitude in her young life. And, they all loved her right back. Family members who had come from North Carolina, Memphis, Washington, DC, Chicago and Detroit had traveled to St. Louis for the annual family feast all welcomed Unique with open arms and hearts. They greeted her with hugs, kisses, and some even brought her welcoming gifts. She was quite fond of an aunt who had come from North Carolina. Finally, Unique happily landed at the Uno table, a game she and Jamie had mastered from hours of playing it when they weren't creating their "line." Jamie felt Unique cheated because she could never seem to win.

Even Kate switched gears for the party. Instead of the kids' babysitter, today she was the official hostess; welcoming every family member at the front door and directing them to the festivities.

Then he arrived—the handsome, expensive-looking man with mischievous, yet kind eyes, whose name wasn't on the guest list Cindy had given her.

He smiled at the puzzled look on the pretty young woman's face. From the expression on her face, he knew she had no idea who he was and introduced himself, "Hi, I'm Al. I'm here for my daughter, Unique."

Kate's mouth fell open. So this was the guy who Cindy said wanted nothing to do with his special needs daughter? Oh, my God! She eventually picked her jaw up off the floor. "Hi, I'm Kate. Usually, I take care of the kids. I—um, apologize, Mr. Al, but this really isn't the best time. It's their—um, annual family barbecue. There are, like, more than a hundred people out back and they believe Unique to be a part of this family. I think trying to stir things up right now would be bad taste, and frankly put, dangerous for your health. So, maybe you could give me your number or something, so Mr. or Mrs. Woods can get back to you? I mean, I know they'll want to talk to you. But, I don't think that's today. Sir— I hope you understand. It's a party, you know?"

Al chuckled at her thoughts, knowing she was right. As an attorney, waiting to make partner—he didn't want trouble. Moreover, Al could read the signs of trouble like a best-selling novel. He pulled out a pen and a small notepad that he carried inside one of his jacket pockets. As he scribbled down his number, Kate twisted her hands together, knowing she was crossing a line, "May I ask you a question, Sir?"

"Sure," Al looked up, ripping off the page and handing it to her. "Now, they can call if this party ends tonight, but I'll be here to get my daughter in the morning. As for your question, ask away."

"I know it is none of my business. But, why now? The Woods—all of us—were under the impression that you, well, didn't want anything to do with Unique."

Al's face reddened, and his commonly controlled tongue was hot. He hated to be falsely charged, so he defended himself. "Ah, I see. Dorothy's delusional fairy tales about me has made waves of lasting impressions. The last years without Unique have been hell. I couldn't find her. I love my child, and no matter what that lying bitch told you or this family, I want my daughter, and I am coming to get her. You know, I should be sharing all this with the Woods. I can see this is a bad time, but I want my child."

This man's apparent anger, disappointment, and sadness tugged at Kate's heart. She had no way of knowing for sure that this Al was Unique's birth father or not, but she knew if she didn't say the right words, he could become irritated enough to force the issue right then, and he could have the cops to back him up. That would be larger than any family the Woods had in the back. Kate offered a few words of comfort.

"Mr. Al, I can't imagine what you have been through, but I can assure you that this family has been taking excellent care of Unique; if that brings you any comfort at all. Dorothy did the right thing in handing Unique over to a loving family, but she was so wrong to claim you didn't want Unique. Please, come with me, Al, and look out back. See for yourself that your baby is doing well. I just have one request. Can you come back tomorrow? Allow Unique to enjoy this day with the Woods family. Please, don't take her now."

Al looked into Kate's light brown eyes. Her eyes showed fear of him ruining the family barbecue. Al always had a hard time telling a lovely

woman no, so he agreed to come back tomorrow. Kate took him to the rear of the house, and he looked out the kitchen window to see Unique smiling and playing. He thought, 'That's the happiest I've ever seen her. She always just existed when she was with her mother, Dorothy. I never actually seen her play as a child while in that house.' Although he saw his child happy for the first time; he desired to have his baby with him.

"Thanks for that, Pretty Lady. Appreciate it. I'll come back and don't forget to give them the number, okay?"

"See you tomorrow," Al responded over his shoulder. Kate blushed and momentarily pleased that she stopped a catastrophic event as he turned and walked back to his Mercedes. Just as he left, more family arrived.

Kate's protective instincts didn't want to ruin the day for the Woods; so, she decided her conversation with Al could wait one more day. They'd have to deal with it soon enough. Finally joining the party, Kate slid right into the "Soul Train" line, where young and old were 'getting their groove on' to Sister Sledge iconic "We Are Family." Unique was in the middle of it, showing off her best moves, surrounded by love. She was cheered on and encouraged by enthusiastic, rhythmic cries of, "Go, Unique! Go, Unique!" In her new family, no one ever made fun of her short, misshapen left arm or its withered hand. No one even noticed. Just a little more than two years ago, the sad, lonely, severely neglected little girl's world was black and white and bleak. Today her world was filled with vivid colors of love, possibility, and joy.

Cindy slipped through the sea of the family to Chuck and wrapped her arms around him. The couple instinctively and intimately leaned their heads into each other.

"We did a good thing, baby," she whispered in his ear, watching Unique dance."

Chuck tilted Cindy's chin up with a fingertip so that they could look into each other's eyes.

"We sure did."

He kissed her on her forehead, grinned and jogged over to the dwindling group of sweaty diehards still playing hoops, yelling, "Let me show you how it's done: fellas!"

Cindy shook her head, chuckling and marveling at her husband, wondering where that man got his energy.

The day and night with loved ones had been beautiful. The cleanup—not so much—working together as a team, Cindy, Chuck, Unique, Jamie, Jerry, Maury, and Kate—who was crashing on the couch—whipped the yard back in shape in no time; with a mountain of stuffed black garbage bags to prove it. Worn out, they all headed for bed that Sunday morning at two-thirty a.m.

CHAPTER 10

A FORGOTTEN FACT

NO CHURCH THIS SUNDAY morning—every member of the Woods family was knocked out, still happily exhausted from their annual family shindig and all the days of prep leading up to it. By ten o'clock, Kate was in full gear, the couch made up and coffee brewing. It was distracting busy work. Her stomach was in knots, knowing what she had to tell Mr. and Mrs. Woods about the man who claimed to be Unique's father. Kate debated over and again with herself about whether or not she should go upstairs and knock on their door; or, wait for one of them to make their way into the kitchen—however, that decision was made for her. The doorbell repeatedly rang, jarring Kate and rudely awakening the entire household, except little Maury, who was out cold. Kate froze, her body not allowing her to answer the door. Cindy rubbed her eyes as Chuck threw off the heavy comforter and swung both legs over the edge of the king size bed. As he slid his feet into his slippers, he wondered whom could that be. Within moments, an agitated Chuck flew down the stairs, still tightening

the sash around his robe, "All right… All right! I'm coming, for God's sake!"

Cindy quickly following behind Chuck, caught the collision of worry and fury on Kate's face, turned to run back upstairs and headed first to the girls' room.

"It's okay. Go back to sleep. We're not doing anything or going anywhere today."

A sleepy Jamie responded,

"Good, Mommy, cause I'm still really tired." She and Unique both rolled over and closed their eyes again.

"Who is it?" Chuck called out, his hands on the doorknob and deadbolt lock.

At the door, a man's voice yelled out, "Al!"

"Who? I don't know any owl; except the ones in the trees."

"It's AL…not owl! I'm Unique's father!"

What the hell? Chuck's mind screamed. Out loud, he answered, "Hold on a second, be right with you."

Kate had run upstairs to warn Cindy, whispering in an urgent voice, "I'm sorry, Mrs. Woods. This Al guy says he's Unique's father. He came by yesterday. However, I didn't want to ruin the day for everyone—I'm very sorry."

Cindy was getting the picture, "No sorry necessary, honey. You were protecting us. I get it. Why don't you run on home now? It'll be okay." Cindy peeked in on her sleeping sons, turned and scurried down the stairs.

"It's Unique's father—or, at least he says he is," Chuck murmured when she reached him at the door.

Cindy partly covered her mouth. "Kate just told me he… Well, Al—stopped by yesterday. She didn't have the heart to let us know with the party going on. What could he possibly want? Dorothy swore he wanted nothing to do with Unique!" Cindy responded, her eyes wide with panic. "Now, he's here; why?"

Chuck swallowed, "I don't know, baby. Hold on, 'cause I think we're about to find out."

With a lump in his throat, Chuck slowly opened the door. As Al stepped in, Kate slid out. Al was a very tall, heavyset—but, shit-sugar-sharp and impressive—man with a Barry White voice.

"Hello, Al. I'm Chuck… and, this is my wife, Cindy. Come on in."

The two men shook hands. Al followed the couple to the living room. His eyes scanned the space discerningly. Cindy sat on the sofa. On guard, Chuck remained standing, keeping an eye on Al, poised to protect his family from any threat.

Chuck cut to the chase. "So, what can we do for you, Al? Why are you here?"

Al turned to face Chuck. "Unique is my daughter. No one ever even bothered to ask me."

"How could we?" Cindy interrupted. "Dorothy never so much as gave us a name when we asked about Unique's father again and again. She simply insisted that you wanted no parts of Unique or her life. Besides your most common name on Unique's birth records—how could we possibly know any information about you if Dorothy would not give it to us? Do you even lived in St. Louis?"

Al shook his head sadly and accusingly, looking from one to the other and said, "Let me guess, you both took the word of a drug-addicted prostitute as gospel because she's so credible. You did no research; You called no social worker; No lawyer; and you didn't even try looking harder for Unique's father, because—well—Dorothy was just—so—trustworthy. Right?"

Cindy was ashamed that—sarcasm aside—Al was on point, "Dorothy signed over the legal guardianship of Unique to us. Of course, it has always been our intention to go through the proper channels to adopt Unique. It's been challenging to keep up with Dorothy, who is the only relative we knew of, except her other children. Time just flew by. We've honestly not had the chance to get started on the process."

Cindy and Chuck shared a sheepish look, knowing that Al was right. They didn't ask enough questions. They both were genuinely concerned and loved Unique so much, and they blindly believed every word out of Dorothy's mouth.

Chuck shook his head, looked at Al and said, "Hey, Man. You're right. We did believe her; but, we had our reasons," Chuck offered.

Al interrupted, "Oh yeah? What reasons might those be?"

Cindy jumped in, "Well, most importantly, we never saw you! You were never there the entire time Unique lived right across the street! So, yes, everything Dorothy said rang true."

Al nodded, understanding, processing and said, "Okay, I get it. But, you've only heard the side of a very sick, very broken woman. It's my turn. Do you mind if I sit down?"

"Please," Cindy waved toward an armchair. "I'm going to get us all some coffee. The kids are still asleep; so, we'll have some privacy. For a little while, anyway."

"Thank you," Al sank back into the chair, relaxing at last.

"I'll help Cindy with the coffee. We'll be right back," Chuck added.

Moments later, coffee in hand, Al opened up, "First, I appreciate the two of you taking the time to listen to me. I stopped by yesterday; but, I left when I realized there was a party going on. The young lady who answered the door didn't tell you?"

"Not until this morning," Cindy answered. "Kate knew how much we all had on our plates yesterday. Please go on."

Al took another sip of coffee before continuing, "Now let me tell you the actual truth. I have always supported my children, including Unique. I loved and wanted that little girl with all my heart. Still, do. I could have pursued legal custody; but, decided against it when I saw how much Unique loved her mom. I lost my mother at a young age and never felt a child should be separated from their mother. So, I thought that I could monitor my child's life, help her with all her needs and be a father without courts and custody battles which damage the child in the long run.

Dorothy was always a good actress. She claims full custody but never has she been taken to court. However, when I found out about her drug usage, she promised me to go to rehab. It worked off and on, and for years we battled over our baby. Dorothy began asking for more money—on top of the regular, monthly child support payments. In return, I was allowed to take Unique home for overnight visits with me and her older sister, Victoria. I ask God, forgiveness because I knew the money was for drugs;

but, I was desperate for any time with my baby girl. One day, she decided to stop the overnight visits; insisting that Victoria and I come to her place to visit Unique. Dorothy said that would run away where I could never find them if I refused. Plus, I was building my career, and I didn't want courts nor Dorothy's drama plaguing my life. I figured I couldn't pay for my children with no occupation. So, I complied. Eventually, Dorothy complained about Victoria always tagging along. I wanted the girls to know each other, you understand? They are sisters. But, Victoria hated the visits anyway; so, she opted to stay with her nanny or mother while I spent time with Unique. "

"I don't get it. "Chuck gave Al a shameful look. "As a man how could you leave your child with that drug addict? Unique was hurt while you claim you wanted her! Where were you? All the time we've lived here, we never saw you."

Al became indignant and said, "I could have reported Dorothy to Child Services. But, she was always street slick. I knew good, and damn well—she would have vanished with Unique and her other kids. So, I did as Dorothy asked. If I just took Unique, I'd be charged with kidnapping. I repeat, that drama—I couldn't have while trying to build my career. The price to see my daughter kept going up. I was sick of being blackmailed to see my own kid; so I refused to give Dorothy another dime to support her drug habit. Even though it stung, I didn't see Unique for a couple of weeks as I weighed all my legal options. The child support was more than enough to cover her expenses, as well as Unique's; but, we all know where most of her cash flow went. I finally landed at a firm; I felt I could build with and had the resources to fight for permanent custody.

Meanwhile… Dorothy made good on her threats. Because of Dorothy's rabid drug habit, her phone service was invariably cut off. I couldn't call so one day I just showed up with legal papers for permanent custody of Unique in hand. Although they weren't filed yet, I needed her to know I was prepared to present my case in court. Dorothy and the kids were gone. The apartment was empty. Even my private investigators couldn't track them down. Like roaches, addicts are well-adept at going underground. I was crushed. I filed the papers for custody; however, without knowledge of the location of my child, and her mother; she

couldn't be served with papers. I could gather no evidence to support my claims of drugs and prostitution. She even had her eldest daughter name on everything—P. O. Box address and everything. We never found Dorothy. The system that I'm a part of had let me down... let my baby girl, Unique, down."

Al took a deep breath and continued. "A friend just happened to spot Dorothy over in Illinois, somewhere. I'll just say that he did what he needed to do to persuade Dorothy to tell him where Unique was. That led me to you. Now, When I found out she was here with you, I was angry at first."

Chuck interjected and said, "Wait." He walked to his office, grabbed the written agreement and guardianship papers that Dorothy signed and returned to let Al view them.

Cindy and Chuck clutched each other's hands, terrified of what was coming next.

Al took a deep breath, hummed and said, "For you—this saddens me. As for Dorothy—it angers me that she would give my child away like some lost puppy. There is no legality to what you and Dorothy have agreed. It makes me appreciate why I do what I do. People need an attorney! You can't go around doing things without legal representation —especially when it comes to family matters. People are taken advantage of every day—and you two—are no exception. Dorothy used you, and this won't hold up in court. Sorry... I mean—I realize Dorothy signed over her parental rights to you. But, I didn't. No one asked me! So, Mr. and Mrs. Woods, thank you for taking care of my little girl. Believe me, I am grateful. But, I want my child. And, I want her today! Dorothy had no right to just hand her over to you."

Cindy and Chuck were devastated—this couldn't be happening! Everything seemed surreal. Cindy stared at her husband in disbelief, tears streaming down her face.

Feeling the heartbreak himself with welling eyes, Chuck lovingly pulled Cindy to him, addressing Al. "You're right, man. You're right. But, you should know, we love Unique. All of us—and, she loves us. She's been happy here."

Cindy jumped in, "Yes, and we made a solemn promise to Unique that we would never leave her, never abandon her," Cindy added, hoping that promise would mean something to Al.

When Al didn't respond for an uncomfortably long time, Cindy with tearful eyes looked at Chuck and repeated, "But honey… We told her we wouldn't ever leave her. Chuck, you were right; we should have stayed out of it. I can't imagine what Jamie and the boys are going to go through with Unique moving." She excused herself to plod up the stairs with leaden feet and a heavy heart.

Both little girls were peacefully sleeping when she tiptoed into their room. Feeling Cindy's presence, Unique slowly opened her eyes, propping herself up with her right elbow when she saw her mom sitting next to her on the bottom bunk bed with tears in her eyes.

Unique rubbing her eyes. "What's wrong, Mommy?"

Cindy couldn't bear to tell Unique what was going on; so she just held her. Unique couldn't have felt more loved.

Downstairs, Chuck was trying his hardest to change Al's mind about uprooting Unique from the family and home she loved. Nothing Chuck said, though, was persuading enough for Al to leave his child behind again. Al was angry, resentful and frustrated with the very thought of Dorothy giving Unique away, even though the Woods genuinely seemed to love and want Unique. He understood why Dorothy immediately took her other children and disappeared into thin air. The legal guardianship would signal red flags. Following protocol after any inspection or investigation, the state would have taken all her children and put them in foster care—a broken system. Then, they would have stopped all of her state government assistance checks. Apparently, the monthly child support payments for Unique weren't enough to feed Dorothy's addiction.

But, none of that mattered now. Just Unique—listening to and observing Chuck and his wife, Al realized the Woods were also victims of Dorothy's sickness, lies, and manipulation. He knew they were nice, compassionate people; and, he felt sorry for them. Nevertheless, he continued to be adamant about his decision to take Unique home with him.

Holding his knees for support, Al lifted himself up from the comfortable armchair, looking Chuck in the eyes the entire time and said, "I am sorry, Mr. Woods. Believe me; I understand how you feel. But, I am Unique's father. I love her—have always loved and wanted her. I won't be that father that leaves my child! I already feel guilty for leaving her with her drug addict mother. So, can you get my child for me? Or, are you going to force me to do things the hard way?"

Chuck was outdone completely, and he knew that Al was right and nodded, "Yes."

He had no choice but to hand Unique over to her father. Heading for the stairs, Chuck prayed Unique was old enough to handle this new reality. Thank God, it was happening now when she was stronger and healthy; not when she first came to their family, fragile as a wounded little bird.

Chuck shook his head in anguish and said, "Just wait right here for a few minutes, okay?" He called back to Al over his shoulder. We'll get Unique and her things. "

Al nodded in agreement, pacing the floor.

Chuck went upstairs slowly, holding his head down and wondering how this entire situation would unfold. He reached the top step of the stairs and choked back tears as he joined Cindy in the girls' room.

Cindy fearfully searched Chuck's eyes for any glimpse of hope. Chuck sadly shook his head, "No." Unique had fallen back asleep in her mommy's arms. Cindy laid Unique on her pillow. Cindy's eyes flooded with tears. "But we promised her, baby—we promised."

Chuck walked to the beds and kissed Cindy on the forehead, and she stood. He said, "It'll be okay, sweetheart. I don't know how; but, it will."

With a firm embrace, Chuck kissed her tears; Chuck knew he had to find the strength to give Unique to her father. The voices stirred both Unique and Jamie awake. Chuck had wanted to gather up Unique without Jamie witnessing any of it.

Jamie went into alarm mode as soon as she saw the tears and woeful expressions on her parents' faces and her mom was gathering Unique's things. "Mommy, Daddy, what's wrong?"

Chuck wanted more than anything to tell his daughters that everything was fine. But, Al was right downstairs, so he had to say to them both the truth in the least painful way possible.

"Unique, there's a surprise for you."

Unique wasn't buying it. Like Jamie, she, too, was sensitive to her parents' feelings; able to read their faces. They thought, 'What kind of surprise makes you sad?'

Cindy said, "It's your dad. He's downstairs."

Unique was confused. "Mommy is silly. My daddy is right here."

Chuck's resolve started to fade, hearing Unique's sweet voice calling him Daddy; but, he continued to explain.

"No, honey, your birth father, Al, is here. Don't you remember him?"

"Yes, I remember. But, that was a long time ago. Al and my mother—my other mother—had a big fight. I didn't see him anymore after that. Is he taking me for a visit to his house like he used to?"

Chuck rubbed his head and said, "A visit? Sweetheart, this isn't to visit. He loves you and has been looking for you all this time. He wants you to go with him to stay at his house."

Cindy chimed in to try and help Unique feel better about the imminent upheaval. "Just think, Honey, you will be with your real father and your sister, Victoria. You'll even have your room to yourself and everything! Won't that be fun?"

Unique was hurt, angry, confused and terrified all at one time, turning to Cindy with her giant, puppy-dog eyes and screamed, "Mommy... NO!"

Cindy turned her back wailing. Unique turned to Chuck, pained tears rolling down her beautiful little face "Daddy? Why? But-Dad? Was I bad? I'll be a good girl, I promise. I don't understand. I don't want to go with him. Victoria always was mean to me. I don't need my own room! I like sharing my room with Jamie! I like being here; this is my family!" Unique cried and squealed so hard, she was on the verge of hyperventilating. "NO, I'm not going! Please don't make me? Please! I will be good. Mommy, you promised me! Nooooooooo!"

Unique stormed up the ladder, hoping to hide in Jamie's bed. Cindy couldn't take it. Unique's pain was killing her. She raced down the stairs to plead with Al once more. Chuck stoically continued to pack Unique's

things. Jamie went behind him, plucking out every single item Chuck threw into the bag.

He gently grabbed Jamie's little hand before she could reach into the bag again, begging, "Jamie, please? I am very sorry. I don't want this any more than you do. But, Al is Unique's birth father. We were wrong about him. And, we can't keep her here; no matter how much we want her to stay."

By then, Unique had climbed down the bed's ladder, stunned into silence. Jamie tightly wrapped both of her arms around her sister.

Jamie cried, "But it's not fair."

"I know it's not, sweetheart," Chuck stopped packing and held both little girls in his arms. "After we get Unique packed, maybe we can see if you could visit her sometimes."

Jamie whined stating her case, "But, Daddy, I want her to stay. She's my very best friend, and she's my sister! Don't let him take her, Daddy, please."

"I know—honey, I know," Chuck whispered.

He kissed both girls, released them and resumed packing. Jamie continued to hold onto Unique for dear life.

Downstairs, Cindy tried to persuade Al, listing all the reasons why he should let Unique stay with them.

"Al, please, just think, Unique requires so much more attention because of her special needs. She's not a baby anymore that you can just coddle. Was she ever with you long enough for you to know how to deal with her when her bouts of depression hit? Are you aware of, or equipped with an incredible amount of patience it takes to compassionately handle a child that suffers from multiple mental illnesses on top of an obvious physical disability?"

Al became defensive. "Don't tell me about my daughter as though I'm not aware of her challenges. I know it's not going to be easy. But, when is raising any child, easy? I love my daughter. I've loved her since the moment I knew she existed; before I even met her. I want her with me—no matter what! I got this."

"I was just trying to explain…"

Al cut Cindy off. Tired of Cindy's mouth. She came off as if she claimed that he wasn't a suitable father. "I know what you were trying to say. Now, please get Unique so that we can go home—where she belongs."

"Fine! She'll be down soon."

Cindy sighed, numb and exhausted in every possible way. Deflated and defeated, she turned to head back up the stairs mumbling under her breath, "There is no reasoning with that man." Chuck was still packing when she reached the girls' room. Cindy's tears were replaced by pain-fueled fury. Unique and Jamie were huddled together on the floor. Ever the loving mother, Cindy sucked it up and plopped down next to them, determined to soothe the terror in Unique's eyes.

"Unique, sweetheart, I need you to do something for me, okay? I want you to be strong. All through your life, there are going to be twists and turns, tough times and disappointments. Know that even when things feel hopeless, you have the strength to get you through even the worst times. Like, I've told both you and Jamie before—it's your superpower. And, believe it or not, in the end, everything will work out just fine. Look at me, Unique. Pay close attention to what I'm telling you with your best listening ears. We're not breaking that promise Daddy, and I made to you, sweetie. This is just one of those unexpected bumps in the road that happen sometimes; but, we are not leaving you! Do you understand? You haven't done anything wrong. You could never do anything that will make us leave you. You can call anytime you want. Maybe even visit. We are always here for you, okay? Always… Remember, to be strong—for me, for you, for Jamie, for all of us."

"Okay, Mommy, I will," Unique almost whispered in a shaky, tiny voice.

"Then, let's go. If anything happens that you don't like, please call home, baby. Deal?"

"Deal." Unique grabbed hold of Cindy's waist.

Jamie crawled into her bed to retreat under the covers, continuing to cry about it 'not being fair.' Cindy and Chuck hugged and kissed Unique as long as they could. But had to rush her along because they knew Al was becoming impatient and walked Unique down the stairs. Chuck carried two bags, jammed with everything he could stuff into them. The couple

held onto each other for support, struggling to put on feigned happy faces as they sent Unique and Al on their way. Cindy stared tearfully at Unique, who was straining to look back while reluctantly following Al to his shiny Benz SUV. Cindy remembered hearing Dorothy's wailing at the hospital when she left Unique with them. At this moment, Cindy was experiencing the same paralyzing pain Dorothy must have felt, letting her child go—no matter how high she might have been. Cindy folded over the front porch's railing, sobbing uncontrollably as Al pulled away with her baby. Just like Dorothy.

Like most men, Chuck was instilled with ignoring any semblance of feelings that might be construed as 'weak' always 'being a man,' staying strong, stalwart and unflappable for his family. Fighting back his own tears, he scooped up Cindy in his arms and carried her back into the house; as she helplessly screamed Unique's name loud enough to wake the dead.

Once inside, Chuck gave Cindy a sleeping pill to help her calm down and drift off into blissful, temporary oblivion. Next, he called Kate, asking her to return and help with the children. Luckily, she lived close-by. Even though she, too, was worn out, Kate loved this family and rushed back over.

As Chuck fully anticipated, the boys were hysterical and inconsolable when they learned Unique was gone. It was a struggle; but, Kate managed to eventually calm down Jerry and Maury, making them a promise that was not hers to make—that they would see Unique again, soon. Chuck sat at Jamie's bedside, rubbing her back until she fell into an emotionally drained sleep. Before her daddy showed up, Jamie had come out from under the sanctuary of her covers; tears and snot running everywhere as she grieved the loss of her only sister and best friend, who was taken away from her.

CHAPTER 11

LIFE WITH AL

AL'S DRIVE HOME WAS guilt biting ride for him, and he noticed a distressed child in his back seat. Unique stared out the window, miserably retreating into herself. Her sniffs from crying were thunderous to Al, and her pain broke his heart; even though, he knew he was doing the right thing by his little girl.

"I've missed you, baby-girl," Al tries to comfort her. "You've grown so much and are beautiful. Unique, I know I wasn't there for you when you needed me most; and, I will be sorry about that for the rest of my life." Al prayed that he was choosing the right words to ease his child's burden of sadness.

"Mr. and Mrs. Woods seem like incredible people. I'm so happy and grateful you had the chance to be a part of their family. And, I know how sad you must be feeling about leaving them. But, you know what? You'll see them again, I promise. And, I promise to make up for all the time we missed together. Daddy's going to spoil you rotten. How does that sound?"

Unique remained silent, her mind and spirit in another world. Upon arrival, she was present enough to observe that the house seemed even more massive than she remembered. She was not impressed back then; and, she wasn't excited now.

Al was apparently very proud of the large Tudor home's renovations over the last few years, hoping that Unique would be, too. Little did he know; to Unique, the giant house with the upscale furnishings felt like a death trap. All Unique wanted was to go back home to her foster parents, sister, and brothers.

Once inside, Al tried to transform the somberness into enthusiasm and excitement, "Hey, want to see your room, Unique?"

"My room is where I was when you took me away."

"Sweetheart, please… I know you're upset. But, I'm your father—your real family. I love you. It's taken me a long time to find you finally. Now that I have, all I want to do is take care of you and make you happy. I don't need anyone taking you from me."

Al knelt down in front of Unique—no easy task—gently taking her by the shoulders.

"Do you think you could maybe give me a chance to do that? Maybe try to trust me a little. Pretty please? That's all I'm asking. Do you think you can do that for me?"

Unique mulled it over a minute, "I guess I can try. My mommy always says to try, no matter how hard things seem."

"Wow, Dorothy taught you that?"

If Unique were a grown-up, she would have blurted out, "No, fool!" Unique graced this new father with an expression of 'how dumb are you?' and explained, "No, not Dorothy. I'm talking about my mommy, Cindy. You know—the one you just took me from."

Al thought about Unique's tone and expressions, and indeed, he felt stupid for entertaining the idea that Dorothy might have said an encouraging statement like that. He assertively chose to move on to something else. He gave Unique an unrequited hug, held onto a nearby table to hoist himself up, and guided her up to her room, which had also been completely overhauled since the last time Unique visited.

"Here we are," Al announced as brightly as he could muster; opening the door to what should have been any little girl's fantasy come to life. Unique looked around her new surroundings. The room was enormous and pink, overflowing with toys, a fancy dollhouse that Jamie would have loved for her Barbies, stuffed animals, and children's books. A lovely, puffy canopy bed was the main attraction. Bright sunlight flooded through a bay window with a padded seat cushion, where she could daydream, read or just look outside.

None of it mattered to Unique, though. No matter what was in the room, to her, it felt empty and cold. The worst part was that Unique didn't have any of her designs or fabric swatches or sewing tools. Unique screamed inside, 'How could she possibly create anything without Jamie?'

Unique's noticeable anxiety wasn't lost on Al, who was feeling helpless. He didn't know what else to do to bring a smile to his baby's face or re-ignite the light that had left her eyes. Al put hope back into his voice and said, "Victoria will be home soon from ballet. She's so excited to have her baby sister here with us. Hey—you hungry?"

"No, not really… But, thanks," Unique remembered the manners Cindy had also taught her. "Can I just have my bags, please?"

Al placed the two bags that Chuck had packed at the foot of the bed. "Need help unpacking?" Unique nodded, 'No,' hunting for her beloved stuffed Teddy bear; the one Jamie had given her. She clutched Mr. Teddy tightly to her chest, climbed on top of the bed fully dressed and fell asleep in the foreign room and house—praying that when she woke up, it all will have been just a terrible nightmare that would have vanished.

❧

Victoria stormed in and slammed the door behind her, screaming through the halls for her Dad. Unique slowly walked in behind her older sister. Saying nothing, she just went straight to her room, as usual.

"Dad, Dad! Where are you?"

Victoria ran through the halls, searching for Al. Finally, it dawned on her to check what she dubbed his getaway space. She ran down the curved

staircase and through the family area to Al's study. Breathless, Victoria tapped lightly on the door, hoping her dad wasn't on a business call. She was spoiled and unashamedly bursting to give him a piece of her mind! Fretful and incorrigible, Victoria threw open the doors when she didn't get an immediate response from the other side. Al was, indeed, in the middle of a call. When he looked up, startled by Victoria and the insistent look on her face, he ended the call.

"What is it, Princess?"

"Daddy, I just can't take it anymore," Victoria complained. "I want Unique to go! Why does she go to school with me, anyway? Shouldn't she have her own school for kids like her?"

Al sighed and pulled Victoria closer to him. "Sweetheart, we've talked about this a hundred times. Unique is your sister. She's smart as a whip, so she doesn't need a particular school. I enrolled her in the same school so that you can look after her. Unique has had a difficult life. That's my fault… Other kids are going to bully her, maybe hurt her because she is special. You are the strongest, most stubborn girl I know. I can't think of another person who comes even this close to having the power to protect her. And, as Unique's big sister; it's your job, honey. Can you do that for Daddy?"

Victoria pushed away from her dad, folding her arms, madder than before. "No, I don't want to look out for her; or, have her anywhere near me at school. I don't even like her hanging around me here at home. We don't like any of the same things. All she talks about are making clothes and her sister, Jamie. And, if you ask me, she should go right back to Jamie."

"Well, I'm not asking you, young lady. I'm telling you. Again… And, I don't want that smart lip—not one more time." Victoria was taken aback and pouted. Her father never spoke to her like this.

"For the last time," Al continued. "This is not a request. You are the older sister. It is your responsibility to protect your younger sister. Comes with the territory, like it or not. If you just gave Unique a chance, you'd find out that she is a lovely girl. She wants to be a good sister; but, you've got to meet her half-way, Vickie. Haven't you noticed how she loves you and looks up to you?" Victoria rolled her eyes.

Al became uncharacteristically firmer with Victoria. "Plain and simple, you're my princess, and I expect you to act like one. Princesses are always gracious and kind. So, can't you put a bit more effort into getting along better with your sister? Be my princess?"

Victoria whined with frustration, "Daddy, it's not fair! I didn't ask to be an older sister. I didn't ask for a sister who looks like that, and I didn't ask her to love me or like me. I don't like her, Daddy; and, you can't make me!"

Before Al could open his mouth, Victoria ran out of the study and straight to her room. Al couldn't believe his ears. In many ways, Victoria was a lot like him. But, she had a cruel, selfish streak that he didn't have, or like in his daughter. Al pondered in his thoughts, 'How did I raise a child who was so self-absorbed, with no family values? Was it my fault for over-indulging her to compensate for her mother's absence?' If Victoria's viciousness was an inherited trait, that's where Al pointed the finger at her mother, an evil bitch-on-wheels. Al petitioned God for a miracle—or, any divine intervention—to help his two daughters bond.

౧

Al increasingly became more agitated with the refereeing between Vickie and Unique. He was very close to his dream of making partner at a prestigious law firm and desired it so much that he could taste it. Al rolled his eyes upward in his head. He was experiencing a complete elevated level of stress. He had been so distracted struggling to keep the peace at home; it was taking him much longer than it should have to complete a significant brief he'd been working on for days. The deadline was looming just hours away; and for the first time in his career, Al wasn't ready. He shut his office door and transformed into automated attorney mode, flipping the script; focusing all of his concentration on completing this brief. Al became so engrossed in his work; he nearly jumped out of his skin when his intercom buzzed.

"Mr. Jacob, your nanny is on line two. She says it's urgent. Should I put her through or take a message?"

"Yes, put her through, please. Thanks." Al massaged the space between his brows. "What's the problem, Ms. Maple?"

"It's Unique. I'm sorry, Sir…"

"Again? What the hell happened now?"

"I'm sorry, Mr. Jacob, but the child's been running a high temperature all day; despite the cool baths and fever-reducing medications. Just to be on the safe side, I think she needs to return to the hospital."

"Oh no! Unique… Yes, of course, Ms. Maple. Thank you. I'll meet you there."

The last couple of hours of concentrated focus had paid off. Al only needed a few more minutes to put the polishing touch on the brief. Throwing papers into his briefcase, he instructed his assistant to print the document and make sure it made it to Mr. Clark's desk ASAP. Rushing to get to Unique, Al asked her also to cancel the rest of his afternoon; and inform Ted Clark, the managing partner, that he had a family emergency. But the assistant reminded him of the board meeting.

"What shall I tell Mr. Clark about the board meeting already scheduled?"

"Well, I plan on making it back for that."

Al couldn't get to his truck fast enough. His heart racing, he tossed his briefcase into the back seat, strapped himself in, then dropped his head to the steering wheel for just an instant. 'What have I done?' Al admonished himself. 'How much longer can I scramble my world to hold on to a child who is more miserable than ever? How fair is that to my little girl? Unique hates living with me. And, Victoria is only making it worse.' He took a deep breath, turned the key in the ignition and drove off. Forty-five minutes later, Al was hunting for a parking spot at Children's Hospital. Inside, a front desk receptionist directed him to Unique's section, floor, and room. The pediatrician on-call ran into Al just as he approached Unique's room.

"Hi, I'm Dr. Gomez. You must be Unique's dad."

"Yes, I am. What's going on with my daughter, Dr. Gomez? It feels like we were just here a few days ago."

"Mr. Jacob, why don't you come with me to our consultation room? You can catch your breath; and, I'll give you a full update on your daughter's situation."

Al followed the doctor to a cheerfully painted private room. Al wanted to get right to the point, pushing the second-guessing about his brief to the back of his mind. Unique was his only priority right now.

"Mr. Jacob, physically, Unique will be just fine. She has an ear infection that we're treating with antibiotics; so, it will improve in no time. But, what concerns me the most are her mental challenges. How aware are you of their severity?"

Al felt as though he'd been punched in the gut. Cindy's pleading and efforts to explain Unique's mental and emotional issues came flooding back. All he did was brush her off.

"What specific mental illnesses are we talking about? I just recently gained physical custody of my daughter. It's complicated, and I don't want to dig it all up right now. Just know it's still a learning process for both of us. So, please, tell me what we're dealing with and how I can help my little girl."

"Of course. I understand. Don't worry; I'll walk you through everything. First, to the best of your knowledge, has there been any major stressful event or trauma in Unique's life recently?"

"Yes, I'm afraid so." Al cringed. "Why do you ask?"

"Your daughter—Unique, suffers from manic depression, also known as bipolar disorder. I ask because manic episodes will become a mania, which are severe swings in a person's mood, energy level, and activity level, can range from extreme highs or the lowest of low. An episode can be triggered by sleep deprivation or something as routine to most people like a change in circumstances. You know, marriage, divorce, changing jobs, moving, having a child, the death of a loved one—life. But, to someone suffering from this disorder, like your daughter, a major life event is processed as trauma and can produce dangerous levels of stress and becomes mania causing her to react with madness, and delirium. That's where Unique's mental state is right now: critical." Dr. Gomez's trained eye recognized the stress level rising in Al.

"I'm not trying to scare you, Mr. Jacob. I intend to help you by educating you. The bipolar condition can be successfully treated with medication and therapy, allowing affected people to live full lives. However, if it goes untreated, it can lead to possible suicide attempts.

Your child is still very young. The highest suicide rate is, sadly, among teens whose illness—for whatever reason, isn't treated. It's your job as her father to be vigilant. Stay on top of the illness so that Unique never falls into that statistic."

"Suicide! What? No!" Al held his head in his hands. "Oh, Dear God, I know she's sad; but, something as drastic as trying to commit suicide—at any time—never crossed my mind."

"How much time have you spent talking to her about her feelings?" Dr. Gomez asked gently.

"I—'m ashamed to admit I haven't spent much time talking. I just thought if I gave Unique space and time that she needs, she'd come around, learn to be happy again, with me."

The unfamiliar sensation of tears stung the back of Al's eyes, threatening to spill.

"Jesus, how blind could I be? Unique comes home from school with nothing to say, locks herself in her room—doing her homework, I assumed—and stays there until dinnertime. Her sister, Vickie, babbles away at the table. Unique only speaks if she's spoken to. Plus, she's eaten like a bird since she's lived with me. What can I do to help her, doctor? Please, I'll do whatever it takes."

Dr. Gomez explains further to—what appears to be a terrified father.

"The usual treatment for bipolar disorder is lifetime therapy and mood stabilizers. Meds like lithium, carbamazepine, or divalproex valproic acid can be lifesavers for people suffering from the disease. Often resulting in a dramatic decrease in manic mania and reduces the risk of suicide."

He continued. "I'm going to give you some literature, Mr. Jacob. But, I encourage you to learn as much on your own as you can about this illness from therapists, the Internet, books, or support groups. Let's make sure Unique is under the care of a trained team of caring medical and mental health professionals. I will prescribe some meds for the depression, right now. Once the meds are in her system, Unique should experience considerable relief.

Meanwhile, I want you to make appointments with both a psychiatrist and a psychologist who specialize in treating children." Dr. Gomez pulled

a few cards out of his white jacket pocket. "Here, these are good people to start with."

Al accepted the cards, grateful and overwhelmed.

Dr. Gomez had more. "Encourage exercise and interactions with other children. Comfort Unique any way you can. Actively show her plenty of love and reassurance. Call me if things don't improve in a couple of weeks. We may have to adjust her meds to find the ideal combo and strength. Any questions?"

Dr. Gomez studied Al's face, wondering if this hulk of a man could handle a sick little girl, who required so much more than meals, a nanny and a fancy roof over her head to thrive. Al buried any nagging pricks of uncertainty and assured Dr. Gomez that he and Unique would be just fine. Within the hour, he was able to complete all the necessary paperwork and take Unique home. Mrs. Maple had stayed with Unique at the hospital and accompanied them back home. He asked her to stay with the girls overnight; but, made it his business first to tuck Unique in, administer the meds and hold her until she fell asleep. Al kissed her little forehead, whispering over and over how much Daddy loved her. Al's heart lightened a bit when he detected a faint smile just as she drifted off.

Al walked into the office late but with his head low. He had missed the board meeting—not good. It was typical for all of the firm's attorneys to burn the midnight oil several nights a week; so there was a full house when Al made it back to the office late that evening.

The legal brief he'd prepared was for one of the firm's most critical and complicated clients. If they won this client's case, Al's partnership was a sure thing. But, even with his entire legal career riding on it, Al found it difficult to concentrate. Instead of working, crunching numbers, Al was at his desk looking at information about bipolar on the internet. Guilt was eating him alive. He couldn't get Unique off his mind. She needed him. Al re-packed his briefcase, deciding to return home to work.

Just as he was about to leave, the managing partner strolled into Al's office, shutting the door behind him. Ted Clark looked serious. Al sat back down at his desk. Ted placed the short brief on his desk.

"Jacob, you haven't been yourself lately. I put you on the Hendricks case because you're one of our best, a rising star. I've mentored you myself, and this is not your best work. What's going on?"

"Just a lot of pressure at home, Ted, sorry. I've been distracted; but, I've got my head clear again. That's why I was taking a brief home with me. Sick kid."

Ted nodded, "Understand. We've all been there. But, I still need you 150%. Do you think you're up for it? If not, I can put Stephens on it. A lot is riding on this, as you know."

"Yes, Sir… That's why I'll be working on it all night. I'll have it ready first thing tomorrow morning."

"Alright, then… I'm counting on it—hell, we all are… A-game, remember."

"You got it. Thanks, Ted."

Ted Clark nodded with an expectant look, got up and added, "Hope your kid's better." With that, he was out the door. Al unpacked his briefcase and placed its contents back on the desk. He discerned that going home wasn't the best thing to do. Al had no time for Victoria's interrupted temper tantrums— Or, the nanny's fear over Unique's every move. Al drank pots of coffee that night, giving the brief his full attention, except for the times he checked in on Unique. Something had to give. He couldn't continue like this. Neither could Unique. He loved and wanted his youngest daughter; but, keeping her with him was selfish. It was killing her: literally.

Ted came back and peaked his head through the door to Al office.

"Al, we rescheduled the meeting for tomorrow morning at nine. I understand that you've got a situation going on at home but you must be present or Stephens will be the go-to guy."

Al rubbed his face, "Ugh! The meeting…! Unique has an appointment at the same time. I can't be in two places at one time!"

Al picked up his phone to call the nanny but instantly remembered; she had an appointment also and requested off for the day. Al slammed the phone back down and rubbed his head with both hands out of frustration. Leaning back in his chair, he then thought about Cindy's words; she had tried to warn him of the seriousness of Unique's illnesses. She stressed how hard it would be to take care of her. After what felt like hours of soul-searching, Al knew what he had to do. He picked up his office phone once again; this time, he called Cindy.

"Hello, Cindy?"

"Yes, it's me." Cindy sounded puzzled as she tried catching the voice over the phone.

"This is Al, Unique's dad."

Upon hearing Al's voice, Cindy immediately suspected that Unique was ill, and he didn't know what to do.

"Is everything alright with Unique?"

"Yes, everything is fine. I just need some help. Unique has an appointment today, and I was called into an emergency meeting with my job that I can't miss, but Unique's appointment is at the same time. Can you take her for me? Plus she misses you terribly."

"I can rearrange my day. Give me directions to your home, and I will take her."

Al thanked Cindy and gave her directions to his home. He informed his nanny about the arrangements for Cindy to pick up Unique.

Cindy was over-the-moon that she got Al's call for help. She was at Al's doorstep within the hour. Unique was dressed and ready for her follow-up doctor's appointment that morning. She was stunned to see her mom walk in, lit up and flew into Cindy's arms.

The two enjoyed a perfect day. Cindy masked her concern for Unique's mental state after being briefed by Dr. Gomez. He, however, noticed a marked improvement in the child already during the exam, recording it in her chart. Afterward, Cindy took Unique to their favorite ice cream parlor, where they had a chance to laugh and catch up on what everyone in the Woods family was doing. Unique only had questions for Cindy. She had nothing to offer about staying with Al—except that she didn't want to be there. She wanted to be home with her real family.

Cindy hugged and kissed Unique when she returned her to Al's. She kept everything as light and promising as she could, "But, sweetheart, this is the enjoyable part. We get to spend time together now. And, you can come and visit with us sometimes. Maybe we'll have sleepovers. Now, you have two homes! How cool is that?"

Unique refused to be consoled. As soon as Cindy left, bursting into tears once she slid into her car—the light again went from Unique's eyes. She was back in what felt like her gilded prison.

In the following weeks, Unique's manic depression grew and was at the most dangerous level. Her state of mind became dangerously unpredictable and awkward. Al began to lean on Cindy more and more. Cindy took Unique to all her doctor's appointments. She responded readily to every late night call whenever Unique had fits of mania. Unique's volatile mental state was more than Al could handle. Cindy was the only one who could calm her down. But, Cindy had three, young, birth children with disabilities who required her attention. She was spreading herself thin, making sure Jamie, Maury, and Jerry were taken care of, as well as her husband, Chuck—trying her best not to neglect either of them. It was Monday, at 11:15 pm, when Cindy's phone rang. Al was at his wit's end. After unbearable fits of screaming and crying, Unique was balled up in the corner of her room, rocking, with her right arm wrapped protectively around her knees. Al couldn't take it anymore.

"Please, Cindy, I need you. Can you come? She's never been this bad. I don't know what else to do. I've got a big day at the office tomorrow. At this rate, I won't be any good to anyone."

"I'm on my way."

Cindy hung up, grabbed her keys, Blackberry and purse. Throwing a coat over her pajamas, she jumped into her truck and took off.

As soon as Al opened the door, Cindy flew up the stairs to Unique's room and plopped down on the floor beside the little girl, taking her in her arms. She rocked and soothed Unique until she fell asleep. Cindy scooped her up and tucked the sad, sick, little girl back into her canopy bed.

It was time for a heart-to-heart with Al. She joined him downstairs in the living room, nursing a scotch to calm his nerves.

"Look, Al, I love Unique. That's why I drive all this way to do whatever I can to help her—and, you. But, this is getting out of control. You love her, too. I know that. But, this—steadily running here when she's sick, doctor's appointments or having fits has gone too far and has to stop. There aren't enough hours in the day, and this is making all of us crazy. Unique is still miserable. I remember all I had to do was walk across the hall when she had her fits or nightmares—now, I have to drive across town! I'm just going to say it, and hope to God; you understand."

Cindy continued to fuss. "You are entirely selfish. Yes, you love her—she is your daughter. But, she is not a possession! She is a little girl with special needs who requires—and, deserves—special care. The longer she is here, the more severe the symptoms of the bipolar disorder are, despite the medication and therapy. She sees me—I drop her back off here—Unique progressively gets worst. Surely, you understand that."

"Wait a minute, Cindy," Al interrupted.

"No, you wait, Al! You can't keep toying with your child's life like this. And, dang it—all, you can't keep turning my life upside down, too, because you can't handle this little girl. I tried to tell you when you barged in demanding to take Unique away from us. Now, I can't eat or sleep; hoping and praying to God my baby doesn't try to commit suicide because she is so desperately depressed. You did that! I feel her pain—all of it—my poor baby."

Al held his head down in shame. He took Cindy's hand and led her to the sofa. Cindy was shaking with anger, but she took a deep breath and sat at the edge of the couch. Al sat next to her.

"Every single thing you're saying is right, Cindy. I was, am… selfish. I try my best to be unlike my colleagues who I work with daily. Most have no real family values; They only care about what appears on the outside, and nothing comes above the job. I find that I am just like them—selfish, but I refused to only care about outside appearances. Demanding my way is okay for my line of work; not my family. You are right to call me selfish, but I'll work on that. When I found Unique again, I didn't want to be accused of being a deadbeat dad who would abandon his child. Yes, those outside appearances; I talked about. It was more about me, at first—not Unique. Yes, I love her. Yes, I want her. Yes, the family is imperative to me. And, I honestly thought I was doing the right thing by my daughter. I couldn't have been more wrong. My baby girl is suffering because of me. The pressure of trying to maintain has allowed everything that's going on at home to affect my work. I'm not giving 100% to anyone. So, bottom line—you were right, Cindy. You were right all along. Can you ever forgive me? Can you please, help me?"

Al's emotions got the best of him. He tried to man up; but, the tears had already escaped. Cindy was touched by the raw vulnerability of this

giant, powerful man. She could also see from his critical red eyes that he hadn't slept much at all.

He struggled to get out the words, "I've failed Unique. I'm not capable of taking care of her; no matter how much I love her. And... she doesn't want me. I think she might even hate me. Unique wants and needs to be with you. If something worse happens to my baby, it's on me. I can't live with that. It's wrong of me to try to hold onto her."

Cindy got to the point, "So, what exactly are you saying, Al?"

"I want to relinquish my parental rights to you and Chuck. I've already spoken with a social worker about the process; and, I've retained a family law attorney to handle the entire procedure. Of course, I'm paying for everything. I only ask that I be allowed to visit my baby; and, that you'll let her visit me some weekends—if she wants to. I would also like to continue to support Unique financially. I understand now how hard it is to raise special needs children like mine; and, it's not cheap. Will you and Chuck at least let me do that for her? Even though Unique won't be my child legally; I want her always to remember how much I love her. And, I pray to God that my baby will forgive me one day for what I've done to her. I am so very sorry."

Cindy slowly lifted her head, tears of joy rolling down her cheeks.

"She won't hate you. I'll make sure of it. And, of course, I forgive you. Thank you, Al. I know how hard it was for you to make this decision."

To lift the mood, Cindy added with a wink, "To tell you the truth, I thought you'd never get your head out of your butt."

Al half-grinned, "Ouch. Harsh; but, true. I'll get the ball rolling immediately. Meanwhile, I'd better let you go before your husband starts wondering if I stole you."

Cindy laughed. They agreed she would be back by the time Unique woke up later in the morning; so they could tell her the news together.

On the drive home, Cindy gave thanks. She overflowed with gratitude and fulfillment. Her baby was coming home and returning: legally. Unique would finally be a part of the family she always needed. And, the Woods family would, at last, be complete with Unique.

CHAPTER 12

A LEGAL RETURN

CINDY RETURNED AT SEVEN the next morning, as promised. The life and sparkle instantly returned to Unique's beautiful eyes as soon as she realized what Cindy and Al were telling her. She was going home but thought it to be a weekend visit, and they didn't know exactly when. Unique hugged Al—as tightly as she could with her right arm and partial left one, whispering in his ear, "Thank you."

Dave McDaniels, Al's attorney, had already prepared the paperwork to legally surrender his parental rights to Unique over to the Woods. Al stopped by McDaniels' office first and signed the legally binding agreement without hesitation, to get the adoption ball rolling. Even with wet eyes, he knew he was doing the very best thing he could for his baby-girl. Al was asked to track down Dorothy.

At his office, Al tapped on Ted Clark's door, the Hendricks case brief in hand. After clearing the air with Cindy last night, it was as though the

weight of the world had been lifted from his shoulders. Al had spent the rest of the evening and early morning hours laser-focused on his work.

Expertly scanning the document now, Ted nodded with approval. He had known all along that Al wouldn't let him or the firm down. "Great, Jacob—and welcome back. So, if you don't mind my asking, what work changed in the last 20 or so hours?"

For the next 15 minutes—they indulged quick catch-up talks because there was no such thing as burning up valuable, billable hours—Al gave his boss the thumbnail version of what had been going on in his life. As the founding and managing partner of the firm, Ted Clark didn't make much time for his family. Hell, that's why he had a wife. And, Mindy Clark thoroughly enjoyed the high-roller lifestyle Ted provided; so, she happily played the role of dutiful wife and mother. He could, however, empathize with Al, now understanding why one of his sharpest associates had temporarily lost his edge. Ted had made the right choice in already deciding to make Al a partner in the firm; but, with partnership came additional stress and responsibility. The partnership announcement could wait until Al had a better grip on his personal life.

After the talk with Ted Clark, he knew he had better find Dorothy sooner than later.

Al had jumpstarted the search for Dorothy by calling every old phone number he had for her; all of which were 'no longer in service.' He'd even hit every dive, hang out, drug den and 'friend' of Dorothy's, coming up with nothing.

A couple of days later, frustrated with Dorothy's disappearing act, Al stormed through his front door, throwing his briefcase on the floor and dropping his keys on the foyer table.

"Damn it!"

The sound of his powerful voice echoed throughout his house; sending both Victoria and Unique running from their separate corners.

Victoria reached him first.

"Daddy, what's wrong?" She asked, puzzled.

Unique caught up and stood next to her sister.

Al looked down at his two angels, instantly regretting bringing his frustrations home. They both had the biggest, brightest, honeyed eyes.

Their faces were so innocent and sweet. For the first time, Unique felt her dad's love and was genuinely concerned for him.

Al stopped and wrapped his hulking arms around them both in a big bear hug.

"I'm sorry, girls. Just a little upset with some grown-up stuff. Nothing for you two to worry about. How are my two beauties today?"

With each arm wrapped around a girl, Al escorted Victoria and Unique to the family room and the over-sized sectional. Al pointed the remote; turning the television off. After placing it back on the table, he took a seat in the middle, Unique and Victoria on either side.

Victoria went first, with her usual whining, "I'm okay, Daddy, but you said to be the older sister. I am—but, she won't do what I tell her."

Al remained patient, "Yes, I did say that. But, being a good big sister doesn't mean you get to boss Unique around. It means setting a good example for your younger sister and looking out for her."

As usual, Unique said nothing. Al continued, "So what is your sister doing that keeps you so hot and bothered, Miss Victoria? Let's just get it all out in the open, right now."

Victoria fiercely stared at Unique, "Well, for one, she wants to play dress up all the time. I'm too old for that. She thinks she's some kind of fancy designer or something. Unique thinks she can make my clothes look even better— dresses, pants too. Do you know she had the nerve to rip apart my favorite blouse and piece it back together the way she wanted? My favorite, Daddy!"

Al tried hard not to laugh out loud, "Well, but how did the blouse look after the makeover?"

Victoria defiantly crossed her little arms and pouted, "Destroyed!"

This time Al chuckled, "That's it? Well, maybe you two just have to find something you both like to do together. Meanwhile, I can buy you more clothes, honey."

Victoria didn't see the humor, "That's not the point! I don't want you to buy new clothes. She has just got to stop ruining the ones I have!"

Al laughed again, Victoria rolled her eyes, gritted her teeth, and stormed up to her room.

Ignoring her, Al turned to his youngest daughter, "Unique, honey, can you please just stay out of your sister's closet? To help keep the peace?"

"She has junk in her closet."

Al laughed again. Unique continued, opening up with Al for the first time.

"I was just was trying to make it better. Vickie doesn't like what I like—that's fine, Al. But, at home, this is how Jamie and I play all the time. Victoria is just a plain, ole' mean, know-it-all! All she knows or cares about are her so-called friends at school and those messed-up clothes in her closet."

Unique scrambled up from the deepness of the sectional, folded her arms, looked directly at her father, and asked, "Can I go now—Al?"

She began to tap her toe as she waited. Al didn't allow her little attitude to scare him off from being her dad.

Al was almost proud of this little act of attitude, "Unique, sit back down, baby. I need to talk to you." It was his first real attempt to reach out to Unique as a parent.

"Sweetheart, I know you don't want to be here with me. That's why Cindy and I are working it out. I also understand that you haven't seen me for a long time and you don't know me all that well; but, I am your father. And, as your father, you can call me Dad, Daddy, Pop or Father. But, not Al— never again... Is that clear?"

Unique's attitude changed at once. She answered with respect and obedience.

"Yes, Sir..."

Al smiled and kissed her on the forehead. "I learned something new about you today."

Unique tilted her head, questioningly.

"You like to make clothes; and, I would love to see your creations!"

Unique lit up, her entire demeanor changing right before Al's eyes. Unique's voice became stronger and vocally expressed her excitement.

"Yes, I do! My mom met this lady named Naomi. She has her own store and everything, and taught Jamie and me all about designing and making clothes! Jamie and I made this blouse I'm wearing all by ourselves.

It's what I want to do when I grow up, Dad. And, guess what Jamie wants to do?"

Al had never heard his daughter talk so much, or seen her this excited and passionate about anything. He was thrilled, "Well, don't keep me in suspense. What is Jamie going to do?"

Unique's entire little face smiled, "She's going to be a model. She wants to walk up and down a runway to show off the clothes I design."

Suddenly missing Jamie terribly, Unique's face fell, and her enthusiasm faded, "Dad, why can't I leave tomorrow?"

Feeling that he and Unique had finally made a connection, Al's heart hurt to realize that she was still eager to leave him.

"Because you aren't going just for a visit, sweetheart. I just want you to be happy, and the Woods love you as much as I do. And, I hope you know how much I love you, Unique. But, Cindy and Chuck aren't going to be your foster parents anymore. They are going to adopt you legally. They will be your parents. We just have to tie up some loose ends first."

Unique was a sensitive child and saw the sadness, and the love for her—in Al's eyes.

"Please don't be sad. I'm sorry I gave you a hard time and got sick."

Al enfolded Unique's tiny body in his mighty arms, "Can you promise not to forget your father? You know—me?"

"How could I do that, Dad? I look just like you."

Al grinned at his creative, intelligent, funny little girl. At that moment, he realized Unique did look like he spat her out. And, she was whip-smart like him, too.

"Yeah, you sure do," Al said proudly. "And, baby-girl, you have nothing to be sorry about. You becoming sick is my fault; and, I beg your forgiveness for being so selfish about you. I am so very sorry, Unique. For everything—I wish to God things were different for us."

Unique hugged him back, as tightly as she could.

Al held her by both shoulders, staring into her eyes, "I want you to remember something else, sweetheart. It doesn't mean you, and I won't spend time together. It can be as much—or, as little—as you like. I am still your father; and, I am never leaving you. Whenever you need me, I am always here for you. Promise you won't forget that."

Al kissed Unique on her small forehead once more. Unique grinned at Al from ear-to-ear, ran to her room and started jumping on the bed, singing, "I'M GOING HOME!"

Al sighed, knowing he was doing the right thing and that gave him a euphoric feeling. Unique's pure joy outweighed any twinges of pain he felt. "Now the hard part," he thought aloud. "How the hell am I going to find that damned Dorothy?"

∾

A few days later, after Cindy had picked up and taken Unique to a routine doctor's appointment, they headed for their usual ice cream date. Cindy usually had Unique strapped in the back seatbelt, but Unique was tired and had her ice-cream to go. She wanted to make sure Unique didn't make a mess. On the drive to the parlor, Cindy spotted Dorothy on the street talking with two other women. Cindy almost didn't recognize Dorothy. Dorothy was even more drawn and gaunt than before. Her wild nest of hair was dyed Bozo-The-Clown red. Cindy's heart raced with excitement. She knew Al had been hunting for Dorothy to complete the adoption process. Cindy drove slower to make sure it was, indeed, Dorothy, as she passed the trio of women. Thank God, traffic was clear. So, she placed a protected arm across Unique and whipped a U-turn to pull right up next to Dorothy. A cigarette was hanging from her drool-encrusted mouth, Dorothy caught sight of Cindy. She noticed Unique was seat-belted in the front. Dorothy stumbled over to the car's passenger side window. Cindy let the front passenger side windows down.

"Wow, Unique, you don' grew, girl,"

Dorothy observed through her drugged-out haze rubbing Unique on the head. Unique cringed at Dorothy's touch. Hey, ya'll. How things goin'?"

"Things are fine, Dorothy. Can you hop in the car? We need to talk about some things. Don't worry; I will bring you back here to your friends."

Rubbing her nose, Dorothy glanced over to her peeps.

"Nah, now's not the right time. I got some business I'm handling."

Oh, hell no, Cindy's mind screamed. She was not taking 'no' for an answer. Cindy looked at Dorothy's hooker—junkie colleagues. Lost souls—waiting on johns to pay for their next fix. She realized sadly that their wait was like a starving person in the desert waiting for a Happy Meal and a Coke. Desperate… Cindy understood that Dorothy only spoke one language; and, quickly promised to compensate her for the time.

Dorothy slurred, "Okay, just wait a sec. Be right back." Dorothy conferred with her girls for a moment, then jumped into the rear passenger seat of Cindy's shiny truck.

Knowing Cindy never tried to interfere with her life, Dorothy asked, "What's so important?"

Cindy had hit the automatic child safety locks as soon as Dorothy got into the car. She grabbed her Blackberry and speed-dialed Al, gesturing 'Just a minute,' to Dorothy with the pointer finger of her free hand.

Dorothy understood and laid her wild head on the cushy, upholstered headrest, not saying another word to Unique.

"Al, hi, it's me. I found Dorothy."

Dorothy wasn't so high that she didn't jump out of her stupor when she heard Al's name.

"What the fuck?" Dorothy yelled, "What kind of Muthafuckin' game is this, bitch? Why the hell you callin' that fucker? Let me out the truck! Now! Y'all trying to lady-nap a Bitch! How to open this damn door?"

Cindy ignored Dorothy's ranting, pulling off with her free hand, "Yes, meet me at my house with the lawyer, right away. I have Dorothy in my truck, so hurry."

Cindy disconnected the call and glanced at Dorothy while keeping her eye on the road, "Look, Dorothy—. "

"Don't 'look, Dorothy,' me, Bitch! What you doin' is lady-napping—I ain't no damn kid! You locking doors, windows and shit! What the fuck you and Al asses want with me?"

"Please stop using that language. Chuck and I want to adopt Unique legally, and we need you to do that. Al has agreed to the adoption. You are the only missing piece."

Dorothy looked at Unique, then back at Cindy, and asked, "What's in it for me? Huh? I gave her to you. Now you want me to go to court and

all that? Hell, I try to stay my ass away from that shit. So like I said, Cindy, what's in it for me? And, don't give me any of your sacred bullshit about it being best for my child."

Cindy knew Dorothy was high and itching to score. Her need for the next fix was obvious. Reasoning with Dorothy wasn't going to work at all. Dorothy only understood the means to her end. Drugs… And, obtaining the money for her next fix by any means necessary; which meant selling her body. She didn't even care to hold back the cursing in front of Unique.

Cindy had promised Dorothy monetary compensation; so, bribery was the only way to go.

"Dorothy, Al and I will come up with some amount of money that will help you along. We can even handle the legalities of the adoption without you ever having to step foot in a courtroom. Do you mind me asking where you are staying, just in case I need to reach you?"

Dorothy sucked her teeth, rubbed her nose, and rolled her eyes at Cindy as though that was the dumbest question ever.

"Do it look like I got some place to go? I live where I live."

Cindy felt ashamed and sorrowful compassion for Dorothy. It was the worst she had ever seen her and couldn't help but wonder about Dorothy's other children.

"What? Now you concerned about them too? They're all right. My oldest is in charge. I sign over all my public assistance for her to take care of them. Don't see 'em much. May and I agreed that's best right now. I allow all my money to go to a card. May is the only one with the passcode, so I don't fuck with it. I am surviving on what I make out here, which is almost nothing. That's why I can't go with you unless I'm paid. Time is money. For real…"

Cindy had a clearer understanding of Dorothy's situation; but, she knew she had to stay focused.

"Dorothy— Are you hungry? I got food at the house, or we can get Chinese."

Dorothy grew increasingly irritated, "How long is this gon' take? I got shit to do. And, if I don't find a place to sleep by six, I will be on the park bench tonight again, and I ain't trying to do that."

Cindy tried to hold on to Dorothy as long as possible before going to the house because she wanted Al to have a chance to get there. So, she chose the take-out route.

"Look, Dorothy, you are skin and bones, Girl. I haven't seen you in a while; and, I want to make sure you eat something, okay?"

"I do look kinda' skinny, huh?" Dorothy looked at her spindly legs, embarrassed. She mulled over Cindy's kindness, not remembering the last time she ate.

"Signing the papers for the adoption won't take long," Cindy continued. "We can pick up some food now; and if for some reason, signing takes longer than expected, you can stay the night with me."

Dorothy recalled how sweet Cindy was. But, Dorothy had been a junkie con artist too long to pass up this opportunity. An overnight meant easy money. That house had to be filled with all kinds of expensive shit she could steal. She looked down at her concave belly surrounded by painfully visible ribs, and responded, "Deal. How 'bout that food?"

Cindy turned the corner and headed for the neighborhood Chinese restaurant.

Meanwhile, Al had called his lawyer, instructing him to rendezvous at Cindy's house with the paperwork. Dave McDaniels and Al were waiting outside Cindy's house when Cindy, Dorothy, and Unique pulled up.

Kate was inside with Jamie, Maury, and Jerry. Chuck wasn't yet home from work. Cindy didn't miss a beat, "Gentlemen, why don't you and Dorothy make yourselves comfortable in the living room? I'll be right there with a big ole' plate of everything for you, Dorothy. Okay?"

She turned to whisper to Kate, after quickly kissing each child, "Kate, grab one of these bags of Chinese with some paper plates and everything else the kids need. Please take Unique upstairs with the others. And no matter what you hear, please keep them occupied."

Always excited to see each other, Unique and Jamie were eager to help. Arms full, Kate and the children headed upstairs for an indoor campout with one of their favorite dinner treats—next to pizza—and a Disney movie.

Cindy got Chuck on the phone. He'd be pulling into the driveway in two minutes. Dorothy was so busy wolfing down her food, she was

oblivious to Al and everyone else. Once settled, McDaniels began pulling documents out of his briefcase.

"This adoption process should move swiftly if all of you are in agreement."

Mouth full, Dorothy blurted out, "I need to chat about something first. So, can you excuse yo' self for a minute, Mr. Lawyer?"

McDaniels made eye contact with Al and Cindy for affirmation. "Sure… I forgot something in my car anyhow. I will tap on the door when I get back."

Cindy nodded to the lawyer. She knew what Dorothy wanted, and hadn't had the chance to talk to Al or Chuck about the compensation. She had no clue how Al was going to take Dorothy's request for money, and a place to sleep for the night. Cindy remembered Al had tried to pay Dorothy in the past but stopped because he knew he was only feeding her addiction. Cindy hoped that wouldn't be an issue today because this was a different situation. Unique's life depended on it. If all went well, he wouldn't have to deal with Dorothy at all anymore. Chuck stepped through the door just as Dave McDaniels was walking out. Cindy stood up and greeted him. Chuck kissed her tenderly. Then he said hello to Dorothy and Al.

Dorothy chortled, at the smooching. "I see you two still at it, huh? Anyway, I want to know, what's in it for me? I need money. And if this here goes on too much longer, I'm gonna need a sleeping bag, too."

Al stood up, sliding his right hand down his face, seething.

"Same ole' Dorothy…! What's in it for you? You mean, besides having a permanent, steady home with a good family for your daughter?"

Dorothy swallowed another mouthful of food and jumped up, "First of all, with yo' think-you-too-good ass, I don't have a bed to go to lay down. If I'm late for the shelter, I'm outside for the night. If I weren't here, I'd be makin' money right now. So yes, overdressed—asshole, I want to know. What the hell's in it for me? And, stop judging me. Why are you signing her over to the Woods? Is it too hard for you to take care of her? Hold up! Or, is it she's too different from yo' other precious daughter, Victoria? Wait, I know, it's because of yo' fancy lawyer job, right? You ain't no better than I am, so don't stand thur—like you are all that and have

been such a great father. You ain't shit; just like me. I want to know what you and Ms. Cindy plan on doing about my money and a place for me to sleep."

Al was ready to jump in Dorothy's ass. But, Chuck broke it up before it began.

"Look, guys, no one is here to judge or fight. We are here to solve a problem that will give an innocent child a place she can call home."

Dorothy wasn't having it, "I'm here to get some money, first." She fiercely eyed Al. "Shit, I know Unique is gonna be fine because of the Woods and not because of her selfish-ass daddy."

Al almost let Dorothy get a rise out of him again.

"Dorothy, I love my daughter; that's why I'm here. Let me ask you a question. How much do you need?"

Dorothy thought that was a trick question, so she answered with a question. "How much you got?"

Al dropped his head down and slowly lifted it back up.

"This is what I'll do. You said you've missed out on making money tonight. So, I will give you four hundred for that. I will also pay you two hundred for coming, and signing the papers with no argument. When everything is completed, I will open a bank account for you with another thousand for any other immediate expenses. I will also pay—in advance, directly to the establishment—for a motel room for you until all this is over. That way, you've got a safe place to sleep, and I can find you if, and when, I need you. I will also provide a temporary, pre-paid phone to contact you."

Dorothy's mouth fell agape, as though she'd hit the lottery. "Hell yeah, I can agree to that. You got lawyers and shit, so I want all that in writing."

Cindy and Chuck were as surprised as Dorothy at Al's generosity.

Al looked over at the Woods' and said, "For whatever it's worth. I want my baby to be happy. I want my career, but I would give that up if she wanted to be with me. I love my girls." Al addressed Dorothy, "Both of them!"

By then, Dave McDaniels tapped at the door. Relieved this was almost over, Cindy welcomed him back inside.

The lawyer had all the necessary legal documents. They all signed for the adoption to proceed. As Al had promised Cindy, he agreed to pay a gracious amount of child support for Unique, more than enough to take care of her every need. It was the very least he could do for his child.

Al tearfully thanked Cindy and Chuck in front of all who were there and said, "I know there is a God because God is protecting my baby by placing people like Cindy and Chuck in her life. Cindy, while my baby was with me, I found out she loves to design and make clothes. I want to ensure she has all she needs to do whatever she wants, so I have an excellent package being delivered tomorrow for her."

❧

The next day, UPS delivered what seemed like countless packages from Al. Cindy was in awe at how all-out Al had gone for Unique. Cindy directed the driver and his helper to Unique's room with all the boxes. It was a good thing Unique was out with Kate, Jamie, and her brothers because they would have been in the way of the delivery. Cindy thanked the men and tipped them. As they were leaving, Chuck arrived. He and Cindy went through the boxes. Al had sent everything he even thought Unique might need. A personal computer, a laptop, a state-of-the-art sewing machine, computer software, online courses, fashion designers' kits, scissors, an awl, L square pattern snips, and a French curve. He also sent pattern-making supplies, pastel fabric marker sets, sketch pads, super airbrush sets, and three gift cards to fabric stores. Al believed in education, so he went further by sending applications for Unique to go to two schools: one for helping her master her reading, writing, and math skills, and the other for fashion. Cindy opened the letter that came with the amazing gifts from Al.

It read: Cindy, I am thankful for you and your husband. Please don't hesitate to call me if you need anything. I never told you this, but when Unique expressed her interest in fashion, I saw her special gift, and as her father, I want to make sure I do my part to assist her with her dreams. Unique is bright and lovable. I am proud to say she comes from me. A long time ago, someone told me that God gives every person an extraordinary

skill that enables him or her to take care of themselves. I think Unique's expertise is in designing, so I support her. Please assure her how much I love her. Can you make sure she knows that for me? Again, thank you. ~Al.

Cindy called Al to thank him for all he had done and assured him that he would always be a part of Unique's life. Al had done just as he had agreed with Dorothy. Three months later Unique was legally Mr. and Mrs. Woods' child. They threw a giant family party to welcome her as an official member of the Woods clan.

Shortly after all was done with Unique's adoption, Al made partner at his firm.

CHAPTER 13

A TRAGEDY AND A PROMISE

IT WAS MIDWEEK—WEDNESDAY. OUT of habit, Jamie jumped from the top bunk to the bottom. Climbing next to Unique with her little legs folded underneath her, Jamie leaned over and began shaking Unique—her hands on each of shoulder.

"Get up! It's time for school!"

Unique pushed Jamie off and said, "I don't go to school today." She wiped her eyes while continuing to explain, "You forgot—I have a doctor's appointment today," Unique stated as she sat up on the edge of the bottom bunk.

"Oh yeah, I forgot." Jamie pouted, "Did you forget we're having a pizza party for the whole school today? I wonder who the special guest is going to be."

"Jamie, I have no idea who it's going to be, but if it's another rapper—I'll be disappointed. Why don't they have a special guest that design clothes?"

"Right," Jamie agreed. "They could invite models too. You know what, Unique; one day we should put a show together. You design, I model, put a rapper in the mix, and we will be hot!"

"Well, it sounds good, but I don't think I can design all that much. Even though my father has given me all this stuff to work with, I am having trouble. I have so much to learn."

Unique felt a bit overwhelmed and unsure of her abilities, but not for long because Jamie always knew how to get her motivated again. Unique stood from her bed, stretched and sat on the floor and Jamie followed.

"Are you kidding? I love your designs." Jamie declared. "Don't forget what Mom said, 'we can and will do anything we want.' She said, 'we would have a hard time, but if we stick to what we want, we can do it.' Don't you believe her?"

"Sure, I guess." Unique wiped her eyes. "I'm just sleepy still, and I am a little nervous about this new fashion school my father has me starting. They keep me busy with all these schools."

"Well, wake up and let's make a pinky promise."

Facing one another, sitting Indian style, Unique and Jamie tied their two pinky fingers together and looked each other in the eyes.

"Okay, Unique, repeat after me." Full of enthusiasm Jamie tightened her pinky with Unique's and said, "I promise to be a fashion designer of clothes and try my hardest to make it."

Unique repeated, "I promise to be a fashion designer and try my hardest. Now you promise, Jamie, to be a fashion model and try your hardest."

"I promise to be a fashion model and try my hardest."

Jamie and Unique let go of each other's hands. Jamie stood up, looked at Unique on the floor and said,

"Don't forget Unique. Oh, I have one question. Who's going to be the rapper?"

Unique laughing aloud said, "I know… Jerry and Maury…"

"NO Way! Unique, I have to get ready for school. I wish you could go."

Unique frowned and said, "Me too… but you know Mom will say I must keep my appointments. I'll be here when you come home, and we can work on that new skirt—I was making just for you."

"I'll look so cute in it. Just like this one I'm wearing today—great design. Oh no, here comes Mom, and I'm not even dressed."

Jamie ran out the bedroom door heading for the bathroom. Cindy walked in as Jamie ran out. Unique saw the disappointed look on her mom's face, aimed at Jamie. Unique quickly distracted her mom by asking a more important question.

"Mom, what time is my doctor appointment?"

"We have to arrive thirty minutes before your appointed time, so nine o'clock sharp. Hurry and get ready."

"Oh, Mom, can I wear the new blouse I made?"

"I thought you wanted to wait and let Naomi's friend Pat have a look at it first."

"I did, but I would like to wear it to see how much attention it gets from the people at the clinic."

"Okay, Unique, that's fine—just get ready now so that we won't be late."

Cindy kissed Unique on the forehead and walked out of the room. Simultaneously, Chuck was walking out of the boys' room. They glanced at each other with that, 'love you, but I'm busy' expression. Jamie walked out of the bathroom; now all three were in the hallway.

Cindy looked at Jamie and said, "Wow, you have grown taller. I can definitely see a model in you. You know Unique won't be at school with you today, so after school—run straight home as soon as you get off the bus. Okay?"

"I know the routine. Love you, got to go."

Jamie hurried off to her room, but Cindy called out to her before she entered, "Jamie, your dad will take you to your bus stop today."

"Oh, Okay Mom… I hope Dad hurry up. I have a fun day today, and I don't want to be late."

"Well, I suggest you help him get your brothers things to the car."

"Right… got to go."

Jamie skipped going into her room and grabbed her book bag. When she came back out Cindy was still in the hallway. Jamie ran to her and

wrapped her little arm around her mom for a quick farewell hug. She then ran off to help her dad. Chuck took Jamie, Maury, and Jerry to their bus stop before going to work. Cindy and Unique left their home forty-five minutes after Chuck. On the drive to the doctor's appointment, Unique noticed her mom was unusually quiet.

"Mom, what's wrong?"

"Nothing baby, I'm fine. Why do you ask?"

"Because you're so quiet. It's like you're sad about something."

"Now, what will I have to be sad about?" Cindy assured Unique that all was all right, by smiling and crinkling her nose at her. "I am a bit tired, though, and it feels like something is out of place or that I forgot to do something."

Cindy had an uneasy feeling but didn't know what it was or why she felt that way, so she thought that she was tired, and plus she'd never want Unique to worry about anything. She was always afraid of Unique getting sick mentally.

After the visit from the doctor, Cindy couldn't wait to tell Chuck the good news—right away, she gave him a call.

"Hello, babe—what's up?" Chuck sounded a little busy.

"Sweetheart, Dr. Gomez stated that Unique was doing surprisingly well and he reduced her medications. He also said that Unique is learning how to handle life's disappointments better. I am happy about this news. And fewer prescriptions also means more money in our pockets."

"Dr. Gomez just made me a happy man. I thought I saw a huge change in Unique. She's more in tune with her responsibilities lately—she is happy. I hope our putting her in a fashion design school will not build up more pressure on her. Anyway, I got to get back to work, honey; we will talk later."

They both disconnected from the call. Cindy didn't know what disappointments Unique would have to face but to know Unique could handle it better gave her great joy. She felt a sense of progress. During the drive home from Dr. Gomez's, office, Unique had fallen asleep in the truck, and Cindy's cell phone rang. It was Chuck again.

"Hello, baby, I forgot to tell you—I won't be able to make it on time for dinner. I have to do extra at work today. Someone at the chemical

plant has been stealing supplies, and we will be doing an audit all week. They will be putting in new security cameras as well. My office is a mess with papers everywhere. I am sorry, my love, but you will have to get Jerry and Maury from school today."

"No problem, I'll get them from school. Dinner will be running a little late anyway. Kate is supposed to stop in to help. Unique is tired, honey, so I think I will drop her off at home then I'll go to get the boys and groceries for dinner."

"Cindy, I am so behind in work here. I'm playing catch up. I love you, honey. Bye, for now…"

Cindy arrived at the house. As soon as she drove up, Kate was at their house sitting on the porch waiting for Cindy and Unique. Kate walked down to the truck to greet them, and Cindy said,

"I am sorry for running late. Traffic was heavy. Something must be going on downtown. Kate, how long were you waiting?"

"Not long at all, Mrs. Woods—can I help?"

Cindy handed Kate the bags while she clutched Unique to wake her. Cindy helped Unique up the stairs and allowed her to lie on the front room sofa because she was exhausted. Cindy used the bathroom and then left out to go to the grocery store for the remaining items needed for dinner.

Unique didn't stay asleep long. As soon as she woke up, she began telling Kate all about her visit to the doctor and how many compliments she got on her blouse. Also, Unique explained why she could not say where she got it because her Mom said not to tell to protect the design. She then asked if she could have a snack out of the kitchen. Kate was spreading the peanut butter on the bread when it suddenly dawned on Unique that Jamie seemed to be running late coming home from school.

"Ms. Kate— shouldn't Jamie be here at home by now?"

"Maybe she stopped at that corner store to sneak in some candy. It wouldn't be the first time."

"Yeah, but Mom told her to come straight home. She had better be here when Mom gets from the store, or she will be grounded again."

Unique took a bite of her sandwich but looked worried as her small mouth moved with delight chewing her meal. Kate thought another glass

of warm milk would help Unique relax and not worry so much about Jamie.

Meanwhile, Kate was right—Jamie had stopped off at the corner store after getting off her school bus. Jamie watched as the busload of screaming children drove past her—revealing the corner store with all her favorite candy. The temptation of the sweet taste was too much for Jamie to bear. She had made up her mind that she had to have a taste. Jamie looked at the green and white awning and the green front door of that store as she convinced herself that she would make it home in time, and her mom wouldn't know that she had stopped by the storehouse for a bit. Jamie ran across the street into the store. She knew she had to hurry, but there were so many different types of candy to choose from with the two dollars she held tightly in her hand. Jamie finally decided what she wanted and paid the store clerk. The clerk smiled at his loyal customer—giving her the candy and the receipt. Jamie put the receipt and extra candy in her skirt pocket and ran out of the shop while taking the wrappings off a piece of candy.

She stood outside the store's door; she couldn't wait to taste the sugar candy stick. Right then, Jamie smiled at the thought of Unique's reminders about how calories, modeling, and candy don't go well together. Jamie popped the candy into her mouth, closing her eyes for a moment; the candy tasted good. After reopening her eyes and looking up — she knew she was running late. Jamie figured that she would take the shortcut through the alley which would lead her to the rear of her house instead of the front. She remembered her mom would always drive down the street—parking in the front. Jamie hoped to reach home and sneak through the back unnoticed. What her mom said about coming straight home ran through her mind, and she began running to the road for that shortcut.

Jamie ran so fast that by the time she got to the alley, she needed to stop and catch her breath. She took out her asthma inhaler while bending over holding her knees, and as she was about to take a puff—she noticed the look of this alley. It had several vacant houses with empty garages, barking dogs, and big trash cans with trash in and out of them. It was scary, but not more frightening than getting home late and being on punishment for weeks at a time. Before she could place her inhaler in her

mouth—Jamie noticed three males had surrounded her. Jamie looked at the guy in front of her. He caught her eyes first because he had on ripped up jeans and his shoes were dirty, completely covered in mud. Fashion never left her mind.

The person with the ripped jeans looked nineteen and seemed to be the leader of them. He was at least six feet tall, muscular, with multiple tattoos; however, the design of the massive eagle on his biceps and triceps was most noticeable to Jamie. He continued to flex his massive arm muscles at the other two; letting them know he was in charge of them, and the new pending situation.

Another was of a medium build and looked a bit younger. The second guy had tattoos on his face like teardrops under his eyes. Jamie had no knowledge of the teardrops but thought them to be strange. He had the darkest eyes she had ever seen and greasy hair. He seemed violent and impulsive, and he kept looking at the older boy for approval.

The third appeared to be around fourteen years old, was thin, just over five feet tall, with a frightened look on his face. Jamie knew he too was afraid of the others; nonetheless, she knew they were trouble. Jamie was very scared. She dropped her inhaler, and as it fell to the ground; she tried to run as fast as she could down the scary alley. She almost got halfway down the alley before they caught up to her. The three guys took Jamie into one of the several empty garages located in the middle of the block. It was so raggedy with only one broken window; it looked to have been painted white at one time, but now all the white had faded away—leaving nothing but white splinters.

The oldest with the ripped jeans showed he was the leader by covering Jamie's mouth with his right hand so tightly—she literally couldn't breathe. He lifted her from the ground with his arm strapped across her shoulders, holding her mouth. Jamie tried to fight back by kicking. He tossed her lower body like a rag doll. The leader gripped Jamie even tighter with his big muscular arms; his eyes widened, and he acted as if he had just caught his prey,

"Yeah fellas, look at what we found. Young—never been touched pussy. This… right here—is just what I've been lookin' for. Tight pussy,

tight ass, and you know this gonna be good fellas. Come get some of this shit—Nothin like fresh fish, fellas."

He began ordering the two guys with him around. "Get that mattress and drag it to that corner of the garage. Just in case someone walks down the alley—no one can hear or see anything."

The seventeen-year-old grabbed the mattress while the leader held his hand over Jamie's mouth. He stood holding her in front of him—her back was against his stomach. Jamie's eyes were red as fire; she trembled in deep fear, watching the guys prepare to hurt her.

She managed to get a bite into the dirty claw he called a hand. The foul taste of salt was disgusting, but she continued to bite down as hard as she could—hoping the pain would cause him to let go. Instead, it just provoked him to do more harm without any conscience.

"Ouch! This little bitch bites! Hurry up with that mattress!"

He pressed Jamie's mouth even tighter—causing her to make whimpering sounds. Keeping her mouth covered, the leader slammed Jamie's little body on the dirt-filled mattress so hard that the dirt from the mattress billowed through the air, and her head hit the ground through the mattress. Jamie continued to fight back; she kicked the leader on his left leg. The violent one saw the kick and punched Jamie in the stomach—knocking more wind from her small airway. He then grabbed Jamie's bare legs and held her mouth for the leader. The leader undid his pants with one hand, and with the other—he yanked off Jamie's little panties. Tears were flowing down Jamie's face. Jamie called out to God in prayer in her mind—asking him to help her. The leader saw the tears and took out his penis, rubbed it back and forth with the one hand.

"Don't worry... you gonna like what I got to give you," he told Jamie, with a very foul-smelling breath.

Then the leader looked at his boys and noticed the youngest not doing his part—he was just watching.

"Wimp, get yo ass over here! This is sweet pussy... not like the others. Come taste it."

The youngest spoke out, "Man, I don't like this. Let her go!"

"Let her go! You stupid or sumthin? There's no letting go! You wimp! Get over here! Lick that little pussy and spit on it, so my dick don't get stuck."

The wimp had a hard time getting his penis to harden, but once inside it did. He too pumped on Jamie until he had to ejaculate. The leader made sure they all raped little Jamie. Jamie's wheezing became louder than before, and the youngest boy looked at Jamie's eyes; they were red and bulging out even more.

"Oh man, we gotta go!" he urged, in spite of his fear, "I don't think she can breathe."

The leader responded telling him to shut up, but he knew the wimp was right. Jamie was very low on oxygen. They started yelling at each other in a panic. They planned to rape—not kill her. They quickly stood up and tucked their penises into their pants. All three had assaulted and beaten Jamie for more than an hour until she passed out. They all ran off when she stopped moving. Although Jamie appeared to have nothing left—she managed to take a breather and began coughing. Limping, bloody, and with hardly any oxygen, she slowly pulled her body up.

Meanwhile, back at the house, Unique was sitting on the back porch swing—in their backyard. She was so scared, not knowing what was taking Jamie so long to come home. It was driving her almost to tears. Although her mom was late—she knew her mom would soon be walking through the door.

Jamie managed to stumble and drag herself through the rest of that dreadful alley to her backyard. She was all beaten up and bloody. Her skirt—she and Unique had designed was full of blood, semen, and dirt. Her panties were still in that garage. Her face was red from the grip of her attacker's hand. She had a busted eye and lip from her abusers' slaps and punches, and there was blood running down her legs.

Unique caught sight of Jamie and started running toward her while screaming for Kate. "Kate!"

Jamie collapsed on the ground; looking at Unique. Unique put Jamie in her arms—crying, and begging God to help her sister.

Kate ran out viewing this horrifying moment from the back porch and saw Jamie all bloody as Unique's held her in her arms. Shaken up, Kate screamed, "Jamie!" She ran back into the house, grabbed the cordless phone, and called 911. She stood on the back porch watching Unique and Jamie as she gave the dispatcher needed information.

While Kate was talking on the phone—Cindy walked in with Jerry and Maury behind her. She had picked them up from school as planned and they had groceries in their arms. Cindy threw her keys on the table and began walking down the hall towards the kitchen. The house had an eerie feeling, and Cindy had had a bad mood all that day, so she told Jerry and Maury to put the bags down on the front room floor and to go upstairs to start on their homework. Before Cindy got to the kitchen, she could see the back door wide open. Kate caught sight of Cindy and with profound fear—she hung up the phone.

Outside, Unique continued holding on to Jamie—then Jamie spoke in a very faint and weak tone.

"Promise me…"

"Promise what?"

Unique held her tighter.

"Promise me you will design and do our show."

"Jamie, I promised. I will. And you still gonna model right?"

"I, I, love your…"

As Cindy approached the kitchen—she saw a terrifying expression in Kate's eyes. Shortly, after seeing Kate's eye—Cindy heard Unique screamed,

"Jamie, NO-OO-OO-OO-OO-O-O-O! PLEASE!"

Outside, Jamie's body went completely limp, and her breathing faded away.

Cindy ran out the back door. Her stomach was knotted up, her heart felt like a truck had run over it, and breathing was difficult. She saw Jamie's limp body as Unique held her in the yard. She ran to them, screaming.

"What happened? Oh, Lord! NOT MY BABY! Oh God, Please! Jamie get up, baby! Wake up!"

Cindy grabbed Jamie's limp body from Unique and cradled her head—slowly rocking back and forth. She knew her baby was gone.

The paramedics arrived with their equipment and tried life-reviving techniques, but sadly, Jamie's spirit had gone from her body.

Pronouncing her D.O.A. dead-on-arrival—one of them looked at Cindy and said, "I am sorry, Ma'am, there is nothing else we can do."

Cindy pulled Jamie's body even closer—a piece of candy fell out Jamie's pocket when Cindy gripped her. Life seemed to go in slow motion. Cindy's eyes focused on the candy, and then her baby.

She screamed from the top of her lungs, "Lord! Why my baby? Jesus, help me, please! My baby, Lord, why my baby? Jamie! Mommy loves you! Jamie! OH GOD! HELP ME!"

Unique sensed her mom's continued cries to the Lord as she lay there in the dirt next to her sister's dead body. Unique went into shock, fell out and began convulsing. The paramedics noticed Unique shaking and started giving her medical attention. They put Unique into the ambulance, and Kate called Al, asking him to be at the hospital for Unique when she got there.

The two boys heard all the crying and went down the stairs. Kate saw them and asked them to go back up. Jerry grabbed Maury's hand and turned back around. Jerry knew something terrible had happened. Kate got the phone again, this time calling Chuck at his job. Kate was careful not to give him information. She just told him, 'there was an emergency.' She did not want him to have an accident on the way home.

The police and detectives arrived soon. They started taping off the area because the vicinity was a crime scene. Cops were all over, retracing the steps they assumed Jamie had taken from the time she got off her school bus. The detectives found a receipt near the garage where she was raped and beaten, and they put a folded number by each piece of evidence: the receipt, Jamie's inhaler, and Jamie's panties. The cops, detectives and other crime officials filled the scene and thoroughly collected every ounce of evidence.

The head detective called in to investigate was Detective Frank Burk. After conversing with the other officials and reading their notes—Detective Burk walked over to Jamie's covered body. He noticed the mother sitting in the dirt next to the body. He felt her pain but needed to look at the Child's body for himself. Detective Burk pulled the cover back—revealing Jamie's small, brutalized body. He noticed some of her fingernails ripped off from her tiny fingers. He assumed she was clawing the ground. She suffered blunt trauma over most of her body.

He stooped down, took Cindy's hand and whispered, "I am sorry for your loss, Ma'am."

Cindy eyed him with anger and replied, "You find the person that did this to my baby. You find him!"

The usual response to Cindy's request from the detective was, 'I'll do my best,' but not this time. Detective Burk never promised a victim's family to find the murderer; but, he told Cindy, "I will find them." He covered Jamie's body again and walked away to catch his overwhelming emotions.

The authorities finished collecting all the evidence to assist them in apprehending Jamie's murderer. Jamie's death was a homicide, and all murders must have an autopsy. The coroner placed Jamie's body into a body bag, after checking for the basics—Cindy watched as they slowly zipped the bag. Still sitting in the dirt, she stared at the coroner as they took her baby's body away. All the detectives and police had left. Detective Burk gave his card to Kate for Chuck to call with any questions.

Kate assisted Cindy in her bedroom. She slowly climbed into her bed and curled up, asking God to forgive her. Over and over—she thought that if she had just gone to get Jamie from her bus stop, she would still have her child.

Jerry and Maury had done their homework as their mother and Kate told them. Although they were hungry, they knew something was seriously wrong, so without asking for food—they fell asleep.

When driving home, Chuck wondered if one of the children had gotten sick. Finally, he arrived and opened the door to a highly unusual sound of complete silence. Once Chuck walked through the front foyer— he felt as if something worse was going on there. He noticed the groceries still in bags on the floor and no aroma from Cindy's cooking. Kate looked at him with tears in her eyes as Chuck approached her in the front room. Afraid to ask what was wrong—he took a deep breath.

"Kate, where is everyone?"

Tears fell from her eyes. "They're all upstairs asleep."

She looked as if she was in a daze or another world. Chuck was in fear of his next question, but regardless, he went on to ask it.

"Kate, what happened? Why did you call and tell me to come home due to an emergency?"

Kate looked at Chuck, stood up and said, "It's Jamie; she was raped and beaten on her way home from school."

"Where is she? Where is my baby?"

"Chuck, sit down."

"I'm fine. Where is Jamie? Kate, where is my little girl?"

Kate's voice and her whole body were trembling.

"She didn't make it. She died in the backyard in Unique's arms."

Chuck fell to his knees. Crying and in rage—he stood up and started throwing things off the mantle.

"I am the protector of my family. How did this happen to her? My baby's gone, is that what you're telling me? Huh!"

Kate sadly nodded.

Chuck screamed, "NO! NO! Not my girl!"

Cindy heard Chuck's cry and ran down the stairs to his arms. She tried to comfort him, but there was no comfort for either one of them. They started to pray together asking God for the strength because they had none of their own.

Although the police and detectives had gone—there were a few more questions Detective Burk had to have answered to start a substantial investigation. The police knocked and asked more questions about that day. Kate had responded to the majority of the officers' questions due to Cindy and Chuck's devastation.

For the first time since the tragedy, Cindy wondered about Unique and asked Kate where she was.

Kate reached for Cindy's hand, aiding her as she sat on the sofa while Chuck continued holding his hands over his head as he sat on the floor, dealing with his grief.

"Cindy, I called Al to go to the hospital with Unique. The paramedics took her to the children's hospital because she had passed out and begun convulsing. Al will contact us soon as he has some information on her. Try not to worry about Unique. She is strong, and I know she will be all right."

Kate had been a blessing that day.

"Kate, thanks so much for being here with me. I must ask something else of you, I don't have it in me right now to do, but I need to contact the

others in the family to make them aware of what has happened. My phone book is in the study, on the desk. All of our friends' and family's numbers are in it. Use the house phone to call everyone. I am hoping Al will call me about Unique on my cell."

Kate listened to Cindy—her voice became lower and lower with every word. It seemed so hard for her to talk or focus on anything else but her loss of Jamie. Kate was tired and emotionally drained as well, but she knew she had to hold up for the family. She was walking towards the study to find the phone book when Cindy's cell phone rang. Kate stopped in her tracks to listen—trying to understand what Al was saying about Unique.

"Hello Cindy, I'm sorry about Jamie. I am calling to tell you Unique is fine; however, she is heavily medicated. If you don't mind, I can take her with me for the night or as long as you need."

"Thanks, Al, for your help, but I think I would rather have her here with me," Cindy said.

Al understood. "Okay, I will be there shortly with her. The doctor stated that she would be sleepy for a few days and to give her the medications he prescribed. Again, I am very sorry, Cindy. You are in my prayers."

Cindy disconnected the call. She turned her attention to Chuck still sobbing on the floor and said, "Husband, let's go to our room."

Chuck looked up at Cindy and knew when she called him husband—she was looking to him for strength. Therefore, he got off the floor, and they held each other up as they headed to their bedroom.

Kate started calling the relatives and friends. She was in between buttons on the phone when Al knocked, bringing Unique home. He assisted Kate by taking Unique to her bedroom; putting her in the bottom bunk. Al covered Unique with her blanket. Kate said she'd be right back. She had to check in on the boys across the hall. While Kate went into the boys' room—Al stood there, observing Jamie and Unique's room for the first time. It hit him like a ton of bricks as he slowly eyed all the contents of the bedroom. His baby just lost her best friend and sister. Al started wondering how this could happen to them as the God-fearing couple that they were; knowing they had done nothing but help others. Anger began to set in on him as Kate walked back into the room.

She saw the tears in his eyes. Al was a larger man with big emotions.

"Al— I know what you're thinking. I know anger has set in your heart against God. I almost blamed God myself, but I know this is not the doing of God. Nothing bad or evil comes from Him, but all things happen for a reason. God will help this family, and He will help you understand."

Al felt encouraged by Kate and was grateful she understood his thinking and was willing to correct him in this situation.

"Kate— I thank you for that. Take care of my little girl for me. Unique's prescriptions are in the bag with the directions. Tell Chuck and Cindy that I said if they need anything—not to hesitate to call. By the way, I can have my nanny help out for a few days until things get a bit easier."

"I need that, and I am sure Cindy and Chuck wouldn't mind me having help. Yes, send her right away."

Al smiled; walked out the front door, and called his nanny as soon as he got to his car.

Shortly after Al left Chuck and Cindy's home, there was another knock was pecking on the door; it was Al's nanny. Kate answered and was so happy to have help. Together they put the groceries up, cleaned the home from all the invading cops, straightened the yard up as best they could, and finished making all the phone calls to family and friends. They also cooked food for that night and the next day, for when friends and relatives came to express their condolences. Kate knew there were two more family members she had to give the bad news to but was unsure how to tell them or if she should leave it up to Cindy and Chuck.

Later that evening, Jerry and Maury woke up hungry. Kate took them to the kitchen for something to eat.

Jerry said, to Kate while his mouth was full,

"Kate— what's wrong, why doesn't this day feel right?"

Kate looked like she went into shock as she said,

"Jerry, I…"

Chuck interrupted Kate when he entered the kitchen. Chuck walked to the table, pulled a chair back, and sat in it.

"Jerry and Maury— there is no easy way to tell you this, but I know I must. Do you remember when we go to Church, and we hear the preacher talking about how some people we love go back to God when they die?"

Maury just sat there and listened.

Jerry replied, "Yeah Dad—I remember him saying that but who do we know that died?"

Chuck took a hard swallow and said,

"Jerry, your sister Jamie has gone to be with God."

Maury looked confused. Jerry gave his dad a look as if he had told a bad joke and said,

"No, she isn't with God. I saw her in her room next to Unique before I came down to eat. Why are you saying that! That's not funny, Dad…"

Chuck was now looking confused, but he stressed Jamie's death even more and decided to take the boys to Jamie's room. They went up the stairs, and Chuck opened the door. They saw Unique sleeping, but Jamie wasn't there. Maury started crying and ran to his room.

"I don't get this," Jerry cried out, "I know I saw Jamie. She was here before I came down to eat! If she's with God, why does He want her? We need her here with us. Dad, this is not real, is it?"

Jerry cried, broke from his dad's arms, and ran to his room with Maury. The entire house was quiet, and Kate felt they couldn't do anything else, so she told Al's nanny to go home. Kate thanked her for all the needed help. Kate was drained, and she hadn't had a chance to grieve herself, so she went into the guest room, wept in the darkness, and went to sleep, for she knew the next day wasn't going to be any easier than that day. The next day they would have to begin making plans for the funeral.

CHAPTER 14

THE FUNERAL

A SORROWFUL AND UNUSUAL vibration echoed in the Woods'
home the evening before they placed Jamie in her final resting place. The
neighborhood referenced the home as 'The Woods'— or, Momma C's
house. Cindy's mother told her the horrifying stories of her childhood
with no parents and the struggle for food. Cindy became like her mother
vowing never to leave a child hungry and quickly developed a reputation
for taking care of the neighborhood children. She supported Dorothy's
children most but did not neglect any children. The ice cream truck made
a fortune every day from Cindy's need to make the neighborhood kids
happy. The entire community grieved for the Woods Family.

The Woods' made the arrangements and notified the family, friends,
and community. Kate had been outstanding in helping the Woods through
the painful process of planning the funeral. Unique had trouble with
going into the room she and Jamie once shared; somehow, her brother's
room felt reassuring. Unique walked into her brother's room, and they
both were in a daze; just sitting and not saying anything.

"Can I stay in here with you?" Unique quietly asked.

Little Maury got up and ran into Unique's arms.

Laying his head on her shoulder, he began crying, "It's not right that Jamie left us."

Jerry looked at them both, turned his back, and lay quietly in his bed. Jerry was infuriated, but he always had trouble letting others see his emotions. So he held onto all of the anger and frustration he was feeling.

The family was in disbelief as the evening continued without Jamie and the household had gone to sleep. Unique had fallen to sleep on the bed with little Maury when she heard sounds of shredding garments ripping—loudly. Removing her arm from around Maury—she curiously followed the sound. The vibrations became more defined as she approached the door. The noise was very familiar; it was the reverberation of an old curtain being ripped up to make doll clothes—the exact sound she and Jamie enjoyed for it meant a new design. Unique slowly opened the door, and it crackled. It was very dark; the night light from the bathroom was the only illuminating source as she peered out into the hallway.

The noise had suddenly stopped, so Unique started to close the boys' door back, but before she could, she heard Jamie's voice calling out to her. Unique's eyes widened, and she became very stiff. Part of her was afraid, but the other part was hoping it was Jamie, and somehow all this was a dream. After three callings, Unique finally answered Jamie's voice.

"Yes, Jamie, where are you?"

Unique closed the door to the boys' room, hoping not to wake them. She moseyed into the quiet, dark hallway.

Unique asked again, "Jamie—where are you?"

"Over here…"

Unique hurried and turned toward the voice. She saw Jamie in white, smiling at her. Unique began to cry when Jamie's form spoke again.

"Don't cry, Unique. I'm fine. I can't finish my work here, so I need you to do it for me."

"What work? Jamie, can't you come back to do this job you're talking about?" Unique was extremely puzzled.

She couldn't see past her pain to know what Jamie's vision was speaking about, and she became disturbed.

"Listen carefully, Unique— I don't have much time. The work I am speaking about is our dream—designing and modeling the clothes—our show. Remember, you must complete our mission. You won't understand now, but that show will be distinctive, and God wants it done. Remember your promise."

"I love you, Jamie and I don't know how I can do this by myself." Unique's tears were flowing so much until her pajama top was thoroughly wet.

"You can do it, Unique. And you won't be by yourself. Remember, I made that same promise. You won't see me, sister, but I will be with you all the way."

Suddenly a light lit up on Jamie, and she continued to say, "Remember your promise, Unique."

Then it was dark again with the one night light. Unique woke up in her bed, in her and Jamie's room. She jumped up, got out of the bed, opened the door, and looked into the hall. It was not dark at all. The light in the bathroom shone through brightly. Unique figured it was a dream, but couldn't for the life of her figure how she remembered every detail of it. What was more, how did she go to sleep in Maury's bed but wake up in her bed? Then she suddenly realized she wasn't uncomfortable in their room any longer. Unique began looking at the vision and thought it to be a real event that had taken place and was encouraged.

"Jamie," she said aloud. "I promise. Please God, make me strong."

Unique turned the light on, then looked around at all the things in her room to make clothes, and again said,

"Jamie, I promise."

Tears fell onto her cheeks. Unique turned the light back off and got back into her bed to finish getting her rest until dawn broke.

⁊

Finally, the Woods' dreadful day had arrived, and being busy helped them through a very emotional morning.

"Unique, honey… Are you ready?"

Cindy asked this with grave concern for Unique. She was so afraid Unique would revert to her previous mental and medical problems due to her losing her sister and best friend. Before the tragedy, Unique had made much progress in handling the pressures of life, but death was the hardest challenge in life. Even though Cindy was having a rough time dealing with losing a child, she felt God was giving her the strength to pay attention to the ones she still had. Cindy looked at Unique with such love and realized Unique was now her only girl. She felt blessed to have her.

Cindy walked into the girls' room. Unique was sitting on the top bunk bed where her sister Jamie had slept. Tears were rolling down her face.

"Mommy, I don't know how to say goodbye to my sister. I don't think I can go."

Cindy knew Jamie's death was painful for Unique and so she tried to think of something to say that would help her baby deal with her loss.

"Sweetheart, you need to go and say your final goodbye to your sister. Jamie would want you to move on with life, and it's hard to do that if you don't say goodbye. Baby, a person, never dies as long as someone holds them in their memory. She will live forever there as long as you remember her. You just won't see her in the flesh. Let's ask God for help."

Cindy called Chuck, Maury, and Jerry into Jamie and Unique's room. She asked Chuck to say a prayer for strength and help to overcome the present challenge.

Chuck prayed: *"Dear Lord, please God help us in our time of need. We can't do this on our own. We need your strength, guidance, forgiveness, and love. Father— the Creator of all things—help little Maury to realize even though things don't seem fair; you are the one that can make it right. Help Jerry to deal with his pain. Let him know it is okay to cry. Crying just cleanses our soul. Help him, Father, where he needs it."*

Chuck began to raise his voice in prayer. Tears flooded up until they started falling freely down his face as he thought of Unique.

Chuck continued: *"Father! Father! Father! PLEASE! Help Unique. She just lost her sister and best friend. We all know the special relationship the two girls shared. They gave each other hope. They shared the same dreams. They were so lively because they were together every day. They separated temporarily*

once, and a piece of their spirits fell sick. I ask, Father, that you help Unique deal with this. Help her not to get sick because we don't want to lose her too. Give her strength beyond normal. Father, Creator of all things, will you please help my wife. There is truly no pain like a woman's pain from losing her child. It is even more than my pain because she felt the first movements in her stomach and shares the overwhelming connections to Jamie. Help her. I must not forget your love and Christ's love. 'For you loved the world so much you gave your only begotten.' You; as Father felt pain when Christ sacrificed himself for us. Thank you for him and that sacrifice. Father, I also pray for myself, for I am fragile. Help me to forgive the ones that took my baby from me. I know you say vengeance will be yours. Help me, Father, for I am also outraged. We love you. We thank you. In your son's name, Jesus Christ—we pray."

They all stood for a family hug, wiped their tears, and immediately felt God's strength. They were dressed and headed to the funeral.

The outcry and community support reached past their neighborhood. Chuck and Cindy saw cars lined up for miles with intent to follow the funeral. She was blessed, and her love for children everywhere did not go unnoticed. The owner of the candy store Jamie had last visited placed flowers and Teddy bears all around their property. Candles and signs of love and prayers were engulfing the home and the hearts of the Woods' family. Cindy cried, but this cry was a thankful one. She knew God was with them. The limo driver escorted the entire family into the many serving limos.

Kate was at the funeral home early to greet the Woods family. She had to be sure all arrangements were correct.

The scenery was beautiful upon arrival as blue and ivory flowers filled the room. Jamie was in a beautiful ivory casket and dressed in her favorite color, blue. Her hair was in beautiful curls and appeared as a beautiful child asleep. There were two wall-mounted screens—located on each side of the auditorium for all to view Jamie's once active life. As they entered the ceremony, Cindy and Chuck walked closely behind Unique, Maury, and Jerry. They all observed Jamie's body at the same time. Maury and Jerry held their heads down after seeing their sister.

Unique made no noise as she looked at her sister, but her tears were endless. Unique took out a blouse that she and Jamie had made together

and placed it into the casket beside Jamie's body and uttering the words, 'I promise.'

Cindy got close enough to see her baby lying there, and her legs became weak. Her stomach felt sick, and she began gasping for air. Chuck grabbed her and carried her to her seat.

Suddenly Cindy caught her breath and screamed out, "LORD NO! My baby—Oh Lord!"

Chuck held her closer and began saying another silent prayer to help his wife. More friends and family started showing up at the funeral home. They walked by to view Jamie's body and gave hugs, cards, and support for the household. Unique's biological family was there to show their support. Al arrived with his daughter, Victoria. Dorothy and her children: Ben, Sarah, May, and Jasmine walked in almost immediately after Al and Victoria. They all hugged as if they were one big happy family. Tragedies bring people together even if it is only for a short time. All of them were feeling some pain for the Woods' loss.

Others knew the Woods family for their kindness and love. It seemed so unfair for that family to go through such a tragedy. All walked by to view Jamie's body. Dorothy walked up to Jamie's little casket. It did something to her to see Jamie lying there. All kinds of emotions ranging from extreme sadness to a guilt-filled soul. She looked at Unique and observed that it could have been her child. She thought back to all the times she had allowed Unique to walk the streets at two and three in the morning. The guilt nagged at her so severely that it motivated her to fix her problem with the drugs. She vowed to herself that after the funeral she would check herself into a rehabilitation center.

The funeral began immediately after the wake. The service started with a song, sung by the choir, called "Lord, Help—Me—Now" and "Better Days by Le'Andria Johnson." The minister—a man who had been with the Woods family for years, gave the eulogy. He began preaching, doing his best to comfort the family and friends with the words from the Bible. He talked about little Jamie and her lively personality. He mentioned how the family had been long-term members of the church and how he knew the Woods to be a kind, God-fearing family. He encouraged them not to become hardened as a result of this tragedy and assured them of God's love.

After the eulogy, Kate stepped up to the platform to do the reading of the obituary. She had a time doing so because she had been babysitting for the Woods family ever since Jamie was three years old. It was hard for Kate to read about the baby that she'd helped raise, but Kate managed to pull off the reading. She muscled up the strength by thinking of the pain Mr. and Mrs. Woods were going through as parents.

The choir sang another song, and then the pallbearers took Jamie's casket to the car and drove her to her final resting place.

The minister said another prayer. They laid roses on top of the closed casket. Shortly after that, they lowered the coffin into the ground. Holding each other close, Cindy and Chuck walked back to the limo with Jerry and Maury holding hands in front of them. Unique wandered behind them, once more looking at the gravesite.

"Jamie, I promise." She repeated—looking to the heavens.

They all got in the vehicles headed to the repast where the entire family and friends gathered to eat and give more comfort to the grieving family. Soon the Woods was back at home trying to put their lives back together, even though losing Jamie had put an enormous hole in their lives.

❧

Weeks later—after the funeral, Detective Burk knocked at the door of the Woods family. Kate was in the kitchen about to take a sip of her ice-cold soda pop, but as the glass touched her lips, the doorbell rang. Kate placed the glass on the counter and walked swiftly to answer the door. She knew Cindy and Chuck were upstairs resting, and she didn't want them disturbed.

"Yes, who is it?"

"It's Detective Burk. I needed to talk with Mr. and Mrs. Woods."

Kate opened the door, showed the detective into the front room, offered him a chair, and excused herself to get the Woods. The detective took his seat as Kate went upstairs to tell Cindy and Chuck they had a visitor. Cindy and Chuck asked Unique to stay upstairs with the boys.

Kate, Cindy, and Chuck headed down the stairs to see what the detective had to say. He stood as they walked into the room, showing them he had respect for the loss of their beloved child.

In a quiet voice, Cindy said to the detective, "Please, have a seat."

"What brings you here, Detective Burk?" Chuck asked once they were all seated. "Is there anything new?"

The detective looked Chuck in the eyes and said, "I recognize that nothing I say would bring you any comfort; However, it may help you move on knowing the perpetrators who hurt your baby is locked up."

Cindy started to cry all over again, a bittersweet cry. Kate sat closer to Cindy, taking Cindy's hand into hers.

Chuck asked detective Burk,

"How did you find the ones responsible?"

Detective Burk sat up straight on the Woods' sofa.

"Many factors lead to the apprehension of the three males that took part in the assault; however, the most damaging factor was a confession from the youngest of the group. The young guy, too, was a victim, but also a party to the crime. He gave a great confession, and the collected DNA evidence will put them away for life. I don't mean to take up any more of your time. Just wanted to personally let you know we apprehended those responsible for your loss."

Chuck thanked Detective Burk for coming by and showed him to the door. Chuck and Cindy walked up the stairs and hugged each of their children. Each parent found themselves praying every minute, and they made sure to shower the three remaining children with all the love that they could mustard together.

CHAPTER 15

THE BANK

THE SERVICES OF JAMIE was complete, and it was time for the family to move on with life. Dorothy went back to her kids. She tried living and taking care of them. Her oldest child, May was happy her mom had come back; she was tired and had given up her youth taking care of the younger ones. Overall, May was one who just got it done. She didn't complain; although, her life has seemed dramatically affected by Dorothy's bad choices.

Saturday morning, Dorothy needed to go to the bank to withdraw some money. Unlike the regular withdrawals for her drugs and liquor; Dorothy was paying bills. Also, she had planned to check herself into a rehabilitating center in a few months, for a few months, and did not want herself or her children put on the streets when she returned home. She desired to tell Ben on the way back from the bank, so she asked him to get into the car with her. Ben looked completely puzzled because his mom never allowed him to go anywhere with her.

"Come on, Ben, let's go. Don't bring that football with you; we will be right back soon."

"Where we goin?" Ben asked.

Sarah spoke before Dorothy could answer. "It's— 'Where are we going.' You dummy!" They started at each other while Dorothy continued looking through the drawers for her wallet.

Ben retaliated, "You dumb, and you ugly. Sarah, you look like a Mike and Ike with pigtails."

Sarah popped him on the head lightly and ran off yelling, "At least at fifteen I knew how to speak proper English."

Dorothy found her wallet and instructed them both to shut up. She looked at Ben and said, "Not another word—"

"But Ma—"

"Let's go. We're going to the bank."

Ben still had questions about why he had to go. He had planned to hang out with his two best buds, Donald, and Ralph.

"Why do I gotta go? You never ask me to go nowhere with you."

Dorothy shoved him in the right shoulder, "I need to tell you something on the way back from the bank."

Dorothy's friend, Diane, had been waiting in her car patiently for them to come out. Dorothy and Ben got into the car. On their drive to the bank, Ben listened to Dorothy's complaints about not having enough money for anything. Arriving at the bank Ben went in with Dorothy. The place was different. He had never seen the inside of a bank before. He slowly looked around. He was outdone when he saw people walking up to the teller and getting money. Never being exposed or taught anything about money; he didn't know how it worked. The closest to understanding anything about money came from playing the board game Monopoly. However, just as it was in the game; banks had all the money. It was Ben's first time thirsting for the green paper—money. Dorothy then got back into the car with Ben and looking over her shoulder to eye the kid.

"Ben, baby… I am sick, and I'll be checking myself into a hospital for a little while. I know you want your mama to stay home with you and I will: later. Right now, I have to get better so when I come back—it's for good. I don't want to hear about you giving May or your sisters any

problems. May is in charge, and you need to do what she says. Do you hear me?"

"Yes, Ma'am… I may have to slap Sarah back mom. She's always putting her hands on me."

"You won't do no such thing! I told you-you're going to be a man and men don't hit girls. Only no good scum do stuff like that."

"All right, Ma… But you need to tell that girl to stop hitting me in my head."

"I'll talk to Sarah about that. We're home now—get out—go inside and be good like I said."

Ben looked at his mom as she and her friend Diane, drove off to pay the bills. Ben had just closed the front door when his two cronies, Donald, and Ralph, knocked on the door. Ben grabbed his football and ran out of the door.

"Man, where you been?" asked Donald, "We're late playing the game because of you."

Ralph wanted to vouch for Donald's anger, so he added, "Yeah man, where was you at, dude? The red team called us faggots because we had to wait on you. Plus, you got the football."

Ben was not even concerned with the neighborhood football league. He couldn't wait to tell them about his visit to the bank.

"I went with my mom to the bank," Ben said with excitement, "I never seen so much money. People walked up with a piece of paper and got back envelopes filled with money. Have you ever been inside the bank before? It was just as quiet, as the school library."

Ralph wasn't amused because his mom went to the bank all the time, but he had to admit he only went through the drive-through. "My mom drives up to the window with paper, and they give her money out of this tube." He said.

Donald was becoming disturbed because he still wanted them to hurry so they could catch the other guys to play ball. Donald placed his hand heavily on Ben's shoulder.

"I never been to the inside of a bank and don't care to. I do want to play football so let's run to the park before all the guys leave."

Ben put the bank in the back of his mind right then and began running with Donald and Ralph. As soon as the game was over, they began casting blame on why they lost. Ben got back to the thought of the bank.

"Hey, Ralph, when your mother gave them her paper at that window, what does it say?"

"I don't know. I think it tells 'em how much money my mom needs."

Ben was frustrated at the process. "Well, whatever they gave my mom; it wasn't enough for her."

Donald disagreed, "It's not that easy—the paper must say something else, or you may have to be a certain age to get money from the bank."

Ben got excited and said, "I'm almost 16 in a few days. That must be old enough. I look grown up enough too."

Donald had to admit; Ben did look older than most 16-year-olds did. "Man, we all look grown enough, but we're not, so drop it!"

Ralph, the youngest, looked at them both as he circled them, poking fun, and said: "I look grown, and I get the grown women, unlike you two nerds."

Ben and Donald looked at each other, and then at Ralph and started chasing after him until they ended up back at Ben's place. They said their goodbyes with their best bud super-duper handshake.

Ben continued to think about the bank and all that cash.

CHAPTER 16

THE ACT

Two weeks later—Donald and Ralph began knocking at Dorothy's door early Saturday morning. Still half-asleep and dragging her worn down footwear across the rotted wood floors, Jasmine answered the door. Upon opening it, she saw Donald and Ralph.

"It's too early for you two dummies."

She shut the door back in their faces and turned around, calling out, "Ben! Ben! Fred Astaire and Liberace are at the door for you."

Ben ran down the stairs and asked Sarah, "Who?"

Sarah was up eating a bowl of cereal, so Jasmine answered for her, saying, "Your two dumb-dumb friends are at the door."

Ben opened the door to Ralph and Donald, and there they were, looking stupid.

Donald wasn't at all happy with the everyday reception from Ben's sisters. He pointed at Jasmine as the two entered into the home saying, "Man, your sisters get on my nerves."

Ralph did not mind the negative attention. He gawked at Jasmine and said, "Jasmine can call me whatever she wants, spank me when I'm bad, tell me to bark like a dog. I will do whatever just to get a look at all her loveliness."

Jasmine saw the look from Ralph and ran upstairs to get out of his sight.

Donald laughed at Ralph and said, "Dude you're sick with it—Jasmine doesn't think twice about you."

Ralph grabbed his collar and gave the sound, clearing his throat. "Not now, but one day she will be calling me Daddy."

Now Ben was very agitated with Donald and Ralph's conversation about his sister. "All right... Shut up about my sister."

Ralph could not let it go right then. "Sorry dude, your sister is fine as he—,"

Ben gave Ralph a look that caused him not to complete his sentence. Ben abruptly said to them both, "Let's go."

Donald wondered what was up. Ben was acting a bit strange, and so Donald asked, "Go where? Without a football?"

Ben smiled at Donald and Ralph and said, "I got an idea that will give us all our own new football."

Ben said two magic words: new and football. They were all ears.

Ben rubbed his hands together and explained, "We can write down all the things we want and the price and give the bank a note. After we get the money, we can go to the store and buy the football."

Donald wasn't the oldest of the three, but he knew something about Ben's plan didn't make much sense. "Man—you can't get money that easy from no bank. Everybody would do it if it were that easy. Right?"

Ralph was mesmerized still with the thought of a new football deal and the thought that if he had money, he might get a chance with Jasmine. One thing Ralph did know was that most girls like money.

Ben plainly said, "Look, I want my own football and some money to help my mom pay some of her bills. If the bank's got money, they wouldn't mind giving us some." Ben then went gangster, "If they don't give me the money, I'm gonna take the shit."

"What else you need money for?" Donald asked, realizing Ben was completely serious.

Ben let them in on a little secret he had been holding to himself and confessed, "I want to help my mom. She's putting herself into some kind of hospital because she's sick—and the bank won't give her enough money to take care of the bills. If I get some from the bank, my mom won't have to worry while she's getting well. I been talking to someone that said he would tell me how to get money from the bank, but I need help to do this."

Donald was the first to answer, saying, "Yeah man, I'm down, and for whatever you need."

As Ben and Donald did their handshake, Ralph didn't want Ben to think he wasn't down, so he hesitantly agreed. "I'm down man—let's just plan this thing, the right way."

Ben's friends were down, so now he had to build a plan. Ben knew Dorothy's friend's son, Lionel, was a real street hustler. He went to him to learn how to get money from banks. He trusted Lionel to keep a secret. Lionel always told Ben that 'snitches get stitches.' He then told Ben all about the banks. Lionel informed him that they would have to rob it to get the money. Lionel's advice struck Ben as a doable situation. In his mind, there was no backing down, for two reasons: One, he had seen where the bank's money was stored, and two, his sister, Unique, had everything money could buy from her other parents, and he wanted some. Lionel went even further by giving Ben an unregistered nickel-plated, 25 automatic handgun, just in case things got out of hand. Ben looked at the gun and took it with haste; flipping it back and forth, examining it, and pretending it wasn't his first time holding a gun. He did not want to appear weak in Lionel's eyes, for fear of him taking the gun back. Lionel saw Ben was not afraid of the weapon; however, felt he had better give Ben a little hardcore advice.

"Hey, little man, don't point that at anyone you don't intend on killing. Don't forget: If you get the money, I want my share."

Ben looked a bit uncomfortable. Lionel saw the look, so he explained further. "This isn't a toy or video game. Once you point and pull the trigger the person at the other end of the barrel is dead. Do you need this, little man?"

Ben didn't want to seem weak, so he confirmed he understood and was ready for whatever. Ben tilted his head, while pointing the gun, and said, "I got this, man. Get at you later."

Ben walked out feeling as if he was as big of a street hustler as Lionel was. Only he didn't get why Lionel had all the tattoos; there wasn't a part of his body free from ink. He figured the women were okay with all the body art because Lionel had no less than three girls with him all the time. Ben took the gun home and hid it under his bed. That night, he sat on his bed and planned in his mind how everything would go. The next day when his friends arrived, he told them all about the plan that was going to go down the following Saturday. Ben suggested doing things peacefully first.

"Whoa, Ben," Ralph cut in. "What if things don't go like we planned?"

Donald agreed, "Yeah man, nothing ever happens as planned. That's why people have a plan B. You know—?"

Ben realized he had better let his friends in on his secret. "Remember when I said, 'if they don't give me the money, I'm gonna take the shit?' That's plan B. The bottom line is this; we are not leaving there without money. I got a surprise for you."

Ben reached into the back of his pants and pulled out the unregistered gun to show them. Ralph was at a loss for words; he had only seen guns on television and video games. Donald loved guns and always wanted to hold one for real. Ben handed it to him. Now Donald was in for sure. Ralph had doubts, but he felt that no matter what, they were friends, and friends stuck together. Donald handed the gun back to Ben, and they all did their friendship handshake and nodded.

"Saturday," said Ben.

"Saturday," Donald affirmed.

Ralph tried to sound sure.

"Saturday."

❧

Saturday quickly arrived for Ben and his friends. Donald was a bit nervous that morning. As soon as he opened his eyes, he had thoughts of how to get out of the upcoming mess of trouble that he had agreed. The idea of backing out was more overbearing than getting into trouble. He also had a strong desire to hold and fire the weapon Ben had in his possession.

Donald sat up on the side of his bed trying to make up his mind that morning, thinking, 'What the fuck am I going to do?'

He stood at a snail's pace—dragging his feet on the bare floors filled with splinters. Donald's feet were already hard-core. The splinters were no threat for his feet. Heading to the bathroom, he picked up his weeks-worn smelly pants and shirt. Carrying his smelly clothes across his left forearm, he scratched his head with the other hand. He dressed swiftly and headed out to get Ralph. Donald noticed Ralph half a block away, sitting on his porch. Donald knew Ralph had a lot on his mind because he wasn't a morning person. Ralph caught sight of Donald and waved. Ralph was signaling Donald to come on his porch. It was evident Ralph wanted to talk about what they were about to do.

Donald gave him their friendship handshake and asked, "Hey, Ralph man—what's up?" Even though Donald already knew, he wanted to open the conversation for Ralph to say what was on his mind.

"Donald, man—I don't know if doing this is cool, dude. Ben got this crazy idea, and things might go wrong. I don't think I want to go."

Donald was always the main one to advocate the three musketeers, all for one and one for all attitudes.

"Dude, I am not sure about this either, but I do know that I won't be letting my boy do it alone. And besides, this just might work. Let's go get that money, man."

Ralph needed reassurance, and Donald had done that.

"Let's go get Ben. Hold up. Let me lock my raggedy door."

Ralph fastened his door, and he and Donald started the walk toward Ben's place. Again, they saw Ben already waiting on his porch a half block down. Ralph leaned and whispered to Donald, "If he changes his mind, let him."

Donald nodded and responded, "Fo`sho—"

As they approached, Ben's first words were, "Y'all ready?" With a firm and assured look in his eyes, he added. "Let's do this."

Donald and Ralph looked at each other, hunched their shoulders, and they both instantaneously and simultaneously said, "Ok. Cool."

"Where we headed first, Ben?" Donald asked.

Ben decided to pull one of his sister's tricks to make them feel a bit inferior and to make him feel like the leader.

"It's 'Where are we headed first?' And, we are going to the park to make sure all the details of what we got to do are all together."

Ralph and Donald, the two dumb-dumbs, as Sarah called them, said together, "Oh, the plan-n-n-n-n."

Ralph, Ben, and Donald laughed as they walked to the park. After talking over the plan, Ben surprised them when he pulled out two more unmarked guns that he had gotten from Lionel. Ben's eyes had lit up when Lionel had given him what he called, 'a man's gun.' It was a 45-automatic. The other gun was a small one indeed, a 22 revolver. Ben instantly knew he was handing the 22 to Ralph. Ben gave the nickel-plated 25-automatic handgun to Donald.

Ralph looked at the small gun and asked, "Man, what the hell I supposed to do with this little ass gun? Shoot pigeons or some shit. Why y'all shit bigger than mine?"

"My dick's bigger than yours too," Donald joked, "dude! Just take the gun, man."

"Ralph," Ben reminded him, "you're just the look-out man. You don't even need a gun, dude."

Ralph was not pleased but agreed. "Fine, but when this is over, I want to shoot the ones you two got."

Ben then thought about the money they would have after the robbery, "Shit, man… I don't know about you two, but I plan on spending all that cash afterward."

All of them were trigger-happy, and now they were ready. The three buddies did their handshake and headed for the battlefield. The bank had the money, and they were determined to get some of it. It was now nine o`clock Saturday morning. They knew not many customers would be at the bank that early. Donald, Ralph, and Ben were going to keep a watch for anything in the area from a safe distance. They chose to watch from the gas station directly across from the bank. They acted as if they were hustling to pump gas for the station's customers. Ben walked across the street into the Fourth National Bank, in his first attempt to take the

money. Ralph and Donald were to look out and come over to the bank in ten minutes.

As he entered, Ben's eyes were wide open, and instantly he began taking a mental note of all that he saw around the inside of the bank. There were only two tellers at their stations. The bank had one customer who was already talking with the tellers. He looked for the cameras and could point out three. The security guard was missing, but he knew the guard was somewhere around. The bank was quiet and clean as usual. Ben walked up to the bank teller with a smile, and before handing her the note, he looked at her work badge.

Ben gave a sexy smile and said, "Becky, is that your name?"

Ben looked at the teller from the waist up. He couldn't help but notice that she was quite good looking. The thought of pleasing an older woman brushed through his young mind. It was a brief but pleasant feeling. He now had to get to his business.

"Yes, my name is Becky. What can I do for you?"

Ben looked at her seductively and handed her the note. Becky reached for the note, slightly touching Ben's hand. While slowly opening the note she had thoughts of her own. Ben was 5 feet 11, with wavy black hair, hazel eyes, and a smile to die for with just one look. Becky would always say to her girlfriends; she was all for putting it down on a younger man, as long as he was legal.

Because it was odd being handed a note, she instantly thought the inscription would read, 'I want to date you' or something like that. Lionel had written the note out for Ben to use and told Ben to make sure the teller continued to smile. The writing asked for $4,500 cash, and if she did not give it to him, he would take it. He also mentioned he was carrying a gun and would use it if she did not give him the money. It said for her to continue the conversation with a smile.

Becky's smile dropped, and Ben gave her a wide-eyed look with a head nod as if to say, "How about that smile?" Becky smiled and began doing as told in the note, but all her insides continued to say, 'I can't believe this shit!' Ben's partners walked in the bank as the bank teller began putting money into the envelope. The sloppy security guard, still struggling to buckle his pants due to his protruding belly, finally emerged from the

restroom. After fighting with his too little pants, he looked around and noticed one adult customer and three teenagers in the bank. Teenagers in the bank were a bit odd to him, but what was odder was seeing one of the teens with the teller like a grown customer. The guard looked at Becky, and even though she was smiling, he began walking over their way to make sure all was all right.

"You are a bit young to be doing banking, aren't you?"

Now being close enough to see the teller's hands shaking in fear, the guard knew that something was wrong. The guard pulled out his weapon and warned, "Son, step away from the teller. Let me see your hands."

Donald stopped in fear as the hold-it-down man who was to back Ben up when something unexpected happened and to make sure no one entered or exited the bank. Though Ralph's original job was to look out, now that Donald had frozen up, Ralph saw that he was the hold it down, man. Ralph locked the doors and pulled the shades. The doors required keys, so Ralph put a nearby umbrella through the inside handles so no one could come in freely. Ben looked at the teller and quietly demanded,

"Keep doing what you're doing."

The teller continued to fill the envelope, but slowly. Ben sucked his teeth as he turned slowly to face the guard. The teller realized the cheesy-looking guard had distracted Ben. She reached down with one hand, feeling underneath the shelf for the little black silent alarm button. She was so nervous; it seemed as if she were looking for a needle in a haystack. Her hands were shaking dramatically in fear. It was Becky's first encounter with a real-life robbery. Finally, she felt it and pushed it several times while silently praying that Ben didn't turn around to see one of her hands not visible. After she had realized she had successfully pushed the silent alarm, she resumed doing as Ben had told her. She was just in time, too because Ben took a quick look back at her before responding to the guard.

"What are you doing asking me about my age? I'm here to get my money from this bank."

The guard now was briefly confused and rubbed his greasy, matted hair that looked as if it hadn't been washed in years. His thoughts were rushing through his minimum-sized mind, and he began asking himself if he saw what he thought, or if this guy was just another young-looking

adult. Suddenly, he then snapped back into reality. He knew Ben was a teenager because he had young eyes. He always felt the eyes never lie. Even though his voice was usually an irritating one, all in the bank could appreciate his voice on a day like this one.

"Young man, please step away from the teller and leave this bank now!"

Ralph was about to freak out and started panting, but when he noticed the only customer was trying to leave after hearing the guard, he made sure to do Donald's job as the hold-it-down man.

"Where do you think you're going? Get on the floor. Face down, bitch! Stretch out your arms and hands."

Ralph remembered a scene in a movie and only repeated the line from the film. To his surprise, it worked; she complied.

Lying on the floor; the customer was now only able to see Ralph's dusty ankles and the holes in his jeans. She wished she had stayed home.

Ralph ran over to the door, flipping the open sign on the bank's door to the closed side. He then moved quickly to pull the rest of the shades. Trigger-happy Donald jumped back to the reality, pulled his gun, and started giving orders to the guard. He walked up to the rear of the guard and pushed the gun in the back of his head.

"Step off now!" Donald ordered him, "Put your gun down and get away from my boy! Give me the keys!"

The guard handed Donald the keys without turning around. Donald then threw them to Ralph, and Ralph locked the door. Becky began crying aloud. Ralph ordered the other teller to come and get in the same position he had put the customer in. They lay there on the floor next to each other sobbing. Ralph felt powerful, and in charge, even though he had the smallest gun. Immediately after throwing the keys to Ralph, Donald got loud with the guard.

"Give your gun to my boy! Now, BEAST!"

Ben looked the guard in the eyes, snatched the guard's gun away from nervous hands and said, "Man, give me this gun. How you get this job anyway? You look like the only guarding you been doing is at the donut shops."

Ben slid the guard's gun next to his on his back. His pants now had two guns pressing against his lumbar. Ben started pulling his shirt over the two guns, and Donald continued to point his gun at the guard's head. Donald began laughing at Ben's jokes, rousing shame in the guard. The guard then got cocky, thinking how bad it would look if he let three punk, teenage boys overtake him. The guard turned quickly to reach for Donald's gun. Seeing, that—Ben reached for his gun. Donald's gun went off, missing the guard's head, going into his shoulder. On his way to the floor, the injured guard snatched Ben's gun away. The guard then fired the weapon at Ben and missed. Ben had ducked out of the way, tripping over a chair in the process. Ben got up and panicked after seeing the guard shot.

Ben looked at Becky and said, "I never meant for this to go this way. I just needed money for my mom because she's sick and needs money for the hospital. I didn't mean it to be like this."

Becky's facial expressions changed toward Ben as she looked into his eyes. Donald fired his weapon, reshooting the guard, this time in the leg. When the alarms from the bank went off, Ralph began crying. The police were now present and circled the bank. Not knowing the situation inside, they started asking the robbers to come out with their hands up. "Come out! You are surrounded!" The three boys looked at each other in fear. They watched movies and hearing the instructions over a loUPSLeaker was a clear notion that they had failed and it was over for them. Ben looked at the wounded guard and the frightened hostages. He knew what they had done, the trouble they were in, and it hit them all like a brick wall.

Donald grabbed Ben by the hand holding the gun. Donald took all the guns, wiped them off with some tissue and tucked them against his lumbar. Donald took Ben and Ralph aside so no one could hear and he whispered,

"It's over man! We have to give up. I shot the guard. I know I am going down. I am going to say I had this all planned, and you and Ralph followed behind me. Stick to that story no matter what."

Ben walked over to Ralph; he was crying hard and shaking in complete fear. He said, "I'm sorry, dude, for getting you in this. Donald, I love you, man."

Donald told them both to be on the floor as if they were hostages and to wait until the police confronted them. Then Donald put all the guns on the floor next to his feet, stood back up, and sauntered to the doors; opening them so that the police could see him. He put his hands in the air and followed the instructions of the police.

The police arrested all three boys. Ben was facing a robbery charge at age 16 and was charged as an adult. Donald faced charges of robbery and attempted murder in the first degree. At 15, he too—was charged as an adult. They charged Ralph with the robbery but tried him as a juvenile at age 14.

ʗɔ

Janet had just come in from gardening in her backyard. She was wearing a pair of her raggedy old jeans and a white t-shirt with an underwire bra to kill the maker for designing. That bra was pinching the hell out of her. She was so happy to be done with gardening but proud of the outcome. Those elephant ears were beautiful to her. She had finally gotten a chance to plant her elephant ears near her patio steps. She was standing at her kitchen sink washing her gardening tools when the phone rang. Janet looked over at the phone as she began to wipe her hands dry from the water. She then pulled the knob to shut the water off and walked over to the phone that hung there on her kitchen wall.

"Hello,"

"Hi, Auntie Janet… It's me, Ben—."

Janet was not quite sure how she felt about receiving a call from Ben. The last time she had gotten a call, he was in trouble with school and wanted her to bail him out of a tight jam.

"Ben, Hi baby, what's wrong?"

"How did you know something is wrong?"

"Because that's the only time you call me."

Ben felt so ashamed, for he knew that to be true. He was in trouble for sure this time as well.

"I'm so sorry for that, Auntie. If I ever get out of this mess I'm in now, I promise you, the next time I call you it would be something going on that would make you proud of me, or to simply, just hang out with you."

Ben's promise moved Auntie Janet. She was quite lonely most of the time. None of the children by her sister Dorothy came over to spend time with her. They only called or came by when they wanted something from her.

"You know, I would like that. However, what's the problem now?"

"Well, Tee Tee," Ben muttered, "I'm in jail."

"In jail! For what?"

"Robbery—."

"Oh my God! Jesus! Is that right?"

"Sorry, Tee Tee, it is. I wasn't trying to hurt anyone, but everything just got out of hand."

Ben was crying over the phone, and Janet could not remember ever hearing Ben cry. She knew her nephew was in serious trouble.

"Ben, baby, just hang in there. I will get in touch with your mother to let her know what happened. Meanwhile, just hold on, baby."

The guard began signaling Ben that his time was up and to end his call.

Ben acknowledged the guard and put in his last words to his aunt.

"Auntie, let the family know that I'm sorry, and I love them. Make sure my mom is okay because she has to go to the hospital; she said she's sick. I have to go now. I love you, Auntie—even if I never said it. Bye…"

Janet stood there holding the phone, looking at it in disbelief. She finally put it back on the hook and sat at her dining room table, wondering how she was going to find Dorothy. For many years, Janet had felt jealous and disdainful because she couldn't have children, and her sister had five but didn't take care of any of them. Then she thought that Unique's adopted mom Cindy might be able to find Dorothy a lot easier than she could herself.

Janet instantly stood up and trotted to her bedroom to look in her bedside table drawer for her phone book. She remembered getting the number from Cindy at Jamie's funeral. Fumbling through and bent over, Janet placed her left hand on her back as she continued to search using her right hand through the drawer. She let out a sigh of relief when she found

the book, she shut the drawer and begun flipping through the pages for Cindy's number.

Janet jumped and said with excitement, "Ah ha... Here it is."

Janet loved her silk comfort set on her bed until she tried to sit in the big slippery slide. As soon as she sat; she slips and plops right to the floor—her hair curls bounced in her face as she hit the carpet. That irritating curl flew in her mouth, so she blew it away with a huff of air from her parched lungs. The family knew Aunt Janet was the clumsy one and a bit goofy.

She roared with real frustration, "This is more trouble than it's worth! I have gotten too old for all this drama."

Opening the book again, while on the floor, she once again found Cindy's number. Janet picked up her phone that sat there on the bedside table and began calling Cindy.

"Damn it!" She shouted aloud at the busy signal. She started looking for Cindy's cell number.

Meanwhile, back at Cindy's house, Unique had been getting into new design software on the computer, and web browsing—tying up the phone lines. Cindy and Chuck had bought her more software to help her get back into designing clothes after the tragedy. Cindy was helping Maury and Jerry with extra schoolwork while Chuck was at work. They were sitting at the kitchen table with papers and crayons extended across the table. Cindy heard her cell phone ring and jumped from the kitchen table in a hurry to catch it before it stopped ringing. Cindy knew Unique was using the home phone line for the internet, so she thought it was Chuck calling from work.

"Hello, hello?" Cindy rushed to answer.

"Hello Cindy, this is Janet. How are you?"

Cindy was a bit confused. She couldn't think who Janet was right on hand, and she hated to ask but felt she had no choice. The voice and the name rang no bells in her memory.

"Janet? Janet, I do apologize, but I haven't a hint of who you are. Please, refresh my memory."

Cindy began making her way back to the kitchen and looking down the hall at her boys to see if they were still working on their schoolwork.

As she made her way down the hallway, Janet started to explain who she was and why she was calling.

"I'm sorry—my name wouldn't ring a bell for you considering I only met you briefly and under difficult circumstances. I am Dorothy's sister, and I met you at your daughter's funeral."

Cindy got quiet for a second. The thought of Jamie had torn into her soul again for a moment. Now she was concerned about the call.

"But anyhow," Janet continued, "I need to get in touch with Dorothy. It is an emergency involving her son Ben, but I have no clue where to look for her. Please, I don't want to be a bother, but can you help me?"

Cindy had become quite nervous from so much drama that seemed to follow her and her family now. She was quick to ask what happened, and now, she felt she wasn't intruding because when she adopted Unique, she and Chuck had been so involved with Dorothy and her other children that they felt like family. Unfortunately, it was the family everyone wanted to deny, but they were still family.

"Janet please, can you tell me what's going on with Ben? I just talked to him last week about his friends being a bad influence on him. Unique came home with some issues with one of his buddies. I thought he had listened to my advice and was doing fine."

Without hesitation, Janet told Cindy the trouble. "Honey, Ben is in big trouble this time. He robbed a bank with two of his comrades, and they got him on a robbery charge, and the charge of attempted murder are pending. They say one of the children shot a guard."

Cindy reflected on the news she had glanced at earlier. "Oh my God… I saw that on the news. I didn't know that involved Ben. He is in big trouble. I will find Dorothy. I think she would be visiting her friend today. I'll give you a call when I find her."

Janet was euphoric that Cindy would help, and she felt some relief. She felt the genuine love Cindy had for their family and knew her family was an extension of theirs.

"Sure—and Cindy, just in case you forgot, if you ever need anything, you can call me. Call me anytime."

Cindy smiled. "I will, and I promise to remember who you are from now on. Thanks for calling, and I will get back to you."

They ended their conversation. Janet went to prepare her meal and prayed for Ben—while Cindy headed straight to make other calls to find Dorothy. She first called the station for the necessary information about Ben. Cindy then called Dorothy's friend Diane. The first attempt proved to be successful. For the first time, Cindy didn't have to look hard to find Dorothy.

Dorothy's friend Diane answered her phone.

"Hello, Diane, this is Cindy. I hope I'm not bothering you, but I need to find Dorothy right away, and I was hoping you knew where she's at."

Diane was usually a bit hostile with stuffy people calling her phone for someone else; however, this was not the case for Cindy. Dorothy had already informed Diane about Cindy, and it was not a surprise to hear her egotistical voice jamming her phone.

"Hey, what's up, Cindy? I'm looking at her big head ass right now."

Diane took her cell phone and gave it to Dorothy. Dorothy slapped Diane on her behind, in a friendly gesture, as she took the phone out of Diane's hand.

Dorothy placed the phone to her ear and asked, "What's wrong Cindy? Is everything all right?"

Cindy cleared her throat as she prepared to give Dorothy the bad news. She could sense that Dorothy was trying to get herself together and was unsure how well she would do taking the news about Ben.

"I'm sorry, Dorothy, everything isn't all right."

Dorothy got excited and interrupted Cindy with another question: "Is it Unique?"

"No... Unique is fine. It is your son Ben. He is in jail."

"In jail... What the hell is he doing in jail?"

"He robbed the Fourth National Bank with two of his friends."

In shock, Dorothy realized aloud, "He was the one they were talking about on the news!"

"Yes, sorry to say—but that was Ben. They're charging him with robbery and maybe attempted murder. That's not all..."

Dorothy started pacing the floor, filled with anger and disappointment with her son, but mainly disappointed in herself. She immediately felt a

pang of overwhelming guilt. Fear of asking the next question was present, however; Dorothy mustered up the words.

"What else?"

"Well, I already called the station, and they're trying to charge him as an adult."

Dorothy Repeated, "An adult! But he's just a boy."

"Yeah," Cindy sighed. "And his bail was set at $50,000. We need a lawyer to help him before his court date."

Dorothy flopped down on Diane's bed. "That is like coming up with $50 million for me. Okay, Cindy, thanks for calling. I'm gonna go see about him right now." Dorothy hung up the phone.

Diane had come out of the bathroom waving her hands and joking, "Whoa, girl; don't go in there!"

Diane then saw the expression on Dorothy's face.

"Dorothy, what the hell's wrong with you? Every time you talk to Mrs. Booshie, you have something wrong. I don't think you should take any more of her damn calls. She always got some bad news or sumthin. What the hell is it now?"

Dorothy was in a daze and said, "It's not Cindy; it's my kids and me. My life is all kinds of fucked up, girl! This time, it's—Ben."

Diane's eyes got big. So she stopped pulling on her breasts; trying to lift them out of the bra to reveal more cleavage and said, "Ben? What that knucklehead done?"

"That robbery we were looking at on the news. It was Ben and his two Bozo the Clown friends."

"Hell naw! That boy always wanted to be on TV."

"Diane! That shit ain't funny!" Dorothy grabbed Diane's wrist, headed for the door and said, "We're going to the station."

Diane was not trying to be funny; she thought she was stating a fact. Diane picked up her purse and keys and followed Dorothy out the door. Dorothy received the very same information Cindy had given her. Her rushing off to the police station had done her no good. She was utterly frustrated, an emotional mess, and felt hopeless. Diane saw all this in Dorothy's face and fought for the words to say, but none came to her, so she just took Dorothy's hand and led her out of the station.

Diane and Dorothy were walking down the stairs of the station when they heard someone calling their names from behind them.

"Dorothy and Diane—"

It was a crooked street cop named Charlie, who had no real regard for justice. He had purposely forgotten the oath he had taken to serve and protect. He was the type that only served himself, and his badge gave him the right to do so. He was a good tipper, but the freebies were at an end because Dorothy was through with his harassment.

Dorothy asked with an attitude, "Charlie, what do you want?"

Charlie was looking around nervously, making sure none of his fellow officers were looking at him talking to two known prostitutes. He whispered,

"Who busted you two this time?"

Dorothy answered, "We're here on other business. Why are you talking to us on these grounds?"

He knew Dorothy was right. He had no business chatting with them at the station. Charlie cleared his throat, looking them up and down, and said, "I might want to pick up a package tonight at the same spot. Diane, you owe me from the last package. You were a little short."

Diane got a bit angry at Charlie's comment and spoke, with her eyes piercing his privates, "A little short? That is the problem! You are a little short!"

Charlie started to look nervous. Diane was attracting attention with the yelling, the snapping of her neck, and the rolling of her head when Dorothy interrupted before things got out of hand. After all, they were still at the station, and Dorothy did not want any more problems.

Dorothy gave her girl Diane a look telling her to calm the hell down.

"Look, Charlie," Dorothy asserted, "I won't speak for my girl, but as for me, I'm out of business, so find you another whore."

Diane looked at Dorothy as they turned and walked away from the crooked cop. After Dorothy had made that statement, for the first time, the silence seemed to fall upon them both. Diane fumbled with the keys to open the car door. She could not get her eyes off Dorothy, wondering if she meant what she said. They both got in the car. These two always ran their mouths like running water, but there was nothing except the highly

unusual silence for a good ten minutes while Diane drove Dorothy back home.

Diane finally broke the silence. "Dorothy, is you for real about quitting the business?"

Dorothy held her head high and then looked over at Diane, confidently stating, "I have never been more serious about anything, but this, I am serious. I'm tired of this, girl. I can't do this anymore. I've not only destroyed my life, but I have also ruined any chance for my children to have a decent life. I did too many things wrong. I've been on this dope and selling myself since they could remember. It wasn't a wake-up call for me when I gave my baby Unique away so she could have a chance. It wasn't a wake-up call for me when I saw Jamie in a casket. That could have been Unique. I let my poor baby roam the streets at all times of the night so that I could get a fix.

Now, because of me, my son's locked up. I wasn't there to show or teach him anything. My eldest child doesn't have a life of her own because she's taking care of my kids and my issues. I think it's long overdue—it's time for me to wake up! None of them has seen me do anything worthwhile, or honest. It may be too late for them to listen to me now, but I need to change for them to know how sorry I am. I need to change for me. I hope you understand, Diane."

Diane had never heard Dorothy talk like this, so she well knew Dorothy was for real this time, but at the same time, she could not help but wonder what she was going to do because Dorothy had always been right next to her through everything.

Diane took a deep breath and said, "I do understand. Dorothy, you know I am here for you, and I promised whichever way you would go, I would follow. I didn't just mean in these streets. I meant in life, period. So what are we going to do? I'm not staying in these streets without my sista; please tell me you knew that."

Diane turned the corner. Dorothy saw a tear fall from Diane's face as they were pulling up in front of Dorothy's place. Diane put the car in park.

Dorothy grabbed and held Diane's hand and asked her, "You mean that?"

"Yeah, I mean it. So what are we doing?"

Dorothy smiled and explained, "How I look at it Diane, if we are gonna do something, we need just to do it. I don't want to waste any time because I can easily talk myself out of doing the right thing. It wouldn't be the first time. Therefore, I am going to say goodbye to my oldest child, put everything in her care, pack a small bag, and grab my pamphlet to the rehabilitating clinic. I'm checking in today. Now, you still want to follow your sista?"

Diane's eyes were wide open. She was very nervous. Strangely, she felt like someone was rescuing her from a storm and was eager to follow Dorothy.

"Yes, I am sure," Diane said, holding Dorothy's hand tighter, "But so I don't change my mind after you come back out, let's go straight to the center. I don't need clothes."

Dorothy was shocked at Diane's response and kissed her on the cheek. They rushed out of the car, were back in ten minutes, and were on their way.

CHAPTER 17

A STRUGGLING FRIENDSHIP

DOROTHY AND DIANE ARRIVED at the center. Dorothy shut the car door, looked at Diane and said, "Let's do it."

They did not know what to expect but had high expectations for whatever it was. Looking up at the building—Diane and Dorothy held hands and walked into the rehabilitation center together, hoping and praying this place would give them the help they so desperately needed.

The center put them in separate quarters, and they had to take medications to help them through the withdrawals. Their bodies were in torment during the detox period: sweating, no appetite, shaking, and the pain in their bodies almost became unbearable. Dorothy had done the most damage to her body, and the doctors were concerned about her heart during the detox period. While the thought of Dorothy's children

kept her going—the hope of a new life was the only thought that kept Diane going.

ↁ

Several months later at the center—Dorothy and Diane were in the second stage of their treatment. They had group sessions held twice a week with eight people. The same group of individuals would be their support once they left the center. During a group counseling session, Diane showed anger toward Dorothy for the first time. She was now looking at Dorothy sober, with no drugs in her system, and for the first time in years. The counselor asked a group question that brought out some terrible feelings Diane had for Dorothy. Being high all the time made her neglect what was really on her mind, and it wasn't on her agenda to even talk about things. Now, Diane had to give Dorothy a piece of her mind.

Diane peered over at Dorothy and griped, "All this is your fault, Dorothy!"

Dorothy interrupted, "My fault! Why?"

The counselor stopped Dorothy by telling her to let Diane finish.

After an initial uprising with the others in the section; they listened intently to Diane's complaint against Dorothy.

Diane continued, "Yes—your fault… I was on my way to college after high school. I had high hopes and dreams. You took me to that party—I said I didn't want to go. You convinced me that using one time wasn't going to hurt, or stop me from going to college. Next thing you know—it was like quicksand. I lost myself when I started getting high. A little bit of me didn't want to face college without you. I knew there was no persuading you to go with me, so I stayed with you. I can't understand it, but I could never see myself without you being with me. It has been like that for me since we were six years old. You wouldn't follow me to college. Instead, I followed you to the slums; now look at where this has led me. I hated my love and dependency on you. Now, I have to thank you too because you led us here for our second chance.

This time, I am determined to stay straight, go back to school, get a career, and live out the rest of my days happy. If you choose to go back

to our past life, I won't be following you this time. I mean it, Dorothy! I won't be following behind you! It's either you come with me—or, I will have the strength to leave you behind. You got that?"

Diane was in tears as she told her friend her thoughts. Immediately after Diane spoke, the group and the counselor began to clap for the progress of Diane. Dorothy was shocked to see her friend's strong willpower and was very proud of Diane's strength as she told how she felt. Dorothy thought back on their life as friends together and realized she was just as dependent on Diane's love.

"Diane—" she said, "I am sorry for the past. I promise to follow you this time, and I promise not to let you or me fall to our past life again. I love you. I also want what you want, so let's do this."

Diane was thankful to hear Dorothy's assurance of their future together, but she was hoping her friend would not change her mind, especially when times got hard. Diane gave Dorothy a hard look, got up from her seat, walked over to Dorothy, and sat in the seat next to her.

"I had to ask myself," Diane said. "When did my dependency on you started? I remembered back when I was eight; I walked through the backyard through this alleyway to your house. I knocked on the door, and your brother Kenny said you went to the corner store. I tried to catch you at the shop. I ran around the corner, skipping down the street, suddenly, this man jumped out of the alley and dragged me in with him. I screamed with all that I had, and you came running to my rescue. I would never forget how you kicked that man in his balls so hard that he fell hard to the ground. Then I remembered when I was ten, and you spent the night over at my place. You went to the bathroom, and when you came back, my uncle had tried to rape me again, but this time, you were there, and you stabbed him in his thigh with a pencil. He never raped me again after that, and I had you to talk to, about him raping me. At first, no one knew, he had been abusing me every weekend for several months—I felt safe with you. That's why it wasn't easy for me to just go and do what I wanted. I love you so much, Dorothy, and I am thankful for you. I will never turn my back on you, but I will never follow you to the pits again either. I hope you mean what you're saying because I'm sincere and determined—I won't return to that life."

Dorothy hugged Diane and said, "I mean it—we're going to do it this time. It's you and me together for good times and no more bad ones. I love you, and I can't see my life without you either."

They hugged with tears and had hope for the first time, and in a long time. The counselor was so proud of the two; she knew they were on their way! She wished them much success in their rehabilitation. Dorothy and Diane became the talk of encouragement for the whole center, and they left the center fully charged with vigor and a new zest for life. The two vowed never to return to their past life. They both enrolled in an education program referred to them by the center, and they moved in together for additional support. Staying off the drugs and the streets was a continuing battle for them, but being committed to it together made it more doable.

CHAPTER 18

TIME TO WAKE UP

"Unique! Unique—honey, it's time..."

Unique continued to hear the same words—first muted and hushed, then more and more pronounced and lively until she became fully awake.

Cindy was now yelling.

"Unique... Wake-up!"

Unique opened her eyes, looking at Cindy as she yawned, "How long was I asleep, Mom?"

"Too long... Unique, there are things you must do. This show is your show, baby."

"I'm awake and revived, Mom. Let's do this." Unique stood up, all excited to get started.

Cindy then told Unique, "Vickie is here, and she has your surprise with her. She wants you to come out to the auditorium."

"Okay, Mom," Unique said, even more excited, "Just let me wash my face."

Cindy handed Unique a wet towel.

"Wipe—now, let's go."

Unique walked out to see hundreds of workers, all moving around getting the show ready. She saw major progress. She checked the time—it was now eleven in the morning — the media stationed themselves all over the place in and out of the building. The sheer, white draperies were elegantly decorating the stage, and the runway was completely lit up. They removed the two HD TV's, replacing them with two high-definition projector screens. The engineers had replaced the original sound system with a more profound one that included earpieces for the entire staff for communication. It was indeed a beautiful sight.

Seeing all these things going on, Unique thought this must be the surprise Vickie had talked about with Cindy. Unique finally caught sight of her sister. She walked in the auditorium dressed in a creamy white dress that Unique had designed for her. Victoria had her long black hair pulled up in the back. She walked into the place with style and charm. She was even more beautiful to Unique because her personality had changed for the better. Now, Victoria's outside appearance matched her inner beauty.

Victoria caught sight of Unique as well. Her eyes lit up when she saw her little sister—Victoria was so proud. Witnessing her sister's talent had blown her mind. While Unique was napping, Victoria had already gone to the back dressing rooms to view some of the items Unique had designed and put together. Victoria was amazed at her gown—wearing the design by Unique, not only felt, and looked good, but it formed to her every curve. The other designs and fabric choices for the others in the show was fabulous too. Victoria also looked in on all the dresses, and devices Unique had designed for all the physically challenged children used to help them with their everyday lifestyles and mobility. There were wheelchair covers, and wheelchair strap bags to match whatever the child was wearing. These bags were also of help for the transporters of the children because no longer did they have to grab a separate bag. The bag could easily be attached to the wheelchair. She had designed devices to fit on the underarm and handle of crutches. These materials not only highlighted the child's clothing, but they also gave comfort to the child using the device. There were shoes, clothing, and jewelry, all made to accommodate the physically challenged with more comfort and style.

Seeing Unique's work, Victoria knew it took love, dedication, and a gift to do what Unique had done. Victoria was so proud that she dropped a few tears—her emotions had caught up with her. A model crying was against the model-diva-rule because tears do not do well with makeup. However, upon seeing Unique taking control over the show from a distance, Victoria couldn't hold back. They both briskly walked toward each other after spotting one another from across the auditorium. Victoria grabbed Unique in her arms and hugged her very tightly. Pushing Unique's hair behind her ears, Victoria tried orally enunciating her thoughts.

"Unique, I am so proud of you. Words can't express how I feel right now."

"I'm proud of you, too, Victoria," Unique said.

Victoria's countenance dropped as she asked Unique, "Me? Why would you be proud of me? I haven't done anything right."

"Yes, you have! Vickie—Do you know how hard it is for a person to change how they think? Some people never do, but you have changed. That's a courageous thing to do, and I'm proud to have my sister in my life. I can't tell you how long I waited to spend time with you. You have become the real Vickie, not the pretend one. Do you remember that time we pretended we were Santa Claus, and we took Dad's shaving cream to make the beard?"

"Yeah, I remember that," Victoria said, laughing. "I told you it tasted like whipped cream, so you licked some. The look on your face was priceless." Vickie was laughing hysterically.

"You see, that's the real Vickie, my sister. I finally got her back. That's why I am proud of you. I promise—I never want to lose you again. I will put up a fight."

Victoria wiped her tears and uttered, "Enough of the mushy stuff, I've got a surprise for you before your show."

"Vickie, stop… You have done enough. This show will be complete because of you. I am thankful, but—"

Victoria interrupted, "Unique, this show is not complete until you see my next surprise. Go over there and sit in the front row, right there in the middle."

Unique no longer put up any fighting. She knew it was useless anyhow to fight with her older sister, so she did as she was told.

Cindy and Chuck were in the front row waiting for Unique to get there. As she walked, she looked at her parents and yelled back across the room to Victoria.

"I see you got my mom and dad in on it!"

She smiled as she walked in front of the seat she was to take. Still standing—Cindy put a black blindfold over Unique's eyes. Chuck guided her into her seat.

CHAPTER 19

BEYOND EXPECTATIONS

STANDING THERE, WATCHING CINDY fumble with the blindfold, trying to fit it carefully over Unique's eyes without messing up her hair, Victoria now began to reflect on all the hoops she had gone through to bring Unique this gift. Victoria felt this surprise for Unique would let her know that she was genuinely sorry for all the sick and undeserving treatment she had given her. Unique would know she had changed for the better.

Victoria had found Dorothy. She had gone to Dorothy's home one day around noontime. Victoria needed to tell her all about the things Unique was doing because she wanted to get Dorothy to come to the show. Victoria knocked on the door. She clutched her purse in front of her, petrified of the neighborhood where Dorothy lived. Diane looked through the peephole in the door and called out to Dorothy.

"Oh, my goodness! Dorothy, I think it's for you. Looks like Al's daughter Victoria is here."

Dorothy had all kinds of thoughts running through her mind about why Victoria would come to her neighborhood and visit her.

She anxiously said to Diane, "Please open the door, Diane, before her narrow ass gets lynched. You know she ain't from the ghetto."

Diane opened the door, looking Victoria up and down. "Come on in."

Victoria, still clutching on to her purse, looked at Diane as she was shutting the door behind her. Dorothy walked into the small front room with stained walls and dirty, smelly carpet. Dorothy saw that Victoria was still standing in the middle of the room clutching her purse as if she was afraid the dirt was going to attack her. Dorothy had on her robe with a glass of red Kool-Aid in her hand.

"Do you want a seat, Victoria? It ain't the Hilton, but it's home to me. It's all I got."

Victoria realized she was in her old ways of thinking. She wanted to change that part of her personality, so she took the offer to sit.

"Thanks, I thought you'd never ask. My feet hurt in these pumps."

While Victoria took a seat, Dorothy was shocked that she would. Victoria put her purse next to her on the raggedy couch, licking her lips, and looking at Dorothy's Kool-Aid. "You got any more Kool-Aid?"

Now, Dorothy began tripping and snapped, "Okay, Victoria, why you here? Al dead or somethin? You know damn well you don't drink Kool-Aid! The sugar alone will make your skinny ass throw up. Why are you here, Victoria?"

Victoria sat up straight, looking up at Dorothy, "No — my dad is okay. I'm here because of Unique."

"Unique?" Dorothy swallowed a sip of her Kool-Aid. "The last time I heard, you put my baby out of the mall, and stations when she tried to see you! What about Unique?"

Victoria held her head down when Dorothy mentioned that. "I am sorry about that," she said. "We have moved on since then. She has a fashion show coming up, and I wanted you to come to it."

Dorothy looked at Victoria with suspicions, "Um—Oh, I see, now."

Victoria stopped her in her tracks and interrupted Dorothy's thoughts and said, "I am trying to help my little sister. I'm not mentioned in Unique's show, but I am doing my best to earn her forgiveness. I need

her to know how much I love her. I need your help for her to know that I have changed."

Dorothy's heart had softened towards Victoria. She, too, was looking for forgiveness from Unique as well as her other children. Dorothy blamed herself for Ben going to jail. Dorothy's eyes faded.

"Victoria, I do understand. I'm looking for forgiveness from all my children, especially Unique and Ben."

Victoria hadn't heard about Ben, so she asked, "Why with Ben? What happened to him?"

Sitting on the couch next to Victoria, Dorothy said, "It's a long story. I will not go into details, but he is in jail for attempting to rob a bank. He has been there for almost ten years now. I know because that's how long I've been off the drugs and the streets."

Victoria's face lit up when Dorothy mentioned she was off the drugs. "I am proud of you, Dorothy; not that me being proud even matters. I know that it was hard for you to get to this point. I am sure they would be proud of you too."

Victoria was the first family besides Diane that knew of her accomplishments with the drugs. She felt good to mention her accomplishments aloud to someone.

"Thanks, honey," Dorothy said, smiling. "It's an everyday struggle; the craving is not so bad, but I have to deal with the emotional anguish that I am in daily on my own. I cannot run to the drugs to numb the pain anymore. I am making it through with prayers, and I hope the day will come when I know that all my children have forgiven me. I just want them to know that I am sorry for all the damage I have caused in their life." Dorothy was tearing up, but she remained tough.

Victoria realized she had lots of work to do and boldly stated, "I want all Ben's information. I won't promise anything, but I want to see if I can help."

Dorothy didn't think Victoria could do anything for Ben. Nevertheless, she did promise to get herself and the rest of her kids to the show early for Unique. Victoria hugged Dorothy and then stood up, straightening out her blouse. Dorothy walked Victoria to the door. Victoria looked out the door.

"Hell naw! Where the fuck is my truck!"

"Shit, Victoria," Dorothy said. "You sound like the hood now. Those damn dope heads probably stole your car."

Diane walked out from the bedroom saying, "Damn, Dorothy, I thought somebody else was in the crib. Did that just come from Victoria?"

Dorothy gave the nod. "Yep—"

Diane continued, "I guess what they say is right; you can take the girl out of the hood, but you can't take the hood out of the girl." She looked straight at Victoria and said, "You ghetto."

Diane laughed and went back into the bedroom to watch 'All My Children.' Victoria knew there was some truth to what Diane had said and laughed too. Victoria reached into her purse, grabbed her Blackberry to call her a cab, and she notified the police and her insurance company. The cab finally got to Dorothy's house.

As she exited, Victoria told Dorothy, "I am moving you out the hood because I will not be back to visit you here."

Dorothy smiled—she knew Victoria was not joking.

Victoria went back to her hotel, and she decided to stay in the same state until she completed her mission. She had to figure out how to get Ben out of jail in time for her sister's fashion show. Praying was major; Victoria had not prayed so hard in all her life, until now. She knew it would take God to help her with this one. Victoria had given every lawyer and political leader that she knew and called on every favor due her. She asked for them to extend their calls for helping her situation. Seeking advice on the situation with Ben wasn't going to be an easy task, but Victoria wasn't taking no for an answer either. No calls had returned to her for several days—this made her nervous about the continuing challenge.

Victoria was about to leave and to visit Ben when her cell phone rang. It was an attorney from New York City offering to help. He wanted to meet with Victoria in three days. She agreed to fly there to meet with him.

She then got into her replaced rental car and drove out to see Ben. She was very nervous because this was her very first time visiting a prison. The department took her belongings, and they sat her down in a big room with only a few tables and chairs. After waiting twenty minutes, they escorted a man in with chains on his ankles and cuffs on his wrist. After

he had entered the room, the guard removed the restraints from his ankles and wrists.

Victoria had not been sure how Ben would look. She had not seen him since he was eight years old. The man they had escorted in was tall—at least six feet five inches. He looked to weigh two hundred thirty pounds. He had smooth light caramel skin, rooted wavy hair. His body was massive in its build, his chest was broad, his arms were thick and muscular, his eyes were deep, and his lashes were long.

Victoria thought to herself, "This man can't be Ben. This man is in the wrong place—whoever he is; he should be a model. He is fine as hell."

The attractive man approached her and Victoria looked up at him. She felt weaker because as he got close, she saw his hazel eyes; instantly she knew this was Ben.

He sat down in the seat across from her and said, "Hello, Sissy, I haven't seen you in years."

Victoria's eyes widened, and she began to stutter. "Be— Ben?"

"Yes, Vickie, it's me. I know I look very different from the last time you saw me. What was I? Eight years old?"

"Yes, about eight… WOW! You are very different now. Ben, you are fine as hell. Why are you here?"

"All I can say, Sissy—young and dumb."

Victoria smiled, "You haven't called me Sissy since we were young. When I hear you call me that brings back a lot of old memories."

"Memories are all I have in this place," Ben said sadly. "I hold on to them to keep my hopes up. I got my G.E.D in here, and I have been studying medicine, never enough books on the subjects though. I am looking for a better life once I get out."

"Ben, you have really—grown," Victoria continued, still amazed, "I mean, not just physically, but mentally. I can't believe you are a man now. The time has passed by quickly."

"Only for you, Sissy," Ben corrected her. "In here, time seems like forever. Anyhow, what made you visit me? And, why did it take you so long?"

Victoria looked down and said, "I am sorry, Ben. I let you down just as I let Unique down. I tried to forget about family. I tried so hard to

leave behind everything my father taught me—next to God—family is the best thing. I heard that so much that it became a statement with no meaning—until now. Unique woke me up to reality with some things she said to me. Regardless, I am here to see if I can help get you out. Unique is having a fashion show, and I want all of her family there to support her. That includes you."

Ben was surprised to hear Vickie take an interest in Unique. He remembered how badly she treated Unique when they were young.

"Wow, you have changed. I remember—"

Victoria interrupted, very upset, "Ben, don't you dare remind me of how bad I treated Unique. I know I got a lot to make up for—"

Ben overlapped Victoria's thoughts again: "Victoria, stop. We all have something we have done wrong to Unique. I think all of us were guilty of that while growing up. We know what you did to her, but you don't know what I did to her. Do you?"

Victoria shook her head.

Ben continued, "I know you don't know because I never told anyone about the dirt I did to Unique. I don't even think Unique knew my role in her first heart-breaking crush.

"After Jamie died, I got a chance to see how Unique lived. I went over to her new family's house one time only. I was angry because she had everything and I had almost nothing. At that point, the only parent I had was messed up most of the time, and Unique had four parents. I wanted what she had: money and family. I became very jealous of everything Unique had. Unique was always sweet to me, but because of the jealousy, I hated her.

"Unique had a crush on one of my friends I used to hang out within the hood. His name was Donald, and he is one of the friends who's locked up with me for that bank robbery. I asked Donald and Ralph to play as if he liked Unique to get some things from her like money, candy, and food whenever she came by to see our mother. Unique started to like Donald, and I egged it on all the way. One day, Donald took things too far and started roughing Unique up for more money. Unique had given Donald the last of her money, and he got upset because he thought she had more. I watched as Donald groped my sister... He punched her in the stomach

several times and teased her terribly. Unique kicked him in the balls and ran out. The thing about Ralph—he did like Unique for real, and she never knew because of me and Donald.

"She never knew that I saw what Donald did and that I did nothing to stop him. Unique never came to revisit our mother after that, and I never saw her again after that. I beat myself up every day that I am in here for allowing that to happen to my sister. I read the Bible when it said, 'Whatever a man sows he shall reap.' I think that's why I ended up in here. Donald got the worst sentencing. I was sure sentencing us went in order of the crimes we had done, not just the bank robbery, but also our treatment to Unique. I found out in here that God watches out for all of his people. My friends and I were hurting Unique. We all are reaping what we sowed. I want to tell Unique—I am sorry, too. I have God's forgiveness; now I need hers.

"So, Sissy, we all got a lot to make up for in dealing with Unique. It's not just you. Not to mention all the name-calling and slaps I gave to her growing up. I ask the Lord for forgiveness for all the wrong I've done especially to my sister Unique. Please, Sissy, get me out of here so I can see Unique."

Victoria realized that Unique had not just endured the harsh treatment by her, but by the whole family. She could see that Unique was a very strong-willed person. She also thought Ben's past actions might be the reason Unique hadn't dated anyone.

Victoria took Ben's hand and said, "We all have a lot to make up for and making upstarts with us getting you out of here. I talked with an attorney, and he's looked into your case, and I know you are up for a hearing soon. I will be there to help. Your lawyer is from New York, but he has jurisdiction here as well, and I hear he is the best at what he does. Just keep up the prayers because no one or no circumstance is stronger than God."

"I don't know how to thank you. And, if this doesn't work, I am so happy to have seen you at least, Sissy."

"You are done with the life of crime, right?"

"You know it. I learned my lessons. I was almost 16 years old when I got into this trouble. I didn't know any better, honestly. Now, I am 25

years old, and I want more out of life now. Being in this place gives you time to find the Creator. I have been studying the Bible too."

Victoria had her motives for helping. She went on to ask the questions that were dear to her heart.

"Well, I do need something from you."

Ben looked puzzled and asked, "What's that?"

"I need your forgiveness," Victoria said, reaching for his hands, "And I need you to forgive your mother."

"I already forgave her. I heard she has been off the drugs since I've been in this place. By her doing that, it showed me she was sorry."

Victoria thought back to Dorothy's and her conversation and asked, "How did you hear that? I thought no one knew that she has been off the drugs."

Ben smiled. "Her friend Diane visits me on a regular basis. She told me everything, and she explained why my mother hadn't been up here to see me. She said my mom feels she's responsible for me ending up here, but she isn't. I was just young and dumb; that's why I am here. Can you tell her I love and miss her? As for you, Sissy, there is nothing to forgive. I still love you. When you see Unique tell her, I miss her."

"I will. I will be in touch," Victoria promised.

The time had run out, and it was time to say good-bye. The two were not supposed to have any physical contact, but Ben had the favoritism with the guards, so he asked, with a gesture, and the guard allowed Ben to hug Victoria goodbye.

☙

Victoria got on her phone to get tickets out of Lambert Airport to fly to New York City to meet with the lawyer. She was amazed at her motivation. Victoria paid her assistant well to do all the things that she was doing; of course, it was on a much smaller scale. A few days later, Victoria was in New York meeting with the lawyer that she had talked with over the phone. She finally was able to put a face with his name. The attorney, Mr. Jeffrey Gates, was an older man in his fifties and, Victoria thought, quite good looking. He reminded her of the actor Sean Connery.

After reviewing the case, he smiled at Victoria and said, "I think I can help you with this one."

He explained that a judicial waiver occurs when a juvenile court judge transfers a case from juvenile to adult court to deny the minor the protection that juvenile jurisdictions provide. He mentioned that it was a good thing that Ben is from Missouri. All states except Nebraska and New York currently provide for judicial waiver and have set a variety of lower age limits. In most states, the youngest offender who can be waived to adult court is seventeen or eighteen. However, the offense must be particularly egregious for the case to be dismissed judicially or it must be a long history of malfeasances.

Mr. Gates rubbed his chin, "From the file, I read your brother was fifteen, almost sixteen, and they tried him as an adult. I can argue this case due to his age, as well as the fact he had never gotten into trouble before. He did not have a previous record. I will also argue the facts of his mental evaluation at the time of the offense, stating he needed rehabilitation, not incarceration. He was simply a misguided teen, caught up in the system without guidance. I will use his time served to his advantage. The statute of limitations may possess an individual challenge for us, and I won't promise you, but your brother has a good chance of leaving after his hearing, on probation only."

Victoria was so happy to hear that and began praising and thanking God aloud.

⁊

The day of the hearing had arrived. Victoria was ready for the great news. She had prayed for good news that day. It was just as Mr. Gates had promised but even better. Mr. Gates was able to put in questionable evidence that was neglected and testimonies that appeared tampered. Because of all these factors Ben was being released without prejudice and released as time served. Joy overcame Victoria in court, and she shouted out, "Thank you, God!"

She wanted to keep Ben's release a secret from Unique. Victoria arranged things, making sure Ben had everything he needed.

She had now become so engulfed in family affairs that her life had taken second place. She was in constant contact with her agent, turning down events for her to attend. She asked her agent to give her time to take care of her family. The agent had no family responsibility, so he gave Victoria a hard time about her decision; however, he knew Victoria well enough to know that when she said something was important to her, there wasn't anything else that could take precedence over what she was trying to do.

After seeing the entire family except for Unique, Victoria took Ben to a hotel room for his temporary stay. She and Ben talked about him attending college and finding employment. However, Victoria continued to stress modeling to him because he was very nice looking. Ben kept telling Victoria that he was the shy type, and his heart was in medicine, so Victoria gave up and agreed to let him make his choice. She knew she had to settle for Ben being a doctor.

❧

Cindy's voice snapped Victoria back into the scene. "Okay Victoria, she's ready. Go get the surprise."

Victoria walked over to the end of the stage, and she signaled all the family to come in onto its platform. She put one finger over her mouth to gesture for them to keep quiet as they got onto the stage. Victoria arranged them in order, and she placed in the first row Al, on the right side next to Dorothy. Next, it was Cindy and Chuck. In the second row from right to left, it was herself, Sarah, Jasmine, May, Ben, Jerry, and Maury. Now they were all set for Unique's two designer teachers, Naomi and Pat, who went down and stood on either side of Unique. They each took one of Unique's arms and assisted her in standing. They removed the blindfold, and the photographers captured every moment with the snap of their cameras. Unique first adjusted her eyes. She looked upon the stage; viewing her entire family together for the first time.

Then Unique wailed loudly, "OH! MY! GOD!"

She saw both of her fathers Al and Chuck, and her mothers Dorothy and Cindy. Dorothy was completely sober and drug-free. She saw all her

siblings. Then it hit her; that tall, good-looking person in the middle was her little brother Ben. Unique started crying and yelling his name. She ran onto the stage to grab him. There wasn't a dry face up there. It was a river of tears. From all the struggles, fights and endurance, Unique finally had her family, the family she loved so dearly. In the middle of the hugs and tears, Unique stopped and asked everyone to hold hands as she began praying and thanking God for the blessing.

"All things are possible with you, LORD. My sister, Jamie, told me this day was coming; Jamie knew of God's plan. I didn't know it then, but it is evident now. Please, God, tell my sister; WE DID IT! Tell her thanks for not letting me give up. I thank you, God, for showing me the way. Thank you for sending my beloved sister to tell me. Thank you for your son. Thank you for my entire family. Amen…"

They all let go of their hands. Victoria walked over to Unique, hugged her, and said, "Unique, I need to know that you forgive me for all the wrong."

Unique held her head down for a second, and as she lifted it back up, tears again filled Unique's precious eyes.

"You are my sister, Victoria. There is nothing to forgive, but if you need to hear me say it—yes, I forgive you. Thank you for coming back. I may have lost a sister in death, and she will never be forgotten, but it feels so right to regain the one I lost in life."

Victoria was euphoric. She then said, "Let's go. We got Unique's show to get on the way."

Everyone took his or her place in helping. They all were moving around like busy little bees.

CHAPTER 20

THE SHOW

EVERYONE TOOK THEIR PLACE, and everything was ready for the spectacular event. The stage was lit up. The runway lights were gleaming. The two substantial projector screens were displaying words in big black bold writing, and the name of each mental and physical illness flashed one word at a time; giving a dramatic effect. BIPOLAR DISORDER, SCHIZOPHRENIA, ADHD, ANXIETY DISORDER, PANIC ATTACKS, ACUTE STRESS DISORDER, NARCOLEPSY, ANOREXIA, ASPERGER'S SYNDROME, ATYPICAL AUTISM, ANTISOCIAL DISORDER, AVOIDANT PERSONALITY DISORDER, BEREAVEMENT, BINGE EATING DISORDER, DOWNS SYNDROME, MENTAL RETARDATION, MOOD DISORDER, just to mention a few. The music was playing as the two screens reflected the many mental and physical challenges people face.

The many guest tables were set-up divinely. The sheer white material was streaming from the ceilings down to the stage, composed flawlessly.

The hanging material from the platform also coordinated with the decorated table covers. It was plain to see that lots of thoughts had gone into it.

All the media, magazine representatives, and writers had assigned stations and were to arrive early, settled into their proper stations, have their equipment set up and have the private interviews with Unique done before the start of the event.

The nurse's stations were ready and completely equipped. The ambulance, fire, and police were on standby outdoors.

The models were waiting to hit the stage. They were applying the last minute makeup and jewelry. Everything was in place and ready to start. Unique gave the signal to her two fathers to open the doors.

Reporters from all over were interviewing the celebrities on the red carpet as they arrived. The question many reporters asked was, "Who designed what you're wearing?" Others asked, "Are you wearing something Unique designed?" Surprisingly, some were able to say yes. Some even elaborated how they asked her to create something just for them, and she was able to do it. They said, "She was amazing!"

Ben made sure Unique knew the crowd was massive. He anxiously said, "Unique! It's many people out there in line. I think I saw the actor, Smooth!"

Ben was entirely ecstatic for his sister, but Unique reminded him to keep on his assignment, which was to make sure people were in the right sector and seated correctly. Different sections were different prices. All takings from the show—tickets sold and food, were for the cause and served as a donation. The tickets were color coordinated, showing what area and seat they were sitting. Front seats were the royalty seats, also known as the platinum package. In this package, a guest received front stage seats, unlimited food, drinks and alcohol beverages, as well as servers to assist any needs they might have. Tickets for this section were burgundy and gray. The next seat arrangements were the silver section. Its tickets were royal blue and silver. In this section, the guest received a meal and two alcoholic beverages. Next were the general admission tickets, which were white with a peach lining. These seats were furthest from the stage although all seating areas had a great view. Tickets in this section meant

guest had to purchase their food and drinks separate and must stand in the banquet line to be served. Therefore, it was important for the attendants to seat people properly. Ben saw Unique take charge and willingly obeyed. He got right to his assignments.

Meanwhile, Unique had to trust everyone to do their assignments because her primary goal was to make sure the fashion models wore her designs correctly, and her special needs models were comfortable. She made sure the speech and sign language interpreters were in their proper place, and their devices were working correctly for the interpretations. She also wanted to ensure her opening address was correct. She prayed she would not get so nervous that she would forget her lines. Very prestigious people packed the show. All who were there supported the cause and hoped to raise as much money as possible for Unique's nonprofit organization.

The presenter announced Unique.

"Thank you all for coming out to the Unique Design Special People runway show, also known as the UPSL. This foundation is truly a unique one. Its donations will reach millions that have challenges from a disability whether it is physical or mental."

The applause started. The announcer continued,

"It does me great pleasure to introduce to you a person with incredible strength. An individual who has stood firm with her battles, and somehow she manages to think of others like herself to bring this fantastic show to you.

Ladies and Gentlemen—Please—Welcome Ms. Unique Woods…"

Applause filled the auditorium with shouting and whistling, and the noise covered the entire place. All-the-while music played as Unique walked onto the platform. Unique saw for the first time how many people had come. She was in awe because it was a full house. She thought she would lose her grip and run off the stage, but she didn't. The applause she received made her feel welcome, and she knew the people wanted to hear what she had to say. She thought of Jamie and pressed on like a pro. Thousands had shown up for this event, and Victoria had set up a telethon as well. People were able to tune into the live broadcast and donate freely from the comforts of their home. Unique was dressed in her favorite design, made from a European fabric. Lavender was Unique's

favorite color. She glowed as she slowly walked out onto the stage with plenty of shimmers.

Unique spoke with authority and wisdom. "Hello, I would like to thank you all for coming out to the UPSL runway show. Your support will help millions of people who have daily challenges with the many physical and mental illnesses out there. I encourage you to take a look. Be determined not to turn your own back on the suffering right here in your backyard. Thousands have a least one member of their family who is challenged by mental or physical limitation. How about you? Can you think of any? One out of five people here in America are challenged from some form of disability currently, and fifteen percent are born with the disability. I want to let the world know, with your help, we can make a difference. Millions of children in our country who are never given the opportunity to achieve their dreams because of mental and physical disabilities—most children with disabilities receive little—if any—direction after high school; which is one of the leading causes of crime. Far too many young adults who have ADHD, bipolar disease, and schizophrenia end up in jail or dead; misunderstood by the police. It is widely documented—males with mental illness have a high rate of criminal activity; while females have a high rate of sexual misconduct. Turning a blind eye to these children and their special needs only compound the problem. The encouraging news is that law enforcement officers are finally being trained to recognize persons with mental illnesses; and how to handle them with compassion vs. violence."

Unique focussed on a different camera and continued, "Physically, emotionally or mentally challenged children are different, and their talents are different. All differences should be embraced, not hidden. It is the endless tapestry of human differences that make the world beautiful. Special-needs children require—and deserve—extra love, support, and resources to achieve their goals well beyond high school. Parents and families with physically challenged children need love and support also. To live successful lives, special needs young adults need the involvement of more organizations dedicated to posting high-school independent living support, employment and socialization. Take a walk in their shoes of everyday challenges. Those provocations impact the families of

special needs children; especially low-income families who struggle with emotional roller coasters and expensive medications. Sometimes, family/caregivers turn to drugs and alcohol for temporary relief from the mental, emotional and economic desolation that is often their lives."

Unique gestured when she addressed the audience.

"We all feel better when we are dressed up. Clothing is a way of expression, and these children tonight have plenty to express, as you will see. Thank you, and enjoy the show."

They dimmed the lights and placed the spotlight on the famous R&B singer, Bounce. Wearing one of Unique's top designs, she elegantly graced the crowd with her hit song, Rainbow in the Clouds. Bounce rattled the crowd as her voice penetrated through their souls. This song described how beautiful we all are, no matter what illnesses we may have. Just as the rainbow with its many colors put all together is so lovely.

Unique's first model was a beautiful girl from India. Her challenges were from bipolar disorder. Some would have never known because she strutted out like a princess. She expressed to Unique that she didn't like the welts from her cuts on both her wrists where she had attempted suicide. Unique's designs were set and designed based on the needs of each person. She was dressed in a sky sheer blue blouse and dragonfly pants with matching bracelets designed by Unique.

Next was seventeen-year-old Beth. Unique jazzed Beth up in a black and silver dress and silver high heel shoes. This teen appeared as if she were ready for the prom. Beth had muscular dystrophy. Her wheelchair design was colorful with shimmering streams that floated in the wind as her aide pushed her onto the stage. The disabled accessories were designed for comfort as well as style. The aide was in a beautiful V-neck dress designed by Unique. Many more models paraded the stage all night. Each model was wearing Unique's designs and moving to the beat on the runway.

People were also excited at the many live talents—singers, dancers, and rappers. Many were there to represent for the cause—Down Home Southern Blues, Hip-Hop, Rhythm & Blues, Country, and Rock & Roll. The excitement filtered through the crowd as they viewed the fantastic designs by Unique. They loved the designs though some were saddened to learn the stories behind what each model wore. Many tears fell on this

night; some were tears of joy, and some were tears of sorrow. Everyone would leave that night feeling informed about the different illnesses that beseeched so many and their joy at the opportunity to wear proper designer clothes. After the last model had exited the stage, Unique walked out once more, dressed in another one of her designs. She was now about to give her special thanks.

Unique spoke, "If we can't take the pain away, we can make it a little easier by designing the outer person to reflect the inner person beautifully. Thank you all for coming out. I hope you enjoyed the show."

The audience began standing and clapping; moreover, some people had tears of joy in their eyes.

"I would like to give special thanks to many. I would start with God because without him; nothing's possible. He gives you the strength when you feel you can't go on. I want to thank my sister Jamie who is no longer here in the flesh but is always with me in my heart and mind. My mothers, Cindy and Dorothy, and my fathers, Al, and Chuck. They helped me through."

Unique gave a pause and took a deep breath before she thanked her sister Victoria.

"Ladies and Gentlemen, I would like to give special thanks to my sister, of whom I am so proud of—Ms. Victoria Jacobs!"

Unique signaled Victoria to come onto the stage. She reluctantly obliged and stood up as the spotlight hit her and followed her onto the stage. She and Unique hugged.

"Yes, the rumor is true; we are sisters. I would also like to thank all my family. I want to thank all of you for your incredible support. Please, look on my website for future shows, designs, and for personalized designs to fit the needs of any individual. You can contact me through the site for any of your custom designer needs."

All the family walked on the stage, took a bow, and said, "Good Night." The show ended on a very positive, tear-filled note.

CHAPTER 21

REVIEWS AND
BARBECUES

Unique's UPSL (Unique People Special Lives) runway show was a success! The sensation of having a blended, united family gave Unique and her family a feeling of contentment they had never experienced before. It was dark and late, and although they all felt drained entirely, everyone lingered around talking and planning future family events, making promises to stay a family no matter what came.

The show was an accomplishment not only for Unique but also for all those who were going to benefit from her work. Every child with a physical or intellectual disability now had another advocate out there to help raise the money it would take to get him or her through this life. Unique's show also was one with a lingering positive message that gave many examples of people with disabilities reaching a level of success beyond measure. The UPSL event caused all who came and all who watched to look into their

hearts. If they saw something they didn't want to see or something they wished they could forget; it taught them to look at it and act with love for all who faces these challenges. The delivery of it touched the lives of the poor, the working class, the middle class, the affluent and famous. Unique's show had brought in over a million in donations that night, and it was certain that more was to follow. Unique has plans to continue her campaigns every year, setting up her non-profit organization under the title UPSL. She also donated to learning disability foundations that had already been established across the globe and were known to be a strong foundation. Unique had big plans for her future. She had prepared to set up shops in different states, allowing people to purchase her designs. Her central location would be local in St. Louis, Missouri. All sites would be ready to accept donations. She planned to do a press release at every opening of each shop, allowing more donations to come in.

Vitoria changed from a villain to angel for doing the right thing and changing her ways quickly. The family admired her for that because they knew it usually takes years for people to make their minds and hearts over. Dorothy stressed how hard it was for her to change and to stop blaming everyone else for her problems.

In many ways, Victoria hoped to become more like Unique. Unique always made time for personal bonding with family and friends, and this inspired Victoria to be like her. Unique was adamant and had very gentle qualities in her personality that were able to manifest themselves at the same time. Victoria had become deeply involved in the life Unique created for herself. The two sisters had so much to catch up on as they learned more about each other so they talked so much that no one else could get in a word. Victoria felt Unique had helped her to see and feel what life was about and she remained grateful for that quality.

Cindy and Chuck let them all in on the family barbecue, but Chuck spoke out while they all were gathered.

"Now, this is a family! This family is your family! We are all family! A family connected by a special person in our lives, one whom we all love, Ms. Unique Woods!" They all gave applause, commending her job well done. Chuck continued, "We—right here, right now—have a tradition to keep up, and that's the family barbecues. We will do this every year, and

we need all of you to think of it as a—must-do; because like Al always says," Chuck paused and gestured for all to speak it at the same time.

"Next to God, the family is the best thing!" Laughter filled them all after saying that.

Chuck continued, "Before we start rushing back to our life's responsibilities, we are starting our tradition this following weekend at our house."

Although tired, everyone was excited about the family barbecue. It was the first of many to come.

⁊

The weekdays had passed, and Saturday's sun was shining brightly. It was a perfect day for a barbecue. All was ready, and everyone was geared up for their first family barbecue as one family with the entire family attending. There was no longer an adopted family and paternal family; it was just a whole family. Just as Chuck always did, he went all out for this barbecue. The amazing part was that he put it together in less than a week.

The green lawn was about to be trampled on. Cindy was quite proud of her gardening skills. She made sure her flowers were out of the way but could still be viewed by all the family and friends.

Chuck had three grills going at the same time. He wanted it hot and ready as people were arriving. He made sure to have every category of meat selections.

Cindy's mother, Grandma Carolyn was quite excited about all her grandchildren. She loved to bake, and new family members that had never tasted her cakes and pies before could praise her for her baking skills.

Cindy talked with Dorothy and Diane; it turned out Dorothy was great at cooking pasta, and Diane was great with coleslaws. Cindy was surprised when Dorothy brought big pots of smoked sausage primavera, chicken Alfredo with fettuccine noodles, and what every barbecue must have: spaghetti smothered in tomato sauces, green peppers, green onions, and ground beef with blends of seasonings. Dorothy had outdone herself. Diane brought two big bowls of flavored coleslaws, one spicy and the other sweet.

Victoria was in charge of bringing different types of bread. The bread job was a first for her, and it showed because Victoria brought loaves of bread nobody had even heard of until that day.

Al brought in all the drinks. Cindy made sure she took care of the salads.

Jerry had made sure all the sports that they were about to play had the appropriate area and gear. The children's water games could not interfere with the football, and the card table couldn't be near the water sports and the kids. Jerry knew the language from the adults' card table was too heavy for the kids' ears, and the kids' water couldn't get on the cards, so he had to think things out. He also had to make sure there was plenty of room for the family Soul Train line. Jerry had used the space to its max, and everything had its place.

The entire family arrived early for a full day of family fun and barbecue. The Soul Train line was up and popping. They danced down the line to their traditional song, 'We Are Family,' by Sister Sledge.

PART 2

UNIQUE LIFE

TAKING A LOOK INTO A UNIQUE LIFE

CHAPTER 22

ANOTHER PROMISE KEPT

THE SHOW AND THE family barbecue had passed, but Victoria had more things she wanted to accomplish before returning to her work, and so she extended her stay in St. Louis. Although the hotel came with all the necessary comforts, it was difficult for Victoria to adjust—she'd grown accustomed to lavish hotels and penthouse suites.

She had gotten in contact with a credible realtor named Susanne Jenkins. Victoria instantly bonded with the agent because Susanne seemed quite honest about the market when they spoke over the phone. The two had gone out to see several homes in the safest neighborhoods of St. Louis County; however, none seemed to impress Victoria. Most had that cookie-cutter architecture or no color. Victoria wanted a home for Dorothy that was available to live in and had some life to it, but on their first outing, Susanne had shown her no home that made her ready to buy.

Another day arrived, and again, the agent had taken Victoria through seven homes on a hot, and muggy Thursday. Victoria had to quit for that

day—drained completely of her strength, she decided she'd have to find the place tomorrow.

She had to admit the reason house hunting was so involved was that she was looking as if she would be living in it. Victoria grasped that she had to change her outlook and realize this home was for Dorothy. She slid the card to open her hotel room door, shut it behind her in slow motion, dropped her purse at the door, wobbled over to the sofa, kicked off her heels, and closed her eyes. Victoria fell asleep for only a moment— suddenly there was knocking.

Victoria peeled opened her eyes. "Why didn't I put a sign out to say, 'do not disturb me?'"

She got up, lugged herself to the door and asked, "Who it is?"

"It's your dad, Girl—open up," Al said with his forceful voice.

Victoria wondered why her father didn't just call her. She figured it must be something wrong again.

Opening the door, she greeted her dad with a tired hug and said, "Hello Daddy, what brings you by?"

Al looked at Victoria. She appeared exhausted to him. Then he noticed her hotel room.

Al rubbed his head and said, "This is different for you. Usually, I have to go through big doors and catch elevators up to the penthouse."

Victoria agreed with her dad with a nod, "Yep—I wanted to be simple while I was here. And besides, Ben was in another room down the hall from me. I didn't want to overwhelm him with my style of living. Think about it, Dad; he was used to inadequate space."

Al got the point Victoria was making, and they both took a seat on the sofa in the sitting room area.

Victoria got to the point because she was tired. "So Dad, what's up?"

Al said, "I had some things I needed to talk to you about, and I have some papers I wanted you to see. Before I bring this up, I need you to know how proud I am of you for putting your family first. It's time for you to get back to your business now. I know about your promise to Dorothy, and that's one of the reasons I am here. I am your father, and my job is never done when it comes to protecting you."

Victoria looked muddled, worried about where Al was going with this. "Dad, what are you saying? I should break my promise, go back on my word, and NOT get her the home? If so, Dad—that's not right—I don't want her there, it's dangerous, and…"

Witnessing her distress, Al intervened. "NO, sweetheart—I would never ask you to break your promise. I know Dorothy, and I have a rocky history, but we both have moved on from the past, and I still wish her the best. I just want you to make sure you put clauses in the contract when purchasing the house for her. I also wanted to help with the cost."

Victoria was shocked that her dad wanted in on this. Her mouth was open wide.

Al said, "Close your mouth, Victoria—I know this is strange, but that sister of yours has brought out the best in all of us. Plus, I am so proud that Dorothy is off the drugs and the streets—I want to do my part to keep it that way. That is why I want you to put a clause in the contract that states if she returns to her drugs the house returns to you or Unique."

Victoria asked, "Dad, do you think she would ever go back to that?"

Al hunched his shoulders, "I can't be sure. I pray and hope that she stays on the path she is, and as long as she's on the right track I want to help her. Victoria, just as much as I love your mother, I love Dorothy also because they gave me you and Unique, and I will always be grateful for my two girls. This clause is a just-in-case, to protect you. Did you find a house?"

Victoria poked out her lip for fun, "Nope—I will find it for sure tomorrow because I got to get back to work. My agent has been waiting patiently for my call, and I got to find a new assistant."

Right after that statement, another knock came at her hotel door. Al got up to answer. It was Ben. Ben said hello to Al and gave him a man hug as he walked in.

Seeing Victoria on the couch, Ben said, "I hope I am not interrupting you, but I was going to see Unique in an hour, and I wanted to ask if you wanted to go because they're playing our game of Moo-O-Mop-Pol-Y."

Al said, "Ben you're not interrupting, in fact, I had an idea to throw at you and Victoria."

Victoria and Ben looked at each other, wondering what could be on Al's mind.

Al continued, "Ben, you need to enroll in a college but need a job as well, right?"

Ben agreed, with a nod of his head.

Al continued, "Victoria, you are in need of an assistant—right?"

Victoria understood where her dad was going with the questions.

Al continued, "How I see it; Ben can go to school in your hometown in Florida while working as your assistant, temporarily—until you get a new one. As for the travel aspect of the job—do things by phone until you get a full-time assistant. At least you know he could be trusted because he's family."

Victoria liked the idea, and so did Ben. It felt comforting to Ben to hear Al address him as the family.

Victoria and Ben both said at the same time, "I like that idea."

Victoria said, "Yeah Dad, that would work, plus I had a school I thought would be just right for Ben in Florida. I hear they have some excellent professors."

Al jumped in and said, "This works out best for you and Ben, but as far as medical schools are concerned, Wash U is the best to me."

"Dad, you are just all about St. Louis. Everything is better in St. Louis." Victoria giggled.

Ben was in disbelief and excited that schools for him were a discussion. He rubbed his face and said, "I can't believe it. Sissy—just a little time ago, I had no hope and was locked up. I had no understanding of how my dreams of being a doctor could come true. I loved my family, but I felt they had forgotten me. I want you to know, I will work hard for you, and you won't be disappointed in me. I will be the first doctor in our family."

Al said, "You bet your ass you will because we need a doctor in this family."

Al then turned to Victoria and said, "I almost forgot the other reason I came to see you. My firm has tracked down the ones responsible for wrongfully editing that material, and we have set up the lawsuit. We are pressing forward with this to teach them a lesson. I need you to sign these papers, and I will be on my way."

While Al looked in his briefcase for the papers, Ben asked Victoria, "You never found the person responsible for the misguided leak?"

Victoria tilted her head and said, "Nope, I had an idea but never found proof."

Ben then asked, "Do you want to know?"

Al interrupted, "It doesn't matter. We are going to the magazine and media that edited the material wrong. I don't want you to be bothered by unnecessary things. Now sign these papers."

Al handed Victoria the pen, and she signed. Al kissed her and shook Ben's hand, and headed out of the hotel.

After Al had left, Ben asked, "So Sissy, are we going to play Monopoly at Unique's place?"

Victoria mind was still on wanting to know if Brenda was the leak.

Ben could see something else had taken over Victoria's thoughts, "What is it, Sissy?"

Victoria looked at Ben, "I know my dad wants me to move on from this. He thinks a lawsuit will settle things, but I don't blame the magazine or the media. They were just doing their job. I blame the person that recorded me in the first place. I blame the person that deceived me; I blame the person that I thought I could trust. I can't just let this go, Ben. Is there a way to find out who the leak is?"

Ben gave a sexy, sinister smile as he looked at Victoria, "I think I can, Sissy. Finding information is one thing I can do, to thank you for all your help."

Victoria asked, "How will you discover who it was?"

Ben explained, "It's a long story, but I will shorten it. Victoria, no one must know what I am about to tell you. Promise me you will keep this secret."

Victoria, wide-eyed, said, "I promise Ben, I won't say a word, and I also promise if you find out whom it was that betrayed me, I will never tell that you were my source of information."

Ben was satisfied, and begun to explain and said, "When I robbed the bank; a sexy lady working as the teller of that bank caught my soul. She and I fell in love, just by looking into each other's eyes. I stupidly went on robbing the bank, and, of course, they locked me up. I thought she must have thought I was a horrible person, but I noticed her sitting in on all my trials and with the same gaze she had in her eyes as she looked across

the room at me. I first thought she was there to testify against me, but she didn't. One day, I had a visitor, and it was Becky. I was shocked to see those big bright, bold eyes of hers, and her body; she was breathtaking. I couldn't understand why she wanted to see me. She explained that she fell in love at the bank. I assured her the feelings were mutual. Her life turned her to politics, and all the while, she continued to visit me. I knew she had political pull when our visits developed into a time where we could hold hands, kiss and ultimately we were able to make love—with privacy—of course, and I married this lady."

Victoria spits out the juice she was sipping on.

"You're married? "

Ben continued to explain, "Yes, I married her, but we are not married now. We got an annulment, not because we weren't in love, but because it didn't look good for her political career. When you helped me get out, I called her up. She has the pull to get any information I need."

Victoria cleared her throat and said, "Ben, I am so happy to hear that you have love in your life. Honestly, I thought you were gay because I didn't see you looking carefully at women when you got out."

Ben abruptly interceded, "Hell naw! Sissy— I know people in jail ended up that way, but I was able to escape that mainly because I worked hard to build my muscles, kicking ass at first, and my wife Becky that had political pull. Soon as I was out of your sight, you had better believe Becky, and I was making up for lost time. That's why I wasn't looking at others; she had me so worn out, I couldn't focus on other girls."

Victoria and Ben had a good laugh at that.

Getting back to the original topic, Ben said, "Sissy, don't worry—I will find the one that betrayed you. But first, let's play Monopoly?"

Victoria did the lip out thing again and said, "I can't. I have to get some rest because I have to find a house for your mother tomorrow, and it's the last day to do it. And don't you think you are a little too old to be that excited over a game of Monopoly?"

Ben smiled and said, "One of the biggest lessons I learned while locked up is that life is short and every moment a person has, they should be enjoying themselves. Monopoly isn't just a game for me. It was the best

times in my life when we played as kids. You never could beat me in the game."

After a pause, he said, "Anyhow, I'd better get going."

Victoria almost forgot to tell Ben something, so she called out before he could touch the doorknob. "Oh Ben, the house is a surprise for Dorothy and Diane, so don't say anything to anyone, okay? Also, I always thought you cheated in Monopoly. But, you're correct that life should be enjoyed. I'll play another time. I have to rest."

Ben agreed and excused himself so that Victoria could rest.

❧

Victoria closed her eyes and before she knew it; the next day was invading her need for more rest. Her phone rang, and Victoria eyed the pesky thing with one eye open. It was Susanne; she wanted to get an early jump on house hunting. Victoria got dressed and was out the door to meet Susanne at a pancake house for breakfast. After eating their fill; Susanne took Victoria to a nice quiet neighborhood with stores and shopping within walking distance. Victoria thought that'd be right for Dorothy, and the exercise wouldn't hurt her either. Character and charm filled the neighborhood. Victoria spoke to a few people around the area and in the stores to see how friendly or helpful they were. She certainly didn't want to put Dorothy in a neighborhood that wasn't welcoming.

Victoria smiled at Susanne and said, "This community has passed my test. Let's find a house."

That was music to Susanne's ears. She took Victoria to a two-story home with great character. It had an excellent outer appearance, but when she got inside, the house needed some work. The paint was awkward, and the floors were carpeted with stains throughout the place. Dorothy's present place had stained carpet, so when Victoria saw the carpeting, she let Susanne know there was no need to go on any further.

A ranch property hadn't been first on Victoria's mind, but once Susanne mentioned one nearby, Victoria got excited.

"I think a ranch property might actually work out better for Dorothy."

Susanne took Victoria to a ranch home that not only had charm and character on the outside, but it had color and curb appeal. The landscape was beautiful. It had a beautiful designer oak front door. It also had a two-car garage. As soon as Victoria stepped in onto the tiger hardwood floors and viewed the granite fireplace, she was half-sold on the home. The rest of the walkthrough displayed three bedrooms, two and a half bathrooms, a beautiful kitchen with stainless steel appliances, and a fully finished basement with a game room, ideal for entertaining and a large family. This home had everything Victoria could want in a home for Dorothy. The only thing missing was laundry machines and furnishings. Victoria wanted that house, and Susanne was thrilled to be done with the hunt. Victoria had the realtor draw up a clause in the contract that stated if Dorothy returned to illegal drug use that she would lose the house.

The house was lovely but had nothing in it, so Victoria called Al, and he sent over his designers. He paid for all the furnishings, a new washer, and dryer for the laundry area.

Sunday arrived, and Victoria had to look at the house's final designs. She went in and was pleased with the furnishings and the color choices Al's designers had chosen. Everything was done, and now Victoria had to show Dorothy her surprise. Victoria called the whole family over to the house. They all stood in front of it, holding a big red ribbon wrapped around the entire building. Al picked up Dorothy and Diane from the hood. Once halfway to the new home, Al demanded they put blindfolds over their eyes. He helped them out of the car, facing them in the direction of the home with the family standing in front of it.

Al next ran over to be with the family and yelled out, "TAKE THE BLINDFOLDS OFF!"

Dorothy and Diane reached to pull the blindfolds down, adjusted their eyes, and saw the house with the whole family standing there. Dorothy didn't know whether she was crying about the house or the fact she had a family that had forgiven her and loved her. Diane too cried because she was part of this beautiful family that took her in as the family. Diane looked at it and thought that if people knew the secret about what made a family, they would be just like Dorothy's family. The two were overcome with tears and joy.

Victoria took Dorothy's hand and said, "Let me escort you to your new home."

Dorothy grabbed Victoria and kissed her, then took her hand. With Victoria beside her, Dorothy was first into the house, and the rest of the family followed behind them. Dorothy cried as she entered every room. She thanked Victoria and Al the whole way through. After the tour of the house, the family wanted food, and Ben wanted games. It was Sunday, and Victoria knew this would be her and Ben's last day in St. Louis, so she was ready for some more family time. They ordered pizza and Chinese food because Unique and Victoria didn't like pizza, and their figures were not to be altered. They all ate while enjoying the new house. Ben declared victory at the game of Monopoly he had played with Unique and Victoria. Al and Chuck discussed sports while watching a game on the new TV in the family area. Cindy couldn't part with Dorothy's new kitchen. She had thoughts of upgrading her kitchen at home. Sarah had already established herself in college living in the dorms, and Jasmine lived with Dorothy, so Sarah made jokes about moving back home. Jerry and Maury joined Chuck and Al's conversation on football. Jerry bragged about his skills in high school, and soon his college skills were to follow. Dorothy felt safe already in the new neighborhood.

Al asked to speak to Dorothy in the kitchen. Al clenched Dorothy's hand and said, "I just wanted to tell you how proud I am of you. I thought I would never see this day."

Dorothy remembered why she loved Al at one time and said, "Al, I never thought this day would come either. Now, that it's here, I want to thank you for everything. I promise to keep it together for myself, my kids, my extended family, and you."

Al got to the real point of calling Dorothy to the kitchen and said, "Dorothy there is something else; the house is fully paid for, but cannot be sold. It is yours as long as you don't return to the drugs. Now before you speak, I just want to say, I believe in you; this is just a clause."

Dorothy looked at Al with nothing but love. Al was looking for the old Dorothy to go off on him.

Dorothy reached for Al and hugged him, saying, "Al, I am just thrilled to be out of the hood. Living here makes it so much easier not to return to my bad old ways. Baby, thank you, and I understand your clause."

They both walked into the other room with the rest of the family with all smiles.

Unique caught sight of her mother, Dorothy and said, "Mother, I am proud of you, and I have never seen you this happy. I know what you must be thinking; at one time I thought it too."

Dorothy wasn't sure what Unique was about to say. Dorothy asked Unique, "Oh yeah? Tell me what I am thinking."

Unique said, "You think you don't deserve this; after all, you feel you have caused too much damage to your family. Am I right?"

Dorothy looked at Unique as if she was asking how this child knew this.

Unique continued, "I understand how you feel. I felt the same way at one time, but then I went to church one Sunday, and the preacher talked about Jesus' sacrifice, and how he did all he did for us. We knew we are sinful and didn't deserve his sacrifice and his grace, but he gave it to us anyway because he loves us—just like we all love you. Besides, we all have fallen short of perfection. I just want you to know Jesus loves you and that the gift he gave wasn't given because we're deserving, and that gift is so much better than any other gift we can give. Mother, do you believe in Him?"

Dorothy's eyes watered, and she saw Unique as a very spiritual, intelligent woman.

Dorothy took Unique's face in both her hands, kissed her, and said, "Yes, sweetheart, I believe. I thank you, baby, for your love and forgiveness. I always loved you. Unique, do you know that?"

Unique hugged Dorothy and said, "I have never doubted your love for me, Mother."

Ben walked over to them and took Unique's hand. He restarted the Monopoly game—he wanted to win again, but Victoria burst his bubble when she reminded him that it was getting late. Victoria knew she and Ben would have to fly out to Florida the next morning. Al, Chuck, Cindy, and Unique had to go to work early. Jerry, Maury, and Jasmine had to go to school the next morning, and Sarah and May had to go back to college; the two were to board a plane early the next morning. They all had another great family evening, this time at Dorothy's house, but life had

to go on, and they had to disperse and say goodbye. Dorothy and Diane had to clean out and pack up their old residence, and happily, move some essential things to the new one. Dorothy and Diane made the second vow—to hold things together and never return to the drugs. Their family inspired them to do something with their lives. Dorothy and Diane talked into the morning about their childhood dream of a house cleaning service. Diane always wanted to own her own business, and Dorothy always liked cleaning the homes of others, so together they thought of a way to better themselves. Diane agreed to go to college to get that business degree she had always wanted. Finally, around two thirty in the morning, Dorothy and Diane drifted off to sleep. Dorothy, Diane, and Jasmine had a good night's rest in their new home, in a safe neighborhood.

CHAPTER 23

BACK TO WORK

VICTORIA AND BEN GOT off the plane in Florida. Ben filled his lungs with crisp air and took in the sunny blue skies. He realizes his pleasure for such beauty was taken for granted when he was young. Now, he vows to enjoy every moment of what life has to offer.

Their driver arrived, and Victoria assumed Ben would be hungry so stopped by a local snack bar near the beach. Ben looked around and saw a bunch of beautiful women all around: walking, jogging, skating, and biking. Panicking, he said to Victoria, "I thought—I would only see things like this on TV. Why are all the ladies in this city so skinny?"

He instantly missed the thickness of Becky, and he viewed Becky as his own personal Betty Boop with ass.

He continued, "We should take them to the STL, and fatten them up."

After obtaining their food, they headed back to the car, got in, the driver shut the door, and Victoria laughed. "I'll make sure I stay out of the STL because I know I've gained a few pounds since my visit. All that soul food that I was eating went straight to my hips."

They were now at the door of Victoria's house—Ben walked into her residence with his eyes wide open, in amazement at her home.

Ben looked around and said, "Damn Sissy—you doing it big, huh. I like your place, and you got some exquisite taste. Are you sure you don't mind me staying with you? I mean this place is very fancy—I'm afraid I might break something."

Victoria laughed at Ben as she put her bags down next to his in the foyer and assured him, "No, I want you right here with me. It's been a long time since I had any company, plus we have lots of catching up to do. I want us to eat popcorn and watch movies together before we get back to life with my business and your college."

Victoria was so thrilled to have Ben there with her. She continued to talk as she made her way into the kitchen—Ben following behind her.

"I can't wait to meet this Becky that you keep mentioning. Let me give you a tour of the place."

Victoria went back to the foyer and grabbed Ben's bags. Ben laughed hard at Victoria trying to lift his bags. He prevented her from hurting her back and handled them for her. He followed her as she showed him to a huge bedroom, which she referred to as his quarters. It had its private lounging area with a mini bar set up, separate from the elegant bed and bathroom and plenty of closet space.

After Ben had dropped his bags off at his quarters, Victoria continued the tour.

"We have a housekeeper named Ms. Ruth—she has been with me for years. She will arrive early tomorrow."

Victoria continued to take Ben on the tour of her place, and suddenly Ben looked sick like he could vomit.

Victoria asked Ben in an anxious tone, "Ben—are you all right?"

Ben's eyes looked like droopy puppy dog eyes. He held his stomach and uttered, "I don't think so—Sissy. I had never been on a plane—I don't feel so hot."

Victoria stopped the tour and took him straight to his quarters. She wanted to watch movies and eat popcorn, but now she realized Ben needed to rest and get better because the next day meant work and college.

"I have something you can take for nausea," Victoria said. "I'll get it. What you are experiencing may be jet lag. Get your PJ's on so you can relax, and I'll bring you something for that nausea."

Ben looked at Victoria and still couldn't believe how friendly and loving she'd turned out to be. Ben grasped his bag and took his PJ's out and put them on. He pulled the covers back, noticed how delicate the comforter was, and thought to himself, 'I hope I can sleep in this bed. It may be too soft. And, why so many covers?'

Victoria knocked at Ben's door, walked into the room with a glass of water and pills for his nausea, and saw Ben tugging at the covers.

Victoria laughed and told Ben, "I know, it seems a bit much, doesn't it? But you can throw some blankets on the floor. Get some rest, Ben. I'm going to watch television in my quarters. I hope we both drift off to sleep soon. We got a big day tomorrow."

Victoria closed the door and went to the kitchen for popcorn. After that—she went to her bedroom for a movie. She slid "The First Knight," in the DVD player. It seemed too early to go to bed. Halfway through the film, as Lancelot grabbed the kiss he desperately wanted—Victoria was fast asleep. Ben felt better and went to sleep as well.

❧

It was an early bright Tuesday morning. Something about being back at home made Victoria yearn to get back to work. Ms. Ruth had already arrived and had breakfast on the table. Victoria had already called Ms. Ruth ahead of time to inform her that her brother would be her guest, but she did not tell Ms. Ruth what type of breakfast the young man would like, so Ms. Ruth did what she knew best. She cooked a bit of everything. The smell of that delicious cooking permeated the house. Victoria hurried to get herself together. She wanted to escort Ben to the breakfast table. After getting divafied, Victoria headed for Ben's quarters to see if he was awake and ready for breakfast. She knocked lightly on the door, and there was no answer, so she knocked again, but this time she called out his name simultaneously. Finally, she heard some movement.

"Come in, Sissy."

Victoria was surprised to see Ben had moved onto the floor.

He looked up at Victoria with those big eyes and said in a deep crackling voice, "I didn't sleep so well. I am sure this bed is supposed to make you sleep like a baby, but for me—right now, it's too soft, and the floor gave me more comfort. I have to get unused to the rocks I slept on in jail. Anyhow, do I smell bacon?"

Victoria smiled, "Yes, Ms. Ruth has breakfast ready. She's probably cooked everything. I had better watch it around her because I could put on the pounds. Ms. Ruth is an excellent cook, and she thinks I am too skinny. Well, I'd better let you get cleaned up."

Victoria headed for the door, and Ben said as she touched the doorknob, "I think the same as Ms. Ruth. You are a bit thin, Sissy."

Victoria briefly looked down at her body and replied, "Of course, I am a model—I get paid to be thin."

Ben shook his head and articulated, "I understand your career, but I will never understand why being thin is so popular. Nevertheless, I'll get my shower, and I'll be at breakfast soon."

She chuckled and headed for the kitchen to see what all Ms. Ruth had cooked.

With a bright morning smile, Victoria said, "Good morning, Ms. Ruth."

Victoria was happy to see her, and she gave Ms. Ruth a huge hug before taking a seat at the breakfast table. Ms. Ruth asked if Victoria wanted the paper. Victoria declined because she had her brother to talk with about the future work that was in line. Ben walked into the kitchen still semi-wet from showering. He had a towel wrapped around his neck for his long hair to drip on but with no shirt—displaying all his chest muscles and a pair of black dress slacks on. Ms. Ruth had her back to Victoria, filling a bowl with food at the stove and didn't see Ben as he walked in.

Victoria introduced them, "Ms. Ruth, this is my brother, Ben—."

Upon hearing Victoria, Ms. Ruth turned around from the stove with a towel and serving spoon in her hand. Ms. Ruth uttered, "Oh damn!" She dropped what was in her hand directly on the floor. Ms. Ruth's eyes were fixated on Ben.

Ben then began to apologize, "I am sorry for not being completely dressed. My hair is long and still wet from showering. Please, forgive me."

Ms. Ruth blushed and said, "Hello Ben, I must apologize. Victoria didn't tell me how good looking you were."

Ben blushed and flashed a breath-taking smile at Ms. Ruth.

Ms. Ruth addressed Victoria, "You can't do this to an old woman— you got to give me a warning or something. It's not every day I see a man that looks like this."

She then told Ben to take a seat and enjoy breakfast. She leaned over to get the towel and spoon off the floor but checked back to see if Ben was into older women. She silently said, to herself, 'I would if I could.' Victoria sniggered because she knew what Ms. Ruth was thinking. Victoria had to get back to work, and Ben had to check out the colleges, as well as start training on the job with Victoria.

In the middle of Ben sipping his juice, Victoria said, "Ben, I already called the college. You are scheduled for a tour today, and immediately after breakfast, your training to become my assistant starts. If you like the college, your classes will commence in the next semester, and that's considerably soon unless you plan on waiting until the next term. I think you will like the college. I also have in my office all the things you will need to begin your job as my assistant. We will get to that right after breakfast, so eat up."

Ben looked at Victoria and said, "Wow, you did all that already? I am going to have to step my game up or else I won't be able to keep up. I am ready for the challenge, Boss."

Victoria took a sip of her tea and said, "I sure hope so because we got lots of work to do. I hate to play catch up. One week out of the game is like one month. You can't imagine the amount of work we have to do. Oh— Ben, don't forget to find that information we talked about."

Ms. Ruth knew Victoria was speaking in code, so she excused herself from the kitchen.

Ben whispered, "I am all over it, Sissy. Do you think Ms. Ruth could have been the leak?"

Victoria quickly downplayed that thought, "No, she has been loyal all the time she's served. I am completely sure it wasn't her."

They finished their breakfast and headed straight for the office. Victoria was aggressive at training Ben in all of his duties. The call-book, the appointments, the arrangements for her travel, interview setups, clothing lines, makeup, and so much more. Ben hoped he could keep up.

Next, he looked at Victoria and said, "Sissy, I have one thing to wear, and I don't know if that is suitable for my tour at the college."

She already knew he was going to need clothes. Victoria smiled and said,

"Put that one thing on, and let's hurry to go shopping. We must head straight for the college after we find clothes."

Victoria and Ben did just that—at the store everything Ben tried on looked sexy on him and Victoria bought it all. While on tour at the college—Victoria's phone continued to ring, so she excused herself from taking care of things while Ben continued with the tour. Victoria had spoken to her agent, Diamarious Tucker. Victoria only talked business with him, never getting into talk about one another's personal lives, but she sometimes wondered whether he dated men or women.

Diamarious did sometimes caution Victoria about her private life—only to the extent that it blurred with business. He wasn't for Victoria's choice to let her brother assist her. He felt Ben wouldn't be able to keep up. Victoria agreed to find a suitable assistant as soon as she could, but meanwhile Ben was it.

Diamarious yielded, "Well, he will need some supplies. I will have them at your house in three hours. I have several things to set up for you, and I have the latest information on what you have been doing with your sister's show, and how it has affected you. So I will be there to introduce myself to your temporary assistant, bring what he needs and to give you updates."

Victoria agreed to be at her home with Ben when he arrived. The phone rang again. Victoria was so happy to see Unique's number when she looked at her cell.

She answered, "Hey Unique, what up?"

"Hey, big Sis—I know you are busy, but I had something to ask you. I wanted your opinion about the shops I'm setting up."

Victoria was so pleased that Unique would call her about her opinion. "Okay, I hope I can help."

Unique continued, "Do you think it's lame to name my shops after Jamie? Do you believe it's a sign I haven't moved on?"

Victoria lightly bit one side of her lip—thinking, while she hummed, then said, "I, believe that it's a splendid idea, but I feel that you need to incorporate your name into it also, so people will remember all the things you do as well. I think you already showed strength in moving on from the tragedy by continuing with your dreams."

Unique loved that she could call her sister up and get her opinion, "Thanks, I just needed the reassurance of my first choice. Love you so much—Vicky."

Victoria told Unique about the morning with Ms. Ruth, and they both laughed. Unique was quite busy herself and understood Victoria was too, so she hurried off the phone after thanking her for the advice.

Ben and Victoria chatted about the college almost the entire ride back. Ben loved the college and was excited to be starting classes in the fall.

"Hey, Sissy... Do you think I can get the medical books ahead of time? I know I've studied everything I could get my hands on when I was locked up, but it sure would be nice to see what's in the medical books out here. I want to be prepared. I'm excited can you tell?"

Victoria laughed, "You think... Yes, I know you're excited, and sure we will get those books asap."

"Thanks, Sissy."

Victoria tilted her head, "No problem but, I still think you should be a model too."

Ben gave her the eye implying, 'No' and he knew to start classes in the fall gave him some time to become the best assistant he could.

They had just arrived home—Ms. Ruth was starting their dinner, and Ben had gone to put his bags and books in his quarters—when the doorbell rang. Victoria had forgotten to tell Ben that her agent, Diamarious, was coming over. Victoria opened the door to view Diamarious' indeterminate facial expressions. With him—he had his assistant, tailor, hair stylist, makeup artist, and fashion designer, not to mention several bags.

Victoria asked as she invited the crew into her home, "Diamarious, what is all this for?"

Victoria had never seen her agent this devoted, and he was aware of that, so he explained, "This is what I feel we need right now. You don't look as if you have been taking care of your skin, hair or nothing, Girl."

Diamarious' phone rang, and he stopped talking with her. He gave Victoria a 'wait-a-minute' finger and then answered his phone. He told the private spa people to come on up to the house. They were in charge of her manicures, pedicures, massages, facials, etc. The dietician was with the spa people, and they told her to come on in also. After he had hung up the phone, the doorbell rang again. This time, Ms. Ruth went to the door, letting the spa personnel and the dietician into the residence. The dietician asked Ms. Ruth right away if she was the one who prepared Victoria's meals.

Ms. Ruth looked at all the confusion and said, "Yes."

The dietician then told Ms. Ruth to show her to the kitchen so that they could talk about nutrition. She wanted to know exactly what foods Victoria had been putting in her body.

Meanwhile, Diamarious had hung up his phone and continued to explain to Victoria what was happening, "I can tell you haven't been paying much attention to the media reports and all the things that involve you. I am here to get you ready for more interviews and shows. Your involvement with your sister's cause has heightened your career. We have almost every clothing line asking you to model their line. We have virtually every morning show wanting to hear about your family. I even had writers call, asking if they could write the story of you and your sister. I really would like you to think about telling your story to a writer I trust. Her name is April Floyd. I will give her contact information to your temporary assistant. To top that all off, I have taken calls from movie producers who want to make a film about your family. I am excited, but I need to know where you stand on all this."

Before Victoria could answer him, another knock came at her door. Ben heard all the commotion and walked into a whole crew of people. He was unsure of what was going on but knew he had to answer the door because Ms. Ruth and Victoria were all tied up in conversations. Ben walked past Victoria and Diamarious to respond to the door.

Diamarious stopped in the middle of talking to Victoria and asked, "Who in the hell is that? Is he a model or for you?"

Victoria said, "Diamarious, that's my brother Ben. And no, he's not a model."

Diamarious immediately said, "Well, damn—he should be."

She laughed and stated, "No, believe it or not; he wants to be a doctor, and there's no talking him out of that."

Ben had let in a man with a package for Diamarious, and he needed a signature. Ben pointed the man in the direction of Victoria and Diamarious. Diamarious signed his name, and the man gave Diamarious a small box. Ben was walking back to his quarters.

Before Ben could get away, Diamarious called out as if he had known Ben for years, "Hey, Ben—come over here."

Ben complied. He was unsure about who this man was and what role he had in Victoria's life, but he seemed cool.

Victoria apologized to Ben, "I'm sorry—I forgot to tell you about my agent, Diamarious."

Ben reached out to shake Diamarious' hand, and Diamarious put the box in the hands of Ben. Ben looked puzzled—not knowing what this meant. Ben opened the box, exposing keys.

Diamarious saw his expression and explained, "You are Victoria's assistant, aren't you? You won't be good at the job unless you have these. The technical person is over there, and he will show you how to use that state-of-the-art phone and headset. I am sure you know how to drive the car that's in the driveway. Go check it out."

Ben was in awe and went to see the technical personnel and the car right away.

Overwhelmed, Victoria said, "Look, Diamarious you are moving too fast—I can't just tell my story or talk about my family without them knowing and consenting—you know that. And what I did with my sister's show wasn't about me. Why are you buying stuff already? What if I don't get my family's consent to talk about our life…?"

Diamarious interrupted Victoria, "I am one of the most precise agents alive. I would never bring you an idea that doesn't have any backbone to it. I know you would never talk to anyone unless you had the okay from

your family. So I went to them first, and if I may say so, your father is an awesome attorney. Your family wants this for you, and they all gave you their blessings. In fact, Unique has agreed to go on some interviews with us. You were also right about her—she is one of a kind. She has offered to do all she could to help with the story. Oh, and as for the car and the phone, I didn't buy them."

Victoria looked shocked. "Who did? Diamarious, tell me, who?"

Diamarious smiled and said, "Your father—the awesome attorney paid for it—out of the fee he got from your lawsuits with the media's wrongful print about your family. They settled yesterday, and your dad called me to do this for him. He said he would fly down to finish the suit, and bring you your portion tomorrow. Victoria, you have what most people would love to have: Your family is great!"

Diamarious knew this was going to be a lot for her to take in. Also, he had work to do with Victoria. He snapped his fingers and ordered the spa personnel, hair stylist, makeup artist, and fashion designer to get to work on Victoria and her new assistant. As for Diamarious' tailor, he wanted him to measure Ben and make all his suits. Diamarious gave his deputy the okay to start agreeing to interviews, all that their schedules would and could allow. As the crew left Victoria's home that evening, Ms. Ruth looked as if she'd had class 101 with that nutritionist. Ben was tired from all the technical learning, and he had to adjust spa, hair, and nail treatments. He was working with a supermodel and apparently he had to represent her well. Victoria was put to bed for beauty sleep because the days ahead would be brutal for her.

CHAPTER 24

BACK IN THE HOOD OF THINGS

A NEW DAY AND a new adventure emerged for Ben as Victoria's personal assistant. Ms. Ruth hadn't come in and started on a nutritionally balanced breakfast for both Ben and Victoria yet.

Ben had been instructed to call Diamarious as soon as it was morning and before the sunrise, so he had gone to the study to make that call. He had many questions and found Diamarious to be more than helpful. Diamarious planned a meeting for the next day to make sure everyone else had the details on the new schedule and its layout. Over the phone, Diamarious had informed Ben that he should get Victoria's affairs in order because they would start the interview process right there in her hometown in Florida and move Victoria from state-to-state while the story of her family was hot and in the media airwaves. It was evident she would not return home for a while. Ben learned a lot in that brief phone call to Diamarious, but he had another call to make in the early morning hours.

Ben made a call to his secret lover: Becky. He needed to know if she could find out who leaked the information about Victoria to the magazine and media and he wanted to have the call done before Victoria got up.

Ben knew Becky was an early riser, because of her career so that it wouldn't be a problem calling her first thing in the morning. He cleared his throat before uttering a word. Everything about Becky gave Ben butterflies in his stomach—especially her voice. Ben's phone calls to Becky would always be brief because just the thought of her made him rise. Ben was missing his secret lover but knew he had to stay focused.

He whimpered at her sexy voice when she answered the phone.

"Hello, Ben. I have been waiting for your call. How is Florida?"

Becky knew Ben wasn't for the small talk. She never stopped trying to get him to communicate better.

Ben had an agenda, so he engaged in the small talk, "So far, I haven't seen much of it. We have been on the move non-stop since I've been here. I start college in the fall, and I'm my sister's personal assistant. It's just temporary until she finds someone she can trust. I sure miss you, boo."

Ben could tell from Becky's brief silence that she was missing him too.

"Ben, I miss you so much. I've been thinking—maybe, I should take a chance and say to hell with what this world thinks. I just want to quit this job so I—"

"Becky, my Becky Boop—I love you, and I know how you feel about me, but I would never want you to feel that you have to take that step to prove your love to me. No one can take what we have; it's real. From the moment we laid eyes on each other, it was real. You and I will keep our love to ourselves, as long as we need to. When the time is right, we will let the world in on the greatest love story ever to exist, next to the love of Jesus. You love me, babe?"

Becky's heart was now pounding, and her voice seemed winded as she said, "You know I do, and hearing your voice just makes it harder to be away from you. All I can think about right now is what would be going down right now if I had you here. When will we make that happen?"

Becky sounded anxious and had a compelling need to feel Ben deep inside her. She had a longing for his touch, and the sexy wet bites that he greeted her with every time he kissed her. She knew her thoughts were

getting out of control as she abruptly felt herself about to have an orgasm. She slightly bit one side of her lip as she quickly asked Ben to hold on the line for a second. She inserted one of her hands in her panties to make sure she hadn't let go.

Nevertheless, it was too late, and her fingers were very slippery from the release of her bodily fluids. Becky placed the phone back to her ear. As one hand held the phone to her ear and the other she couldn't stop from sliding back and forth under her panties.

Ben, also—felt the yearning to touch and kiss his long distant secret lover. He longed for the feeling of the tight grip of her insides, as her juices flowed down his shaft onto his testicles.

Ben knew Becky was losing control and decided to assist her mentally in finishing her orgasm, so he said, "Becky, boo—I understand how you feel. I will see you soon, but right now, I need you to lean back in your chair and close your eyes: Are they closed?"

"Yes, baby, they're closed." She replied.

"Now take your panties off." He demanded.

"They're off, Ben." She whispered.

"I am right there with you, boo, do you see me?" He asked.

"Yes," She replied.

"I am in between your legs, baby, so open them: wider. Yeah, wider— like that. Now, baby—let me in. I'm kissing those sexy-ass thighs of yours slowly. You like my bites, baby?" He asked.

"Um ah, yes…"

Ben then demanded, "Tell me you like them."

"I like it when you bite me, baby. Bite me harder."

Ben was excited to hear Becky talk dirty to him. He asked,

"Can I taste that wet pussy?"

"Um huh." She moaned.

Ben voice deepened, "You taste good, baby. Sweet, oh baby, I'm licking that clit just the way you like it. I want you to rub your clit harder for me—take two fingers and rub it. You know my strength in my body extends to my tongue, right? Rub it, baby—just how I lick it, and how I suck it. Yeah, my long tongue is in that sweet tasting pussy, now. Damn! Did you just give me a drink? Fuck! You taste good. Do it again."

Becky began to squirm in her chair, and she started panting with every breath she took. She stimulated herself as Ben unceasingly maximized her sex drive with his voice.

"You want this big massive dick, don't you?"

"Yes, I love that fat cock. You want these lips around it, don't you?"

Ben felt like Becky was taking over.

He whispered, "Yeah, baby—I want your lips on… Oh hmmm—Becky; suck this big, thick dick. Try to put all that in your mouth. I know it's hard—it's thick, but you can do it."

"I'm sucking the tip—Ben." Becky used slurping sounds—the same tones used when she does it for real. And, it took Ben to a new level of phone sex.

Ben was about to burst as he gripped his penis firmly from his pants and began rubbing it, imagining Becky sucking it.

Becky continued taunting him, "Grab my ass like you usually do, spread my cheeks. You see that cute ass hole—don't you?"

Ben uttered in a low tone, "Yes, It looks good."

"Do it! Ben, make me cream from my ass with your tongue first."

Ben lost all his words at this point, and could hardly breathe.

Becky knew he was a goner for sure, so she kept at him, "Touch and tease my asshole with the head of that huge dick. Can you see me cramming by the ass, baby?"

Ben manages to say, "Oh shit! Yeah…"

Becky needed to drive him home, "Put that cock inside me and let my pussy grip it. Push it harder, Ben—Oh, harder."

Becky rubbed herself into a wild orgasm and squealed as she pleasured herself.

Meanwhile, Victoria was now awake and went through the house looking for Ben. She heard his voice coming from the study and smiled with pride, knowing her brother was up early and hard at work at his new job as her assistant. She uttered to herself, 'Ben is up early, getting off to a good start.' She placed her thin fingers on the gold door handle, opening the door to the study. Instantly, she saw Ben was hard at work and getting off to a good start, but it had nothing to do with him being her assistant. Ben was releasing himself, with his dick in one hand and phone in the

other. Victoria couldn't move, she was in shock from two sights—what Ben was doing and the size of Ben's thick and long penis. Victoria had never seen anything like this before. Ben's semen was plentiful, and it burst across the room and down his hand from the shock of Victoria walking in.

Ben yelled, "Oh damn!"

Victoria stormed out of the room, breathless. Becky, still being on the phone, thought Ben was just excited, so she asked, "It was that good? I wish I could lick it up."

While putting himself up, he told Becky, "Baby, let me call you back."

Ben hurriedly hung up the phone, rushed to the nearest restroom to clean himself and then quickly tried to address Victoria with apologies, "Victoria—please forgive me. I am very sorry."

Victoria was still just looking at him—not saying a word, so Ben knew she was shaken up. He continued to try and get a reaction from her and said, "Sissy—please say something, I am sorry. I just got too involved on the phone with Becky. To disrespect, you and your home weren't my intentions. Sissy, would you please talk to me?"

Victoria blinked, looked at Ben, and screamed, "What the fuck, Ben? My study is not your quarters! How...? Why...? What were you thinking? I have never been so humiliated in my life! I've got to have this area disinfected. My study, Ben! My study has your massive fluid all over the damn place! Damn it! Ben! Go clean yourself up, with bleach."

Ben looked very shocked and yipped, "With bleach?"

Ben returned to his quarters and instantly remembered how it felt to be the little brother again, with sisters who always corrected him, and he was profoundly disappointed in himself. He started the shower, and as he cleansed his body, he thought of leaving Victoria's home and starting his life with Becky. Ms. Ruth had come in upon the yelling and Victoria stomping through the house. Ms. Ruth knew the two would have it out. It was a natural thing for brothers and sisters to argue, but this was early, even for Victoria.

Ms. Ruth asked, "What is going on, Victoria?"

Victoria didn't want to say because of the nature of the argument, so she said, "It's personal, Ms. Ruth."

Ms. Ruth gave Victoria a look like the one a grandmother does to tell her grandchildren they ought to know better. Ms. Ruth said, "Look, I am like family, and I'm old, so there's nothing that I haven't heard before—talk to me."

Victoria told Ms. Ruth the details of her morning discovery, and then Ms. Ruth helped Victoria to see things differently and said, "Victoria, you are just getting the sense of what family is all about. It's not just the good and bad moments. It's the shocking moments as well. This one is a shocker. That's your brother and, no matter what—you must be there for him because of where he's just come from—jail. All it takes is something this small to make him give up. Just think, this can cause him not to become that doctor, your assistant, your friend, and your family. You know you don't want that. And besides, Ben had come accustomed to phone sex with whoever that was on the phone with him. It will take more than a few days to get that out, literally." Ms. Ruth chuckled.

Victoria had to admit she didn't want to repeat her past. She thanked Ms. Ruth for the talk, went to Ben's quarters, and knocked on the door.

Ben answered, "Come in—It's open."

Victoria opened the door slowly. Ben had his bag opened on the bed and was putting clothes in it. Victoria thought about what Ms. Ruth had just said.

She took the shirt Ben had placed in the bag back out and asked, "Ben, what are you doing? Little brother—we are going to fight at times—you do know this, right? It doesn't mean—my love for you has changed. It doesn't mean—I don't want you around. I need you just as much as you need me. Please, don't leave me."

Ben now was in shock and had to ask, "Why do you feel you need me? I don't want to disappoint you, Victoria."

Victoria sat on the bed with her head down and said, "Ben, I need you because you are my family, and I need to continue to learn how it feels to have a family. You know, the ups, the downs, and even the shockers."

Victoria looked at Ben with a smirk and laughed. Ben sat next to her on the bed and asked, "Sissy—please don't tell anyone about this shocker, okay?"

Victoria laughed again and joked, "I don't know, this might be one of those, must tell tales—at the family reunion. I'll call it the large-and-in-charge tale."

Victoria laughed harder as she got off the bed and stood up.

Ben said, "You wouldn't."

He pulled her by the waist back to the bed, tickling her. Laughter filled the room, and then Ms. Ruth yelled, "Breakfast…!"

ೋ

Several weeks had passed, and Diamarious hauled Victoria and Ben around to every interview he could fit in within each city they visited. Ms. Ruth had decided to stick with Victoria on the road until she got the extra pounds off and to keep her in touch with a daily workout routine. Ben had studied up on personal assistants. He wanted to make up for what he had done in Victoria's office, and he was profoundly thankful for all she had done for him. Astonished with how fast Ben caught on, Victoria saw that not only was he proficient and aggressive, and he had a great sense of the fashion world. Diamarious was aware of Ben's talents as an assistant. He tried his best to get Ben to stay on full-time.

Additionally, he thought—Ben was marketing material for modeling. Ben continued to stick to his love for the medical world. Becoming a doctor, next to Becky, was all he thought about and wanted.

Victoria's career had taken them to the city of Atlanta. When they arrived at their hotel suite, Ben could see Victoria was tired. He knew he had to tell her about the conversation he'd had with Becky earlier, but he decided to let her rest that evening.

The next morning, after breakfast, Victoria went to the gym to work out. Ben's conversation with Becky had confirmed who had leaked the story about Victoria's family. Ben wasn't surprised to know it was Victoria's last personal assistant. He was relieved that it wasn't Ms. Ruth or anyone presently close to Victoria. Victoria walked in the hotel with a blue sweat suit, running shoes, no earrings and with her hair pulled back in a ponytail. Ben looked at her as she opened the doors. After entering, Victoria caught the look and instantly stopped wiping her sweat with her towel.

She anxiously asked, "What is it, Ben?"

Ben joked first, "Well, you have dressed appropriately for what I am about to tell you."

Victoria's eyes widened, "No one is here but us, so tell me what's up."

Ben stood up from the edge of the sofa arm and said, "Becky called me and told me who it was that leaked the information to the magazine representative."

Victoria anxiously yelled, "WHO?"

"It was your ex-assistant, Brenda. She privately recorded you and sent in the recording. There is something else — the person who helped with your father's case against the media was this guy named Jason—said to be Brenda's ex-boyfriend."

Victoria's facial demeanor changed into a hardcore thug appearance as she wrapped her mind around all Ben had said, "That means my dad knew who betrayed me. Jason must have decided to do the right thing. I told that bitch if I ever found out for sure it was her I was going to beat her skinny-cow ass! And, I never break a promise."

After breakfast, Ms. Ruth had gone out to get more food items to prepare their healthy meals. Just as she entered the front door, Victoria stormed out the front room into her bedroom suite.

Ms. Ruth looked over at Ben with bags still in her arms. "Ben, what is going on? Before you say, 'Nothing,' Boy, you better speak nothing but the truth to me."

Ben took the bags out of Ms. Ruth's hands with a fearful look on his face, and they headed for the kitchen. Once the sacks were placed on the counter, Ms. Ruth said, "I'm ready. What just happened?"

Ben knew he couldn't lie to Ms. Ruth.

"I told Victoria who leaked the story about our family."

Ms. Ruth covered her mouth, then spoke, "We already knew who did that. We decided it was best for Victoria to move on without knowing because that girl doesn't think when she gets angry. She doesn't care what she will lose when she's furious, Ben—. It's our job to keep her from getting that way because she has a lot to lose."

Ms. Ruth sounded very troubled after hearing what Ben said and asked, "How did you find out?"

Ben knew that question was coming and said, "No matter what—I can't tell you that, but I can tell you an investigator was used, so the information is accurate."

Ms. Ruth and Ben heard the front door slam as they were talking. They both ran to the front, calling Victoria's name. Ben checked the bedroom and, seconds later, moved back to the front room with a look of fear in his eyes and said, "She's not in here; she left. Where would she go here, in Atlanta?"

Ms. Ruth's eyes lit up. She remembered Brenda lived in Atlanta.

"Brenda lives in this city!"

Ms. Ruth grabbed the phone and called Al. Ben looked up the address to Brenda's home. He grabbed his cell phone and called a cab to take him to the location. Ms. Ruth got no answer from Al. Therefore, she left a detailed message; in the meantime, Ben got in a cab, headed to the location, and thought, 'What have I done? I believed Victoria was sound in mind. I didn't know she would go out like that. Her ass is just as crazy as the rest of us.'

Ben told the cab driver, "Hurry up, man, get me there!"

Ben tried to call Victoria's phone—there was no answer, so he called again. After the third attempt, he finally got an answer, but it was Ms. Ruth. Victoria had left her phone at the hotel. Then Ben started thinking like her assistant and called her driver to see if she was in the car.

"Hey Mike, this is Ben, Victoria's assistant, and brother. I am looking for Victoria. Did you drive her and is she with you now? Wait, do not say it aloud—just say—yes or no."

Mike said, "Yes."

Ben continued, "Okay—Mike. I need you to stall her mission. Drive her around until it looks as if she is calm. If she gets irritated with you, go ahead and take her where she asked you to take her. Can you do that? Please, Mike—just say, yes or no."

Mike said, "Yes."

Ben asked Mike to say yes or no in confirming the address of Brenda. Mike confirmed again with a simple, 'Yes.'

Ben called Ms. Ruth, keeping her informed. In the intervening time, Victoria had gotten more upset with her driver.

"Mike didn't we just go this way? Get me to that address right now, damn it! Now, Mike!"

Mike headed straight for Brenda's house with no more stalling. Al got Ms. Ruth's message and purchased a flight to Atlanta. Victoria finally arrived at Brenda's home—she got out of the car, shut the door, and told Mike he could leave. However, instead of going; Mike parked around the corner and called to see how far away Ben was from that address. Ben felt helpless because he was hung up in traffic. Mike decided to stay parked until Ben got there. He, too—had never seen Victoria like this. Mike was very nervous—thinking about what could happen. After seeing Mike drive off, Victoria turned her attention to Brenda's home and walked up the steps slowly, filled with anger. There was not one rational thought going through her mind. She just wanted to beat Brenda's ass. She knocked on the door as hard as she could. Brenda pulled the curtain back to look out her front door window and saw Victoria's face. Instantly Brenda remembered what Victoria had said about kicking her ass if she ever found out it was her who leaked the information.

Brenda decided not to open the door but to talk through the door. "Why are you here, Victoria?"

Victoria knew she couldn't kick her ass unless she could get in— therefore, she tried out her acting skills.

"I am here in Atlanta on business. I thought about you, and I wanted to let you know that I know about you leaking the story to the press. I talked with Jason, and he told me why you did it. I wanted to let you know I understand and that I am sorry too."

Brenda's heart melted as soon as Victoria said Jason's name. That would always be her weak spot.

Victoria continued, "Brenda, I don't like talking through doors. Please—open up so we can talk."

Brenda glanced at Victoria, and she looked sincere. Brenda unlocked her door and said, 'Come on in.' Victoria walked in, and as soon as Brenda sealed the door, Victoria balled up her fist and swung as hard as she could—striking Brenda in the jaw. Brenda instantly grabbed her jaw and ran into the front room of her shanty house. Victoria moved close

behind her—talking and shadowing until Brenda's body swathed on her sofa, and Victoria stood erect over her.

Victoria yelled, "You bitch! You pretended to be my friend! You recorded our conversations! I did so much for your ungrateful ass. That's why Jason left you."

As Victoria balled her fist up to strike Brenda again, a small cry came from the next room, stopping Victoria in her tracks—just as a deer stops when he thinks he's being hunted.

Hearing her baby cry in the next room, Brenda pleaded with Victoria crying, "Please, Victoria—I deserve all this, and I am sorry. Please, don't hurt me, because I live for my baby now. I only care about her."

Victoria's anger high calmed down at the mention of a baby girl. She was no longer angry with Brenda. Now, she was mad at herself because of her actions. Victoria grasped Brenda's hand in her own—straightening her up on the sofa.

With a shell-shocked expression, she told Brenda, "I am sorry, Brenda. Will you please forgive me? I can't believe what I just did."

Brenda sat up—holding her jaw and said, "I can believe it. You have always been very feisty. I forgive you only if you will truly forgive me."

Victoria looked at Brenda—remembering all the great times and smiled, shook her hand and said, "That's a deal. When did you have a baby? Is she Jason's baby? Does he know?"

Brenda smiled as she stood up and said, "You're the same ole' chatter mouth—aren't you? Ask me one question at a time, girl. She's only four weeks old. No, she is not Jason's baby. Oh, I don't think he was able to have children because you know we were humping like rabbits, and we didn't use protection all the time, but I never got pregnant. When he left me, I felt so bad about all the things I had done to you, Jason, and my family. My family was at their wit's end. I wouldn't eat or sleep and screamed uncontrollably, so they put me in the hospital for depression. That is where I met a male nurse named Emanuel Rite. I made out with him and ended up getting pregnant, but he claimed she wasn't his— probably because he knew he wasn't supposed to have relations with the patients. I got better and stayed away from mental hospitals. So it's just my baby and me now. Do you want to see her?"

Victoria's face lit up with joy—she secretly loved the idea of having children but didn't want to sacrifice her career and her body for them. Victoria smiled, and said, "I sure do."

Brenda went to the nursery and brought out little Free, placing her in the arms of her Victoria. She was beautiful, about nine pounds with a head full of hair. Her eyes were gray looking, and her skin was a shimmery white color. The two were sitting on the sofa, enchanted with little Free when Ben knocked at Brenda's door. Victoria remembered her family—they must be frantic at that moment.

Brenda looked out the curtain and yelled to Victoria in the next room, "Girl, it's some fine-ass guy on my porch."

Victoria stood up with the baby and said, "Oh girl, that's my brother, Ben. Can you let him in?"

"Hell, yes! He can come in."

Victoria laughed, "Same ole' Brenda…."

Brenda opened the door. Ben stepped in, out of breath and asked, "Is everything all right here?"

Ben asked this before taking notice of his sister holding a baby. Brenda sensed Ben's need to chat with Victoria, so she took little Free from Victoria's arms and took her back to the nursery.

Once Brenda was out of sight—Ben yelled at Victoria, "You may be the oldest, but not today. You are acting insane. Did you put your hands on her or is the bruise on her face old?"

Victoria held her head down, "I hit her one time, but then I stopped because the baby started crying. She said it's okay and that she would forgive me."

"Let me guess, you believed her?"

Victoria said, "Yes, I think she was for real about forgiving me."

Ben let out a sigh. "No wonder God brought me into your life. You can't trust people's words anymore—Victoria. Especially, individuals who have a betrayal track record like Brenda. I will take care of this. You get in the car. Mike is out there waiting for you, and I'm not done talking to you about this. We will finish this later."

Victoria walked to the car, realizing Ben just made her feel the same way she usually feels when her dad disciplines her. Brenda stayed in the back room, but she could clearly hear what Ben said, and Ben knew it.

Ben called out to her, "Brenda—."

Brenda walked out from the back room after closing the door to the nursery slowly.

Ben had no trust in Brenda. He opened the front door wide so Mike and Victoria could view him talking with Brenda.

"Brenda, I don't beat around the bush when talking, so forgive me if I seem too blunt. After what you've done to my sister—I don't trust you. Victoria is a very forgiving person and a bit naïve. I'm in her life now to make sure no one takes advantage of her—never again. Now, she said you were going to forgive her about the punch in the jaw. Is that right?"

Brenda could hardly get past Ben's gripping appearance, but his words penetrated through her like a two-edged sword and felt very sharp when he said that she was untrustworthy. She realized that even if Victoria forgave her no one else around her would ever trust her again. She wanted to start on the right track for her child.

Brenda tilted her head toward the floor. "I deserved this. My record is evidence that I can't be trusted. I know this, but I do mean it when I say I will forget about Victoria striking me. How can I prove it?"

Ben said, "It's simple—put it in writing."

Ben ran to the car, opened his briefcase, got out his writing pad and pen, and wrote out a quick statement. He asked Mike to be a witness to the note—he signed it. He then ran back to the house to get Brenda's signature. He handed the paper over to Brenda, and she signed it after he.

Ben then said to Brenda, "Thank you. Just so you will know it, it is illegal to record someone without their knowledge of it. I will make sure Victoria doesn't file suit against you for doing that in the past. I also want you to sign another statement—saying that we won't bring a lawsuit against you for that."

Ben noticed the sadness in her eyes as she signed.

"Brenda, hold on for a little while—I am sure Victoria will be your friend again."

Brenda said, "I hope so, Ben. She was the only one I ever had."

Ben nodded, "Thanks again, Brenda."

Ben walked out, and Brenda shut the door behind him.

Victoria was silent during the ride back to the hotel. Ben had gotten on the phone and arranged for Al not to board the airplane, and for Ms. Ruth to have food ready. He also called the spa crew to do some work on Victoria when they got back to the hotel. They had several appointments the next day, and she had lots of work to do.

As soon as they walked through the door at their hotel, Victoria plopped down on the loveseat.

"Do I need to tell you what it was like in jail?" Ben asked, his voice milder now. "Moreover, how I let my emotions put me in a situation that I couldn't get my ass out? Look around, Victoria—you could have lost everything you have worked hard for tonight because you allowed your emotions to tell you what to do. Your family would only be able to see you through bars. You would have to use the nastiest toilets imaginable. Do I need to say more?"

Victoria cringed, "No more needed. I got it—thanks for being there for me."

Ben kissed her on the forehead, "No problem, call your dad to smooth things over with him. Ms. Ruth is in need of an apology too. I need you to eat because the crew will be here soon to get you prepared for tomorrow."

Victoria did everything Ben said. She was thankful to have him in her life again.

CHAPTER 25

UNIQUE ON THE RISE

Back home in St. Louis, Unique had worked the hardest she'd ever worked—after her show. The business had taken off fast, and she sometimes she found it hard to keep up with all the orders coming in daily. It was suggested by Cindy, Naomi, and Pat to Unique to hire more help. Once she had thought of her storefront's name—Naomi, and Pat felt all other things would fall into place for Unique. It was Saturday—during the late fall season when Unique suddenly remembered the times she and Jamie would play with their initials—U & J. They designed it on papers and Unique had them. She found their childhood art! She thought of using its symbols on the clothing line and as the storefronts' name.

Unique shouted out as she exited her room to the study,

"That's it! I got it! The U&J Designer & Accessory Gear…"

She started up her personal computer. She had to get going on the graphic design for the newly found name and scan their childhood

art. Excitement flooded throughout her, and she knew she was on to something.

Unique was in a very crowded room with fabric, sewing machines, paper, and books. She would always bump into something trying to get to something else in that small space. She and her family had outgrown that home, and it was time for a new one.

Unique was a bit torn about the idea of leaving the only home she had ever known, but she was starting to realize it was time to move on. Though this home had many memories of her sister Jamie, she needed more space to get her and Jamie's dream off the ground. Unique resolved to bring it up to her family though she had no idea how her mom and dad would react to the suggestion.

Cindy came in from her garden; Unique was at the kitchen table drinking her favorite—apple juice.

Taking off her gardening gloves, Cindy gave Unique a mothering look and said, "Okay, Unique—what is it?"

Unique smiled. Her mom knew her too well.

"Mom—I love this house, and I know we have lots of good memories here, but I have every spot in this house covered with my things. It's just not enough space. I know I should be moving on my own, but I am just not ready for that."

Cindy walked over to the sink and washed her hands. She paused for a few minutes with her back turned to Unique. Of course, this made Unique a little uneasy as she waited for her mom's response.

Cindy turned to eye Unique and said, "I haven't even entertained the thought that you would one day leave home. Honey—I am not ready for that. As far as moving, I thought you would never ask. I didn't bring it up because I didn't want you to feel we were rushing anything, and I know how you feel about the memories of Jamie here. I was hoping you would want to move one day. You are correct; it is too tight with all your belongings. This location is not so good anymore because everyone knows you stay here. The media, neighbors, and the perverts can easily harm us—free access. Therefore, for safety reasons, I would also like to move. Jerry is expected to be gone to college soon, so I think we should tell your dad about this, and let's see what he says."

Unique was excited and called Victoria, who was in Chicago being prepped to go onto the set for her interview when her phone rang.

Before Victoria had a chance to say hello, Unique said,

"Victoria, I know you're busy, but I want you to get in touch with the agent that found Dorothy her house. I think we are ready to move. We need more space; much larger than what we are dealing with now, and my mom thinks it's unsafe living here."

Victoria gave her cast a wait-a-minute finger and continued her call with Unique. She said, "That's good news, Unique. I'll have my assistant—Ben to call you with that number, right-a-way."

Unique chuckled at Victoria—then said, "Ben must be doing a great job, huh. Well, I'd better let you get back to business. Oh, and Victoria, I love you."

Victoria was so happy to hear her sister remind her of the love she possessed for her and replied, "I love you too. I'll chat with you later."

After disconnecting the call—Unique went right back to her computer to start looking at properties. Later that evening, Chuck walked through the door and instantly started saying sexy things to Cindy. Unique heard his comments from the next room.

She leaned back in her chair—looking into the next room at her parents and said, "This is another reason moving to a larger home would be best. I really, don't need to hear all that."

Cindy started teasing Unique, "One day, we may be hearing you talk that way to someone."

Unique was at unease with where that conversation was going. "It won't be too soon. So, don't be knocking on wood for me, yet."

They laughed while Unique picked up her laptop to go into her bedroom, but Chuck stopped her with a gentle tug and a surprised look and asked, "You want to move?"

Unique grinned, "Yeah Dad—this place has great memories, but we have outgrown it, and I think it's time to move on—don't you?"

Chuck looked at Unique. She continued to impress him with her strength. After gathering his thoughts, he said, "Wow, sweetheart. Moving is an excellent idea—you got my vote; let's do it."

Unique smiled with the knowledge of having approval from both her parents.

She continued, "I'm getting in touch with the agent that Victoria used to find Dorothy's house. I also wanted to see if she could help me find properties for my shops. Dad! You know, what?" Without allowing Chuck to respond Unique continued. "I thought of a name for my shops. Are you ready?"

Chuck and Cindy were arm-in-arm, and they both said at the same time, "Yes."

Unique continued, "What do you think about U&J Designer & Accessory Gear?"

Cindy said, "I like it!"

"It's catchy and easy to remember. I think it would work," said Chuck.

Unique smiled ear to ear with gratification, "Okay, U&J it is."

She went upstairs to her room to do more work and search for houses over the web.

୧୬

The next day, Ben called to give Unique the number to the realtor and to tease her about never being able to win in Monopoly. Unique teased back about how he was never able to beat her in UNO. They quickly ended the call so Unique could get a move on finding properties for her shops throughout the Metro area. She had carefully selected four prime locations for her shops. That following evening, she gave Susanne Jenkins a call, and they set up a meeting for the next morning. While Unique was on the phone—she became irritated by the noise going on in the background while she tried setting up her appointments.

After hanging up her call with Ms. Jenkins—she addressed Maury and Jerry, "You two get out of this area when I am on the phone. So Jerry, why are you home early? Don't you have practice or something?"

Jerry irritated his sister even more—bothering her hair.

"I have no practice today or tomorrow. I get to torture you for two days."

Unique was officially irritated and snatching Jerry's hand away from her head. She roared, "Oh, no you're not! I have work to do. I'm already behind, and, besides—where is that girl you believed likes you; what was her name?"

Now, Jerry felt crossed, "You must be referring to Jessica. I thought I told you about her."

Unique looked mystified and declared, "No, Jerry. I don't remember you telling me anything. You know—I am continually making sure I listen when it comes to the ladies. Tell me what happened,"

Jerry hunched his shoulders and articulated what happened. He explained, "Unique, it's like this—I am torn between two loves, but I know I can't give my all to them both—so I'm forced to choose which one I'm going to love."

Unique interfered, "Whoa, you have two jars of honey after you—at the same time?"

Jerry swiftly struck down Unique's thought, "Unique, I am speaking about girls and football. I like Jessica, and when I am around her—I get these goosebumps. I start to stutter my words, and sometimes I can't speak. I know she feels the same for me. However, I know if I got on the football field—she'd be the only thing on my mind, so if I love football, I feel—I can't love her too. Plus, I have to be fully in the game, or I can injure myself for life, and I'm not trying to be another statistic on that front. I think I just made my mind up. I'm going to let the ladies go until I reach my full potential in football."

Unique had to admit Jerry wasn't just another cute guy; he was a smart person as well.

"It sounds like you know what you have to do. If Jessica is for you, then she'll be available when you're ready."

Jerry appreciated the reassurance from his sister about girls.

"Unique," Jerry added, "I know you have lots to do, but Maury and I were thinking that maybe you could take a little time to spend with us. I am going off to college soon, and I'm going to miss being at home and talking to you. I know I'll be homesick."

Unique closed her phone and laptop and said, "You know what? You're right; let's get out and do something. Did Mom and Dad tell you that I'll start looking for a new house for us tomorrow?"

Jerry appeared shocked, but happy, "No, they didn't mention it yet. It's about time—this place has become too small with all your junk."

Unique laughed and agreed, "You're right about that. You have tomorrow off, so why don't you go with us to search for our new home? However, today, let's go to a movie."

Jerry frowned, "I am down for looking for a house tomorrow, but not a movie. I don't like to sit for hours—looking at someone else's stories. How about we go bowling?"

Unique suggested, "How about we ask Maury, and whatever he decides, we'll do."

Jerry agreed, and they both ran out of the room calling for Maury to see what he wanted to do. They found him in the kitchen, eating again. After putting the question to him—he said, "I want to go swimming."

Jerry and Unique gazed at each other and said, "Swimming it is—let's go swimming."

Unique then said, "I forgot! What about my hair?"

"Oh well," she continued—after seeing Maury's face, "It's time for a new look anyway."

They packed the swimming gear, and as they left—Unique gave her parents an expression—as if she knew, having them all away at the same time was what their parents wanted, and she understood that they needed some quality time alone.

⁊

Early the next day—Susanne called Unique. Unique got the family up and told them the house hunt would start at six thirty. Everyone asked Unique the obvious question: "Why are we starting so early?"

"I need us to find one and move on to finding properties for my shops," she explained to them. "Plus, I want us to find one together before Jerry goes to college. So come on, let's do this."

Everyone was ready and had eaten breakfast when Susanne showed up with copies of every property they were to observe for the entire family. They viewed each page in the car as they were on the move. Unique had a

printed page for the agent of all the things they wanted in their new home and the max amount they could afford. The new house was to have an open concept, with front and rear foyers, a living room, a dining room, a study area with internet access, and a lower level or finished basement for Unique. The area for Unique would serve as her work area—internet access throughout the home was necessary, a green room for Cindy's garden and a work garage or space for Chuck. Jerry and Maury wanted a basketball hoop, and the house needed to be sitting on at least ten acres of land. A curved driveway and four car garages were a necessity as well. However, the price Unique thought she could get all this for was entirely out of sorts with Susanne.

Susanne boldly stated in the car, "Unique, your list doesn't add up to the price. What you are asking for in a home may cost you double of what your budget allows."

Unique replied, "Okay, Susanne—find us a home that we all like, and we'll talk about the price. Our chief objective is to find a house that feels like home."

Cindy and Chuck gazed at each other because they were used to modest living, and they were hoping Unique wasn't over her head. However, they weren't confident that they should jump in either. Unique was indeed in charge. Susanne took them to two houses, and they all said it didn't feel like home for one reason or the other. Then Susanne got a call from her office stating that a home she thought was sold hadn't gone through and was back on the market.

Susanne instantly got excited and said, "I think I just found your home."

She swiftly turned her truck around and headed for the property. This house had a previous contract on it that hadn't gone through, so the seller was willing to drop the price dramatically because of the financial burden of keeping it. Every day the house was on the market; cost the owner money. It was a must-sell situation: Susanne knew this, and because she wanted the continued business of Unique's family, she was willing to work hard getting the price down. As soon as they pulled up into the driveway, the Woods' felt at home. This home had private gates before entering—this is something Cindy had wanted but did not mention. Beautiful hills

and greenery filled the landscape as they opened the gates. The curved driveway up to the front entrance was great. The Woods' was ready to buy this home because it had all the space they needed and more—plus they also felt completely at home with the place. Chuck had gotten very excited thinking about how lovely the family barbecues' would be if this were their home. They had acres of property to play a real game of football. Jerry always looked forward to the family football league. Maury was excited to see a pool! He loved to swim, and now he could do it at home.

They all got excited and looked at Susanne, saying, "This is it! We know this home is for us."

Unique took Susanne in the next room to ask its price. She didn't want to overwhelm her parents with worry that they couldn't afford the home.

Susanne smiled big and said, "This home is only one hundred thousand over your budget—unlike spending twice your budget as I thought earlier. This home was three times your budget, but they must sell it. So what do you say?"

Unique wanted it all—the house and her four stores, but she knew doing so could put her in financial trouble, so she told Susanne, "I'll take this home, and I'll adjust how many stores I'll open. Maybe, instead of opening four stores, I'll start with two. I can bring in the income, and then I'll open more. I'd like you to handle the selling of my parents current home, and that income helps us as well. I'll always call on you as my agent, so don't worry about the sales. Continue to get us what we want, and you'll always be the agent for my entire family."

Susanne said, "I am delighted to have served your family. Let's get the paperwork done and get you guys into your new home."

❧

They all piled into the truck and headed for Susanne's office. Unique didn't want a large mortgage, so she paid most of the home off. Unique had secured four contracts with major companies, but she hadn't told the family yet. Sitting on more money than anyone knew about made Unique a shrewd businesswoman.

Unique needed all their things moved from the old home into the new home. She asked her parents to take on the task.

Cindy called a moving service and schedule pick up and drop off. She and Maury worked tirelessly to pack the majority of the contents in the home. The excitement of the new home was their drive.

Chuck called Al for the team of home designers whom he used to service Dorothy's home. Chuck wanted to make sure they threw out everything that wasn't needed in the new how and replaced with new furnishings to make the new place look fabulous and serve them all with the comforts of home.

Jerry had to pack up some of his things for college, and the rest of his things went to the new home.

It was moving day and Jerry as well as Chuck, unitedly directed the move. Cindy and Maury unpacked as it came in.

Unique was busy trying to find properties for her new stores while continuing to make and design her clothing lines. She had a deep need for an assistant as well. She set up interviews for that position, as well as staff positions for her stores. She had to get her life settled in a hurry—after all, she was under some major contracts.

Finally, when it was time to go home—she was able to go to the new home. Jerry only spent one night in his new house. The next morning, Jerry had to go to the airport to college.

"Go get 'em, Tiger," Chuck said, giving his son a manly hug.

Maury was sad to see his brother leave—being a couple of year behind Jerry. Maury knew he was next in line for college, so he told himself not to show any tears. Cindy and Unique—being the emotional females they were—crying was inedible as they waved farewell.

❧

Several months had passed—Unique's business was quickly on the rise, and so were her charitable funds. Unique's show had made millions in donations. Her success was emanating. The more she went on talk shows, and interviews with Victoria, the more Hollywood pressed her for contracts and putting their money where their mouth was profound.

CHAPTER 26

LOVE IN THE AIR

MOVED BY UNIQUE—VICTORIA STRIVED to improve in the way of allowing personal bonding. In every interview, Victoria thanked Unique for being the greatest sister ever. She felt Unique had helped her to see and feel what life was about and she no longer felt the need to fear personal relationships outside her immediate circle.

Victoria's career had now taken her to Charlotte, North Carolina. Ben—as her assistant—was with her but Ms. Ruth had gone home to rest. Victoria was to do a photoshoot on each of the ten best beaches in North Carolina. This job was tremendous, and strenuous—due to them needing all the shots taken in four days, but Victoria had three extra days in North Carolina before her next job. Ben had already made plans to hook up with Becky for his extra three days there. Victoria had to work with photographers whom she'd never worked with before. All but one intensified the urgency of getting the shot.

Victoria wanted a break and did not feel at ease asking the director, and so she shouted out to the photographer who gave her the impression that he was a kind and compassionate person, "Hey, you!"

He pointed to himself asking if she was referring to him, "Who me?"

Victoria nodded, 'yes.' All-the-while, using hand gesturing for him to come to her.

He approached Victoria and said, "My name is Dave."

Once Dave got close to her she couldn't help but notice how good he smelled, his dark gray eyes, well-maintained haircut, his tall and slender cut body, and overall sex appeal.

She spoke as if her tongue thickened and she had slightly paralyzed language. "Yes, Dave... I was hoping... maybe, I can... you see—I..."

Dave smiled and inquired, "Victoria, do you need a small break?"

Victoria sighed, "Yes, please—Dave."

Dave looked her in the eyes, "Ten minutes—okay? I'll deal with the director and tell him my equipment need maintenance or something. Ten minutes, only..."

Dave took a large beach towel, wrapped it around Victoria, and simultaneously yelled aloud, "We are taking ten."

He walked her off the set and showed her to the restroom. Victoria almost could not take her eyes off Dave, and he had the same issue. After completing the job, it had gotten a bit dark. The entire crew was done and packing up. Ben had said a farewell to his sister and told her that Becky had already flown in, so he was out for the next three nights.

Dave strolled over to Victoria and plainly said, "I hope this doesn't sound strange, but I have been searching for the feeling you give me all my life. I started to believe it didn't exist for me. Please, don't be offended."

Dave gave the impression he was afraid to let her go without saying what he needed to say. She almost felt like her breath was being taken away as Dave spoke.

Gazing into his deep gray eyes, Victoria took a chance that she had never considered before, "I am not offended; I feel the same."

The entire crew had gone, and the two were on the beach alone. The moonlight was shining brightly this night and reflecting across Victoria's face. Dave couldn't help it; he reached for Victoria's head placing his hand

behind her neck and drawing her lips to his. Victoria and Dave kissed with all the passion they could draw up. With heavy breathing—they heated up like a new furnace. Caught up at the moment—they ripped each other's clothes off. The photo shoot session reserved the beach for the entire day and evening, and Dave knew it, but not once—did they stop to see if anyone had stumbled onto the beach. Dave kissed Victoria in every spot on her body, causing her to moan outward in passion. They continued at it until midnight. Dave realized the beach was no longer theirs—the private time had run out.

Victoria felt shame and regret because of all the unknown things about this man. She then thought, 'I am a tramp! Oh My God! I didn't use protection.'

She had all kinds of concerns, and the expression on her face communicated her distress to Dave—she needed comfort. Dave reached his hands out to hers; he picked her up and walked her to his SUV. She got in, sat there, and watched him as he walked over to get in the driver's seat. She wondered why or how this happened.

After sitting, Dave turned to her before starting the engine, "Victoria—I know you didn't expect this, and neither did I. I want you to relax because unless you don't want me—I'm yours for life. Saying this may seem sudden to you, but I fell in love as soon as I saw you. It was as if, I already knew you and I belong. Does this seem strange?"

Victoria gazed into his eyes again, and she felt like she was being hypnotized and replied, "I have never felt this way—and I am scared. I only hope this is real because it's an amazing and exciting feeling."

Victoria and Dave began kissing over and again—the flames of desire besieged them. Before they knew it—Dave reached over and took Victoria's breast into his mouth. Throwing the seat in the reclined position, Dave took over—slipping into Victoria's wet vagina. They were thrashing each other back and forth until they both erupted in passionate love-making again in the truck. Finally, Dave and Victoria made it to her hotel suite— where they continued to make love and learn about each other. Victoria learned all she could about her newly found love. He learned all about her—the intimate lifestyle that was not in the media. She learned about where he grew up, what he did besides photography, his likes and dislikes,

his last relationship, and his hiccup in life, that he was unable to have children of his own. This news from Dave didn't bother Victoria at all. She always said that if she had a child, she would adopt and didn't want to take her body pain by giving birth. If possible—Victoria wanted to work in her profession until she'd expire.

***

Meanwhile, Ben and Becky were in another suite in the same hotel making up for lost time. Becky made the sacrifice to come to North Carolina—passing up some important political dinners, but she couldn't go another day without seeing Ben. Becky had another agenda also—she had to discuss if there were any hopes for their future together as husband and wife. What would it look like if she married a former inmate? As soon as Becky entered Ben's hotel room—they removed their clothes and made love. They were in an intermission, and they were both in bed, turned face-to-face when Becky asked Ben something that had been troubling her heart.

Becky stared into his eyes while gently touching his face with her slender fingers and said Ben—will we be able to pull our love off and keep our careers? What I mean is my career. I'm afraid to lose all that I have worked so hard for; and, at the same time, I'm worried I might lose you too. The long-distance relationship is tearing me down. Sometimes—I lay in my bed crying myself to sleep because I miss you so much. Ben—how long do you think we can hold up to this? "

Ben threw the covers back and sat up on the side of the bed with his head down. He gripped his face with his left hand, rubbing downward, showing complete distress over the reality. Becky moved closer to him while still in bed. She leaned her head on his shoulder.

In a quiet tone—Ben expressed, "I love you so much. I know I can do what it takes to become a doctor. No one would think anything, and if they did, would it matter? Would it?" Without allowing a word he continued, "I miss you too, but I want to be able to be with you and not in the shadows. Not being able to see you or touch you when I need to hurt me every day, but it also gives me the strength to do what I have to so that my life becomes what I want it to be. I am halfway there—baby. Can you hang in there with me for the rest of the way?"

Becky was melting at Ben's words, and his manliness, his gentle eyes, his body, his voice, his equipment, his walk, everything about Ben turned her on, and they were back at it again. They made love as if it were the first time.

***

Back in Victoria's room, she and Dave talked as if they had known each other for years. Victoria expressed to him that she was a pampered model, and she didn't cook. Dave told her she should learn the art. He loved the taste of food and thought he might one day own a restaurant instead of a camera. Both Victoria and Dave laughed at the notion of him being a chef.

The day had come when Victoria and Dave had to part ways for a little while. It was six o'clock that morning in North Carolina, and life had never felt this great to Victoria. She was emphatically in amazement about her life as events continued to enhance it. Victoria thought about how it all started with her returning love to her sister, Unique. Now, she was waking up with this gorgeous man's arms draped around her, giving her a feeling of being complete—something she had never been able to feel. She prayed and thanked God for all he had done. God had shown her patience as he continued expressing his love for her, through his grace.

Dave took a deep breath upon waking up, looked over at Victoria, "Good morning, beautiful."

In a spooning position, Dave gripped her even tighter, making sure there was no space between them. Victoria hated that the three days were almost over.

She clutched his hands, "Good morning. Do you want breakfast? I can't cook, but I can order room service."

Dave quietly chuckled at this, "Yes, babe—that would be kind, but I want something more than food right now."

Victoria pretended she hadn't noticed the sensation of Dave's third leg penetrating through her legs. Victoria made a suggestion, "Let's get cleaned up, eat, and get back to bed."

Dave understood that all models hate dirt, and he jumped in at the mention of soap and water.

"Yes, baby—we need a shower, and you need to eat because you're going to need your strength to deal with me for the rest of this day."

Victoria joked, as she broke from his grip, she stood putting her robe on and headed for the shower, "I think it's you that's gonna leave here limping."

Dave gave his sexy, quiet laugh again and declared while on his way out of the bed, "We shall see."

After Victoria had started the shower, she hollered out to Dave, "I'll be out in a little bit."

Dave wasn't into wasting time because he knew they didn't have much of that left.

"Okay, I'll order the room service."

Dave got on the phone, ordered their breakfast, and put a note on the outside of the door saying to leave the food at the door if they didn't answer. He then went to the restroom where Victoria was taking her shower. He saw her silhouette through the shower glass, and instantly his eyes fell, and his penis rose. Victoria was reaching out for some shampoo with her eyes closed. Dave placed the shampoo in his hands and got in the shower with her—Victoria was hoping he would join her. Dave poured a substantial amount of shampoo in his hands. He placed his hands on her head and washed her hair. Eyeing the suds as they fell past her face, and long neck to her breasts causing him to desire her even more. He knew she was craving him too— her nipples had become erect. Dave got on his knees, placing one of Victoria's legs over his shoulder. He then took her with his tongue. Dave filled up with passion and turned Victoria's back to him. She gripped the wet shower wall with no success while he powered his way through her repeatedly until she, with him, exploded. Victoria's legs were utterly feeble, so Dave picked her up, put her robe on, and took her to the bed.

He slowly replenished her skin with moisturizer, and every time Victoria tried to assist him—Dave said, "No, baby, let me do this."

After their shower, Dave retrieved their breakfast from the outside of Victoria's hotel suite. Back in the bedroom, Dave fed her and kissed her throughout the entire meal. The two used the three days to the max as

they continued to chat, laugh, and make love. They promised to talk every night and to see each other as often as they could.

***

Ben was continually reassuring Becky of his love and commitment to what they have. The two woke up on the third day on the floor, next to the bed. Becky loved to sleep on Ben's broad, muscular chest, and Ben continued to enjoy the floor for sleeping.

Ben woke and kissed Becky's head, "Hey, baby, do you want some breakfast?"

Becky slowly opened her eyes, wishing she could stay like that forever, "Yes, I could go for some breakfast."

Ben stood up and went to the hotel phone to order breakfast while Becky went straight to get her shower. Ben had so many thoughts going through his mind as he placed the covers back onto the bed. Ben wondered if Becky loved him as much as he loved her. Her job and what people thought—ran her life, and he hoped he could compete with that. Ben went to the second bathroom and took a bath, afterward putting his cologne on and moisturizing his skin. He laughed to himself because he thought Victoria was wearing off on him. He remembered their conversations on how to take care of his body. Ben threw on his robe, and Becky had hers on also, looking in the trays at the breakfast nook. Ben walked up behind her.

He embraced her waist with a snug grip and suggested while kissing her neck, "How about we go out for breakfast? I saw something at a store I want to buy you before you go home. We can stop at the store and be back here shortly after lunch."

Going out for breakfast was a splendid idea to Becky because she wanted to go for a walk. Ben needed to get them in a position to talk and not allow their passion for each other to get in the way of the critical discussions that they needed to have before time had run out for them. They quickly were dressed and headed out for breakfast. They went to a secluded beachfront property that had an open restaurant. It was breathtaking, relaxing, romantic and quiet. Their waiter put their meal on the table as the two gazed into each other's eyes. They both knew there was so much to say but didn't know how to start the conversation. The waiter

left—Ben took Becky's hand, dipped her index finger into the whipped cream and sucked her finger slowly. Becky then took a strawberry and licked it slowly and seductively.

Ben's breathing became brisk as he said, "Damn, baby, I love you. Oh shit—just looking at you turns me on—with my size, it's always evident, so I can't stand up or walk right away."

Becky laughed in a sexy, seductive way and asked, "Let me see."

She looked under the table to see between Ben's legs. She thought she was going to see his imprint through his pants. She was surprised when he had unzipped his pants—allowing his dick to expand fully. She jumped her eyes back to him.

He then blamed her, "What? I can't hold him in the tent. You do this to me all the time—it's your fault, and you know it's too large to be cramped in my pants. It would most likely rip my pants. You wouldn't want me to walk around with a hole in my pants, not there—right?"

Becky licked her lips, and then gently bit one side. Ben knew her every thought when she did that.

Ben took a deep breath and guessed at her demands, "Stop that! Don't do this baby. We're in a restaurant."

Becky then switched the blame on him, "Oh, no… Daddy—you started this by pulling that thick dick out. You fully understand that I have no control when you let that monster out. Besides—it's not fair to be able to pull yours out for relief, and I have to cream my shorts and feel the wetness while trying to eat breakfast. Do you think that's fair?"

Ben was now licking his lips, "You're right. As soon as I can, I'll put him in the house, and as for your cream, finish your food so I can eat and lick all my creamy delights."

Becky took in some milk. Ben picked up a strawberry, got out of his seat with his fat dick imprint going down his pants leg and leaned over Becky with the fruit in his mouth. She bit into it, as he covered her mouth with his biting kisses. Becky had a semi-orgasm in her shorts again, and her panties were thoroughly wet.

Ben grabbed his dick because of the pain from being fully erect in his pants, "Fuck breakfast babe. I need you now."

They ran off into the private outdoor restrooms and slid "Occupied" on the door. Ben took down her shorts, lifted Becky onto the sink, licked her thigh, and with one long tongue swipe up to her vagina—he then fed on her juices and rubbed his enormous dick. Ben snatched Becky and placed her on top of him, pressing and forcing his way through Becky's walls.

She gripped and scratched his back while trying to hold down on the noise. "AW! AW! Baby, take me," she cried in ecstasy.

The flow in Ben's penis had maximized, and he was now about to burst. He pumped faster and harder, pulling and gripping Becky's body tight. Becky orgasmed, and it flooded Ben's shaft. She hoped she'd be able to walk after this because she could feel the walls in her pussy swelling.

Ben released himself inside Becky, "Awe baby, Awe boo—damn!" Ben's body jerked, and his legs lost strength. He finally pulled out. "I know—I usually pull out before I come; even when wearing the condom, but your pussy gripped me. I am happy my condom didn't break."

Becky suddenly woke up to reality when Ben said that. Ben sensed a sudden mood change as they were cleaning themselves up as best they could.

He inquired, "What's wrong—baby, what?"

As they walked from the restroom, Becky appeared very distressed. They decided to leave the money and tip on the table, but the waiter met up with them.

He said, "I knew you two lovebirds weren't going to be able to just eat breakfast without eating breakfast." He laughed at his own joke, "That's why I put you in our private section. I'll make sure our restroom is in order."

Ben thanked the waiter for his discretion and handed him a tip to remember.

While walking to the car, Ben asked Becky again, "Baby, talk to me. I know something's bothering you."

Becky got in the passenger seat, and Ben got in the driver seat. Even though the keys were in the ignition, he didn't start the car until Becky began talking.

Her countenance was incredibly sad, "I might be in over my head with this trying to keep us private because of my career. What if I was to get pregnant; then all our secrets will be out. I want to marry you—Ben. I don't think we should have to wait. I am willing to give it up to be happy with you."

Ben felt the weight on his shoulders to do and say the right thing and said, "Becky, that's your love for me talking. You have worked hard all your life to get where you are. I will not be the reason for you throwing your career away. Don't you know how bad that will look? A beautiful woman with a promising career leaves it all behind for an inmate with no degree, no work, and no nothing. I love you too much to allow you to do that to yourself. If you wait until the right time, I promise you can have it all, your career, and your husband. I am ready to make you my wife, but I have to be a man and have a career also. I want to be a doctor, babe, and that hasn't changed. Promise me you'll wait for us."

Becky now had tears drowning her face. Ben kissed them and continued to say, "I love you, baby," over and again.

Becky uttered, "I love you too, Ben. I promise to be strong. I know I've got to allow us to do things the right way. I've learned that you are not one to let anything or anyone to change your mind when you want something. Being a doctor is important to you—I see that, and I don't want to be a distraction."

Ben kissed her again and drove to the store he talked about earlier. He brought her an engraved necklace for her to keep, as a reminder of their love for each other. Back at the hotel, Becky ate dinner and packed her things. Hugs and kisses filled the air, along with heartbreak, every time they parted ways. Ben took her to the airport, gave her his blessings, and said farewell to his love. They promised to see each other as often as they could.

***

Weeks had passed, and Dave had found his way on to many of the sets that Victoria was doing in different cities. Ben liked Dave and asked for his assistance with a surprise for Victoria. Ben knew he would be at school full-time soon and he would no longer be able to see so much of his sister. Dave assisted Ben with his excellent skills in photography, then

helped Ben to get a gig modeling for a prominent magazine. Ben wound up on the front cover posed as a doctor in scrubs. Inside the magazine was a series of pictures of him in scrub pants and no shirt and with the stethoscope around his neck. Dropping the magazine on Victoria's desk, Ben gave a smile, telling her to check out page 23.

Victoria looked at the magazine and started screaming and jumping like a teenager, "Oh my God! Oh my God!"

Ben peered back in the room at Victoria and told her, "I'm going to be a doctor, but I modeled just this once for my sister."

Victoria was so pleased with Ben but knew she soon had to find another assistant because Ben would be working to become the first doctor in their family. Victoria thought about Brenda needing money for her baby and the lessons of forgiving from Unique. She called Brenda up, putting her back to work but with fewer duties because she was a mother.

While being dropped off at the airport to go home, Ben kissed his sister and gave a small warning with love.

"Victoria—Sissy, I love you, and I hope this decision to bring Brenda back in your life doesn't come back to bite you. I wish you well. Don't forget—tell Brenda not to mess up my notes and contact lists. I worked hard at arranging that so keep it up."

Victoria thought Ben was just like her with keeping things organized, and so she knew she was going to miss her brother dearly. She started tearing up, standing next to the car as he grabbed his bags.

"I'll miss you, Ben."

"I'm going to miss you too. I am just a flight away. I have got to do this, Sissy. So—no tears, okay?" Ben replied.

He put his bags down on the pavement and hugged her tight with a rocking motion. As the car drove away, he was blowing kisses to her until she was out of sight.

Victoria was soon on another flight, heading to Alabama to meet with the novel writer April Floyd and more interviews on a major television station in that state were to follow. After Alabama, Victoria was on her way to California to meet filmmakers and do more interviews. Diamarious kept Victoria busy. Dave had Victoria glowing; she finally could say she had fallen in love. Allowing a male in her life wasn't easy,

but it was all worth it. Victoria smiled from ear to ear for the first time whenever someone interviewed her—asking questions about her new love. Marriage talk was in the air for Victoria. Brenda was hard at work trying to prove her loyalty once again.

CHAPTER 27

TROUBLE IN PARADISE

Victoria continued to work hard, but she made sure to call Unique at least once every two weeks—she never wanted to lose contact again. Victoria was convinced—Unique would have stressful situations running a major company, and it would be an uphill battle for her business to run smoothly. She made sure she'd be there for Unique no matter what.

It was a pleasantly crisp and refreshing Monday morning in the city of Memphis, Tennessee. Victoria had a photoshoot with a record company—rich in history—Stax. Many legendary Blues singers started at this company. A major cover story about music history and where today's sound originated from was the top talk in the music industry. The production wanted to use a youthful and stylish image to bring our history to modern times, and Victoria was their model for the job. Victoria knew the history and loved the music, so she was euphoric to have such an opportunity.

The photo shoots lead Victoria to the best spots in Memphis. The famous, Beale Street was intriguing for her, and she was amazed at how the street had become a cultural and recreational median for Blues Musicians all over starting in the late 1800s. From the first artist like 'Young Men's Brass Band' to many legends like 'B. B. King' Beale Street has been the spot of musical masters. She was outdone to learn the first black billionaire in the South was due to the popularity of Beale Street. It was merely a place of magic and blues.

At The Stax Museum, she was able to see and read the history about the artists. Victoria saw the clothes they wore in those days and thought about how the past always ties into the future. She even remembered the music her dad played while growing up. Victoria was surprised when she found out that most of her father's musical albums came from Stax artists. "Love and Happiness" by Al Green was only one of Al's favorites. He would always sing songs like, "California Girl" and "Knock on Wood" by Eddie Floyd and so many others. Isaac Hayes and his style were a force from the future. Victoria conceived after seeing Isaac Hayes car, 'No one to this day has anything like that.' She did her best to fit the role as the photographer gathered hundreds of shots.

While at the Stax Museum for the photo shoot, some of the legends came in to be part of the shoot. She met legendary singers and writer of Stax—Eddie Floyd, Mavis Staples, William Bell, and Booker T and the MG's. After talking with them, Victoria had a grand idea! She wanted to know what Unique thought of a clothing line geared to bring soulful music into today's designs and fashion—something that would merge the two worlds into one. After the final shoot—she called Unique with her idea and views.

Unique was at her desk and answered the phone with her natural greet for customers. Excitement bubbled fourth when she heard her sister's voice, "Hey Vicky, what's up?"

"Unique, I know you have a lot on your plate, but I thought of something that will have a substantial purpose, and in the long run will pay off considerably. Remember, how we always said that this generation never gave props to the person that has paved the way for us to do what we do?"

"Yes, I remember," replied Unique, somewhat confused.

Victoria continued, "Well, it's the same with the music industry. People go on making song after song, losing the soul in the music because they forget where it originated. Let's remind them of a clothing line that displays the art of soul in its designs. I can contact and draw up some contracts for any legendary artist that will go with this, and you come up with some designs. We can do this together."

Victoria was excited with her idea but even more excited to think that she and her sister could work on something together.

"I like the idea," Unique said, "But I want more specifics about it. So, gather more information with detail on numbers—if you continue to think we can do this, I am with you all the way."

"Sure…" Victoria stated, "But—if we do this, I'll pay for it all to get started, but you'll receive all its proceeds. I wouldn't want you to put any more projects into your budget. The last time we spoke—you seemed to have reached your max."

"You know me, Vicky. I never complain, but I find a way to get it all done. Thanks that takes some weight off the project."

"Unique, this project can put you on a new level and having money will no longer be an issue. Plus, you can use some to donate to your charities as well. I just want to help young ones to start appreciating where we got our soul and to be part of something with my sister."

"Awe… You are something." Unique then teased Victoria, "Vicky, when did you have the soul or feel the funk? I haven't forgotten that you dance like your mother, with no rhythm at all."

They both laughed because Victoria knew Unique was telling the truth.

Victoria cleared her throat, "I may have some rabbit in me when I'm dancing, but I know good music when I hear it."

Unique teased again, "Rabbits is not all you have, girl—you look like rabbits, frogs, and horses when you dance. Do you still do that leap when you feel the soul?"

Unique was now laughing harder, thinking about Victoria's dancing. Victoria had had enough.

"All right now, I do my best. The key is I never give up, no matter how bad I am at dancing."

Unique asked, "Vicky, you sound more relaxed and a bit happier now. I don't think I have ever known you to be this excited about life. I can't wait to meet Dave. Anyone that can make my sister love life—I have to meet him."

"Unique, you have become my best friend. I talk to you about everything now." Victoria paused and smiled, "You're right; I am in love for the first time. I allowed my heart to change when you came back in my life—now I have never been happier. I told Dad a little about him, and Ben knows him, but I can't wait until you all get a chance to meet him."

"You're happy because you learned to love and you've opened yourself up to the possibilities that many people never see in a lifetime. Some are too afraid, and some just aren't that lucky." Unique continued, "I am so thrilled for you, and I look forward to meeting him. Now, I have to get back to work, and you have to get some rest. I'll talk to you soon, Vicky. I love you, girl."

Victoria gave Unique her love, and they disconnected. Victoria had gone back to her hotel in Memphis when her phone rang. While sipping on her glass of wine, It was just the person she'd been thinking about, deeply.

"Dave, baby! Just the voice I needed to hear. I miss you, honey."

Dave smiled agreeably, "Hey, my love, I miss you too, that's why I am at your hotel door. Open up, sweetheart."

Victoria hopped off the sofa and ran to the door. She leaped into his arms—filling him with hugs and kisses.

Victoria looked down and noticed Dave had bags, so she inquired, "How long do we have together before your next job?"

Dave gave Victoria a dazzling smile and uttered, "You have three weeks to do what you want with me."

In her excitement, Victoria shouted, "Three weeks! That's great…!"

Victoria stated she had to work one more week, but then she would have her second and third week off but would return to work in the fourth week. The two talked about making plans. Now that she had an upcoming two weeks off; her plans to go home were certain. Victoria wanted Dave to spend more time with Ms. Ruth because he had only met her once and it

was brief. She was also missing her brother, Ben. Swiftly, Victoria thought about Ben's studies and did not want to intrude.

Dave came to the rescue with an idea, "How about you and I go to Hawaii?"

Victoria was pleased with that idea, and their plans changed instantly. She grinned, "That will work out. I'll send my assistant home so she can be with her little girl. Then it's just you and me, baby."

Dave wrapped his arms around her waist, "Before we leave Memphis, I have got to taste some of this southern food. I saw some brochures downstairs. I'm going to get one so that we can know which restaurants are the best in Memphis. I'll be back, baby."

Dave kissed Victoria on the forehead and walked out of the suite. Meanwhile, Victoria rushed to style herself a bit sexier for his return.

Brenda had never met Dave but had heard Victoria talk to him on the phone. Brenda was staying on the same floor as Victoria but in another room. Brenda went out of her suite to get Victoria's updated list for her schedule. Walking down the hotel halls with papers in hand, Brenda looked up as she felt a familiar personal presence.

She apprehensively called out his name, "Dave…?"

Dave looked back at her, "Brenda…?"

As she was about to ask him what he was doing there, the thought precipitously hit her that Victoria's new love's name was Dave. Now, Dave simultaneously reciprocated the same thoughts.

Brenda asked, "I think I know why you are here, Victoria right…?"

Dave felt very awkward, "Yes, she's my lady. I guess you are the assistant she talked about."

Brenda felt his implications about her betrayal.

"Yes, I am… I have a question for you: Are you going to let her know about us?"

Dave asked, "What, us? You left me at college, and I never heard from you again. In my mind, there was never anything between us. If I had known it was you she was talking about, I would have suggested that she let you be because—people like you—never change. You weren't loyal to me back then, and you surely weren't loyal to her."

Brenda declared, "You sound angry, Dave. You have no right to be! Your life turned out fine. Mine caused me to stop school, and I lost a child, Dave! Your son! I loved you, but after losing our baby, I couldn't face you again."

Dave's eyes dimmed, "You had no right to go on pretending you were still carrying our child! Then you told me about losing my baby, and you left me! Afterward, I was upset. So, I got in my car and drove far too fast. I was involved in an accident that impaired my reproductive organs. I can't have kids now! So my life has been changed too, and because of you! I'll never have the chance to know what my child would be like."

An angry tear fell from Dave's eyes as he continued, "Now…! Here you are again. I finally found a love that doesn't care that I can't have children. I'm not going to let you mess this up for me."

Brenda interrupted, "The past is the past, Dave. I am sorry about our child and my reaction, but I have a child I must take care of, and I can't afford to lose my job with Victoria again. Please, don't mention our past to her. I have changed, and I don't want to be responsible for ever hurting Victoria again. Brenda started to cry. Please, don't tell her. Please, Dave!"

Dave's heart went out to her, and he too; didn't want to risk losing Victoria.

"I won't say anything. I love Victoria, and I don't see the need to hurt her with this—it's cool."

In the intervening time, back at the hotel, Victoria was wondering what was taking Dave so long. Dave hurried to get the brochure and got back to the suite with Victoria. Upon his entrance to the room, Victoria embraced him with a seductive hug and opened her silk robe revealing nothing underneath. Dave dropped the brochure on the floor—for this day, making love took preferences over barbecue.

The following day, Victoria and Dave were about to head out for some southern food. Brenda stopped by before they left to give Victoria her renewed upcoming schedule. Victoria briefly introduced them. They both shook hands, pretending never to have met. Victoria and Dave then headed out for a good time in Memphis, Tennessee.

Victoria and Dave loaded up and flew to Hawaii immediately after her last shoot. Dave made a bonfire and insisted they stay on the beach

until dark. They watched the sunset together, wrapped in each other's arms. The glow from the blaze illuminated Victoria's beautiful face while lying there on the faux fur blanket. Dave took Victoria's hands and assisted her in standing.

He then dropped to one knee, taking out a ring that he purchased in Memphis.

"Victoria Jacob, I don't know how I got so lucky or why God has favored me. I was sure that a person like you didn't exist; now, I'm convinced that I was wrong. I love you with every breath I breathe. Will you take me as your husband? Victoria, will you marry me?"

Tears filled Victoria's face as she repeatedly replied, "Yes, yes, I will."

They enjoyed the rest of their weeks full of exhilaration and love.

ↄ⍀

Victoria couldn't wait to become Mrs. Victoria Smith, but the two had decided to keep the engagement a secret until they felt the time was right. Almost a year had passed, and Victoria needed to go home to get some rest. She missed Ms. Ruth and Ben; nonetheless, it didn't matter about Ben because he wasn't going to be there—he had already planned a visit to see Becky. Victoria and Dave had prepared to take several months off. They had to make time to announce and plan the wedding. Victoria arrived home on a Saturday evening—Ms. Ruth was excited to see Victoria and to meet Dave officially.

Ms. Ruth gave her approval, "You got you something there. He is handsome in regular clothes. The last time I saw him; although brief, he had on some photography brown wear."

Victoria inquired about Ben, "Ms. Ruth, how is my brother? I miss him so much."

Ms. Ruth spoke with a great sense of pride, "He has been working so hard in his studies. I felt sorry for him at times—he wouldn't even eat because he was so focused. I have never seen anyone work so hard. He wanted to wait for you, but his flight was early. I have your dinner ready and…"

While Ms. Ruth was speaking, the doorbell rang. She went to the door, and Brenda walked in.

"Hello, Ms. Ruth, it's been a while since I've seen you."

Brenda reached out to hug Ms. Ruth and received a very tense embrace.

Ms. Ruth closed the door and chatted as she walked to the kitchen, "I guess—I'll set up another spot at the table."

Victoria noticed Ms. Ruth slowing down. She was looking more tired and older now.

Brenda then approached Victoria and said, "Here's all the information you asked me for."

Victoria thought it would help if she kept Brenda with her to help do some of Ms. Ruth's work.

Victoria then asked Brenda, "How is your little girl?"

Brenda replied, "She's great, just growing up fast."

Ms. Ruth called out, "Dinner's ready." Victoria, Dave, and Brenda went to the dining room and sat as Ms. Ruth placed food on the table.

Victoria continued her thought, "Brenda, I merely thought that you could help a bit more around here. I want you to stay with me for a while, and you can send for your daughter. I want to spend some time with her while I'm off work anyway. There's no need for us to be in separate cities, right now. There's plenty of space here, and besides, we have lots to do: planning the announcement, engagement party, and wedding. Two things that came out of Victoria's mouth had shaken Ms. Ruth. One was that Victoria was getting married, and two was that she wanted Brenda to stay in the house with them. Ms. Ruth noticed Dave's facial discomfort when Victoria said it. Ms. Ruth didn't want to involve her thoughts right then; however, she was sure she would say something later.

Ms. Ruth solely said, "Congratulations, Victoria and Dave, on your upcoming marriage. I am proud of you; enjoy your meal."

Ms. Ruth dismissed herself. Dave looked very uncomfortable as Victoria and Brenda talked about plans.

ϾϿ

It was a dull Tuesday, midday—'Little Free' was running through the house, and Ms. Ruth and Victoria told the child to walk. Brenda was working in the study, and Dave had gone out for a jog. Ms. Ruth then felt the need to let Victoria know how she felt about Brenda.

Ms. Ruth declared, "Victoria, I hope I'm not out of place by saying this, but I think to have Brenda in your home is a mistake."

Victoria thought Ms. Ruth was saying this because of Brenda's past. Victoria gently smiled, "I forgave her, Ms. Ruth…"

Ms. Ruth interrupted, "This has nothing to do with the past. I don't think she should be here while you are with your future husband. I just don't trust her."

Victoria smiled at Ms. Ruth, thinking she was just old-fashioned.

"I don't trust her either when it comes to that, but I do trust him."

Ms. Ruth decided to let it go. She had said her peace on the matter. She went back to her duties. Dave walked back in, very sweaty, and kissed Victoria.

She balked at him—he knew that she hated to touch after his runs physically.

Dave then asked, "Come take a shower with me?"

Victoria looked attracted to his offer but declined, "I can't, babe; I must finish this so we can get things ordered in time."

Dave gave up and kissed her again. She playfully shouted at him as he walked away. The phone rang, and Ms. Ruth answered it. She then approached Victoria with a fearful look on her face, as she handed her the phone. It was Barnes Hospital in St. Louis on the line.

A nurse said, "Hello, Victoria, we have you down as an emergency contact for your father,—Mr. Al Jacobs. He had a heart attack, and we had to proceed quickly with surgery. He is in recovery, and he seems to be stable right now; however, if anything else were to happen, we would need your permission. Is there any way you can get here?"

Victoria was very scared, "I am on the fastest flight there."

She hung up the phone, crying and praying. She screamed to Brenda to get her on the most rapid flight to St. Louis and have a car ready to go once she touched down at Lambert airport.

She then told Ms. Ruth, "It's my dad; he had a heart attack. Can you please gather a few things for me?"

Ms. Ruth, still in love with Al, told Brenda, "Make that flight for two." To Victoria, she said, "I'll pack up for us both. I am going with you."

Victoria wanted Ms. Ruth with her, and there was no talking her out of it anyhow, so she agreed. Victoria had already showered and started to get dressed.

Dave came out of the bathroom into the bedroom while Victoria was getting dressed.

"Babe, what's happening?"

She quickly answered, "My dad had a heart attack, and I got to go to St. Louis."

"Okay, I'll pack up." Dave quickly said.

"No," Victoria replied, "I don't want to have to explain anything concerning us while he's in this situation. I'll keep you informed about what's going on. Plus, I need you to finish what I've started regarding our arrangements. I'm ready to walk down that aisle and become your wife—I'll be back as soon as I can. "

Brenda knocked at the bedroom door and stated loudly, "I got your tickets. You have forty-five minutes to get to the airport, or the next flight is two hours later. The car is outside waiting."

Victoria and Ms. Ruth hurried. Dave grabbed their bags, helping them into the car. They made the flight and were on their way to St. Louis. Upon their arrival at the hospital, Ben met Victoria and Ruth at the door and escorted them to the floor in the family waiting room where they all were waiting for the doctor to return with some updated information. The entire family engaged with mixed emotions ranging from the joy of seeing each other and the fear about Al's condition. Victoria and Unique clenched each other when the doctor walked in the room.

The doctor was very tall, but he had a gentle face.

"You're all here for a Mr. Al Jacob?"

They all said, 'yes,' with their eyes.

The doctor understood and stated, "Well, I got good news. He responded well to the surgery, and he'll soon be out of recovery, then moved to another floor where another doctor will preside over his care. His vitals look good. He is well on his way to a full recovery. I know you all want to see him, but it will be too much on the patient at one time. Once he is in his room, he can only have two visitors today. Maybe more will be able to see him tomorrow, depending on how he's doing. Can I make a suggestion? Will you all allow me to take a picture of all of you here? When he is able—he'll know how loved he is."

The doctor was kind, and he took a picture of the entire family. Victoria and Unique stayed at the hospital while the rest of the family went home, and all the family members who came from out of town extended out, some went with Cindy and Chuck. Dorothy's kids went with her and Diane. Also, some people had hotels.

It seemed to be the longest night ever for Unique and Victoria—waiting to see their dad open his eyes. Victoria went into the family lounge to call Dave and give him an update.

Her voice was quiet, "Hey, baby, I am still at the hospital. My dad is going to be all right, but he hasn't fully woken up yet. I am sorry I had to leave like that. I should be home soon…"

Victoria was interrupted by a nurse—gesturing for her to come quickly.

"I got to go, babe. Love you."

Victoria rushed into the room to find her dad's eyes wide open, smiling at Unique. When he saw Victoria walk in he reached his hand out to her. Victoria walked over and kissed his hand while sitting next to his bed. Unique was on the other side of his bed, holding his other hand.

Al spoke in an undertone, "This is one of the best days of my life. I have my two girls next to me. I am very proud right now."

Tears streamed down the sides of Al's face as he continued, "God is good. I always say next to God; family is the best thing a person can have. I am truly blessed."

Victoria pulled out the picture the doctor took and said, "Yes we are, Dad—truly blessed."

Al looked at the picture and smiled before drifting into a medicated sleep. Victoria and Unique left the room so he could rest. They stayed at the hospital with their dad but in the family waiting room. The next day, the entire family was back out to see Al. The waiting room was packed once more with their members—eating breakfast and drinking coffee. The doctor gave the great news—Al would be able to go home in a few more days.

※

Back at Victoria's house, Brenda was cleaning things up from the mess made on behalf of Victoria and Ms. Ruth being in a hurry to leave. Two days had gone by, and Dave would only receive one call from Victoria each day. He hoped all was going well with her dad, but he missed her. Brenda walked around the place continuing business as usual. Now, it was Friday morning. Dave sat on the sofa in a daze when Brenda walked in to ask him if he wanted some breakfast, but what she had on was impractical, considering it was almost noon, and he thought, 'a see-through nightgown should only be worn in her private room—not for breakfast.' He remembered her perky breasts, long slender neck, and beautiful shapely legs.

He snapped out of his stare and articulated his discomfort, "Brenda! What are you wearing? Let me guess. Your attire is your formal brunch wear. Where is your daughter? Is she dressed?"

Dave was trying to keep his eyes on Brenda's face and off her breast as he waited for a response. Brenda looked down at her gown with an innocent appeal, rubbing the silk with her hands and drawing the garment up more, displaying her every curve.

"Oh yeah, I wasn't feeling much like anything, so I wanted to sleep in—I didn't feel like getting dressed. My daughter is napping. I'm sorry, Dave, if this makes you uncomfortable—I'll change. I just presumed you already knew how I look so why the need to hide or cover up? You have already seen and tasted every inch of me many times."

Dave got annoyed because she was putting him to the test and inside he knew he was failing. Dave stood up from the couch, snapped and

became cynical, "You're right; Brenda—seeing you doesn't bother me at all. You look the same; nothing new. Take off the gown since I've already seen it all. I guess you thought you were worth remembering."

❧

In St. Louis, Victoria got the okay from the doctor's that Al would be just fine. His pacemaker and stents were doing the trick. She arranged for her dad to have around the clock nursing. Midday on Friday—Victoria and Ms. Ruth were packed and back on the plane to Florida. Victoria made no call home to Dave because she wanted to surprise him.

❧

In Florida, the conversations and situation with Dave and Brenda had taken a turn. Dave looked at Brenda while sipping his drink and walked into the kitchen. Brenda felt very cheap and stupid. She went to her room and started packing up a few of her and the baby's things. Dave saw her put two bags in the foyer. On her way to get another bag, Dave stopped her. She had tears falling from her face. Dave had a storm of emotions approaching like small waves on a beach that became a massive tide.

She cried to him, "I am sorry, Dave. I never meant to hurt you then, and I don't want to hurt you now. I am going to go. I don't know how long Victoria will be gone, but I shouldn't be here with these feelings I feel for you. You were my first at everything: my first sexually, and most of all, my first time falling in love was with you. Seeing you again has turned me upside down."

Dave looked into Brenda's eyes. He comprehended the pain she felt because he felt pain also.

He said, "Brenda, I know you have more work to do here for Victoria. I want you to stay. I am going to leave."

Dave picked up her bags and took them back to the guest room. When he was about to walk out, Brenda called out to him, "Dave, I have something to show you."

Brenda reached into her bag, taking out a sonogram picture of their baby. After she had handed him the photo, she explained, "Dave, we had a boy coming. I was three months before I lost him. It took me too long to tell you, but I didn't have the heart."

Dave stared at the image and said, "This was my boy? We had a boy. I had a boy?"

Dave's gray eyes filled themselves with firm tears. Dave always wanted kids of his own. To know he almost had a son tore into him like a lion on a gazelle.

Brenda approached him, gazing into his gray eyes and said, "I want you to have that. I felt ashamed that I lost our baby; I'm sorry I couldn't face you and keep our relationship going."

Dave wiped his tears with his entire hand, rubbing downward on his face. He took a deep breath as he proceeded to try to comfort Brenda.

Dave uttered, "It wasn't your fault."

Brenda cried, "I wish I could believe that, but when the doctor told me I lost my baby due to me stressing—I blamed myself. Over and again, I replay that part in my life with all the 'what if' questions."

Dave grabbed Brenda by both her shoulders, "Listen to me, it wasn't your fault."

With lust and embedded pain, Dave and Brenda locked on each other's eyes and started kissing avidly. Dave couldn't pull himself back. He and Brenda had collided with each other as if they were in college again. They moved away from the sleeping Free in Brenda's bedroom into Victoria's room. Dave slammed Brenda's naked body on the bed and plunged into her with every force he had.

Victoria and Ms. Ruth walked through the doors and noticed the house was tranquil. Victoria almost called out Dave's name, but some bothersome feeling caused her to keep quiet. Ms. Ruth went into the kitchen, and Victoria went into her bedroom. Victoria opened the door and viewed that Dave and Brenda were fiercely fucking. They both jumped when they saw Victoria. Brenda started grabbing sheets to cover up while apologizing.

Victoria screamed, "OH HELL NO! You had gone fuck her in my house! In my BED—too! You two must think I'm stuck on stupid, glued to dumb and tattooed to idiot. You got her nasty ass in my bed!"

Ms. Ruth heard the yelling, and she instantly knew what happened, so she got on the phone right away to call Ben, but got no answer, so she left a message. She told Ben there was trouble at home with Victoria and asked if he could come back right away. In the room, Dave was trying to explain as he tried pulling his pants up. Victoria picked up a vase near the door and threw it across the chamber at Dave's head. It missed his head and shattered on the wall. Victoria was blocking the entrance so that neither one could get out. She had her purse on her arm—reaching into it, she brought out her taser gun and hit Dave in the chest with it. Dave fell to the floor, seizing and foaming at the mouth. Brenda's eyes were big, and she knew she was about to die. Victoria took off her earrings and kicked off her shoes. Always known for leaping, Victoria launched forward and snatched Brenda up by her hair and slammed her to the floor face first, breaking three of Brenda's front teeth. While Victoria was kicking and punching Brenda, Ms. Ruth walked in and saw the damage Victoria had done to them both.

Mrs. Ruth screamed and pleaded with Victoria, "STOP…! Victoria—that's more than enough!"

Victoria's anger had succumbed to tears filled with pain as she leaned her head on Ms. Ruth. Ms. Ruth wrapped her arms around Victoria, led her into the study, and then told her to stay there. Victoria sat down with messed up hair and torn fingernails. Worst was all of the emotions of being hurt for the first time by her first love.

Ms. Ruth hurried to get them up so they could leave. She went to Brenda's room, gathered Brenda's things and put them at the foyer entrance. She then took Brenda a set of clothes—throwing them at her—she shouted, "Get dressed and get your ass out of this house; don't you ever try coming back."

Ms. Ruth then took Brenda by the chin, "If you mention any of this to anyone—I want to remind you that I'm old school, and I would have your ass wiped out. I don't need a written document! I'm from Detroit—Bitch! Do we understand each other?"

Brenda nodded, 'Yes.'

It had been many years since Ms. Ruth let her gangster out. She continued, "Good—you got twenty minutes to be gone."

Dave could not walk because Victoria had used a taser gun on him. Ms. Ruth assisted him into the bed while calling him a stupid asshole. Ms. Ruth got on the phone with her doctor and had him come out and check on Dave.

The doctor checked Dave over and said, "He'll be fine—he has an active heart. Just let him rest up a bit."

The doctor pointed to Victoria as he walked out of the bedroom into the front area. "I am concerned about that young lady, right there."

Victoria was sitting on the sofa in a complete mess. Ms. Ruth looked shocked, but the doctor continued with why he was concerned.

"She seems to be hyperventilating, and her color doesn't look good."

Ms. Ruth explained, "She's distraught, doctor, and I have done and said all I could to make Victoria feel better. Nothing is working. She just keeps crying."

The doctor reached into his bag, took Victoria's vitals, encouraged her to breathe and gave Ms. Ruth some pills and a prescription, "This should help her get some rest. Maybe when she wakes up, she'll be able to deal with her sadness. If not, you call me, and I'll set up her an appointment with a psychiatrist. I want you to pay close attention to her attitudes and stress levels."

Ms. Ruth looked stunned at the thought of Victoria at a psychiatrist, "Thank you, doctor, and I'll keep you informed of her conditions."

Ms. Ruth showed the doctor out—then ran to the kitchen for some water. She came back and told Victoria to take the pills. Ms. Ruth took her into Ben's room so she could rest. Victoria cried herself to sleep.

Brenda—had her baby, her gear, and was ready to go. She looked at Ms. Ruth and said, "For whatever it's worth, will you tell Victoria I am sorry?"

Ms. Ruth was so angry that she told Brenda, "If I weren't a changed woman, I'd spit in your face because that's what your apology is worth. Get out! Let me remind you to let this go or else."

Brenda thought she saw the devil in Ms. Ruth's eyes and knew that was one person she wasn't going to cross: ever. She got in the cab and was gone. Ms. Ruth knew it was for good this time. Ms. Ruth went on to clean up the room Brenda was using—throwing out anything she touched. Meanwhile—Ms. Ruth heard the front door shut. She ran out to see who it was. Ben walked in looking as devastated as Victoria did when he entered.

Ms. Ruth addressed him, "Ben—I'm so glad you're home. Did you get my message?"

Ms. Ruth noticed Ben's appearance was as if he had seen a natural disaster. Ben looked at Ms. Ruth with anger, and he said, "I didn't get any message. I was on the plane, and I came straight home."

Ms. Ruth then knew something was wrong with Ben also. Ms. Ruth asked, "Ben, what's wrong?"

Anger filled his expression, and sadness welled in his eyes, "Becky—she didn't wait for me. She found someone else, Ms. Ruth. Now, what am I supposed to do? I love her, and she doesn't even want me. People kept telling me I shouldn't be serious with one girl, but it's not me to be that way; It's immoral. People look at me and wonder why I don't use my good looks to get what I want; I just can't do certain things. And, cheating—that's one—I won't do. Sometimes, I wish I could have; maybe this wouldn't hurt so bad."

Ms. Ruth was thinking, "Wow, I am running out of bedrooms."

Ms. Ruth then tried to comfort him, "Ben—there's nothing wrong with you, son. Something was wrong with Becky. You don't need to change who you are. You were right not to be with more than one girl. God don't like ugly, and cheating is an ugly thing. Keep your studies up and become the best doctor you can be. Don't let Becky win. She thinks she was your inspiration to become a doctor. Finish school and show her that God was your inspiration. Later, she'll see. Also, son—you must allow God to find you—someone to love, it won't go wrong when God does it. Becky wasn't from God, baby—that's why it ended. I am cleaning the guest room that Brenda was in…"

Ben then interrupted Ms. Ruth, "Brenda? Why was she here, sleeping?"

Ms. Ruth continued, "It's a long story, but Victoria is in your bedroom, sleeping…"

Ben then interrupted again, "Why is Victoria in my room? Ms. Ruth, you said you left me a message—what happened here?"

Ms. Ruth went on, telling Ben the whole story. When Ben found out Dave was still there, he went to Victoria's room—filled with anger about Becky and what has happened to his sister.

Ben opened the door, threw the covers off Dave, and yelled, "Get your skinny—nothing ass—out! I don't give a damn if you can walk or not! You bitch ass, motherfucker! You had better crawl out if you have to because I'm ready to go back to jail for mine! Bitch ass!"

Dave put his hands up gesturing and pleading. He didn't know Ben had been to jail and feared his size.

"Okay, man—Okay… I'm out."

"Hurry up!" The bass in Ben's voice shook Dave up.

He slung his shirt on his back and headed out the door as quick as his maimed body would allow. Ms. Ruth was helpful to have a cab waiting for him, too. She couldn't help but feel pity for the young dummy.

Ben went into his room to check on Victoria. He sat on the side of the bed rubbing her hair. Victoria slowly opened her eyes, noticed Ben.

She swiftly sat up halfway and laid her head on his broad chest crying and saying, "To hurt this bad seems worse than death."

Ben wanted to agree but knew Victoria wasn't as tough as he was so he chose his words carefully, "No, Sissy, death is worse. I understand how you feel. Becky left me too. However, I live because it's a gift from God. We can't let them make us forget how blessed we are, and how good life is. We are going to get through this together, okay?"

Victoria begged, "Please don't leave—stay in here with me."

Ben agreed—he didn't want to be alone either. Ben lay on the floor next to the bed. They both drifted into a resentful sleep.

CHAPTER 28

A STRANGE THING

VICTORIA LOVED MS. RUTH. In fact—Ms. Ruth had become like having her mother with her as she worked. Victoria didn't want Ms. Ruth to waste any more of her precious years in service—it was evident that Ms. Ruth was getting older. Shortly after the Dave and Brenda episode— Victoria processed her healing, and she looked at the person who has never disappointed her—Ms. Ruth. Victoria's love for her superseded that of her biological mother. Victoria's conscience wouldn't allow Ms. Ruth to wash one more dish—no cooking, no cleaning, Ms. Ruth's days of serving were officially over. Victoria watched Ms. Ruth, as she yearned for the love that had slipped away—the love Ms. Ruth had for her father, Al, a love that never got a chance to grow into maturity. Ms. Ruth never stopped loving Al since the trip to Jamaica. Victoria never understood why her dad and Ms. Ruth decided to discontinue seeing each other.

Ms. Ruth was in the kitchen, about to pour a glass of lemonade. Victoria looked at Ms. Ruth with soft, loving eyes and asked, "Ms. Ruth, I need to talk to you. Can you join me in the study?"

Ms. Ruth finished pouring her drink and followed Victoria to the study. Ms. Ruth was very much aware of Victoria's behavior. She distinguished the differences in conversations—when conversing in the study, the subject was of a severe or private nature.

Ms. Ruth addressed Victoria, "Okay sweetheart, what's this about?"

Victoria asked Ms. Ruth to sit on the sofa. Victoria next placed a small gift-wrapped box in her hands. The expression on Ms. Ruth's face was of complete surprise.

"What's this for, Victoria?"

Victoria sat next to Ms. Ruth and gently spoke, "Ms. Ruth I've been thinking for a while; how, I have been so blessed. When you came into my life as an employee, it was perfect because I was so young starting out in my career, and you were—and still are—as a mother to me. There were so many times I would've been lost without your advice and your love. There were things I've asked of you; I could never dare ask my birth mother. You were there when I needed you, and you still are. Why did you sacrifice so much to stay with me? And, why—after meeting my father and falling in love with him, did you not go be with him?"

Ms. Ruth looked into Victoria's serious face with watery eyes, "Victoria, I had a daughter once, and she passed away from cancer when she was only eight. Afterward, I was able to move on from the loss of my baby, but the massive bills that I had to pay hounded me. That's when I got the job as your worker. You paid me more than any other offer I was getting with my limited skills. I also needed to be a mother. I had lost my baby—my only baby. However, when I saw you—I knew I had found a child in need of a loving mother. I don't know how I sensed that, but I did. You weren't a child, but you were childlike because you hadn't been exposed to many things. I knew there would be times when you would need a mother to talk to, and I was jumping for joy at the thought that I could fill some of that role—although, I would never try to take the place of your birth mother. After meeting your father, I knew he loved you so much. We met on that Jamaica trip, but we continued to have very passionate secret trips from time to time."

Victoria was startled, "You and Dad spent more time together after that excursion?"

Ms. Ruth smiled, "Honey, yes! You're all the way grown now; so I would speak the truth to you."

Victoria blushed as Ms. Ruth continued, "Al was the sexiest man I had ever seen on the beach that day. His thickness, height, and his full lips turned me on so. When he spoke to me, I knew he was my love. We shared some exceptional moments together. Then reality hit us both. I worked for his daughter, and he loved knowing that. He was aware that you were safe as long as I was your caretaker. We both didn't want to do anything to jeopardize my position, so I worked, and he moved on."

Victoria was amazed that two people in love would sacrifice what they felt over her and stated, "I understand why you two thought I couldn't handle things like that. The truth is I was very bitter and bitchy back then, but I'm not happy knowing you two stayed apart because of me. I saw you two falling all over each other. I knew it was real because I've never seen my dad smile so hard. You say that you, and he loved each other. I say the both of you were cowards, using me as an excuse not to let your love grow. I mean…. What was I going to do? Either accept it or not, right? The bottom line is this—you two still love each other, and I won't be your excuse anymore. Ms. Ruth, let my dad know how you feel. I have set everything up already. Your plane leaves at 6:45 am. You'll arrive in St. Louis at 9:20 am. A driver will pick you up and take you to get lunch, then your hair and nails, then to the hotel where I have picked out a special dress for you to put on. You should be ready to surprise Dad no later than 5:00 pm."

Ms. Ruth smiled and hugged Victoria very tight. She realized Victoria was right. She only wished she hadn't waited so long. Holding Victoria's hands, Ms. Ruth agreed and said, "You're right—baby girl. Life is short, and you must live it without fear."

Victoria kissed Ms. Ruth on the cheek and said, "I also don't want you working for me any longer. I have been trying to get you to take it easy for years now, and you were persistent about staying on with me. I am not asking—I am telling you; you won't wash one more dish. You are like a mother to me already, so see what you can do to make it official. OH, I almost forgot, open your gift after you have seen my dad."

The next morning, Ms. Ruth said her goodbyes to Victoria. Then went back to St. Louis, to confront her fears of rejection from Al. The statement Ms. Ruth said, about living without fear—got Victoria to thinking about her life, how she needed to grab onto her boots and live her life to the fullest, without fear.

Al was at his home in his pajamas watching sports on the television. Ms. Ruth arrived unannounced and rang his doorbell. Al looked out and was stunned to see who was at his door. His first thoughts were that something was wrong with Victoria. He hurried to open his door. Ms. Ruth was standing there, appearing to be years younger. Her dress fitted tightly against her protruding hips, her makeup, nails, and hair were beautiful—Al instantly knew Ruth was there for him and that Victoria was okay.

Al took her hand and led her into his place and his arms, "Oh, baby, what took you so long?" He said aggressively.

Al kissed her so hard, and with so much passion, it had escaped his attention that the doors were open.

After breaking away from his lips, Ruth joked, "Wow, I miss you too. Your neighbors are getting a full eye's view."

Al chuckled and shut his door. Then he suggested, "This is a time to celebrate. Let's go out."

Ruth smiled and agreed. Al whispered after another kiss, "Let me take my shower, and I'll be out in a second."

Ruth stood in the foyer of Al's home and thought about Victoria's gift, and so she opened it. It was a gold key chain and the inscription inside reads: I love you, Mama Ruth. She walked closer to where Al was— she could hear the shower water running, and the thoughts of their past passion invaded her, 'I don't need to go out. I need him inside me. Right, now…!' Fear ultimately left the building. Ruth took off her clothes and led herself to the shower with him. She opened the shower curtain, and Al's eyes followed her every curve as his manhood instantly rose firmer and stiffer. Ruth hadn't forgotten how Al loved the way her mouth felt. After seeing his very thick, firm penis, she had a strong urge to engulf it. Ruth kissed Al—slid down from Al's lips to his chest—looking at his surgical

wound. She gazed at his passionate eyes and kissed him slowly—tenderly kissing his medical scar.

Ruth stopped, thinking of Al's heart condition. She asked, "Al, baby, your heart—what if…?"

Al interrupted the thoughts of Ruth, "Baby, I am strong. My heart probably gave me trouble, because I lived all this time without you; I missed you so. Sweetheart, if my heart gives out while making love to you, then I died the best way a man can die. No worries, Ruth, I am strong. Let me show you."

Al placed Ruth's hand on his sinewy part, and she seductively smiled; as she proceeded to please him. Ruth continued kissing Al sliding downward until she reached his penis. Ruth placed all of Al in her mouth, and his leg buckled.

He shivered and said, "Oh baby! I missed you."

Al looked down at his love giving him her all. And Al wanted to provide her with the same. He lifted her face to his to kiss her. He draped his massive arms around her as the water glided off their naked bodies. Wrapped together in lust from a long wait, the two entwined together like a pretzel. Al turned her back to him, with one arm gliding between her breasts holding her neck, and the other hand gliding back and forth and through and in her vagina. Al's fingers were gentle but immense—they caressed as they massaged her clitoris. Al needed Ruth to know he still had what it took to please her. Al lifted Ruth and placed his hard thick firm penis into her vagina. Al discerned Ruth hadn't had anyone following him because she was very tight and her body always carried a sizzling temperature when excited. All those years apart; he missed the feeling of being inside her. Al couldn't hold his excitement and began pumping harder and deeper into Ruth. Ruth moaned with ecstasy. Al felt a gush of hot juices surrounding his penis as the fluid fell towards his thighs— instantly remembering why Ruth had been an unforgettable lover; she was his heated waterfall. The passion between the two was very intense; they stayed in bed for two days after their reconnection. The two only felt like youngsters in heart, but the harsh reality was they had aged since their last encounter. No longer afraid, the two started their life without fears.

ↂ

A few years came and went—Victoria's work had slowed down a little, and Ben was very close to finishing medical school. It was on a Thursday evening that Ben came home from school early.

"Victoria! I got some great news!" Ben called out upon entering their home.

"What is it?" Victoria asked, running out of the study.

Ben was excited—he staggered over his words. "Twenty-five percent of students elected to graduate with honors were in, but only ten percent made it; I was one of them. And, the Academic Awards Committee nominated me for all six awards: The Outstanding Achievement Award in Medicine took four years. I got this nomination for my potential in teaching, research, clinical medicine, my demonstrated leadership and academic excellence during both the basic and clinical science years. The Memorial Prize is for my outstanding proficiency in clinical medicine. The Leadership Award is for my standing extracurricular accomplishments during four years in medical school. The Strong Community Service Prize is because I have contributed the most through community service. This award was the hardest to get because I had to do volunteer work with an already tired mind and body. This award will go far in helping me with my years of being a doctor in practice after school; they call it intern years. I look forward to that in my future. They chose me to receive fifteen additional awards from the Clinical Department Awards. These awards are a great deal to me; all my hard work is paying off. Let's do something to celebrate."

Victoria was surprised. She knew Ben was smart enough to become a doctor, but he had genuinely excelled in the field.

"HELL YEAH!" She said, "This is a reason to celebrate. Let's go out."

Victoria took her purse, told the staff to go home, and they headed out the door. Victoria and Ben chose first to go out to eat at a local restaurant in Ft. Lauderdale, Florida. The restaurant they visited boasted an outstanding authentic Italian cuisine. This restaurant was beautifully lit up with romantic candlelight. Its Trattoria was nestled in Victoria Park with a gorgeous view of the Middle River. With its doors opened, they were

exposed to the many tantalizing aromas of fantastic Mediterranean flavors. The atmosphere was full of romance and dynamic character, positioning the two in an abnormal scenery. Seated in this beautiful Italian restaurant, they began laughing and talking about all about his achievements. They always chatted about the day that their first loves hurt both of them. The candlelight was glowing from Victoria's face, and Ben couldn't help but see how beautiful Victoria was. He wrestled with himself inside, thinking his thoughts were not pure.

In the middle of seeing her smile, Ben asked, "Victoria, I recalled a time when I was seven. Your dad had brought you over to be with Unique. You went outside while my mom and your dad argued in the house. I guessed you hated when they did that because you ran out the front and to the back of our house. I remember you fell, hurting your ankle. You had a small cut, and I ran into the house for some tissue to wipe the blood."

Victoria interrupted, "Of course, I remember that day. Eventually— you wrapped my ankle in cloth, and my arms were wrapped around your shoulders as you helped me up. You kissed me, and I kissed you back."

Ben chuckled and declared, "I didn't plan it, and you were my first kiss and my first crush. Did you know that?"

Victoria held Ben's hand across the table, "You were mine too. After that kiss, I got butterflies every time I saw you. Then I didn't see you anymore, but I never stopped thinking about you. Did you know I told your sister Jasmine about us kissing?"

Ben looked shocked then laughed and said, "No, I didn't know she knew that. Wow, I thought only you and I knew what happened."

Victoria continued, "Yes, I told her, but what she said next— overwhelmed me. She said that you and I could never be because we were brother and sister and that's just nasty. When I turned seventeen, it became apparent that our attraction to each other was natural because we weren't in the same bloodline. We don't have the same mother or father. We're just connected because Unique and I have the same father and you and Unique having the same mother. I said that if I had a chance to see you again, I would have been your girlfriend, but I never got that chance. Ms. Ruth told me something before she left that got me to thinking. She said, 'Life is short, and you should live it without fears.' Ben, now—I have

the same ole butterflies that I had when we were young and kissing. Can you tell me why I am so scared?"

Ben's big bold puppy eyes were falling. He gripped her hand more, "It's because of what has been said to us all our lives. We are brother and sister; however, it's not by bloodline. I can't help but be honest with you and tell you why I called you Sissy—which to me meant you were a sister—but not. I never thought of you like my natural sister—I knew I wasn't a pervert because I had other sisters. Unique, Sarah, Jasmine, and May—I never wanted to kiss them! However, you. You were another secret of mine that I held on to, the entire time I was in jail. And, since I've been here with you—I fought every day, not to let you see the lust in my eyes for you. I must say this—Victoria, because it's the truth and forgive me if it's unseemly. There's only one thought that helped me not to think of you sexually. Well, that was until I learned better from my studies. The fact is, I thought I could hurt you—I looked at your small frame, and I knew if I were to make love to you, you wouldn't like it, or worse—I'll hurt you."

Victoria jumped in and said, "What! I know you are a doctor, and I know what you are working with because I've seen it—remember? However, I think you were underestimating my size."

"I can still hurt you if I'm not careful." Ben smiled, "That's another thing I love about you. I don't have my degree in my hand, but you see me as a doctor already. You build me up all the time. I'll never forget what you said when we were both sad over our exes. You said that Becky had lost a magnificent man—I swear I wanted to kiss you and I had to get up. That's why I told you that I needed to study. My dick was growing fast—I didn't want you to see."

Victoria snickered, and agreed, "I had some moments like that. I walked in one day while you were showering. I stood there—staring at your body as if I was in a trance. Thoughts of holding and touching you overpowered me so much that I had to go in my room and release—alone."

Ben then thought about where their conversation was going. And said, "Wait, what are we saying? Is it this place —or, the wine? Why aren't we thinking straight? Loving each other would distress our family. We can't do this! And, thanks to my studies—I know you can handle me.

Well, only if I make certain not to get too rough—I don't think I could be gentle. You might have complications from all this."

Victoria was now thinking—Ben was trying to rationalize why they shouldn't go into a relationship, but all she could think about was how they were already in a relationship, just not sexually. Moreover, as far as the family was concerned, Ms. Ruth's take on it was the right advice.

Victoria eagerly said, "Not this time, Ben—let everything go, let everyone in our family—go, and do what you want—right now."

Ben looked at Victoria—his eyes were holding the question 'Are you sure?' Victoria gave Ben a bold and daring look as she repeated, "Without fear—Ben, do what you want! Right now—this moment: What do you want to do?"

Ben instantly got out of his chair. While Ben came over to her—Victoria briefly glanced at Ben's pants. She saw his large print and got nervous, but only for a moment.

Ben lifted her out of her seat, grabbed her neck, kissed her gently, and said, "Let's go home."

The host from the restaurant said aloud for all in the restaurant to hear, 'This is the place of love.' People clapped as Ben and Victoria exited the restaurant.

Ben was driving, and he moaned, "Oh, shit—this hurts."

Victoria looked over at him and noticed him pulling at his right pants leg. She watched as his penis continually grew—choking against his driver's leg. Ben got on the freeway to go faster.

Victoria licked her lips, took a deep breath, and said, "Ben, you have got to start wearing larger pants."

Victoria then did something he and she would never have thought she would do. She undid his zipper and tugged at his pants until she ripped them and exposed that huge pipe of his. She said, "I hope you're a good driver."

Victoria leaned over into Ben's lap and placed her mouth over the head of Ben's penis and start working it while he drove. Ben repeated, "Oh damn...! Victoria...! oh, baby, damn...!"

He tried not to lose focus on the road. He couldn't believe what was happening. His thoughts raced, 'Victoria was better than Becky was.' He

rushed to pull in their driveway. He jumped out, not even trying to cover himself at all—Victoria did the same. They shut the door behind them. Victoria enticed Ben to follow her to the kitchen, and he did. She stripped her clothing, got on the countertop, and leaned back as she began pouring chocolate down her stomach onto her privates.

Ben licked his thick lips, "You know how I like chocolate—don't you?"

Ben stood between her legs, took both his hands and placed them on her hips, pulling her frame towards him. He kissed and licked the chocolate, starting at her navel—slowly down to her vagina. Ben then took her into his mouth—twirling, and sucking. Victoria didn't know oral could feel that good. Ben was a master with his tongue—Victoria trembled with ecstasy. Ben touched his penis, and it was the hardest he had ever seen it get. Ben got nervous—hoping he could please her but not hurt her. He contemplated on putting it in slowly, and if she cried out, he knew he would take it out. Ben rubbed himself and laid it on Victoria's stomach as a final warning. Victoria took a deep breath. Ben's penis reached past her navel, just below her breast.

Victoria up close and personal with the firm, long, thick coke-cola size extension of Ben. She licked her hands with saliva, grabbed his penis and gave him a hand job. Ben surveyed—giving her another chance to back down, but Victoria wanted him inside her immediately.

Victoria exhaled and said, "I want it. Ben, give it to me—now."

Ben happily complied with her. He took the head of his massive cock, wiped her juices from her backend to the front of her vagina, spit on it and pushed through her very snug entrance. Victoria's inside heated like a furnace that allowed Ben to melt inside her as he slowly pushed through with cautious. Victoria was hotter and more profound than Becky. Ben became more confident that her frame could handle all of him, so he pushed in entirely. Victoria was a perfect fit. Ben eyes widened with shock, and so he became more aggressive. Victoria screamed Ben's name in a frenzy. Ben slid through and pounded in and out of her with uncontrollable passion.

Victoria wondered what she'd been missing all her life and her thoughts invaded the moment, 'Ben is hitting every corner—Dave couldn't fill my space. Plus, Dave was quicker. Ooh, damn! Why was I waiting?'

Ben was hammering away at Victoria. Ben couldn't help but talk while making love to her because the sex was great and his congenial feeling flourish.

Ben whined, "Victoria— Oh, da-a-a- -! Victoria, you feel good. Oh, shit—I can't hold on, baby."

The warmth and deepness of Victoria caused Ben to erupt like a volcano while inside of her. When his sensation burst forth in her, she quivered with the highest intensity of sensual gratification. Victoria thought Ben would be done after he erupted, but Ben wasn't anything like she had ever experienced. While his dick was still hard inside her—he picked her up off the counter, kissing her and sucking on her nipples. He took her to the bedroom. Ben placed Victoria on the bed, laid her on her stomach, and continued to drive hard into her from the rear. Victoria clenched the bed sheets as Ben pushed in and out of her. Ben then changed her position. He placed her on her back and drove from the front. Ben gazed into Victoria's face—staring, and feeling like the luckiest man in the world. He loved everything about Victoria. He held her long neck gently with one hand as he guided his body like a human centipede.

Victoria's thighs and legs tightened up, and she let out a squeal—her breath heavy and repeatedly slurring, "Oh baby, Oh Ben!"

Ben knew she was having another orgasm, and his was coming at the same time. Ben released in Victoria twice—no condoms on at all, and Victoria didn't expect to be having relations, but for the moment—they didn't care what the consequences would bring. Ben's body fell to the side of hers. Ben noticed she looked utterly worn out. Ben got up and made her some bath water so she could soak.

She fell asleep, but he woke her up, saying, "No, babe—you can't sleep without soaking or else you won't be able to walk straight tomorrow."

Ben ran to the bathroom and filled the tub with water and bubbles, then came back to the bedroom, picked her up, and placed her in it. He stayed in there with her because he didn't want her to fall asleep. Ben rubbed her hair and back, then asked, "I hope you can take this every day—several times a day if our schedule allows it."

Victoria, with a weak voice, snickered, "You're a badass, aren't you? I'll handle everything you bring to the table, sir. You are just right, Ben, I

wouldn't change a thing about you. I am tired, but my pussy has never felt so good and swollen. I'll keep up and fill your every need, babe."

Ben kissed her again; his love was growing at a rapid pace. Ben took off his robe and joined her in the tub. Sitting in the back of her—he kissed her neck continually.

He then became aware of something else and said, "Baby, I think I'm in love. How can this happen so soon? My feelings are stronger than what I had with Becky."

Victoria kissed his hand, "You too, huh? However, it's not as sudden as you're thinking. Ben, we have loved each other all our lives. Dave and Becky hurt and cheated on us, but that situation helped us realize— something more was in the cards for us. We would have never admitted how we felt if they hadn't broken our hearts. Let us thank them. I'm so in love with you too."

Victoria turned her body and leaned in—kissing him very passionately. Ben's dick rose, and he pulled away and said, "Oh no... I know—I got to let your body heal."

Victoria gazed into Ben's eye's and said, "Yeah... But— There's nothing wrong with my mouth."

She sucked another orgasm from Ben's enormous penis. After their bath, they went on to bed, holding each other tight.

❧

Sex with Ben was fantastic for Victoria every time. They grew closer than ever, and so did their love for one another, but it tormented them when they thought about their family. They felt they had a forbidden love. They lived in a world of secrets—happy only for the moments alone. They both agreed not to say anything about their love until the time was right. They questioned—if there would ever be a time that was right. The love they shared would have to stand up to relentless ridicule from a three-tier family that would completely freak out—if they knew. Ben and Victoria weren't ready for that type of drama.

CHAPTER 29

A FAMILY TRADITION

SUMMER ARRIVED AGAIN AND several years had passed since the last family barbecue. Cindy enjoyed her new house—especially her vibrant garden. She realized that time had gone by, and she had—had enough of this distant, career-driven family. Chuck had just come in when he saw the stressed look on Cindy's face.

A very concerned husband asked, "Baby, what's wrong? Why are you looking that way?"

Cindy perceived that she and Chuck had been together so long—he knew her every expression. She didn't want to cause him to be alarmed, so she responded quickly.

"Oh, nothing, babe, I just suddenly got upset with this career-driven family. They have all been too busy for our family's traditional barbecue, and they all promised to keep the custom. Unique lives here, but we barely see her—she's on the plane flying everywhere but home; I'm just sick of it!"

"You know opening more stores in different states is important to Unique. She's already opened several shops here in St. Louis, but that wasn't good enough. Now she expanded to the various states, designing clothes for women, men, teenagers, and children, as well as any with physical disabilities, and their disabled accessories."

Chuck was excited about what Unique has accomplished. "Did you know the U&J symbol has set off a fashion fury in Hollywood? I saw on TV how Unique's clothing line had reached the music rappers. They were sporting U&J gear—the actors in movies, as well as well-known singers. Also, our girls' new R&B clothing line is doing well. Jasmine has always been a cutie pie, so it didn't surprise me when Victoria said that she was their model for that line of fashion."

Cindy interjected, "I just hope that doesn't start interrupting Jasmine's last year in college. Victoria has been busy too. She has had too many jobs and interviews, and now she is about to do movies. I know we won't be able to see her once she starts doing that. Ben is always on call. I know he's doing well as a doctor but with all the offers for practice in other states— it's only a matter of time before they move back to a remote city. Jerry's off playing football, and soon he may be drafted into the NFL. Now, Maury is in college, and at one time—I thought he wasn't going. That boy surprised me! Dorothy said May passed the bar ahead of schedule and soon she'll be one of the best attorneys ever known. I was surprised when she said civil rights was her interest. Sarah is a nurse in LA. Oh, and guess what Al has been up to since he got out of the hospital?"

Chuck was grateful to get a word. He asked, "What?"

Cindy said, "Al has hooked up with that charming lady who worked for Victoria; her name is Ruth. I met her at the hospital when Al had that heart attack. She was a beautiful person; I think she fits well into this family."

Chuck declared, "Baby, we don't need any more family members, but if Al is serious about this one, I guess we would know, and she will then be family."

Cindy knew she was wearing on Chuck's ears, but continued anyhow, "I suppose you're right about that. Dorothy called last week. Do you know she asked me if I needed her service?"

Thinking of Dorothy's past, Chuck quickly asked, "What service?"

"Dorothy and Diane started a personal house cleaning service. She and her friend are running a company. Now, they have hundreds employed. This house may be big, but if I didn't have to clean it, I don't know what I would do. It continues to amaze me how Dorothy and her best friend Diane stayed in the house together. They built their lives up. They go to church every Sunday, and they never returned to the habits of drugs and prostitution. Now, that's a true testimony to what God can do."

Chuck clearly understood how Cindy was missing her family because she hadn't stopped talking about them since he walked through the door. Therefore, he made a suggestion, "Cindy, I am going to call Al and Dorothy tonight. All of us together will get these kids down here to the family barbecue."

Chuck kissed her on the forehead, grabbed the phone and started dialing Al first, "Al, I hope you're not busy. I wanted to chat with you for a minute."

Al interrupted in a joking fashion, "Man, Chuck—if this is about you losing at the bowling alley, I won that game,"

Chuck laughed at him and joked back, "Dude—you just want to use any occasion to brag about that match. I got the next one. My call isn't about bowling. It's about our family barbecue. We said we were going to keep our family together and keep up with a barbecue once a year in the summer, but the whole family has been tied up with their careers and school. The last time we were all together was when you got sick. I'm happy that you're better because you scared all of us. I want you to call on Victoria to come to the barbecue and don't take no for an answer. By the way, you cheated on that last game. I am going to win the next game at the alley—you better believe that."

Al chuckled, "No problem, I will call her tonight—and as for the game—we shall see."

Chuck disconnected from Al and immediately called Dorothy, "Hey Dorothy, how are you?"

"I'm good Chuck." The call puzzled Dorothy. "I thought Cindy said that she didn't want help with her house cleaning."

"Oh, no... she doesn't. Anyhow—how's the business life treating you?"

"Business is going well. We have more clients than we can handle sometimes, but I want to make sure my family has a clean house, so that's why I make sure I offer my services to Cindy. That house is big, and of course—I would never charge her. I worry about her?"

Chuck quickly answered, "Dorothy don't worry about her—she's fine. Since Cindy stopped working—she has nothing to do but clean that house, and it's always clean. She's just lonely again and misses the family. I just called because we all have forgotten how essential it is to keep our family barbecue going. I know everyone has been involved in their careers, but as Al says, 'next to God—nothing is better.' I need you to call all the kids for the barbecue and don't take no for an answer."

Dorothy was thrilled and said, "Sure thing, Chuck—I will get on it right away."

Chuck then called Unique, Jerry, and Maury. He firmly told them that he wasn't taking any excuses. They had to come to the family barbecue.

Cindy had gone to the kitchen; Chuck went in behind her after his calls, "Okay it's on. Let get things ready for our family barbecue."

"Really!" Cindy danced with joy in the middle of the kitchen—genuinely pleased with the news. She started making plans right away. It was going to be a different experience because they had park-like surroundings, so space would not be a problem. The new pool area was perfect for the kids with their water sports, and it wouldn't interfere with the card players this time. Jerry and his football players had plenty of rooms to run the ball. They even had a basketball playground and hoop for all the towering cousins who liked to play that sport. Cindy was comforted knowing her plants wouldn't be damaged—having a greenhouse was perfect. Several gazebos were put out for shade. Bug repellents and electric bug stingers covered the entire area for the protection of the pesky little creepy-crawlers. Chuck was very proud to show off his craftsmanship—his brick grill was massive, and he did it with his own hands. This family always did the cooking, and this barbecue wasn't any different. Except, for its location—nothing changed, and it felt like planning a large banquet. Everyone would bring the food. Almost everything you could want would

be there. Cindy hired some help for cleanup from Dorothy and insisted on paying regular price. She also hired a DJ from one of the St. Louis local radio stations. DJ Mack had a reputation for keeping up with the older generations music, as well as the youngsters and pleased everyone in between.

The family mostly flew in the night before the event, but some were there two days ahead of time. However, the day of the event family arrived, as early as seven o'clock in the morning. They wanted the whole day to enjoy themselves.

The family barbecue was on, and everyone was so happy to see each other again. The football players and the basketball players were playing hard. The card table was the loudest, as usual. Unique was eating and dancing most of the time. Maury and Jerry were in the football game until Cousin Jeff hurt his leg and that ended the game. Grandma Carolyn was spoiling all the young ones. Dorothy and Diane were in the food tents, making sure their staff were tending to things properly—after all, this was their family event.

Diane poked Dorothy with her elbow and murmured, "Dorothy, I know—I do not see what I think, I am seeing."

Dorothy, eyeing the direction Diane was looking— highly concerned, asked, "What the hell do you see? Because I don't see anything."

Diane whined, out the word, "Girrrrl, open your damn eyes—look at Victoria and Ben. They haven't left each other's side since they've been here—look at their expressions, girl."

Dorothy took a more extended look and saw the love between Victoria and Ben, but tried to justify what she saw, "Diane, they are together most of the time—that's why they are so close, but I don't think it's nothing like you're thinking."

Diane gave Dorothy a derogatory expression, and rolled her eyes, "Yeah right—one thing I know is when someone is fucking, and they're fucking."

Diane huffed and walked out of the tent—Dorothy followed behind her to enjoy the event.

The DJ was jamming. When he played oldies from Stax musical artists, Al, Ruth, Dorothy, Diane, Chuck and other family and friends

started cutting a rug and yelling, "That's my song!" Jasmine, May, and Jerry were dancing too. Although they were the younger generation—they were raised listening to artists like Eddie Floyd, Al Green, William Bell, and many others.

Ben and Victoria joined in the dance when the DJ played Johnny Taylor. Ben tried hard not to laugh because he saw for the first time that Victoria couldn't dance at all. The entire family was laughing hysterically at her moves. Victoria did her hopping dance step and fell—twisting her ankle. Ben jumped in quickly to make sure she wasn't hurt. He leaned over her and before he knew it, he instinctively kissed her on the mouth and called her babe.

Dorothy looked at Diane; Chuck looked at Cindy; Al looked at Ben; Ruth looked at Victoria; Jerry looked at Jasmine; May looked at Sarah, and Unique was standing with her mouth completely open in a frozen state.

Al yelled out, "Houston—we have a problem!"

Chuck told everyone to keep enjoying themselves, but the entire family was murmuring. Chuck then called a brief meeting in the kitchen with Dorothy, Diane, Cindy, Al, Ruth, Ben, and Victoria.

Chuck was the first one to say something after they all sat at the table, "Okay, family—we're all grown so let's talk about this like adults. I am going to say this is shocking—although, I am not surprised. You two have been through a lot together and have gotten very close. Technically—you are not blood-related, so it's not as bad as some will think of it."

Dorothy then spoke out, "How long had this been going on, Ben?"

Ben answered, "For a while, Mom—look, I know this is awkward, but sometimes falling in love happens. We should feel ashamed, but I am not because Victoria has been the best thing ever to happen to me—I love her."

Victoria was a nervous wreck—her legs were shaking tremendously. She wondered what her dad was going to say. But her heart melted upon hearing Ben confession of love, and in front of the family.

Al yelled at Ben and said, "You love her! You love her? I am glad you love her because if it were anything else…" Al winked at Ben. "I would have been upset with you."

Ben looked thunder bolted and relieved at the same time.

Ruth said, "You two are just going to make the family official—that's all. Victoria, do you remember when I said that life is too short to worry about fears?"

Victoria nodded, 'Yes.'

Ms. Ruth continued, "I wasn't just talking about Al and me. I saw love in both your eyes before I left your home. I prayed as I took courage to be with the love of my life, Al—I also prayed you two would follow your hearts, and I knew you two would unearth things for yourselves."

Ben and Victoria couldn't believe that their family was okay with them being in love. All that time wasted worrying about what would happen—sickened them both.

The two exposed lovers had a sense of relief until Cindy said, "Hold up! Hold up! You two are not out of hot water as far as I am concerned. You held back from this family! We are a family and no matter how bad something seems—you should know you could be open to talking with your family. Holding back is never an answer, Victoria, and Ben."

Al jumped in and arbitrated for the lovers, "That's partly my fault, Cindy. You see, most of Victoria's life she feared that she would displease me. I'm that parent that she admires very much, she cares what I think. I must admit—I love that quality in my child, but I know It was her chief reason for being afraid of how I would react. The truth is—I prepared myself for the secret news when Ruth talked to me about Ben and my daughter. After I had begun thinking how the last person turned out and the pain she experienced—I was pleased that Ben became her next choice because I knew he would love my daughter the way she deserves."

After hearing her dad's approval—Victoria began tearing up and walked over to hug him tightly. Victoria and Ben started apologizing to the family, when Jasmine and Jerry walked into the kitchen hand-in-hand for support, as Jerry tried to explain, "We hope you aren't taking things hard with Ben and Victoria because Jasmine and I have gotten romantically involved since we started to college together. Please, don't be mad."

Cindy abruptly said to Jerry, "Boy! We all knew about you and Jasmine. It was said earlier—this will make our family legit—pending you

all get married. It's like Al always said next to God—family is the next best thing, Right? So we all should be—just fine."

Al said, "Maybe we'll get some grandkids out of all this."

With that being said—Victoria hadn't told anyone her other secret, not even Ben. Victoria spoke out and said, "Family… Ben— there is something else I must tell you."

Victoria walked over to Ben, held his hand, placed it on her stomach, and said, "I'm pregnant. I found out this morning."

Shock filled the kitchen. Ben started weeping, and his emotions freaked everyone out; not because he's a man with tears of joy but because of his muscular exterior—it looked unnatural.

Al looked at Ben and said, "Son, it's cool… You're freaking us out."

Ben got the gesture, straighten up, kissed Victoria and instantly became overprotective.

Al smiled ear-to-ear and said to Ben, "Good job, son."

Ben smiled and said, "Thanks, Dad. There is something else—but I want the whole family to know and see. Let's get back outside."

They were all walking out of the kitchen. Unique was there on the patio, waiting for them to come out. She decided to keep the other family fun going while they talked things over.

She stared at them as they all walked out and said, "I feel like I am on the outside of the courts waiting for the verdict regarding a major case. Well, what's the ruling? Someone— Anyone! What Happened?"

Cindy laughed and told Unique, "All is well. Ben has an announcement to make. We will fill you in on the details later."

Ben walked over to the DJ with Victoria's hand in his. The DJ turned the music down and gave Ben the microphone.

Ben got on one knee in front of Victoria, "Victoria, I know God loves me 'cause He has helped me through a lot. God blessed me with you—I would make sure I remain grateful for the gift God gave me. I love you with all my heart, and I promise never to stop loving you. To know, I have a baby coming brings me joy—I am speechless. I love him already. Please, Victoria, take me as your husband. Victoria, will you marry me?"

Victoria cried and repeatedly said, "Yes, Ben… Yes."

The entire family was thrilled, and tears flowed freely. Ben placed the ring on Victoria's finger. She then concluded that he had planned to tell the family at the barbecue. She was proud to have a man like Ben—a man that wasn't afraid to take the lead. They all had more to celebrate and went back to having fun. The DJ played their family song, "We Are Family," by Sister Sledge. The Soul Train line was popping once more, but Victoria had to sit this one out due to her ankle and her newfound knowledge of pregnancy. Unique observed her united family all together—having fun. She remembered her mother—Cindy, telling her to be strong, never allowing her differences to slow her down and never settling on her dreams. She comprehended how God works things out in the end. Now, she understood the entire process. It wasn't just about her being successful or her making the dream of her sister Jamie come true—it was God allowing her to have what she'd always wanted—a united family. She remembered praying to have a family like the Woods when she was just a small girl. God not only responded to her prayers, but He displayed His love for her—no matter what challenges she faced. Now, Unique realized it—now, she sees in her mind's eye what it all meant. Looking into the heavens with tears of joy—she again thanked God for all he had done and said thanks to Jamie again.

They all danced, ate, played games, laughed, joked around, and expressed love and Dorothy's crew cleaned until two the next morning. The next day they were back to business, but this time—as one united family.

DEAR READERS

THE PHILOSOPHY OF UNIQUE

THERE ARE MILLIONS OF children in our country who are never given the opportunity to achieve their dreams because of mental and physical disabilities. Most children with disabilities receive little—if any—direction after high school; which is one of the leading causes of crime. Far too many young adults who have ADHD, bipolar disease, and schizophrenia end up in jail or dead; misunderstood by the police. It is widely documented that males with mental illness have a high rate of criminal activity; while females have a high rate of sexual misconduct. Turning a blind eye to these children and their special needs only compound the problem. The encouraging news is that law enforcement officers are finally being trained to recognize persons with mental illnesses; and how to handle them with compassion vs. violence.

Physically, emotionally or mentally challenged children are different, and their talents are different. All differences should be embraced, not hidden. It is the endless tapestry of human differences that make the world beautiful. Special-needs children require—and deserve—extra love, support, and resources to achieve their goals well beyond high school.

Parents and families with physically challenged children need love and support also. To live successful lives, special needs young adults need the involvement of more organizations dedicated to posting high-school independent living support, employment and socialization.

I wrote Unique with the hope that readers will experience the unconditional love that special-need children possess. Take a walk in their shoes of everyday challenges. Those provocations impact the families of special needs children; especially low-income families who struggle with emotional roller coasters and expensive medications. Sometimes, family/caregivers turn to drugs and alcohol for temporary relief from the mental, emotional and economic desolation that is often their lives.

Unique will resonate with the 40 million Americans who suffer from some form of disability. Fully 17% of the U.S. population falls into this group… Many, if not most of whom have been mocked and bullied.

This unique novel journeys back and forth in time causing the story to be told through the varying viewpoints of the major characters; giving us a rare glimpse into their thoughts and feelings.

I hope, 'Unique' will speak to your heart to make a difference.

ACKNOWLEDGMENTS

I WOULD LIKE TO thank God. Nothing in this life is possible without Him.

As a mother of three, all who suffered from some form of disability, I would like to thank all the doctors and nurses that were there to pull us through the rough times. I would like to thank wonderful organizations like St. Louis Arc program and Shriner's Hospital for helping me through some horrific battles.

I would like to thank my family for the love and support throughout the years, as I struggled to take care of my children. I would like to thank my three precious children: Malissa Scott, Terry Scott, and Walter Scott, Jr. They are my heart and inspiration for writing Unique. I realized a long time ago that they were the ones keeping me stable. A child's love for his or her mother is a blessing that blossoms as time pass on. The strength I saw in my children, while they were growing up, was incredible. Their love is profound and wondrous. I encourage them to continue thriving and, no matter how hard things seem, continue to fight; because there is nothing left if you give up.

I would like to thank my ex-husband and friend, Walter Scott, for the three blessings we co-created with God, and the support.

I would like to thank my mother, Carolyn Ford; she has always been my biggest fan. My mom believed in me regarding anything I tried to

accomplish. I love you, Mom; and thank you for the support. RIH as I keep my promise and finish my journey.

I would like to thank my father, Benautry Ridgnal. I am thankful for your love and support. RIP

I would like to thank my mother-in-law, Rachel Pinkney, for her invaluable advice and undying love for me.

Thank you to my father-in-law, Eddie Floyd, for his inspiration.

And, a special thank you to the Love of my Life, my wonderful husband, Eddie Floyd, Jr. for loving me unconditionally; and, always believing me in me and helping me to understand that there is nothing wrong being a dreamer—dreamers rule. I love you, baby.

I want to thank all my beta readers for taking the time to be the first ones to experience Unique. Thank you to Lisa Anderson, Tammy Hampton, Barber Jackson, Ricky Jones, Deon Layton, Lisa Sanders, and so many others, for your generous support.

Thank you, Carlito Doss, for your contribution from Nasty Rebel Music Inc.

Thank you, Anna Spies **celairen@hotmail.de** and Aaron Newton and Elaine Young, for your enrichment in great graphic work on our first designs @5creative Graphics Inc and Hopscotch Communications.

I would like to thank Ron Stevens and Joy Grdnic, my supporters at Onstl.com, for giving me the opportunity to write about my beloved hometown, St. Louis.

ABOUT THE AUTHOR

WRITER/PRODUCER/DIRECTOR

APRIL FLOYD IS A dream maker—of her own and the dreams of others. April began her mission with the writing of her Unique novels more than ten years ago. However, within the last five years, the self-made, St. Louis born-and-bred writer, producer, and director began a steady path in production after springing as a blogger, and production associate promoting her hometown for St. Louis at OnStL.com in 2013. The author

has published four novels and is organically morphing into a fledgling entertainment powerhouse—as a stage and film producer/director.

Floyd discovered her writing gift as a middle-schooler: however, when she attended Kirkwood High stories start to dance in her head. Life circumstances could only incubate Floyd's colorful narratives until they demanded release decades later. Floyd birthed her baby, of Unique novels and her third novel, The Link: Christ, Christmas, and Santa Claus, which captivatingly weaves faith, mythology, magic, and mysticism to connect the intrinsic thread of all three. She worked as a nurse's aide and a school bus operator to support her now-adult children. Life was often challenging, as Floyd's remarkable children were born with special needs. With the love and support of her family and organizations like St. Louis Arc, School Resources, and Shriner's Hospital, Floyd was able to help her children thrive, teaching them to "continue to fight, no matter how hard things seem; because there is nothing left if you give up." That fight for her beautiful children lit a fire in Floyd's belly and a passion that would turn into a mission—and a movement. Floyd credits the love and dedication of her husband of eight years, Eddie Floyd, Jr. (son of legendary R&B singer/ songwriter Eddie "Knock On Wood" Floyd, Sr.), with encouraging her to rekindle her early dream to write; all the while, he worked along with her to build on their goals of books and film.

Fueled by April Floyd's first-hand experience of dismissive or indifferent attitudes, lack of resources, cruelty and the abuse children born with physical and mental challenges (17% of the American population) far-too-often suffer, preventing them from living successful lives, she created the character, Unique. In A Unique World, A Unique Life and then, I am Unique film trailer, Floyd takes readers through the heart-wrenching realities of a little girl born with the entire deck stacked against her: a drug-addicted, prostitute mother, physical and mental challenges, poverty, dysfunction, cruelty, and tragedy. Throughout the emotional roller coaster ride, Floyd skillfully infuses goodness, possibilities, faith, the power of love and ultimate triumph that is every human being's birthright.

I Am Unique will soon be coming to the big screen. Together, using their own resources, April and Eddie FloydJr., built a company, FEG-Floyd Entertainment Group, LLC, which now includes their company,

Floyd Books Publishing, LLC to produced their trailer "I AM UNIQUE." April Floyd also partnered with veteran entertainment producer Monica Butler of The Butler Group and Echelon Entertainment. The collaborators have produced plays and formed Film Camp, USA to train young people in all things film production-related.

Spearheaded by April Floyd and her husband, Eddie Floyd, Jr., the partners produced trailers with 1 minute, 3 minutes and 45-minutes for pitching and a short of I Am Unique, to be shown in St. Louis and at film festivals across the country in 2019. Hundreds of St. Louis locals auditioned for roles in the movie, both in front of and behind the camera. "April taught, loved and nurtured more than 80 people from our area during the process of producing this short and trailer," exudes partner, Monica Butler. "I watched her pull out the actor and actress in people who only possessed a hunger and passion to give their all."

##STAY TUNED##

www.aprilfloydbooks.com.
THE END

www.ingramcontent.com/pod-product-compliance
Lightning Source LLC
Chambersburg PA
CBHW061515020726
47502CB00006B/2080